HOOFIN' IT

A Magical Romantic Comedy (with a body count)

RJ BLAIN

HOOFIN' IT
A MAGICAL ROMANTIC COMEDY (WITH A BODY COUNT)
BY RJ BLAIN

All Shane wanted was to get away from the wreckage of his career for a while. He picked New York City to provide him with a distraction from his early, unwanted retirement from the police force.

New York City delivered, distracting him with three corpses and a miniature llama with a spitting problem and an attitude. If he wants to return to a normal life, he'll have to face off against a sex trafficking ring targeting the woman of his dreams, ancient vampires, murderous criminals, his parents, and an FBI agent with a hidden agenda.

Some days, it isn't easy being an ex-cop.

Warning: This novel contains excessive humor, action, excitement, adventure, magic, romance, and bodies. Proceed with caution.

For more information or to contact the author, please visit thesneakykittycritic.com.

Dedication

To the Usual Suspects: I'm pretty sure this is all your fault.

ONE

The next time I took a vacation, I'd just stay home.

THE NEXT TIME I took a vacation, I'd just stay home. While there were cozier places than my apartment in Chicago, it beat being covered head to toe in blood spatter on a busy sidewalk in Times Square. I'd seen a lot of crazy shit during my short stint as a cop, but I'd never seen a body plummet from a skyscraper and crash through the windshield of a car stuck in traffic before.

One body was bad enough, but the victim had landed on the driver and passenger. Maybe if they'd used a real windshield instead of a substitute, the glass wouldn't have broken into razor-sharp chunks and killed them. I'd seen it in Chicago once, when an enterprising idiot had purchased window glass, ground it down, and forced it to fit in his vehicle. I'd heard about it happening back home in Lincoln, Nebraska, too.

Both drivers had died after rear-ending someone, breaking their makeshift windshields, and slitting their throats.

What stopped me in my tracks was the furry head sticking out of the back window, its white fur stained with crimson and its long, fluffy ears pinned back. My mouth dropped open, and I rubbed my eye, blinked, and looked again.

Nothing changed.

A rather angry looking miniature llama glared at me as though I'd somehow been responsible for the corpse falling through the windshield of its car which, by some miracle, hadn't accelerated following the accident. First, I needed to make sure the car stayed put. Second, I needed to call the cops. Since I could do both at the same time, I grabbed my cell, dialed 911, and held it to my ear while I circled the vehicle.

Fortunately, the driver's side window was down, offering me a good look inside. Not only had the driver ended up with a face full of glass, the angle of his head suggested the falling body had broken his neck on impact.

"911, please state the nature of your emergency," a woman answered.

"I'm on the corner of Broadway and West 42nd in Times Square. A body has fallen from a skyscraper and landed on a vehicle. There are two people inside the car, and I'm fairly certain they're dead. The driver's neck appears to be broken. The passenger has severe lacerations to the face and neck and is non-responsive."

"I'm sending officers and EMT to your location, sir. Please stay on the line."

I heard the tell-tale click of the operator putting me on hold. Knowing she'd try to stop me if I told her my intention, I reached in, contorted around the tangle of bodies and steering wheel, and put the vehicle into park, grateful the shifter wasn't part of the center console.

"Officers are on their way, sir. Does it appear there are any survivors in the vehicle?"

"There's an animal in the back." With the car secured from taking off and rampaging through Times Square, I focused my attention on the miniature llama, which had swiveled its head around to glare at me. It snorted, then it spit in my face through the open back window. Green goo smeared over my right eye and dripped from my face.

For the first time since the accident that had sent me into early retirement, I was grateful for my glass eye, a solid blue sphere. My insurance company had been far too cheap to pay for a realistic one.

"An animal, sir?"

I could handle a body falling from the sky and killing two men in front of me. A miniature llama with an attitude, however, crossed every last one of my lines. Lifting my hand, I wiped the gunk off my face. "It just spit on me. It's some sort of demented miniature llama, and the fucking thing just spit on me."

"Please remain calm, sir. What's your name? Do you know anyone involved in the accident?"

"My name's Shane Gibson. I don't know anyone involved in the accident, ma'am." Sighing, I stepped out of the alpaca's range, returning to the sidewalk to wait for the cavalry to arrive, bracing for the wave of questions the woman would ask to get a handle on the situation and keep me calm. I played along more for her sake than mine. I'd seen enough bodies during my three years on the force to last me a lifetime.

Three more and a pissed-off miniature llama meant little in the grand scheme of things.

SOMETIMES I REALLY HATED PEOPLE. The majority of the passersby decided they wanted nothing to do with the trashed car and trio of bodies. Their unnatural lack of curiosity left me as the only viable witness, which I considered absolutely ludicrous. Times Square in the mid-afternoon was a

bustle, and *I* was the one with the full attention of the six cops dispatched to the scene to
deal with me and the angry miniature llama.

The animal spit on three officers before
the youngest one got tired of its existence. He
drew his gun and pointed it at the animal's
head. There was only one thing stupider than
shooting an animal for being an animal, and
that was standing in front of the gun to stop
the shooting from happening.

If he decided to pull the trigger, I deserved
to get shot.

"Killing the animal isn't necessary, sir. I'd
be spitting angry, too, if someone hogtied my
legs together with duct tape and dumped me
in a car. It has no other way to defend itself."

Did the young idiot, who couldn't have
been more than a few months over twenty-
one, really think he could open fire on a busy
street because an animal had spit on him?

Apparently.

The young cop spluttered but holstered
his weapon. Once I was satisfied he wasn't
going to kill the animal, I turned my attention
to one of the older cops, a man with gray-
touched hair and steely eyes. "What's the procedure   for   animals   under   these
circumstances?"

In Chicago, I would have been drawn and
quartered for even thinking hurting the
damned thing, no matter how many times it

spit on me. Unless a sentient was at risk of fatal injury, killing an animal without just cause would result in a suspense and potential loss of badge.

A glob of spit smacked into the back of my head, and I stuffed my hands into my pockets so I wouldn't turn around and throttle the ungrateful animal after standing in the line of fire to keep an idiot from killing it.

The older cop sighed. "Animal control will be by to pick it up and either dispose of it or take it to a shelter. We don't have the facilities for animals like this unless they're sentients or exotics, which this animal is not, so they'll likely euthanize it and dispose of the body."

Bastards.

"All right. I'd rather not see it destroyed for circumstances out of its control. I'd like to make arrangements to claim the animal if no owners are located."

One day I would learn to mind my own business. The cops stared at me, looked at each other, and the oldest stepped away, talking to someone on his radio. The remaining cops resumed questioning me, repeating the conversation five or six times before they came to the conclusion I really had no idea why a man's body had fallen from a skyscraper and crashed through the windshield of a car stuck in traffic.

Or why a miniature llama was hogtied with duct tape in the back of the car.

The oldest cop returned, shook his head, and sighed. "If you want that thing, it's yours. Leave us your contact information should anyone with legal documentation proving ownership comes forward. By law, you are required to keep the animal in your possession for a minimum of twenty business days. If these terms are acceptable to you, you'll need to come to the station to sign some paperwork."

What the hell was I going to do with a spitting miniature llama for twenty business days? Clenching my teeth, I regarded the surly animal still trapped in the back of the car. It glared at me, and the fires of hell burned in its dark eyes. "They're acceptable."

The third time was a charm. It spit; I dodged and went to work extricating the animal from its grisly prison.

MY NEW PET, which I learned was an alpaca rather than a demonic miniature llama, weighed a hundred and ten pounds and hated everyone, especially men, with a vengeance. I spent almost two hundred dollars for a vet to tell me she was a female, she seemed to be young, and would need to be sheared within the next few weeks or her coat would become unwieldy and uncomfortable.

At least my two hundred bought her a round of vaccinations, which she protested with squeals and spits. My hold on her ratty halter kept her from biting anyone. Strips of duct tape still clung to her legs, but I would remove the adhesive with some patience and a pair of scissors later—after I convinced her I wasn't actually the devil.

Then again, once I stuffed her in the back of a rental van and carted her halfway across the country, the poor thing would probably hate me for the rest of her life. Since my hotel wouldn't allow an alpaca to stay in my room, I convinced one of the cops to write me a little note suggesting management release me from my reservation without penalty.

Freeing her from her duct tape bindings must have earned me a few points because the she-devil stopped spitting on me and didn't try to bite me once.

The rental company charged me an extra three hundred to transport an alpaca in one of their vehicles. To add insult to injury, they doubled my deposit due to my vision impairment, making it clear half-blind men were lucky to be allowed to drive. By ten at night, I was ready to hit the road, although I wasn't looking forward to three days of traveling with an animal in dire need of a bath.

At least the back of the van came equipped with mounting brackets, which were perfect for tethering my alpaca so she wouldn't be able to climb over the seats and assault me while I was driving. Once she was secured, I slid behind the wheel and made the phone call certain to add a little bit more suck to an already shitty day.

My mother answered on the third ring. "Hello?"

"Hey, Mom."

"The last time you called, you'd just had your eye scooped out. You refused to bring it home in a jar for me."

At least my glass replacement made it possible for me to blink—and close my eyes so I could enjoy the illusion of normality. "That's disgusting."

"That's what your father said. How could you resist the chance to keep an actual human eye on your desk? It's a trophy. Sure, you lost your eye, but you saved three lives. That's something to be proud of. Come on, Shane. I raised you better than that."

Given five minutes, my mother could always find a silver lining in any cloud. "Why aren't you in an institution yet, Mom?"

"You'd get bored if you sent me away."

"First, I haven't needed to call you because you call me every morning at exactly two minutes after eight. This couldn't wait until tomorrow morning."

"You mean you actually need something?"

I bumped my head against the steering wheel. "Yes, I do."

"Is it my birthday?"

"No. It's not your birthday." Once I popped my question, she'd consider it Christmas in April. "Can you take this seriously for a change?"

"I always take coercion and blackmail seriously, Shane. I thought you knew this by now. If you're asking *me* for help, I intend to get something really good out of it."

To the rest of the world, my mother was an upright citizen, a police officer, and the perfect wife and mother. To me, she was everything right and wrong with my life and half the reason I'd become a cop in the first place. Dad was the other half of the reason, and since I couldn't hear him howling in the background, I assumed he was on duty. "I can't believe you have everyone fooled into thinking you're actually a good cop, Mom."

"Now you're just being snide. Aren't you about to ask me for a favor? I could just wax poetic about how I have such a wonderful son who's a capable, independent adult, who comes home for Christmas, Thanksgiving, and Easter and doesn't bother anyone, not even when he's recovering from losing his eye in a different state."

Unless I got to the point quickly, she'd serenade me with every one of my achievements before circling around to the fact she didn't have my eye in a jar on her desk. If I got lucky, she'd call my grandmother and bring her into the discussion. The only thing worse than my mother on the warpath was my mother's mother joining in.

I wasn't sure if I loved or hated the woman sometimes. "A man fell from a skyscraper, busted through a windshield, and killed the people in the car while I was touring Times Square today. As a result, I am now the guardian of an alpaca for the next twenty business days. I thought I'd come visit you, with my new pet alpaca, for the next twenty business days. Then, because you're such a wonderful mother, you'll help me find a good home for the alpaca I'm legally required to keep for the next twenty business days."

I loved the sound of silence. It meant my mother had short-circuited and her brain was in process of rebooting. Smiling at having dumbfounded her for a rare change, I buckled up and started the van, fiddling with the temperature controls until it was cooler than I liked but tolerable for my new companion.

"You have an alpaca."

"It's like a demonic miniature spitting llama. The vet told me she's female, she needs to be sheared soon, and he gave her all of her important vaccinations. We're both in dire need of a bath, too. By the time I reach the house, I'm sure we'll be ripe for your enjoyment."

"I've raised a terrible child. What did I do to deserve you?"

"But they were going to euthanize her. I couldn't let that happen, Mom. When she isn't trying to spit on me or kill me, she's kinda cute. She's white and fluffy, and she has these adorable little fluffy ears. If she'll let you pet her, she's really soft. I'm thinking I'll teach her to sleep in bed with me. It *is* possible to housebreak an alpaca, right?"

My mother choked. "You'll do no such thing, Shane Gibson!"

"But you're always saying how you want me to come home and visit you. Does this mean you don't want me? I even found a cute little lady to keep my bed warm at night. Isn't that what you wanted for me?"

"A human lady, not a sheep on stilts!"

"Does that mean I have to try to convince my landlord to let me keep an alpaca in my teeny tiny apartment rather than at your nice big farmhouse? You even have a paddock she can run around and play in."

"That paddock is for my horses, young man."

"Mom, your horses are almost thirty years old. I'm sure they can share with a hundred and ten-pound alpaca."

"I don't have a spare stall."

"They had her hogtied with duct tape on the back seat of their car. And the one cop was going to shoot her for spitting on him."

There was a long moment of silence. "You manipulative brat. Fine. You'll clean up after her without complaint, and you'll be in charge of my horses for the next twenty business days as payment for your room and board. Her fleece is also mine. You can't have any of it. I expect you to clean and take care of her so I get the most spectacular fleece. Am I understood?"

Knitters. I could talk them into just about anything with a bribe of soft yarn. I pinched the bridge of my nose and sighed. "Yes, Mom."

TWO

Waking up with an alpaca using me
as a pillow wasn't my idea of a good
time.

I DROVE most of the night before I found a
roach motel willing to look the other way
when I told the desk clerk I needed to bring
in an alpaca for a much needed bath. Securing a reservation took a lot of patience
and a bribe of a hundred bucks, much to my
disgust. It was a good thing I wasn't a cop
anymore because I was pretty sure I was violating health codes in some fashion or another. Mom would turn a blind eye; she liked
animals almost as much as she liked yarn, and
it hadn't taken her long to figure out I was
bringing home a living supply of yarn fiber.

One thing would have to change, though:
at the rate I was spending money on an animal that didn't even like me, I'd blow
through my disability pay within a month.

In the best-case scenario, it'd be a year before I could reapply to join the force for any form of field job; in a few months, I could apply for a desk job. Unless I could afford a custom glass eye, one able to grant me clear vision, my days in the field were over. Since I didn't have a spare two million kicking around, I'd have to put an end to my pity party and hunt down some form of meaningful work.

According to my insurance company, my right eye had a dollar value of fifteen thousand, paid out by the city of Chicago. I also got paid medical leave for two months; if I passed the rest of my physical, I'd get the lowest paying desk job my chief could find. The only good news was I didn't have to pay taxes on my income until after my leave ended. I sighed, shook my head, and led my four-legged companion out of the van, keeping a tight hold on her halter so she wouldn't make a break for freedom.

Neither one of us liked the next four hours of our lives, which involved her standing in the rust-stained bathtub while I cleaned blood out of her fur, used a flea comb to check her fleece for any unwanted hitchhikers, and otherwise transformed her from a disheveled mess to a silky beauty.

I took my time cutting away the duct tape, trying to do as little damage to her coat as possible. Ice helped; chilling the adhesive reduced its effectiveness, which let me pick off the fibers bit by bit. If the motel didn't like me decimating their ice supply, they'd have to deal with it. For the rate I paid for the room, I deserved it delivered in a silver bucket.

Before I finished grooming her, she fell asleep on the bathroom floor, so I covered her with the spare towel and took a shower. It took me an hour to get the gunk out of my hair and feel clean. I barely had enough life left in me to stagger to the bed and flop onto it.

Waking up with an alpaca using me as a pillow wasn't my idea of a good time. Her front legs stretched across my chest while her hind legs flopped across my knees. As though worried I'd escape, she was using my forehead as a chin rest.

Maybe she was warm, soft, and fluffy, but she was heavy, had a drooling habit, and snored worse than my father.

When I had told my mother I was going to teach my alpaca to sleep with me in bed, I'd been joking. Groaning, I squirmed from beneath the sleeping animal, who didn't budge an inch, much to my relief. According to my phone, I had an hour to clean the room and leave. I checked the bathroom and discovered the alpaca had a rather negative opinion of the bathtub. While I agreed with her, I grimaced during the cleanup, grateful for the nearby trash can.

Hopefully, the roach motel staff would realize cleaning a clogged toilet was worse than emptying a plastic bag full of alpaca crap. Besides, the front desk clerk had gotten an extra hundred to deal with any problems.

I resolved to ignore my guilt, cleaned the rest of the room, and petted the alpaca to wake her up.

Sleepy alpacas enjoyed cuddling; I spent ten minutes trying not to laugh while she determined she was too big to fit on my lap. It took work and a bribe of grain to get her moving, but she scrambled into the van readily enough, and since she was behaving, I laid down the back seat to give her some extra space. I secured her lead to the bracket to keep her out of the front, and she seemed happy to stretch out and take another nap.

Two days later, I pulled into my parents' driveway in Lincoln, Nebraska. With a population of over two hundred thousand, there was always a need for cops, even crazy ones like my mother and father. But even the police departments of major cities like Chicago wanted someone like Dad on the force.

Werewolves with perfect control over all three of their forms were few and far between. Add in Mom's skills as a practitioner and hedge witch, and my parents were a force to be reckoned with. Alone, neither were powerful, ranking low on the talent charts, but they were good at their tricks, and their skills were ideal for law enforcement.

I, on the other hand, had been the token low talent freak on the force with a good cop pedigree. Chicago's police department had ignored my general lack of magic in exchange for my memory for detail, my ability to work with just about anyone, and tolerance for the jobs most didn't want.

My alpaca pressed her nose to the window and slobbered all over the glass.

"There's a paddock in the back with your name all over it," I promised, killing the engine and stretching with a tired groan. Driving hadn't done me any good, and my left eye ached from the strain of checking my blind spots, which I suspected was more than double the effort it had used to be. Each day, I'd developed a headache within an hour, and my current one would persist for another four or five before easing. I had made it halfway around the van to let my fluffy companion out when a dark shape barreled off the porch.

Great. Dad was running around on all fours, almost as furry as my alpaca. Since I'd lost my right eye, I'd remastered distances and depth perception, allowing me to plant my boot on my father's chest before he could plow into me. "No. Bad wolf. You will not slobber on me. You will not chew on me, either. You will also not terrify my—"

The alpaca screamed like she was being eaten alive.

I sighed. "Go back in the house and think about what you've done."

For once in his life, my father obeyed with a whine, scurrying to the front door with his tail tucked between his legs.

Apparently, alpacas really didn't like wolves, and she kept screaming until he disappeared, and even then, she trembled so much I worried her legs wouldn't hold her up. I stroked her nose and cooed at her, untying her lead line and taking firm hold of her halter. "Dad's sorry he frightened you. If he knows what's good for him, he'll change to his human shape and stop being a terror."

It took me over twenty minutes to convince her she wasn't going to be eaten, but she refused to get out of the van, forcing me to pick her up and carry her. A hundred and ten pounds of squirming alpaca was a lot to hold, but I managed to haul her all the way to the paddock and let her loose without getting spit on, bitten, or kicked.

It turned out miracles could actually happen.

With wide eyes and ears perked forward,

she explored the paddock, sniffing at the grass and taking curious nibbles.

"That's the damned most skittish critter I've ever done seen, boy," my father growled. "What you doin' bringin' a furry chicken to my barn?"

"I'd be skittish, too, if a corpse decided to crash through the windshield of the car I was riding in. While hogtied with duct tape in the back seat. She's had a rough few days. It doesn't help you're a wolf. She's an alpaca. You know, a prey species?"

"So that's the thing your mom's turning into yarn?"

"I'll find her a new home in twenty business days, I promise."

"Son." Dad's voice dripped scorn. "You brought a furry chicken to my barn."

"She wants to keep my alpaca, doesn't she?"

"Little thing's name's Sally, and your mom's done made me build an extra stall in my barn, boy."

"I already told Mom I was training the alpaca to keep my bed warm."

"There'll be no furry chickens sleepin' in my house."

In normal families, the werewolf would be the one off his rocker. How was it I had the only sane lycanthrope in the state of Nebraska for my father while my mother was the crazy hedge witch? "Her name's not Sally."

"Your mom says otherwise."

"She's my alpaca. I get to name her."

"Better name her Sally, then, else your mom's gonna be skinning your hide. And you're damn lucky Sally's got white fleece because your mom's already gone and ordered her next batch of dyes. So help me, if she decides she needs more of those furry chickens..."

"I've had a long drive, Dad. Can we talk about this later?"

"You got Sally's food in that van of yours?"

I sighed. "Yes, sir."

"Well, haul it on out then, boy. Don't leave poor Sally waitin' for her supper. Horses are already fed and bedded down for the night, so you can start your work in the mornin'. Now, hurry on up and get your ass in the house so I can have my supper."

MAYBE MY FATHER had the strength and endurance of an ox, but I ranked a lot lower on the totem pole, and it served him right to wait. I took twice as long as needed to settle Sally. The alpaca didn't seem too enthused about her new name, turning her ears back enough I kept a wary eye on her so I wouldn't get spit on again.

Hopper and Skunk seemed happy to see me, whinnying and bobbing their heads when I led Sally to her new stall. Either Dad had no idea how large an alpaca was or Mom had demanded a palace, because the new addition offered plenty of space for a Clydesdale.

"What's the holdup?" Dad bellowed from the house.

"Revenge tastes a lot like dinner," I informed the old horses, who bobbed their heads and lipped at me in bids for attention. Spending five more minutes stroking them resulted in my father prowling into the barn in his hybrid form, towering over seven feet tall.

While my father's head was shaped like a massive wolf's and he had a long, fluffy tail, his resemblance to his canine form ended there. Thick fur covered his body, his oversized legs and feet supporting a muscular torso with long, thick arms, and hands equipped with long claws sharp enough to easily decapitate someone.

I'd heard of fainting sheep but never a fainting alpaca. Then again, the first time I'd seen my father in his hybrid form, I'd learned how potent smelling salts were and why they were used to restore someone to consciousness. I'd been four or five at the time, and it was one my first memories. Sally thumped over, and I sighed, opening the door to check on the poor animal.

Her heart raced a mile a minute, and I realized the clever little beast was playing dead. "Dad, so help me, if you keep scaring my poor alpaca, I'm going to find out if you regenerate nearly as fast as you think you do. Don't make me remind you that Mom wants an eyeball in a jar for her desk."

"I'm hungry," my father growled.

"And you just added an extra ten or twenty minutes to my work by trying to terrify the life out of my alpaca. I'll come in as soon as I'm sure she's not going to have a heart attack. Go in the house, and for fuck's sake, at least be human for supper. You know Mom hates when you drool on her tablecloth."

"Furry chicken."

When my father was in his hybrid form, there was only one way to deal with him: with violence. Rising to my feet, I stepped out of Sally's stall, closed the door, and cracked my knuckles. "I'm going to count to ten, Dad. If you aren't in the house by the time I'm done, I'm going to use you as a punching bag for a while. I haven't been to the gym in a month, and I could use the exercise. Once I'm done beating the sense back into you, I'm going to get Mom's shears so she can card your fur and turn it into yarn. That should keep her busy for at least a week. I'll even be nice and buy her the bleaches and dyes she needs and suggest she use the garage as her workshop."

My father's ears turned back and he bared his teeth at me. His dark eyes took on a faint silvery gleam, and he licked his tongue over his three inch long incisors. A better man would've started counting.

I hammered my knuckles between his eyes hard enough he yipped and staggered. My second blow caught him underneath the chin and floored him. With a wince-worthy thump, my father crashed onto his back, his arms and legs twitching. I nudged him with my boot and was rewarded with a groan.

My hand throbbed, and I hoped I hadn't broken anything attempting to beat sense into his thick skull.

In his hybrid form, Dad weighed between four and five hundred pounds, so I grabbed one of the hauling chains hanging from the wall, secured it around his feet, and hooked it to the tractor. After snagging Mom's new electric shears from the tack shed, I dragged Dad to the front porch. I checked on Sally, and when she seemed like she'd be fine, I went to work before Dad woke up and stopped me.

Sometimes I loved my life.

WITHOUT HIS FUR, my dad looked like an oversized mole rat with a steroid addiction and a gym membership. Gathering his precious fur in several garbage bags, I hauled them into the kitchen and showed them to my mother. "I come bearing a gift, Mom."

"What have you done now?"

"I found your electric shears in the tack shed, so I thought I'd take them on a test drive."

Her eyes widened. "You sheared Sally already?"

Grinning, I replied, "Not quite."

The moment realization of what I'd done dawned on my mother, her eyes bulged, she grabbed one of the bags, and peeked inside. "Your dad really let you shear his fur? How on Earth did you manage that? You darling boy. It really *is* Christmas."

"Let is a really strong word."

Mom stared at the three bags before turning her gaze to me. "I should be scolding you for this, Shane. I raised you better. Yet…"

"Yet you have three bags of Dad's fur to card and spin into yarn. I'll even buy all the bleaches and dyes you need so it can be just the right colors for your knitting adventures."

My mother's eyes gleamed with unshed tears. "I truly have the best son."

I set my offerings at her feet and kissed her cheek. "I left him on the porch. I'm sure his concussion will heal after he shifts a few times."

"You're grounded. As punishment, you must eat your supper. Then you'll bring Sally into the house to begin her indoor training. Bad Shane. Don't do it again."

The infuriated howl from outside promised a great deal of trouble, but I laughed all the way to the table, where I dropped onto my seat and waited for the fireworks. Angry werewolves scared sane folks, but only an idiot accused my family of sanity. The sight of the oversized mole rat invading her kitchen reduced Mom to helpless laughter. She slid to the floor, leaning against her cabinets, chortling so hard tears streaked down her cheeks.

"Shane." My father snarled and snapped his teeth at me.

Maybe leaving a little bikini of fur to preserve his dignity hadn't been the best move. The bikini challenged my ability to keep my expression calm and neutral. "You're in great shape, Dad. Have you been working out at the gym lately? You've got some nice muscle tone. That's a pretty spectacular six pack you've got."

"Shane!"

"That said, I'm pretty sure fur-lined

bikinis went out of style years ago."

My mother whimpered and clapped her hands over her mouth, her shoulders shaking as she struggled to regain her composure. It wouldn't work, not this time. No matter what my father said, I'd break one or both of them, and I'd enjoy every minute of it.

If I was digging my own grave, at least I'd make my death memorable.

At the rate my father huffed and puffed, he'd blow the house down or rupture something. "Shane Abraham Gibson, give me one reason why I shouldn't tear you limb from limb and drape your dripping corpse from my porch rail."

"Secretly, you're proud your son dropped you in two hits and kept you down long enough to gift his wonderful mother with sufficient fur to keep her busy for a week. I just gave you a week of peace and quiet. I wasn't even armed, and I didn't scrape my knuckles, either. You should be thanking me."

Wailing, my mother writhed on the floor, kicking her feet. If I hadn't known better, I would've worried she was having a seizure. "Fur-lined bikini," she gasped.

Maybe the fur-lined bikini had been a good move after all. If my mom kept laughing so hard, she'd pass out, and I'd be able to eat dinner without interruption, as my father would spend the rest of the evening shifting between his three forms to grow his fur back.

"Patsy," Dad growled.

"Fur-lined bikini," she countered, as though her words somehow justified her inability to contain her laughter. In some ways, it did.

Howling, my father scooped my mother off the floor with one arm and bounced out of the kitchen. She squealed. Between giggles I could hear across the house, she called, "I'll put the leftovers in the fridge before bed, Shane."

I really didn't want to know what my parents were doing, but if I stayed in the house, I'd find out. A quick check of the stove determined Mom had made beef stew. After careful consideration, I grabbed a few apples from the fruit basket and headed out to the barn.

Hopefully, Sally wouldn't mind some company, because the paper thin walls of the old farmhouse had been half the reason I'd fled to Chicago in the first place. There were simply some things a man didn't want to hear, and male werewolves didn't lose their virility with age.

THREE

Did Dad's fur grow back?

SALLY ACCEPTED my presence in her stall readily enough, although I suspected my ability to drive away a seven foot tall predator was involved. Explaining to an alpaca my father wouldn't eat her was useless, but I tried anyway.

It didn't take long to figure out she viewed me as a provider of food and a living pillow for her amusement. Since serving an alpaca as a bed beat keeping my parents' company for the evening, I dealt with it. In reality, I didn't mind sharing a stall with an animal. When I'd been a kid, we'd all taken turns when Hopper was close to dropping a foal. Skunk's days as a stallion were long over, but he didn't seem to mind life as a gelding.

Instead of coddling a pregnant mare, I had a lap full of alpaca, and she seemed to enjoy attention almost as much as Dad when he was a wolf, which I found amusing. It didn't take long for Sally to settle down, and it didn't take long for the wear and tear of driving to catch up with me.

My mother's chuckles and the whinnying of two hungry horses woke me. During the night, Sally had decided to use my lap as a pillow and curled up beside me. I was grateful she hadn't decided to sleep on top of me again.

"Did you need us to show you where your room is, Shane? You could have slept in the house."

"I thought I'd give you two some privacy."

"Don't be such a baby. I had your father fix the walls last winter. I got tired of freezing my ass off, so he insulated them properly. They're not quite soundproof but close enough."

Miracles really could happen. "Did Dad's fur grow back?"

"Somewhat. He's sulking."

I laughed. "Serves him right for scaring my alpaca."

"Sally."

"You do realize she's my alpaca, right?"

"For now. And you're naming her Sally."

Scratching Sally behind her ears woke her, and she lifted her head, blinked, and snorted, regarding my mother with an expression of utter disapproval. "I don't think Sally agrees. Anyway, I might keep her."

"In your apartment in Chicago."

Without decent pay and with my experience and education dedicated to serving in a police force, I'd have a hard time surviving in Chicago, with or without a furry roommate. Moving was on my list of things to do.

My vacation to New York City had been to escape from reality for a while—and to see if I liked the coastal city. I hadn't.

A night in a barn smelling of horses and hay suited me more than the bustle of city streets and looming skyscrapers. Lincoln, Nebraska had its flaws, but it had plenty of unclaimed land on its borders.

I sighed. "Since I don't have two mil for an eye, I'll be looking for work outside of Chicago. I'll pick a place I can bring my fluffy friend. If you're nice to me, I'll even let you have the fleece whenever I need to shear her. If calling her Sally will make you happy, fine, but she's *my* alpaca. If you want one, get your own."

"But we already built her this nice stall and everything."

"A stall you can put your alpacas in should you get them. You can't have her."

"But you told me you wanted help finding her a home. I found her a home —with me!"

"I changed my mind."

"You're cruel."

"Says the woman who wanted my eyeball in a jar on her desk."

"Admit it, you laughed."

I had, right when I had needed to the most. The doctors had mitigated the scarring, leaving me with a thin line trailing from my scalp, over my eye, and halfway to my chin. Using a little magic, the surgeons had aged the injury enough it appeared a white line rather than a red welt. The scar would never fully fade, but while they hadn't been able to save my eye, they'd spared me from additional disfigurement.

In reality, my eye *was* in a jar somewhere —just not on her desk. For a hundred dollars, the surgical team had preserved it and put it in a medical vault in case I managed to scrounge up the two million required to create a functional replacement. While any eye would do, having the original meant I'd get the best eye possible.

Two million dollars wouldn't just buy me an eye; it'd be an eye with superior vision and potential extra abilities. Some people developed the ability to use their new eye as a magnifying glass or a telescope. Others gained limited abilities to see in the dark.

"It is funny in a sick, demented sort of way," I conceded.

"You're seriously going to keep her?"

"That's my current plan. She's terrified of

Dad. It'd be cruel to leave her here for his amusement."

"He's not going to like that."

I worked my way from beneath Sally, hopped to my feet, and stretched. "That's his problem. Every time he scares my alpaca, I'm going to club him unconscious and shear off his fur. If you encourage him to frighten her, I'll sell the fur to the highest bidder."

"I'm not sure that's legal."

"By scaring my alpaca, he is consenting to being sheared. Animal fur no longer belongs to the animal once it's been sheared off." I smirked. "I suggest he behave himself around my alpaca and earn her trust properly."

My mother's eyes narrowed. "How much do you think you can get for werewolf fur?"

"Not enough for whatever you're thinking."

She pointed at my right eye. "We could take turns forcing him to shift, shear him once his coat grows back, and repeat. I bet we could shear him once a day. If we get more for it as yarn, I can do the spinning if you'll do the carding."

Where *had* I gone wrong in my life to deserve my mother? I gaped at her. "That's awful even for you, Mom."

"So, how much can we get for werewolf yarn?"

"God help me. I don't know, Mom. Go

look it up on the internet. He's your were-wolf. You shear him for his fur and sell it."

"Your concern for my fur is charming," Dad growled from the doorway. "Are you two seriously discussing shearing me *again*? Was the first time not bad enough?"

"We could sell your fur to pay for Shane's new eye, darling. We'll make a fortune off you. Your coat grew in so soft."

Dad stepped into the barn dressed in his uniform and dropped a kiss on my mother's cheek. "I'm afraid to ask. I need to head to work. Colin called in sick, so I offered to fill in for him. Try not to burn the house down while I'm gone."

"My shift starts in two hours. Patrol?"

"Patrol."

"Try not to get shot today. It's annoying." Mom sighed and shook her head. "Shane, try not to burn the house down while we're gone."

"Since when have I ever burned the house down? Why do you think I'm going to start burning houses down?"

"You're related to your father, that's why. You should have seen what he did to my old shed."

I regarded my father with a frown. "Dad's the 'rip it into tiny chunks and tear metal apart' type, not the 'burn it down' type. He probably just smashed the corner, ripped the siding off, stomped on it a while, and finished tearing it down the next day after he cooled off."

When my father refused to look me in the eye, I knew I'd hit my mark. I smiled at my mother. "*You* probably burned what he didn't tear apart the next day so you could roast marshmallows."

"We have an awful son," my mother grumbled.

"We sure do."

"Just take Mom to work with you, Dad. I'll take care of the horses and handle whatever disaster Mom left in the kitchen this time. *Someone* has to be a reasonable adult here."

"And I suppose you think that someone is you?"

"Mom wants to shear you once a day until she raises two million dollars. You'll probably let her try. So yes, I *do* think I'm the only reasonable adult here."

"You started it, son. Just you remember that."

I smiled my best smile. "No, Dad. You started it by scaring my alpaca. You could have left her alone. If you had, Mom wouldn't have discovered you're a walking fur factory. Go to work and take her with you. I have chores to do."

"You're right, Patsy. We do have an awful son."

Laughing at my parents wasn't nice, but it spurred them into hitting the road so I could enjoy some peace and quiet.

WHY WAS THERE a half-cooked pancake on the kitchen ceiling? I scratched my head, wondering how I'd get it scraped off, why it was still up there, and if pancake batter would leave a stain. Did alpacas like half-cooked pancakes? I regarded Sally with a thoughtful frown.

She chewed cud, watching me with wide eyes.

Since my alpaca wasn't going to be showering me with wisdom anytime soon, I sighed, grabbed a chair and a spatula, and went to work restoring the kitchen to a habitable space. Several scrapes later, the pancake splattered to the floor. I scowled at the new mess. "Fuck."

Sally's ears pricked forward, and she approached the ruins of my mother's cooking, sniffing it.

"It's probably poisonous."

My warning went unheeded. Before I could do more than sigh, Sally gobbled down the pancake. Both her ears turned back, and she regarded me with undisguised loathing.

"I tried to warn you."

While she still wore a halter, I'd unclipped her lead line, giving her the freedom to roam around the house. Instead of exploring, she kept close, observing as I scrubbed the ceiling from my precarious perch. Everything went well until I loaded the dishwasher and turned it on. The dishwasher proved as frightening a foe as my father, and Sally bolted for the doorway, her head tossed back and her eyes white rimmed.

"It's just the dishwasher, Sally. It's not going to hurt you."

The machine whirred, which was more than the miniature devil llama could handle. She bolted for the living room, collided with the couch, and scrambled onto it. With a rough application of teeth, Sally snatched my mother's favorite crocheted blanket and hid beneath it.

"Are alpacas just funny looking dogs?" I crossed my arms over my chest, deliberating if I wanted to rescue my mother's blanket. After a few moments of thought, I decided against saving it.

Making a new one would keep her busy—maybe long enough for Dad to keep his fur for at least a few extra hours. I should have felt bad for catalyzing one of my mother's harebrained schemes, but if she wanted to try to raise two million using Dad's fur, that was his problem.

If Dad really wanted to stop her, he could. Then again, he *was* a werewolf. Werewolves tolerated a lot from their mates. I considered myself blessed I hadn't started sprouting a fur coat when I'd hit puberty. Since I hadn't contracted lycanthropy then, I wouldn't, which had given me an edge in law enforcement.

I could handle interactions with enraged werewolves without running any risk of becoming one. Mom would one day, and her infection levels were monitored daily for evidence of her first transformation. I sighed.

In her way, Mom was probably trying to come to terms with my mortality. *She* wouldn't be dying anytime soon, at least not of natural causes. Once the lycanthropy virus became fully active and she underwent her first transformation, she'd exchange some of her humanity for a lengthened lifespan.

In a few hundred years, she'd start showing signs of old age, and I'd just be a dim memory among many.

Sally stuck her head out from beneath the blanket and snorted.

Grabbing her lead line, I clipped it to her halter. "Come on, girl. Why don't we take a stroll? If I stay cooped up here, I'll become as crazy as my parents."

I wasn't sure if she understood me or if she knew the lead line meant we were going somewhere, but she got off the couch willingly and stood still while I folded Mom's blanket and returned it to its proper place. Within ten minutes, I'd locked the house, released Hopper and Skunk so they could enjoy the morning in the pasture, and grabbed the keys for the van. The rental place was two miles away, which would make for a decent walk home. If I needed a vehicle, I'd steal Dad's car from the garage.

I'm sure he'd appreciate me packing Sally in his Corvette and taking her for a ride. One day, I might understand why most folks in the area had a Corvette of some sort hidden away in their garage or barn. Then again, maybe I wouldn't.

As expected, the rental place charged an extra fee for cleaning Sally's fleece out of their van. I got most of my deposit back when the vehicle passed inspection since there was no evidence of despoiling by an adorable alpaca. Bringing Sally had earned me points with the young woman at the counter, although I ended up staying an extra half hour.

"You're popular," I informed Sally.

Sally rubbed her head against me and stared at me with big dark eyes, which earned her another round of petting from me. In the few years I'd been living in Chicago, new faces had appeared in town, although I still recognized many others.

Old Harold, who ran the tiny gas station

across the street, ambushed me before I'd even left the rental place's parking lot. "Hot damn, boy, you're going to end up as big as your daddy at the rate you're growin'. Didn't you learn you're supposed to stop adding inches after puberty?"

Good Old Harold. He was almost as bad as Mom about opening his mouth and saying exactly what was on his mind. "I'm still six inches shy on my toes, old man."

"Didn't hear you were comin' back to town."

"I rescued an alpaca and needed a place to keep her for a bit. I volunteered my parents' place. So, I'm in town for a while until I find a place to board her in the future." I glanced in the direction of Old Harold's gas station. "How's business been?"

"Better than normal. Lotsa folks comin' round these parts nowadays. They're done developin' along the way. Lotsa strangers come livin' 'ere now. Where's your old man? Didn't he bring his truck on down to give you a lift back to the house?"

"They're working. It's a nice day, so we're hoofin' it back to the house. Sally needs the exercise, too."

"Sally's a whatsit now?"

"Alpaca."

"A whatsit?"

I sighed. "Miniature llama."

"She spit?"

"If you corner her or piss her off she will."

"She bite?"

"Maybe."

Instead of heeding my warning he could become Sally's chew toy, Old Harold dug his fingers into her fleece and gave her a good rubbing. His eyes widened. "Well, I'll be, she's right soft."

I kept a close eye on Sally, taking hold of her halter in case she got any ideas. "Mom's already laid claim to her fleece, but maybe you can talk her out of some yarn for the missus if you're lucky."

"The missus don't be needin' any more yarn," the old man grumbled.

Laughing, I bobbed my head in agreement with the sentiment. "They get a little unreasonable about their yarn, don't they?"

"Don't they ever. You sure you don't need a lift over to the house, son?"

"Thanks, but I'm sure. We could both use the exercise."

Old Harold gave a nod, his eyes locked on my scar. "That healed up right nice. You done did us all proud, you know."

The last thing I wanted to talk about was the car accident, but I bucked up, fixed a grim smile in place, and flicked the old man a salute, the one response I could make without insulting him. It was as much an acceptance of his compliment as a signal I'd rather not talk about it.

"Gonna get one of them ones that look like real eyeballs? I hear they're squishy, just like the real deal."

"We'll see."

With a grin that bordered on the demented, he leaned towards me. "Did you put it in a jar?"

Why did *everyone* want to know if I had my eye in a jar? "I didn't keep it."

"Why not?"

Uncertain of how to respond, I stared at him. Sally pawed at the ground and snorted, giving me a perfect excuse to escape Old Harold's interest. "Just didn't. Had other problems to deal with at the time. Anyway, I need to be getting Sally home so I can feed her and bring Hopper and Skunk in from the pasture. You have yourself a good day."

"You, too. Don't be a stranger!"

I refrained from sighing my relief until the old man had crossed the street. "All right, Sally. I hope you don't mind a bit of a hike, because you don't get to hitch a lift in the back of the van this time, girl. You might be cute, but you have to earn your keep, and that means walking home with me."

My alpaca flicked an ear at me and followed without complaint. I gave her some extra line so she could sniff and explore anything of interest along the side of the road. In some ways, she reminded me of a really tall dog with a lot of fur, as she found every single rock and bush fascinating.

Plastic bags scared her almost as much as my mother's dishwasher, and I laughed at her antics. After manhandling Hopper and Skunk most my life, her hundred and ten pounds wasn't much of a challenge, although I had to work to keep her from running away. Laughing, I hauled her in and stroked her neck and back until she calmed.

"Silly Sally. The plastic bag isn't going to eat you. You're as bad as Skunk. He thinks the tractor's sole purpose is for murdering all equine kind. Only time we can bring it out is when he's in his stall where it can't get him."

Sally didn't seem very impressed, but at least she spit on the bag instead of on me. Green goop dripped off her chin, and she stared at me in undisguised horror, smacking her lips as though questioning her actions. Her ears drooped sideways, and she made a pathetic little moan.

"That's not the brightest thing you've done today, fuzzy." I rubbed her ears and led her away from the dangerous bag. A better man would've picked up the litter, but I drew the line at dipping my hands in alpaca spit to spare the environment from a bit of plastic.

Since I was guiding her away from the evil

bag, she was happy to go, pulling on her lead in her eagerness to escape the threat. It'd been a long time since I'd laughed so hard. Sally enjoyed bouncing around, chomping on tall grasses and examining everything with the curiosity of a newborn.

Absorbed in watching her antics, I ignored the vehicle coming up behind us until I heard the crunch of gravel as it slowed. Expecting a curious neighbor wanting to catch up and make small talk, I stopped and turned to see who it was.

A lot of people owned guns in Nebraska. I had enough time to identify the shooter as a middle-aged man in a black suit driving a beat-up Ford before he opened fire. I felt the first round catch me in the shoulder before registering the concussive blast of the weapon discharging. The muzzle flashed a second time, but I felt nothing more before my vision faded to black.

FOUR

Concussions sucked.

MY WOULD-BE killer couldn't hit the broad side of a barn at point blank range, so while the shooter managed to punch a pair of holes through my shoulder, he missed anything important, including my heart and lungs. I'd done more damage to myself when I fell, cracking the back of my head into a rock.

Concussions sucked.

Mages could fuse bone with a little work and time, but organs, especially the brain, were another matter entirely. Some people believed if mages and doctors could overcome the obstacles surrounding the regeneration of soft tissues, they'd unlock the secrets of eternal life. Closing wounds and encouraging skin to heal with minimal scarring was as close as humanity got.

Luckily for me, since gunfire wasn't a common occurrence near my parents' place, several curious neighbors searched for the source of the commotion. Instead of bleeding to death on the side of the road, I woke up in the ER. ID'ing me was easy enough; everyone in town knew who I was, and within ten minutes of my arrival at the hospital, both my parents showed up, still in uniform—mostly.

Dad's had seen better days, since shifting from human to his hybrid form tended to make a mess out of his clothes. Under normal circumstances, I doubted the doctors would have let an enraged, frothing werewolf into their ER, but there were benefits of being a werewolf's son. We shared the same blood type, and if he were going pass the lycanthropy infection to me, he would have before I'd been born. While normal human blood would keep me alive and kicking, werewolf blood would enhance my healing beyond any magics humans possessed, although I'd pay for my hastened recovery with a high fever.

I still had to consent to the risks of contracting lycanthropy, which I found amusing. Mom did, too.

Dad just snarled until Mom tired of his ruckus and swatted his muzzle to make him stop scaring the doctors. While I thought it was hilarious, no one else appreciated my good mood. After everyone in the room had taken a turn scolding me, the nurses began the transfusion process. A pair of doctors did something to my shoulder—something I wasn't invited to watch; they poked me with a needle, and the lights went out.

Growls woke me.

Normal people would have panicked at hearing a snarling werewolf nearby, but having spent most of my life listening to my grumpy father vocalize his displeasure, I ignored his fussing, leaving Mom to deal with him, and moved on to the next interesting thing, a rather obnoxious and steady beeping. My mother had several ways of calming her cranky werewolf, most of which weren't suitable for an audience. I wondered how they'd manage after she had her first shift.

I probably didn't want to know. Actually, I was a hundred percent certain I didn't want to know. I was grateful my mother had found a way to calm him without the risk of giving me a little brother or sister.

One of me was bad enough. I couldn't imagine my parents inflicting another child on Earth. The Earth wasn't ready for another Gibson spawn.

"You two are noisy," I complained. I'd get around to opening my eye eventually. Maybe. "Can't a man enjoy his near-death experience in peace?"

"Oh, baby," my mother whispered, and a moment later, I felt her brush my hair off my forehead.

"You didn't steal my other eye, did you? I

already told you. You can't have either one of my eyes in a jar. I've only got one left, so you can't have it."

While she laughed, her voice was strained. "You're an awful child."

"I try. It's hard to live up to your expectations." I began the systematic process of testing my fingers and toes. Everything cooperated, but my right shoulder wasn't pleased with my efforts. "Some dick shot me and stole my alpaca. I need a gun and an alibi, because I'm going to hunt him down and show him the right way to kill someone. And take my alpaca back. That's important, too."

Issuing threats had seemed a good idea, but my parents only sighed. I did accomplish one thing, though. Dad stopped growling.

"You're going to be stuck here for three days, Shane, so you won't be hunting down anyone and shooting them. The doctors won't discharge you until they confirm you're clean of lycanthropy. Your father donated a substantial amount of blood, so the doctors are worried you might become infected despite your resistance."

"I'd like to file a complaint. Can't they just send someone with a meter to the house in a couple of days?"

Lycanthropy infection wasn't even a big deal. Unless the person was infected before birth, it usually took decades for the first shift to happen. Since the virus levels of the infected were monitored, doctors could reliably predict when the first shift would happen, complications were rare, and the danger associated with a new lycanthrope was minimized.

When Mom shifted, she'd be retired from work until she could demonstrate full control over all three of her forms. With Dad as the source of her infection, she'd become a wolf with the prized hybrid form, and he'd be able to teach her how to control it.

She'd be back to work within a couple of months.

"That's what I tried to tell them, but they seem to think you'd prefer imprisonment in the hospital. Maybe if you tell them, they'll change their minds. Your father's going to growl himself hoarse. He's not going to calm down until he gets you home. I'm sure he'll remember how to speak English given a few minutes or a tranquilizer. I'm starting to think a tranquilizer is the way to go. I don't understand how they think I'll get him to leave in two hours."

I thought about that and realized I had no idea what time visiting hours ended at any of the Lincoln hospitals. In Chicago, visitors were kicked out at ten. "What time is it?"

"Seven. You've been out of surgery for three hours. They brought in a mage from

Des Moines to fuse your shoulder together. Between her help and your father's blood, you won't have any impairment. Your arm will be in a sling for the next week as a precaution. She did some pretty good work."

I grimaced at how much flying in a mage would cost me. "My bank account doesn't thank you."

"Your insurance is covering it. Your father enjoyed having a little conversation with them."

"Isn't Dad limited to growling right now?"

"Emphasis on little. I merely told the agent you were the son of a rather agitated werewolf, and that I was infected, and it'd be absolutely terrible if stress induced my first shift. It'd be like detonating a bomb in a busy public place. A werewolf with the love of his life going through her first shift *and* his only beloved child critically injured during a drive-by shooting isn't a force to be trifled with."

"I'm starting to think you're the reason I'm such an awful child, Mom."

She laughed and kissed my cheek. "Is there a reason you're keeping your eyes closed?"

"You mean he didn't steal my glass eye along with my alpaca? Asshole. So, can you get me that gun and alibi?"

"No, Shane. We're looking for Sally,

though. I was going to call in some favors, but it turns out everyone is already on it. We have a description of the vehicle, and there's quite the manhunt underway. Let us worry about finding the man who shot you and recovering your alpaca while you worry about healing."

Since Mom wouldn't be happy unless I demonstrated I still had one functional eye, I cracked it open and peeked through my lashes. The yellow lights overhead triggered a headache, and I hissed at the discomfort, giving up on the idea of looking around the room. "Let's forget the whole opening my eyes thing for a while. Have I ever told you concussions really suck?"

Dad growled and snapped his teeth together. "Don't listen to your mother. The concussion is the reason you're staying here overnight. You about cracked your skull open on a rock when you went down."

"Hey, Dad. How about that gun and an alibi?"

"I'm thinking about it."

"You're the best father a son could possibly have. Get me a good gun. Something with a lot of bang for the buck. Hollow point rounds for starters, maybe?"

"Calibre?"

"The bigger, the better?"

"You sure woke up cranky. The drugs wear off already?"

"They stole my alpaca." Getting shot was bad enough, but why would anyone kill someone to take Sally? She was adorable, and I'd grown accustomed to sharing my sleeping space with her, but she wasn't cute enough to kill someone over.

Then again, maybe she was. I sure wanted to get my hands on a gun and hunt the bastard down. The ache in my shoulder had something to do with my desire to stir up some trouble and participate in an act or two of violence.

The lycanthropy virus was probably another contributing factor. The bloodlust would fade around the same time the virus worked its way out of my system, which would happen when Dad's blood was replaced with mine. Assuming, of course, I didn't end up with a permanent lycanthropy infection.

What *was* the downside to turning into a wolf capable of ripping people apart with my hands? Ah, right. The control issues and potential of ripping someone apart *unintentionally*. I couldn't even remember the last time someone had gotten ripped apart because the Center for Disease Control had begun monitoring those infected with lycanthropy and providing services to new werewolves.

"When I meant for you to find a lady, fall

in love, and settle down, I meant with a sentient, Shane," Mom complained.

"It's progress, Patsy. He's obviously smitten with his little pet, which proves he is, in fact, capable of loving others. It's our fault we didn't get him a pet while he was growing up. Maybe if we'd gotten him a horse of his own, he'd be more comfortable showing us how much he loves us."

Mom huffed. "He loves me more than he loves you."

"You wish."

My parents settled into bickering over which one of them I loved more. Unless I picked one of them, they wouldn't stop. Picking neither wouldn't help, and picking both wouldn't, either. Of my options, annoying them both seemed more entertaining. "Maybe I actually hate both of you, and you should be arguing over who I hate the least. Compared to Sally, you're hardly blips on the radar. Allow me to present some evidence. Mother, I scraped a pancake off the kitchen ceiling this morning. You know what? Don't even get me started about you, Dad. You're both the reason I'm such an awful child."

"That would explain why he refused to give me his eye."

"I refused to give you my eye because I gave it to someone else first. In a jar, too."

"Shane! You didn't!" My mother wailed. "That's not fair."

Dad chuckled. "Medical vault?"

"Who knew a mason jar and some preservative cost a hundred bucks? Ridiculous, if you ask me. I think they should have paid me to keep my eye. Insurance refused to cover it since they won't even consider an advanced replacement."

"That's my boy, thinking ahead."

"But I asked first!" I was willing to bet everything I owned my mother was pouting.

"Actually, the surgeon asked me if I wanted to store it in the medical vault when I arrived at the ER. I said yes before asking how much it cost. You were the second to ask me. Sorry, Mom. You snooze, you lose."

She sighed. "This is all your father's fault."

"How is this my fault?"

"You convinced me lycanthropy wasn't so bad. You didn't tell me I'd end up with a son like this!"

I laughed. "Just let her shear your fur, Dad. That'll keep her quiet for one whole hour. Go home. It's not like I'm going to get into any trouble here."

"I can't say he's wrong."

Dad sighed. "The instant we leave, cops will be in here questioning you about what happened."

"If they bring me dinner, and something

better than crap hospital food, they can ask me all the questions they want."

"Pizza, tacos, or fast food?"

"Is that Chinese place I like still open?"

My mother groaned. "Unfortunately. How can you stand that garbage?"

"I like it. If they bring me offerings of bad Chinese food, I'll answer any questions they have."

NEXT TIME, I needed to more carefully word my bargains. While a quartet of my parents' co-workers brought me enough Chinese food to feed Dad, they had no interest in limiting their questions to the shooting. I should have known better.

In Lincoln, Nebraska, gossip amongst cops and their families was a way of life. They'd gotten the important questions out of the way first. It didn't take them long to walk me through my morning up to the shooting. One of them even doubled as an artist, and within twenty minutes of the session's start, they had a sketch of the middle-aged man, his junker Ford, and his gun.

"I have to give you credit, Marshal. That's a damned good drawing of that truck." I pointed my chopsticks at the detailing of the rusted-out wheel well. "Why aren't you the permanent artist at the station, anyway? You're good enough."

"And miss partnering with your mother? You've got to be kidding me. Since I doubt they told you, your parents were 'strongly encouraged' to take the next week off work, so I'm stuck with your father's partner for a week."

My dad's partner, a centaur blending a human and a tiger, waved from his spot near the door. I liked Winston Emmanuel. Few had no fear of my father's disturbing strength, tendency to drool, and inclination for howling inappropriately in public. "Don't tell Marshal this, but it's a relief not having to rein in your old man for a change. It's like they expect me to hold him back if he flips out."

"They actually took vacation time?"

Hell had truly frozen over. Even when I'd lost my eye, my parents hadn't taken any time off work. Granted, I held a certain amount of responsibility for that, resulting in early morning calls with my mother each and every day. This time, instead of a phone call, I expected her in person.

"When our chief gives strong suggestions, they're not ignored. It's all right. It's not a suspension. It's just a very flexible shift. One where they aren't expected to show up at work unless called in. Now, the chief *did* suggest they'd get an invitation to the bust if it happened on our turf. That made them both quite happy for some reason."

"Is he trying to make it a blood bath? Because that's what's going to happen, Winston."

The tiger centaur chuckled. "When an ex-cop gets shot in a drive by, everyone wants a piece of that pie, Shane. So, we're going to take it from the top and get to the bottom of this as quickly as possible. I very clearly heard your mother growl that you'd answer all our questions if we bought you that horrible Chinese. We did. You're stuck with us now."

"I don't see why everyone hates this restaurant," I complained. "I like it."

My mother's partner sighed and pointed at my dinner. "That 'General Tao's' is over-cooked chicken meat in hot sauce someone introduced to an orange that somehow turned out crunchy. It's vile, Shane. Anyone who eats it loses their taste buds. They're charred off. It doesn't even taste like General Tao's."

I took a defiant bite of my dinner, which was rather crunchy and hotter than hell. "Maybe that's why I like it."

"You know the routine. How many cases in Chicago were you involved with that may have left someone behind wanting you dead?"

I missed being able to properly perform a

dramatic roll of my eyes. Rolling one just didn't cut it. "Possibly a few, but it's a long hike to Nebraska just to kill a cop with a tendency to leave warnings rather than issue tickets. I let a lot get away with ten over, unlike half the department. There were a few domestic disturbance cases, but none of them were in any position to come hunting me here while wearing a suit. In fact, I'm pretty sure most of 'em wouldn't know what to do with a suit if you gave it to 'em as a gift."

"Ghetto jobs?"

"Mostly."

"What about this alpaca of yours?"

"I picked Sally up in New York after a corpse fell from a skyscraper onto a car I was standing beside. She was tied up in the back seat. The NYPD would have put her down, so I claimed her and took her home. Granted, she'd been spitting mad and nailed one of the cops, but I'd be pretty angry, too, if I were hogtied in the back of a car with three corpses."

"Any reason anyone in the car might have wanted you dead?"

"I sure hope not. Sally was the only living thing in the car. That'd be a pretty awkward situation. Driver's neck broke when the corpse busted through the window-glass windshield. Passenger's throat was cut open, but I'm willing to bet his neck broke, too."

All four cops grimaced, and Winston sighed. "They never learn, do they?"

"They don't get a chance to learn, since both times I've seen it, they died. No one stuck around, so I was the only witness questioned. My history with the Chicago police wasn't brought up. I told them why I was in town, what I witnessed, and that I would take custody of the alpaca. Apparently, my mother has named her Sally. For the record, Sally is *my* alpaca, no matter what bullshit my mother attempts to feed you."

My dad's partner laughed. "How many jilted girlfriends do we have to consider as possible suspects?"

"None."

"What do you mean by none? Even with the scar and false eye, you're not a bad lookin' gentleman, Shane. Surely you have a few girlfriends in the wings."

Since killing my dad's best friend and partner would probably land me in a lot of hot water, I settled for a one-eyed glare. I even closed my right eyelid so he could get a better look at my scar. "I'm the son of a werewolf, Winston. We have a reputation, and it's not one the ladies like. And so help me, if a single one of you cracks a joke about my mom, I'll demonstrate the many ways I can turn my chopsticks into lethal weapons."

My mom's partner grinned. "You're so

much fun when you're high on painkillers and hopped up on the lycanthropy virus. You're definitely cut from your father's cloth, that's for sure. And don't underestimate the ladies. There are advantages to men with the lycanthropy virus—loyalty being one of them. I doubt even an incubus could get your father to cheat on your mother. The trick is waiting for the girls to want to settle down. That's when the werewolves get the lion's share of the bachelorette pool. It's a guaranteed way to avoid most marital problems."

"It's like I have a second set of parents, they're both male, and they're as determined as my mother to have me explore the potential of the opposite gender." I groaned and set my dinner aside. "It's not that I wasn't interested in finding someone—I am. I was just too busy in Chicago. The hours were crazy, especially since I had the lowest magic rating the force would allow. They're more prejudiced against werewolves in Chicago, too."

Winston sighed. "Of course they are. Here, either you're infected, you're related to someone who's infected, or you want to be infected. Those outside of those groups either can't be infected, like us centaurs, or don't care either way. Lincoln, Nebraska. Werewolf Mecca."

Thinking about my utter lack of a love life depressed me. "I figured I'd do my time on the force before thinking about settling down. Actually, I think I was hoping to meet someone on the force but in a different department, but it turned out Chicago was a really bad choice for that sort of thing. They require cops exposed to the lycanthropy virus to wear special badges. Useful for dealing with angry werewolves on the streets but bad news for finding a date."

"They discriminate that much there?"

"Between my low rating and exposure to the virus, let's just say the last rung of the totem pole was an exclusive club belonging to me and only me. I was good at my job, but I was only accepted because I busted my ass. They didn't care I wasn't infected. I'd been exposed, and that was enough to get them riled up. They, grudgingly, have three werewolves on the force, and they only have them to meet their diversity quotas."

The four cops exchanged long looks and remained quiet.

"So, before you get any bright ideas of trying to hook me up with a date, don't. When I want a girlfriend, I'll start looking around to find one."

Dad's partner smirked at me. "You're a virgin."

I smacked my forehead. "I'm the son of a werewolf. Of course I'm a virgin."

Not playing the game often meant I won

the game, and my ready acceptance of the truth, without any evidence it bothered me, stopped the quartet of cops in their tracks. They gaped at me.

"Consider my father. Now take a moment and consider my mother. What do you think would happen if I even thought of having a romp in the hay?"

Enlightenment hit all four at the same time. "Ooooh," they chorused. "A wedding."

I clapped for them. "Well done. You've demonstrated you know my parents. Now, what are you not going to do? Marshal, you're probably the best one to answer this."

My mother's partner laughed. "We're never going to speak a word of this to anyone, especially your mother, as she'll want to start making wedding plans, and you *might* even get to contribute on some element of it. Unlikely, but possible."

"Exactly. Now that we've gotten that out of the way, I have no idea why anyone would have shot me and taken Sally. The vet said Sally wasn't all that old, and while she does need to be sheared soon, her fleece isn't *that* valuable. Not worth shooting an ex-cop for. The only thing I saw in New York was the body landing on that car and killing its occupants. If someone had tossed the body off the skyscraper's rooftop, they would have had to use binoculars to get a good look at me. I didn't see anyone suspicious, just a bunch of New Yorkers who didn't want to have their day blown answering questions for law enforcement."

"This would be a lot easier if you had a long list of enemies wanting revenge on you for landing them in prison, Shane," my dad's partner complained.

I pitied the other two cops in the room. They looked at the door and heaved a pained sigh.

"I can't help that I went to work, got along with the riffraff, and didn't cause trouble for hardly anyone. It's not my fault."

"For once in your life, I think you're right." Winston scowled and beat his tail against the floor while tapping the hospital's polished tiles with his claws. "But why would anyone shoot you to steal an alpaca?"

FIVE

When my mother smiled like that,
she was preparing to cause a lot of
trouble for someone.

WHY *WOULD* someone shoot me to steal an
alpaca?

Nothing made sense. I thought through
every single case I'd ever dealt with in
Chicago and had no idea who might want to
come all the way to Nebraska to kill me. My
inability to make sense of the situation kept
me up all night, resulting in me resemble a
demented raccoon when my mother and father walked into my room at exactly two
minutes after eight in the morning.

"Right on time. Did you just happen to arrive, or were you standing out in the hallway
waiting for the perfect moment? Eight sharp
would have been fine, you know."

"Why ruin a perfectly good tradition?"
Mom stared down her nose at me and
scowled. "Why do you look worse than you

did right after surgery? Darling, I thought your blood was supposed to help, not give him raccoon eyes and rabies."

Dad shot my mother a glare and hooked a chair with his ankle, dragging it to my bedside before sitting. "It seems I am the source of every one of life's problems this morning. Got angsty because you couldn't do anything productive?"

"Got angsty," I confirmed. "I just don't understand why someone would shoot me to steal my alpaca. I've gone over my cases in Chicago about a hundred times. I can't think of a single person who would hunt me down in Nebraska to kill me. If they were after me, why take Sally? It would have been easier to shoot her, too."

"That thought had crossed my mind. Seein' it was right on the way home, your mom and I had a look at where you'd been shot. You left a lot of blood on the ground, son." Disapproval deepened my father's voice. "The shooter didn't leave a scent marker for us, but your Sally sure did. She sure does like spittin', doesn't she?"

Mom stayed in the doorway, crossed her arms over her chest, and smiled.

Uh oh. When my mother smiled like that, she was preparing to cause a lot of trouble for someone. "I wouldn't say she *likes* it. She makes the most disgusted little face after she spits, like she doesn't understand why she'd do something so awful to herself."

"Thanks to her spittin' habit, I was able to find the direction the truck went. I'm thinkin' your mom and I are gonna go on a ride later today."

"On Hopper and Skunk?"

"No, son. Motorcycles. Our poor old horses wouldn't like us taking them on a ride like that. Ain't no one ridden them in years. Harold's gonna watch over 'em while we're gone, and since you'll be locked up here for a few days, I reckon you won't miss us much, right?"

Mom and Dad teaming up for a hunt worried me. Dad pulling out his worst southern drawl meant he fully intended to cause trouble wherever he went. The police department kept them separated for a reason. Alone, either one of them could amass major property damage in a few minutes when left unsupervised. Dad did it with his bare hands. Mom did it with her guns.

Together, I feared for any building they went into. It always amazed me their house was still standing.

"Try not to get arrested. I can't afford to bail you out, and even if I could, I won't." I took my time glaring at each of them. "That means if you find the shooter, you do not beat the daylights out of him. You call the cops in the appropriate jurisdiction and let *them* arrest him. 'Arrest him' is not a euphemism for 'beat the daylights out of him.' Am I understood?"

"If he tries to run, we will restrain him," Dad growled.

"Restraining does not mean beat. Restraining means pin on the ground without excessive force. Remember, you're both cops. Cops are supposed to be good people who uphold the law."

"I told you telling him was a bad idea, Patsy."

"I have awful parents." I groaned. "Go on your field trip, and don't panic when you realize you can't reach me on my cell since I don't have its charger."

Dad reached into his pocket. "This charger?"

"Yes, that charger. I'll forgive you for being awful parents if you find Sally and bring her home safely. Remember, I like her more than I like you, but I might like you a bit more if you return her."

Those infected with lycanthropy were so easy to manipulate. Working Dad over took less effort because his virus was more mature, but my mother's eyes gleamed, too. Wolves craved affection from members of their pack in the wild, and the lycanthropy virus

rewired its host to respond in a similar
fashion.

To them, I wasn't just their puppy, I was
part of their pack.

"Don't you get into any trouble while
we're gone," Dad growled, setting my phone's
charger on the table beside my bed. "Behave."

I saluted my parents. "Have a safe trip.
Don't kill anyone unprovoked. I really can't
afford to bail you out even if I wanted to."

They glared at me on their way out the
door.

THE HIGHLIGHT of my hospital stay was when
I cornered and convinced the nice doctor responsible for me still having a shoulder to release me several days ahead of schedule. A
better son would have notified his parents he
had escaped the hospital.

Me? I retrieved my blood-stained wallet,
filled out my forms, promised I wouldn't bite
or bleed on anyone for the next three days,
and called a cab. The no-biting thing was
more of a precaution than anything else;
saliva didn't contain the virus. Blood and
semen did; a single cut on the gums could
spell lycanthropy for someone else if I wasn't
careful.

Since I didn't have any women in the

wings, I classified as a minimal contagion risk.

Fortunately for me, Mom and Dad had brought a change of clothes, although I didn't think either one of them expected me to need it quite so soon. With my arm trapped in a sling, I wouldn't be doing a lot of heavy lifting, but I could manage most of my chores with my left arm.

When I arrived home, Old Harold was in the barn tending to Hopper and Skunk. "I was done told you weren't gonna be home for a few more days, son!"

"I'm an awful child and escaped prison early," I confessed, flashing him a grin. "A little help keeping these two grass guzzlers fed and groomed wouldn't hurt. I'm under strict orders to take it easy. I'm also supposed to avoid biting anyone."

The old man laughed. "You're in a right good mood for someone who done got himself shot fulla holes."

"Just don't tell my parents I was discharged. I get the house all to myself for a few hours."

The first thing I'd do was raid their gun cabinet and pick a friend to keep me company, and then I'd do a thorough cleaning of the place. Knowing my parents, the instant they got home last night, they had paced their way into a frenzy, resulting in my father dis-

mantling at least one cushion to ease his anxiety. Mom would have scattered half-knitted
projects around the house, and if she had
taken the shears to Dad, there'd be fur *everywhere*. Cleaning would keep me busy so I
wouldn't fixate on what I couldn't do, which
was pretty much anything useful.

"You betcha, son. You go take your tired
self on into the house and catch up on some
rest and heal up proper. I'll make sure the
horses are set out to pasture and brought on
in and fed tonight, so don't you worry yourself none about them."

"Thanks, Harold."

"Anytime. You see anythin' funny around
here, you give me a call. I'll come on by with
the rifle."

To most, rifle meant a hunting rifle, but I
knew better when it came to Old Harold. In
his day, he'd served in the military, and his
rifles could stop a tank in its tracks.

Most people called his 'rifles' grenade
launchers. I thought it better to let him call
his badass guns whatever the hell he wanted
to keep him happy. I also was pretty sure he
had heavier machinery than grenade
launchers kicking around his place, too.
Hopefully, he'd just bring a high-calibre rifle
over instead of his heavy weaponry.

I could justify Old Harold having a machine gun. It'd be a lot harder explaining to my parents why they no longer had a house.

"I'll keep that in mind. Thanks again!"

I escaped into the house, which my parents hadn't bothered to lock. I wasn't surprised. Who was stupid enough to rob a werewolf? A stranger might try, but anyone with half a grain of sense in their skull steered clear of a werewolf's home. Add in the fact both my parents were cops, and no one in their right mind tried anything on their property.

Those caveats didn't stop me from partaking of their gun cabinet, however. They'd probably forgive me. Finding the keys took an hour, and I located them between the mattresses of the guest room bed. Since I'd left home, they'd added to their collection of weapons.

The glittery purple and silver zebra-striped wraps on the machete caught my attention, and I gaped at it. The blade, a terrifying eighteen inches long, could ruin someone's day in a hurry. Since Dad wouldn't be caught dead with anything glittery *or* purple, my mother must have finally taken complete leave of her senses. Lifting the weapon with my left hand, I tested its heft, raising my eyebrows at its weight.

In the hands of a human, a machete could easily kill. A werewolf could slice and dice someone into cubes within ten minutes, leaving even the bones a splintered mess. Shuddering at the thought of so much carnage, I returned the weapon to its spot and went on a hunt for a suitable pistol.

My father's idea of a good gun cabinet had a lot of drawers, each one dedicated to a single weapon. When I'd last accessed my parents' firearm collection, they'd owned sixteen different handguns. The count had gone up to thirty-two, and they'd also added a rack for three hunting rifles.

True to form, they alternated rows, with Dad favoring guns with enough recoil to knock a regular human on their ass if they weren't ready for it. Since Mom handled lighter weapons, I sorted through her collection in search of something a little tamer.

What in the hell was my mother doing with a purple leopard print Desert Eagle? I scratched my head, staring at the drawer with my mouth hanging open. Even her spare magazine was decorated in the horrendous pattern.

The Desert Eagle would punch me in the face if I let it, but I lifted the weapon out of its drawer and checked it over. Why did my mother have a custom Desert Eagle in purple leopard print? Why would she do such a thing to an otherwise manly gun?

Why? Why? Why? *Why* would anyone customize a Desert Eagle to have leopard print of any color?

Maybe a better question was why wasn't I putting it back? I dug through the accessory drawer until I found a holster suitable for a left-handed draw and buckled it around my hips. When my parents got home, making Mom explain why she had defiled a perfectly good gun would be my first task. Then I'd spend at least an hour tormenting my father over my mother's choice of weapons.

I'd have a great time. I looked forward to it.

Until then, I'd do my mother a favor, clean her disgustingly cute but deadly gun, and carry it around in case someone decided to take another stab at ridding the Earth of me.

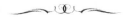

WHAT WAS it with my mother and pancakes? Why would she think it was acceptable to leave two half-cooked pancakes splattered on the ceiling? One day I would figure out how the damned things stayed up there, forcing me to stand on a chair to scrape them off.

Upon closer inspection, I realized the ceiling was mottled with pale stains marking at least ten other pancake incidents. The chore kept me busy, although I made my right shoulder sorer than I liked cleaning the kitchen ceiling and floor.

Realizing I couldn't leave part of the kitchen spotless while the rest resembled a battlefield, I sighed, put on the dish gloves, and went to work. I began with the fridge.

The instant I opened the door, I acknowledged my mistake.

My parents needed an intervention, although I suspected the accident causing the loss of my eye was to blame for their behavior. No one liked cleaning out the fridge, but after a month of neglect, the disaster I faced made me want to throw up—and murder them. The pancakes made a lot more sense.

Pancake batter in a box only needed water, allowing them to dodge the horrors lurking within their refrigerator. Shuddering, I found a garbage bag and cursed them, cursed the asshole who'd shot me to steal Sally, and began throwing everything out, including several of my mother's best pots and pans.

The dishwasher didn't deserve to have such nasty things put into it, and I wasn't sure it could kill whatever the hell was growing in the cookware. One of the roasting pans had turned a rather intriguing shade of green, tempting me to conduct science experiments in the sink.

Halfway through cleaning, with my

stomach performing summersaults because of the smell, I wanted to haul the fridge outside and light it on fire. My phone ringing spared the appliance, and I ditched my gloves in the sink before answering, "Hello?"

"May I speak to Mr. Gibson, please?"

"Speaking."

"This is Detective Steinburg from the NYPD. Would it be possible for you to come to the station to answer some questions?"

I had to work hard not to laugh. "Is there a problem?"

"We have some additional questions about the murder you witnessed."

I blinked. "It's been classified as a murder?"

"Yes, Mr. Gibson. The case has been re-classified as a murder investigation. We're going to need you to come in for additional questioning."

"I'm afraid that's not possible, Detective Steinburg."

"Why not?"

Sighing, I sat at the kitchen table. Since I'd already disregarded my doctor's warning to avoid using my shoulder, I lifted my right hand and pinched the bridge of my nose. "Have you done a background check on me yet, Detective Steinburg?"

"No. You're not a suspect in Mr. Maquire's murder or the deaths of the two men in the vehicle, so the information you provided was sufficient."

"All right. If you contact the Chicago police department, you'll learn I was on the force until recently. I lost my eye pulling a family out of their vehicle during a rather bad traffic accident."

"You're a cop?" Something changed in Steinburg's tone.

"Former. I don't have a replacement eye rated for police work, so I'm retiring. If you need to see me for questioning, it will have to wait several days until I'm out of quarantine." In reality, if I needed to go to New York City I *could*, but all things considered, I didn't want to.

I knew nothing about the man who'd fallen or the other two men killed.

"Quarantine? Why are you under quarantine?"

"Lycanthropy exposure."

"Your file states you've already been exposed."

I sighed. "I required a transfusion, and my father supplied the blood. He's a werewolf, so my virus levels are rather high at the moment. It'll be three days until it can be confirmed if I'm infected with the virus."

"That's rather inconvenient. Care to explain why you required a transfusion?"

Dodging a cop's questions wouldn't help

me in the long run. I muttered a few curses. "Drive by shooting yesterday near my parents' place. I got lucky. I took two rounds to the shoulder. The shooter took the alpaca and left me for dead. Fortunately, he shot me not far from my parents' home, and the neighbors heard the gunfire. Since I'm resistant to the lycanthropy virus, the hospital allowed my father to donate blood. So, until we find out if the virus takes root, they'd rather I stay close to home."

"And you're still in the hospital?"

"No. They flew in a surgeon from Des Moines who handled the surgery. Dad's blood took care of the rest. I was discharged this morning, so I'm at my parents' place."

Detective Steinburg was silent for a moment, then he sighed. "Do you have a contact at your local station I can talk to?"

"Sure. I'll put you in touch with my mother's partner. He can field any questions you have. They already have my statement about the shooting and all the information on the suspect. I'm sure you two can compare notes."

The silence dragged on long enough I fought the urge to tap my toe while I waited. "Your mother's partner?"

"Just be glad I'm not putting you in touch with my father's partner."

"Let me see if I understand the situation. You, an ex-cop, was gunned down near your parents' home, both of whom are police officers."

"Correct."

"And to think all I wanted to do was ask you a few questions about any people you might remember standing near you at the scene. This is not how I anticipated this conversation going, Mr. Gibson."

"That's how I felt when some dumb fuck in a Ford decided to open fire yesterday. I already told you everything I know, Detective. I'm happy to return to New York City in a few days to answer any questions you have. I'm also happy to talk over the phone. I just don't remember anything beyond what I'd already told you."

I gave him the contact numbers for my parents' partners.

"I'll be in touch," the detective promised before hanging up on me. Long after the call disconnected, I stared at nothing. What could I have possibly witnessed that was worth killing me over?

SIX

I'm pretty sure they mugged
someone for a motorcycle and went
on a joy ride.

THE FIRST RULE of the Chicago police department was to stay out of personal cases. Objectivity mattered during an investigation. While I'd had no hope of rising to the rank of detective due to my low magic rating and classification as the son of a lycanthrope, investigations had intrigued me. The entire process of determining the truth lit a fire in my blood.

Personal involvement led to mistakes, mistakes that could cost someone their life.

In Chicago, my involvement with the investigation would have been limited to my interrogation with any other participation in the case strictly banned. Expecting the same principles to apply in Lincoln, Nebraska classified me as an idiot.

At least I'd gotten the kitchen habitable

and the fridge cleaned before the first cop came knocking at my mother's door. I regarded my godfather and my parents' supervisor, Sergeant Lewis Springfield, with a frown. He wore plain clothes, although I saw the lump under his jacket promising he had his firearm with him. "More questions?"

"Are your parents home?"

"I'm pretty sure they mugged someone for a motorcycle and went on a joy ride."

Lewis chuckled. "That works for me. I got several interesting calls today."

"NYPD?"

"And from Chicago. Can I come in?"

"At your own risk. I've decontaminated the kitchen, but the rest of the house worries me."

"They still have you working as their maid?"

I laughed. "They have no idea I'm out of the hospital, and I hope to keep it that way. Come on in, just watch your step. Mom'll skin you if you ruin her fur collection, and one of the bags tore."

Dad's fur completely covered one hallway, but with some effort, I'd be able to gather it back up.

"Bags? Fur collection?"

"Dad scared my alpaca, so I knocked him out and sheared him for his fur for Mom's enjoyment. Someone had a temper tantrum last night for some reason and ripped open one of the bags."

"I wonder why. Kitchen's safe you said?"

I waved for my godfather to follow me. "I even detoxed the coffee maker. I might con someone to pick up some paint for me, as no one told my mother pancakes don't belong on the ceiling. It turns out pancake batter will leave a stain if the pancake is stuck to the ceiling overnight."

"You should probably take it easy on your shoulder, Shane." Lewis pointed at my sling, which waited for me on the kitchen table. "That does you no good if you're not wearing it."

"It kept getting in the way."

"That is the entire point of wearing the sling."

"You're over here in a godfather capacity, aren't you?"

Chuckling, Lewis clapped his hands. "You haven't lost your basic grasp of reality. Well done. I feel a bit sorry for that detective you routed to your parents' partners. Once Marshal got done with him, Winston had a turn, and they grilled him for over an hour. By the time he was passed to me, he'd been rather tenderized. Nice enough fellow for a New Yorker. We got a hit on your shooter from him. Detective Steinburg recognized him from the sketch."

"Seriously?"

"Seriously. The fellow's name is Mark O'-Conners, second-generation Irish-American who somehow found his way into an Italian mafia in New York City. The NYPD has been after him for years. The man who fell from the skyscraper had known ties with a branch of that mafia."

Most large cities in the United States had a mafia of some form; even Lincoln had one, but it specialized in the pixie dust trade. Since the CDC turned a blind eye on them dealing the mood enhancer, the police did, too—as long as the drug didn't become a public hazard.

Lincoln's crime tended to involve petty theft, traffic violations, and domestic disturbances.

"How does this involve me?"

"The branch involved is the mafia's sex trafficking operation."

My eyebrows took a hike towards my hairline. "I'm not nearly pretty enough to be sold in a sex trafficking operation, Lewis."

"I wouldn't know about that. Sure, you won't be modeling anytime soon, but that scar is actually pretty nice. Cheap bastards should have given you a better eye, though."

"At least the color's decent, right?"

"If you were the target of the sex trafficking operation, they would have grabbed you instead of your alpaca."

I opened my mouth, thought about that for a few minutes, and clacked my teeth together. "That's just wrong, Lewis. She's an alpaca."

"No, we have reason to believe she's a human woman who has been transformed into an alpaca."

I again opened my mouth but words failed me. Sally was *human*? "But aren't full-scale transformative magics permanent?"

"Not if it's done by a practitioner using a certain ritual. One of the men in the car was a practitioner known to be experimenting with transformation rituals."

"Wait. One of the mafia's men fell from a skyscraper onto a car containing other members of the same mafia transporting a possible sex trafficking victim?" The coincidence astounded me almost as much as the idea someone would turn a woman into an alpaca to kidnap her and sell her into the sex trade.

The sex trafficking didn't surprise me; Chicago had a huge problem with sex trafficking, although I'd been fortunate enough to avoid being involved.

"You caught onto the gist of it pretty quick."

I thought about Sally's behavior since I'd adopted her, and several things made a sickening amount of sense. If she'd been kid-napped and transformed into an alpaca retaining a human's intelligence, she wouldn't trust anyone—especially not men.

Her behavior around the cops made sense, as they'd been very open about what would happen to her. In her position, I would have been spitting angry over anyone casually discussing my murder.

"You look like you've swallowed a frog, Shane."

"I thought she was rather clever for using the tub as a toilet in the hotels I took her to, and she was pretty cuddly—more so than I expected from an angry alpaca. But if she's a transformed human, she likely realized I was her best bet and didn't want to rock the boat, right?"

"That's a possibility."

"And then she watched O'Conners gun me down before being kidnapped again."

"Had I known she was a probable sex trafficking victim, I would have ordered your father to use his sniffer and hunt her down. While we have plenty of werewolves on the force, his nose is particularly sensitive, and he's familiar with her scent."

"Well, they went on a joyride on a motorcycle to follow the spit trail."

"Does she know your father's a werewolf?"

"Definitely. He terrified the life out of her. She's seen him in all three of his forms." Groaning, I turned and banged my forehead into the refrigerator door. "I've probably traumatized the poor woman even more. Do we have any idea who she might be?"

"No clue in hell. New York has a lot of missing people. Their last count was over four hundred cases of missing women during the past six months. She could be any one of them. She might be someone whose disappearance hasn't been reported yet, too. We have no way of knowing unless we find her and figure out a way to transform her back into a human. With the practitioner dead, Detective Steinburg isn't even sure it can be done."

I banged my head against the fridge a final time before pacing around the kitchen. "So it's entirely possible I'm a target right along with her."

"You were always a quick study. You're more of the 'kill him so he can't talk' type of target, but you *are* a werewolf's son. You'd actually be a good addition to a sex trafficking operation. If you don't become infected, you have many of the benefits of werewolf genetics without the risk of spreading the contagion. If they figure that out, they may want you alive."

Decades on the force had obviously taken

their toll on my godfather. "Why, exactly, do you think I'd be a good addition to a mafia's sex trafficking operation?"

"Do I really have to explain this to you?"

I pointed at myself. "Twenty-seven year old virgin."

"Damn it, Shane. How many times do I have to tell you that your mother isn't going to actually make you marry the first woman you sleep with? You could be a slut if you want with no consequences."

I laughed. Lewis *had* tried to impress on me—many times—my father's one-woman policy didn't have to apply to me. "I wasn't ready to split my time between the force and a woman, Lewis. I was hoping to meet someone on the force, too, but it turns out Chicago's pretty heavily prejudiced against lycanthropes."

"I got the impression they were pretty disappointed you'd been exposed to the virus. I rather enjoyed singing your father's praises—and yours, of course—to the detective I spoke to. I think I startled him."

"They have token lycanthropes on the force, but they're given the most dangerous jobs. Since I didn't actually have the virus, I was usually sent out to deal with pissed off werewolves."

Lewis wouldn't understand my dubious relationship with Chicago's vampire population—or their demonic friends, and he wasn't going to hear about it from me.

"That was actually pretty smart of them. You're still young enough most werewolves will view you as a puppy. It's one thing to get into a fight with another werewolf, but another to pick a fight with a young cop who smells like some pack's puppy. I bet using you limited injuries substantially. All you'd have to do was flinch to bring them in line."

"Ex-cop," I reminded him.

Lewis snorted. "You can take the cop out of the force, but you can't take the cop out of the cop, Shane. You'll be a cop until the day you die, even if you don't ever wear a badge again. Don't try to pull that shit with me. I know better. And so help me, if you start whining about it, you'll never be too old for me to turn over my knee and give you a spanking you'll remember."

Laughing, I shook my head and thumped down onto one of the kitchen chairs. "Now *that's* how you rile up a lycanthrope. You spank their kid. It's a good way to have to clean blood off the walls for weeks. If it makes you feel better, I did tell Mom and Dad 'arrest him' wasn't another word for 'kill.' I also reminded them it didn't mean 'beat.' I thought they could use a reminder."

"How is it they managed to produce someone like you? Are you a parasite? Did you siphon away your parents' common sense and dignity while you were in the womb?"

"I don't think it works that way."

"It would explain a lot."

"All right, Lewis. You didn't come all this way in plain clothes to tell me my alpaca is probably a victim of the sex trade. What are you up to?"

"Know how to ride a motorcycle?"

"Of course."

"How do you feel about being bait? If Detective Steinburg is correct, they're going to come after you again. With the right bait, we might have more luck than our NYPD friends."

After spending my life around cops, I recognized Lewis was playing a dangerous game of one-upmanship against the NYPD, who had a lot more funding, a lot more cops, and a reputation the Lincoln police could never hope to gain.

Sergeant Lewis wanted a piece of the glory pie.

Typical werewolf.

Since I could, I popped my fake eye out and rolled it across the table. "This is a reflection of my opinion."

"That's disturbing. Please don't do that."

Grinning, I returned the glass orb to its proper place and blinked a few times.

"Come on, Shane. You could have washed it off first."

"You're the one who wants me to draw gunfire so you can catch yourself a mafia hit-man, Lewis. I only have two questions for you."

"What?"

"Do you have a vest for me? When do we leave?"

"Yes, and now. I even have a proper gun for you, one that doesn't looks like you got it from a toy store. What is that thing anyway?"

".50 cal Desert Eagle."

"I've changed my mind. Bring your little toy, and make sure you have enough ammo for it."

"Aren't you going to ask me if I have a permit for it?"

"No."

"What kind of cop are you again?"

"The kind who taught his godson how to shoot when he was five years old. Stop your whining and get your ass in gear. We've got work to do."

I only hoped I wasn't about to do something I would regret.

NEXT TIME, assuming I survived long enough for there to be a next time, I would remember my godfather was just as crazy as my parents. When I thought of a motorcycle, I thought of something like a Harley, a bike meant to impress with its roaring engine and massive body.

Lewis had a pair of dirt bikes on steroids in his truck. In my testosterone-poisoned teens, I would have thought they were the coolest things on Earth. Now all I could think about was how much it would hurt when I pancaked myself onto the highway.

"Remember that guy with the real glass windshield, Lewis?"

"I remember him."

"This is the motorcycle version of his windshield."

"Where's your sense of adventure?"

"Hiding with my dignity and planning an escape with my self-respect." I scowled, crossed my arms, and regarded the pair of death traps with my left eye narrowed to a slit. I didn't even care what the hell my right eye looked like anymore. I hoped it creeped my godfather out.

"Don't be a scaredy cat. They only do one-sixty."

I upgraded their status from death trap to incredibly sexy, lethal, and tempting death traps with invisible rockets attached to them. "When you get me killed, my mother is going to have her first shift. Dad's going to froth at the mouth and require treatment for rabies. They're going to eat you. They're going to gnaw the flesh from your bones and use them to decorate their house."

"That's probably an accurate statement. Come on, Shane. I've been waiting years for you to come back so we could take these babies on a ride."

"I need to have a long, serious talk with the chief about the mental stability of his officers."

"He'll probably beg you to take his job. No matter how hard we try, you're disgustingly responsible. When I last checked the dictionary, your face was next to 'good cop.' Live a little!"

I shuddered at the thought of being in charge of a bunch of maniac werewolves, their loved ones, and a city full of rednecks with odd hobbies and a love for high-powered weaponry. "I never thought I'd be thankful for my low magic rating. I'm very thankful right now."

"Admit it. You want to take one for a drive. One-sixty, Shane."

"Why are you trying to kill me?"

"I'm not trying to kill you. I'm trying to let you have a little fun while we play cops. I'm off duty. I'm just doing exactly what I was told I shouldn't do."

Maybe if I closed my eyes and took a lot

of long, deep breaths, everything would go back to normal. "You're disobeying orders, aren't you?"

"Well, the chief didn't say I *couldn't* go chasing after your parents. He may have said something about not chasing after your shooter. He may have also said something about not getting involved with a criminal organization larger than the Lincoln police force could readily handle."

"So basically, you're planning on using me to lure them out so you can honestly say you didn't actually chase after them. We're just going on a joyride looking for Mom and Dad, and we might happen to draw the wrong sort of attention. And since you're my loving, concerned godfather, you suggested I should bring my mother's gun as an insurance policy."

My godfather grinned and hauled the first of the mutant dirt bikes from the bed of his truck. "Admit it. You want to know if these can do one-sixty."

Would I look better splattered alongside the red death trap or the yellow death trap? I considered my choices and pointed at the yellow one. "I think my blood and guts will look better with that one. What do you think?"

"I think you have a morbid sense of humor."

"Lewis, have you ever met my parents?"

"Good point. Forget I said anything. Sure, you can take the yellow one. Just watch her on the turns. She's a bit of a bitch and needs a tune-up. For some reason, she views the speeds between one-twenty and one-forty as optional and prefers to go straight to one-sixty. You might want to keep her below one-twenty until you're used to her."

"Dare I ask what's wrong with the red one?"

"She's just an asshole and views everything up to one-sixty as an obstacle to overcome."

"These aren't street legal, are they?"

"Sure they are. Would a respectable cop like myself drive something not street legal? They're legal. They're just slightly modified."

"Please tell me you have a plan."

"We need a plan?"

"A plan would be helpful."

"I thought I already told you. I'm going to use you as bait, lure them out, and deal with them. Violently. Then we'll save the young lady and make sure she gets home. I'll even be nice and let you take all the credit for the daring rescue."

"Am I the only sane man in this town?" I complained, peering into the back of Lewis's truck for a helmet. Fortunately, I spotted a pair and grabbed the one matching the yellow death trap. I shoved it over my head, muttering curses as I tightened the straps.

"No. You lost your right to say you're sane the instant you decided to actually go along with this."

I hated he was right.

SEVEN

How did he always know when I was
contemplating something illegal?

DID it count as grand theft auto if I was
stealing from my godfather? The little yellow
death trap was coming home with me, and
that was all there was to it. I'd also have a
long talk with him about saying mean things
about the most beautiful piece of machinery
I'd ever laid my hands on.

The bike purred beneath me, and true to
my godfather's claims, she was a bit of a bitch
on the turns, hated being restrained, and
begged for me to put her through her paces.
Until I got her beyond the normal patrol area
of the local cops, I'd keep her near the speed
limit. The last thing I needed was someone
spotting me with Lewis and calling my
parents.

"You can't steal my bike, Shane."

Damn it. How did he always know when I

was contemplating something illegal? "Are you a closet telepath?"

"No, you're just muttering to yourself. The mic in your helmet is really sensitive. I might consider letting you buy her for a reasonable price."

"Dare I ask?"

"How about a promise to enter the dating world and lose your virginity before you're thirty?"

"Did it ever occur to you I wouldn't even care if I stayed a virgin until the day I died?" I did care, but it wasn't anyone's business why I waited.

I knew I could turn myself into a whore if I wanted, but I didn't. When I did settle down, I wanted to follow in my father's footsteps. Maybe my parents were more than a little crazy, but they were still together after so many years.

That's what I wanted, and I wasn't going to ruin my chances by being a dick—or thinking with it. There were plenty of girls in the world who reduced me to drooling, but I recognized the difference between love and lust.

I wanted the kind of love that resulted in a pancake-stained ceiling and a child willing to clean up my messes. That sort of love took a special woman, and I wasn't going to find her unzipping my pants every time a pretty lady took a second look at me.

"Where did we go wrong?" Lewis mock sniffled.

"You really aren't going to give up, are you?"

"Not without good reason."

I sighed. "Fine. I want what Mom and Dad have, and hopping from bed to bed isn't going to get that for me. So, no. I won't turn myself into a man whore. I'd rather wait for the right woman."

"What if she never comes?"

"I die sad, alone, and a virgin. Shit happens."

"You're making it very difficult to tell you to rebel and do all the crazy things you missed out on as a teen, Shane. How am I supposed to do my godfather duties if you insist on being so responsible?"

Since I didn't trust my one-eyed vision enough to shoot a glare at Lewis, I concentrated on the road. I had no idea where we were going except my godfather seemed to believe we'd find trouble east and south of town. Of course, with few main roads connecting the scattered cities and towns of Nebraska, we could be headed west and north via a very scenic route destined to add eight hours to the trip.

With Lewis, I never knew.

"You wouldn't have dragged me out of the house with a busted up shoulder unless you had a good idea of where we're going. What do you know that you're not telling me?"

"Have your parents ever told you you're a spoilsport?"

"No, they just tell me I'm an awful child."

"Well, you are." Lewis laughed. "Actually, you're just an awfully responsible child. We wish you'd come out of your shell. I'm following a hunch. Six months ago, a few sex trafficking rings were busted in Des Moines. Since there was an established network there, it's possible that those rings were related to the one in New York. If so, we might be able to find a lead."

"That sounds like a pretty cold lead to me."

"Please don't tell your parents this, but I may have installed tracking software on their phones. I have been tracking their location with this software, and they beelined it for Des Moines. I figured I'd just piggyback off their hard work."

I really should have known. "Have you done anything nefarious with my phone?"

"Not yet."

"I will consent to tracking software installed on my phone in exchange for my new bike."

"Pull over and pay up."

Torn between laughing and groaning, I obeyed, letting the engine idle while I dug my phone out of my pocket, unlocked it, and handed it to my godfather. "I'm only doing this because the chance of this trip going south fast has occurred to me. That, and I really want this bike."

"Of course you do. She's fast, she's beautiful, and she doesn't talk back, unlike every other woman in your life, right?"

Considering my mother was one of the few women in my life, I nodded. "How does this tracker work?"

"It's something the force has been playing with. Since everyone carries their phones with them, the chief thought it might be a good idea to have an extra layer of protection. Anyway, the cars are tracked, and some of our gear is tracked, but people rarely remember phones are tracked. So, one of the forensics guys wrote an app that lets us keep track of each other. I'll install the app on your phone and authorize certain officers to track your location. For now, I'm giving myself, your parents, their partners, and the chief tracking access. The chief tracks everyone who uses the software. This'll make them feel all nice, warm, and fuzzy knowing where you're at. When this blows over, we can uninstall it."

"I basically just sold my soul and privacy to the devil for a motorcycle."

"Yeah, not your brightest move, kiddo."

"But it's a really nice bike, right?"

"Keep telling yourself that. Now, try to keep your phone charged because we'll only be able to get your last known location if the device shuts off. It'll kill your battery a bit faster than you're used to, so keep an eye on that. Did you bring your charger with you?"

I shot him a glare. "Does it look like I brought anything with me? I have Mom's gun, extra ammunition, my wallet, and my phone."

"Wallet equals cash equals charger. And a change of clothes. Maybe I should have told you to bring an overnight bag."

"Getting shot put a damper on doing my laundry."

"Yet you cleaned your parents' kitchen."

"Toxic wasteland. Priorities, Lewis. The biohazards in their kitchen might have killed me. A little dirty laundry never hurt anyone."

Lewis sighed. "That bad?"

"There were pancakes on the ceiling."

"Maybe I underestimated their stress levels."

"Maybe?"

"Definitely. I definitely underestimated their stress levels. Change of plans. Let's hunt your parents down, make sure they aren't about to go on a rampage, and *then* lure out our bad guy and deal with him."

"I'm telling you the same thing I told them, Lewis. 'Arrest him' does not mean 'beat him within an inch of his life.' Restraining also does not mean beat him. No unnecessary force."

"You seriously take all the fun out of life, Shane."

"Are all werewolves whiners?"

"Yes."

"How wonderful. If I get infected, does that mean I'll become a whiner, too?"

"We can only hope."

I flipped my middle finger at Lewis and muttered so many curses he laughed.

ACCORDING TO LEWIS'S PHONE, my parents were at a hotel in downtown Des Moines. We stopped at a shopping center to buy some extra clothes and get me a new charger before hunting them down. Luck was with us; the place had vacancies. While I understood the reasoning behind sharing a room with my godfather, the werewolf snored so loudly I doubted I'd be getting any sleep for a while.

"Let's wait for them at the elevators. They'll come down eventually," Lewis suggested.

I snorted, pulled out my driver's license, and held it out to the woman behind the counter. "Can you tell me which room the Gibsons are staying in? They're my parents. My godfather and I are surprising them. If you need more proof, my godfather can show off his badge."

The woman chuckled. "Normally, I wouldn't be able to do this, but as Mr. Gibson was rather vocal about his son, who happens to have the same name you do, I'll make an exception. They're in room 406."

"Thanks, ma'am."

I smirked at my godfather and headed for the elevator. "Wise men take the path of least resistance."

"Has it ever occurred to you that you only got away with that because you're a good-looking man with doting parents who sang your praises? If I were a better cop, I'd write her up for that."

"But you're not. And I'm not a good-looking man, Lewis. The whole missing an eye and scar thing disqualifies me." The elevator opened when I pressed the button. Selecting their floor, I considered the best way to surprise them.

Showing up would definitely do the trick, but I'd be a bad son if I didn't try to make my appearance extra special.

"I'd have gotten around to flashing my badge to find out which room they were in."

"Only after we spent a few hours waiting for them to go through the lobby."

"This does not follow the spirit of a stake-out."

"Good thing this isn't a stake-out."

My godfather glared at me. "Spoilsport."

"Think if you knock and I hide to the side and jump out at them we'll get a good reaction?"

"Probably."

"You knock, I ambush."

Chuckling, he nodded and went ahead of me down the hallway. When we reached my parents' room, Lewis listened at the door for a few moments before gesturing for me to come forward. I took my spot beside the doorway, ready to pounce on my mother or father.

After the third knock, the door cracked open. "Lewis? What are you doing here?" Dad growled.

"I visited your child, and since he was worried, I offered to tail you and help out."

By claiming he'd visited me, Lewis explained why my scent lingered on him.

Dad fell for it hook, line, and sinker, opening the door and taking a single step into the hallway. In his human form, he was taller than me by a few inches and had plenty of muscle to withstand my full weight slamming into him. I caught him completely by surprise, and we hit the floor hard, giving me the advantage, which I used to pin him beneath me. "Hi, Dad."

"Shane Abraham Gibson!" my mother shrieked. "What are you doing here?"

I sat on my father's chest cross-legged and grinned up at her. "I stole Lewis's motorcycle. It's pretty cool. I also conned the surgeon into letting me out of prison early. Some weirdo came to the house after I'd finished cleaning the kitchen. Apparently, I'm the bait."

Dad snarled, hooked his arms around my waist, and tossed me over his head. I yelped, tucked, and rolled, landing on my back hard enough to drive the air out of my lungs. Since turnabout was fair play, he jumped me, braced his knee against my right shoulder, and pinned me down in an iron grip. "I left you in the hospital safe and sound this morning. This is not the hospital. This is not safe or sound. What are you doing here?"

If my father had been in his hybrid form, his looming over me with his teeth bared might've been enough to scare even me.

Lewis let himself into the room and closed the door behind him. "Harold called the station to report your brat had escaped. He was worried. Said Shane looked pale and tired, so while he didn't want to impose and barge in, he didn't want to leave him alone, either. The chief suggested I take some time off work and keep an eye on things. When I went to your house, your boy had done a top to bottom cleaning of your kitchen. I couldn't leave him unsupervised. I even put him in a bullet-proof vest before we left. He's already proven himself quite useful, as he charmed the nice lady working the front desk into give us your room number."

"Lewis!" my father snarled.

I tilted my head back and waved at my mother with my left hand. "Hi, Mom. Miss me?"

Yanking my parents' chains came with risks, and my mother planted her bare, smelly foot on my face, digging her toes into my chin. I considered myself lucky she didn't break my nose. "I haven't washed my feet in at least two days."

I shuddered and tried to avoid breathing. It didn't work very well. "I can tell. That's almost as disgusting as your fridge. Come on. Just because I got shot doesn't mean you have to abandon basic hygiene. For fuck's sake, go take a shower. You're going to announce your presence to everyone within a block if you leave here with your feet stinking worse than a skunk."

My parents had the decency to blanch and look embarrassed, with the added bonus of my mother moving her foot to my left shoulder. "You looked in the fridge?"

"Looked implies I, like you, closed the door and ignored its contents. No, I cleaned your fridge. I deemed every pot and pan in there a biohazard and got rid of them. I also scraped two more pancakes off the ceiling. You two are grounded until you can act like the adults you're supposed to be. Obviously, you can't be left unattended, so I'm here to keep you from being dangers to yourselves."

My parents exchanged long looks before Dad sighed, got off me, and hauled me to my feet. The room had a pair of double beds, and he shoved me onto the nearest one. "You do realize we're here tracking down the man who shot you, right?"

"He's aware. He was quite happy to come help. We come bearing gifts of new information." My godfather took his leather jacket off and tossed it onto the other bed. "The NYPD called. There's reason to believe Shane was a target because of Sally, who's probably a transformed young woman in the process of being sold in a sex trafficking ring."

My parents' eyes widened. My mother turned a sickly gray. "Sex trafficking ring? What sex trafficking ring?"

"One involving a New York City mafia with probable connections to a ring here in Des Moines. The NYPD was able to identify

Shane's shooter from the sketch. His name's Mark O'Conners, and he's a second-generation Irish-American with known ties to the Italian mafia in New York."

"And you brought my son where it'd be easier for them to get him?" My mother's voice went up a full octave, and I grimaced.

"Mom, I'm fine. I'm armed. Oh, you can arrest me later. I stole one of your guns from your cabinet."

"Shane Abraham Gibson! What has gotten into you?" She towered over me, planting her hands on her hips. "You did not steal one of my guns. You would never do something so irresponsible."

I lifted my right arm and revealed the holster containing her leopard print Desert Eagle. "Why did you do such a terrible thing to such a respectable gun, Mom?"

"You little shit!" Mom cuffed the back of my head, and I yelped. "That cabinet was locked. How'd you get into it?"

"I told you not to hide the keys between the mattresses," Dad muttered.

"Did you really think I was going to sit around the house unarmed? It's all Lewis's fault."

"How is it my fault?"

"You brought a vest for me, you encouraged me to borrow Mom's gun, and you brought two bikes, helmets, and biker jackets.

I'm pretty sure you begged me to come after them."

"I'm sorry, Patsy. He looked so sad and lonely. I couldn't leave him home by himself. I installed a tracker on his phone, so when we use him as bait, if they kidnap him and sell him as a sex slave, we'll be able to track him."

My parents' eyes bulged, and they gaped at my godfather.

Dad recovered first. "Why would they want Shane as a sex slave?"

"Thanks, Dad."

"You weren't modeling before you got yourself a marble for an eye, son."

"Think this through carefully, Justin. He's your son. Werewolves have a reputation for a reason. If they find out he's a werewolf's puppy, he'll rise to the top of their list of potential victims. Once he decides to settle down and finds the woman of his dreams, she's going to be a very happy lady."

My mom's cheeks turned pink. "You may have a point."

"Mom!"

"Oh, don't you start, Shane. You're a grown man. There's no need to be embarrassed."

"You know what, I'm going to take a shower while you all discuss my future career as a sex slave because I don't want to hear it.

Try to have something resembling a plan by the time I'm done."

"If you want a shower, you'll have to go to your room, because we have a jet tub instead."

If they thought I was going to my room when theirs had a jet tub, they were insane. "I think I'll manage."

EIGHT

Don't break the hotel, Dad.

NOTHING WAS BETTER than napping while soothing jets massaged my sore muscles. A persistent knock at the bathroom door woke me, and I grumbled curses at the cooled water.

"Did you drown, Shane?" my father asked. "Unless you come out or at least acknowledge me, I'll break this door down."

"Don't break the hotel, Dad."

"Get out of there already. We're ready to get to work. Apparently, leaving you in the hotel isn't an option."

I almost regretted missing my godfather arguing with my parents about including me in plans that could get me killed or forced to be an unwilling participant in a sex trafficking operation. I definitely didn't want to be involved unless I was taking part in a raid to destroy it. "All right, all right. Keep your pants on, Dad. I'll get out in a few minutes."

"How about you get out now? You're going to fall asleep again. I'd rather my son didn't drown today."

"So it's okay if I drown a different day?"

"No. Get out of the tub so we can put this plan together."

My mother laughed. "Expect to be cuddled into submission, Shane."

If Dad was feeling needy enough Mom felt the need to warn me, I was going to have to endure at least an hour of him hovering. "You may have *one* hug after I've finished my bath and gotten dressed, Dad. One. Not two, not one that lasts an hour, one normal hug."

"Thanks, Patsy," Dad grumbled. "Five minutes, Shane. Don't make me come in there."

"I'm a grown man. I can take as long as I want in a bath, damn it!"

"You're a grown man in *my* hotel room using my tub. Stop whining."

My godfather laughed. "Give him a break, Justin. The kiddo's had a rough couple of days. He's probably sore and tired. I wouldn't want to get out of the tub, either."

If I didn't get out, Dad would break the door to get in, which was enough to get me moving. Groaning, I turned the jets off, taking a few minutes to check my shoulder while I dried off. Although I still ached, only faint bruising and two pale scars betrayed where I'd been shot. Instead of dressing, I threw on Dad's bathrobe, giving my dirty laundry a kick.

Next time I'd remember to bring my clean clothes into the bathroom with me.

When I emerged, Dad scowled at me. "That's my robe."

"I didn't take my clean clothes into the bathroom." I pointed at my new duffle, which was near the door. "I'll change later."

"But that's my robe."

"I'm just grateful you did your laundry before coming here. What's the plan?"

My parents and godfather stared at each other, and I waited it out, sitting on the edge of the bed. After a few minutes, I wondered if they'd ever get around to letting me in on their scheming.

I worried they'd decided the worst plan was the one most likely to succeed. "I'm beginning to think you want to sell me into slavery."

Dad sighed. "That might be the easiest way to track them down, find out how they turned a woman into an alpaca—if they did turn a woman into an alpaca. Lewis seems to think it's possible. Your mother and I have been informed you're actually a handsome enough man, and that little scar of yours gives you a certain bad boy flair, which might be appealing to certain women looking for a male escort for an evening."

"And I've heard rumors he's rather delicious in a uniform," my godfather announced.

"And the bullshit levels in this room have risen to absurd levels. There are no such rumors about me. Can you three take this seriously?"

"We are." Dad sat beside me, wrapped his arms around me, and squeezed hard enough I squeaked. "At first, I wouldn't even consider selling you into slavery, but then Lewis suggested I might be able to get a good rate for you since you're my son and possess werewolf genes. Since you seem to favor the werewolf way of picking a wife, you'll probably be a beast in bed, just like me."

"Please let's never discuss this ever again. I did not need to know that."

"He can't help that it's the truth," Mom replied.

I groaned and struggled to escape my father's hold. "You're not selling me into slavery."

"It might not be an option. If something goes wrong, you might end up a victim just like Sally."

"Shooting me and leaving me to die on the side of the road leads me to believe they don't want to make me a sex slave. Make a contingency plan in case something like that happens, but why don't we focus our attention on rescuing Sally and breaking up the ring?" I squirmed out of my father's arms, and to prevent him from bothering me further, I fetched my new clothes and headed for the bathroom. "Let me get changed into real clothes so Dad will stop whining I'm wearing his robe."

"You should pose for us so see if you're physique is appropriate for the sex trade." My godfather flashed a grin at me.

I smacked him with my duffle as hard as I could on the way by. "No."

"But we're curious."

"No."

Dad looked me over from head to toe. "Come on, Shane. It's relevant and important. You *are* my son. You'd probably make a good sex slave with appropriate training."

My mother grinned. "I bet a virgin is worth more, too. If they're running a sex trade operation, they have to have an incubus or succubus on board. One look at you, and you'd be a top sell. Between your resistance to the lycanthropy virus and your exceptional heritage, you'd bring in a pretty penny. Add in that scar, and you might even classify as exotic."

"This is punishment for having gotten shot, isn't it?"

Ruffling my hair, Dad gave me a shove towards the bathroom. "We've only begun, boy."

IT TURNED out the trio of troublemakers had a plan, and true to Lewis's initial proposal, I was to serve as the bait to lure out O'Conners and any potential friends. Thanks to Dad's sensitive nose, we even had a rough idea of where he'd taken Sally.

Like many cities in Nebraska, farmland skirted Des Moines. Dad got a rental car and drove us to a cattle ranch twenty minutes beyond the city limits. "This is the place. They breed cattle for slaughter, and the owner is also a heavy investor in several nightclubs in the city. The nightclubs are probably the front for the sex trafficking ring. For your cover, you're looking for a girlfriend—someone you can trust to be loyal."

I arched a brow. "You want me to hit on women in a nightclub."

"I'm not telling you to bend a girl over your knee, spank her, and get her to call you her daddy, son. You're on vacation, looking for love—the usual things a newly retired young man might do. You're just doing it in a way you'll catch attention from our prey."

I could always trust my father to be, well, a werewolf. Sighing, I shook my head. "All right. So I go into these clubs and look for a girl. What do I hope to have happen?"

"We're hoping you'll find someone interested in hooking you up with an escort or a prostitute. Maybe for a night, maybe for longer. Discuss the idea, act a bit uncertain and shy. Show some interest, especially if you're offered something like being matched with a woman for a long-term relationship. Be cautious, but find out how much a match like that would cost you. If you're lucky, they may make arrangements for you to meet some women. That's what we're hoping for." Dad chuckled. "Lewis will be doing the same. We're going to be watching your tracker on our phones."

"What's the probability I'm going to end up a sex slave?"

My parents glanced at each other and said nothing. I turned my glare to Lewis, who shared the back seat with me. "Lewis?"

"Fifty-fifty."

"I'm going to need a spare battery and a pair of boots."

My godfather frowned. "Why?"

"A spare phone is going in my boot with the spare battery. That way, it might actually be useful. It'll have that tracking software installed, too."

"You raised a smart boy, Justin. Where can I get one like him?"

"Take that up with your wife. I recommend begging. Just don't expect her to go through mating more than once. Patsy still refuses to even consider going through it again. I keep telling her it'll be better once she shifts for the first time."

I put my hands over my ears. "I don't want to hear about werewolf mating rituals."

Mom snickered. "It's not that big of a deal, Shane."

Why couldn't I have dignified parents? "You are the reason I'm an awful son."

"Can't say he's wrong," my godfather agreed.

"Stop being such a child about this, Shane," Dad ordered. "First, it's what makes *you* appealing to a sex trafficking operation while werewolves aren't. While you were snoozing in the tub, I talked to some Des Moines cops who've been working on busting rings here. Typical uninfected children of werewolves enjoy heightened sexual prowess without the complications werewolf men face."

"I suppose I should be grateful you haven't explained these complications to me before."

"It wasn't necessary; you've never been infected, so it hasn't been an issue. If you become infected, I'll teach you, as it's very easy for an ignorant puppy to cause his woman substantial discomfort."

I wanted to put my fingers in my ears and hum to avoid the discussion. Instead, I surrendered to the inevitable and asked, "Fine. What complications?"

"Male werewolves share certain physical attributes with mundane wolves," Dad explained.

"That's not a helpful answer. I haven't exactly studied natural wolves."

"I'll explain it, darling. You'll dance around the subject all night long and make him more uncomfortable than necessary. Shane, male werewolves go into a frenzy, and once they start trying for a puppy, they don't stop until certain there's a puppy on the way. Since male werewolves can smell when a woman is fertile, they're rather insistent on ensuring pregnancy. Let's just say your father and I were inseparable for twelve hours. He refused to quit until he could detect the changes in my scent. Fortunately, as I was already infected with the lycanthropy virus, it didn't take as long as it would for a regular human woman. Long story short, it's really not comfortable. Worth it, since you were the result, but not something I look forward to doing again anytime soon—at least not until my first shift. It's supposedly a much better experience when the woman is a werewolf. I'll consider a sibling for you then."

With the unwanted mental image of my

mother and father having twelve hours of non-stop sex to conceive me rattling around in my head, I tried to steer the conversation back towards safer territory. "So why is being a werewolf's son a big deal for a sex trafficking ring?"

"You'll probably be able to have the twelve hours of sex without the issue of being inseparable from your partner. With a bit of work on your part, you'll be able to give women the ride of their lives. Unfortunately, it won't be good for your emotional well-being, as you're like your father. You don't want just any woman, do you? You want the perfect woman for you."

The easiest way to deal with my mother was to tell her the truth. "Yes."

"So there you have it. You'd be a good target if they figure out you're a werewolf's son."

"That's just what I wanted to know. So, what if I were a daughter instead of a son?"

"They wouldn't want you. You'd be useless to them unless you were really pretty. I don't think you'd make a pretty girl."

"Thanks, Mom."

"Anytime, baby."

THE NEXT TIME my parents sent me into a nightclub, I'd remember to ask what type of nightclub before going in. When I thought of a nightclub, I thought of dancing, loud music, and a lot of inappropriate hip grinding. I found the hip grinding, but it involved a lot of scantily clad women on the laps of appreciative men ready to part with their money. Fifty dollars got me in the door, and within five minutes, I doubted I'd ever feel clean again.

Unfortunately, to get to the bottom of the sex trafficking operation and find Sally, I needed to get my hands dirty. With a thousand dollars burning a hole in my wallet, greasing the wheels wouldn't be a problem, assuming I remained calm.

Strip clubs weren't illegal. Prostitution wasn't even illegal. Forcing girls to work in strip clubs or as prostitutes, however, was extremely illegal and fed sex trafficking rings. I should have realized the type of club it was before I'd gotten inside, but I avoided the places as a general rule.

I was oddly disturbed I'd been to more brothels than strip clubs, but my work in Chicago had required me to visit them on occasion. It bothered me the Chicago brothels were more classy and discreet than the Des Moines club. I hadn't been expecting to grease the wheels by paying girls to dance for me. I headed straight for the bar, one of the few places the strippers and lap dancers avoided. I disliked drinking on the job, but I browsed the selection of alcohols, my gaze settling on an old bottle of Scotch.

The barkeeper looked me over, strolled closer, and asked, "What can I get for you?"

Asking for a double of the barkeeper's best Scotch might cost me a fortune but would send an important message about my money and my willingness to spend it. I braced for the damage, put my credit card on the bar, and ordered. Unlike me, the barkeeper was dressed like many of the clients, blending the strict formality of a black suit with a splash of color in the form of a bright red tie.

He looked down his nose at me before selecting a bottle from the top row and snagging a whisky snifter. "How do you want it?"

"Whatever you feel is best to bring out its true potential." Some Scotches needed a few drops of water to make them bloom while others went down better neat. My answer earned me the hint of a smile. After pouring, he dribbled a few drops of water into the glass.

He took my credit card to the payment terminal, and while he swiped, I dug out a twenty for a tip. Then, satisfied I'd begun the process of securing the barkeeper as a new friend, I paid more attention to my drink than to him.

He did the Scotch justice, and I savored the way the whisky's smoke and peat tones partnered with a faint floral sweetness. When the barkeeper returned my credit card, he lingered.

"You know your Scotch." I lifted my snifter in a salute. "You have my thanks."

"You're a new face around here."

"On an extended vacation, so I thought I'd take a drive across the country, get out and see the world, maybe meet a girl worth settling down with." I paused, glancing in the direction of the many scantily clad women working the men scattered around the tables and booths. "Take in the scenery."

"How are you liking the scenery so far?"

I chuckled, making a show of looking over the women. Many of them were pretty and delicate, perfect targets for sick perverts on power trips. I hated myself for noticing them, for knowing some—if not all—might not be working the club because they wanted to. "This is the nicest place I've been to in a while."

Hating myself for the truth wouldn't change anything.

"You'll find the girls are friendly. We have a new one starting tonight. She's a bit shy, but if that's the kind of lady you're looking for, arrangements can be made. She might not be the greatest dancer yet, but if you're looking for some conversation, she might do." The barkeeper nodded towards one of the alcoves deeper in the nightclub.

The dim lighting did a good job of obscuring the young woman occupying the booth, who wore the same barely there style as the women working the tables. Her blond hair was tied into a messy bun, and her attention was fixed on her drink as though she hoped to find salvation at the bottom of her glass.

"And how much is this conversation going to cost me?"

The barkeeper's grin turned sly and lecherous enough I tensed. "Got some proof you're not from around these parts? We're going to have a bit of a party later. I might be able to get you in. Consider it a gift from one Scotch lover to another."

I pulled out my wallet, made a point of tilting it so the barkeeper caught glimpse of my cash, and pulled out my Illinois driver's license. Thanks to my lost eye, I'd gotten a new one—one clear of evidence I'd once been a police officer.

"Ah! Now Chicago's a hopping town. There are some damned fine girls there."

"Sure are," I agreed. "I just thought a change of scenery would be nice."

Resting his elbows on the bar, the bar-keeper leaned towards me, tapping my license on the polished wood. "Here's how it works. Since you're a first timer, seven hundred gets you a good bottle of Scotch and the girl's company for the rest of the evening. I'll send the pair of you up to the VIP lounge. Relax, take a load off, enjoy your conversation."

The way the man put an emphasis on conversation implied I'd be doing most of my talking below the belt. Since there was nothing illegal about buying an expensive bottle of Scotch and talking to a girl who wore the equivalent of a skimpy bikini, I pulled out my credit card and handed it over. "What kind of bottle will fifteen hundred get me?"

The barkeeper's grin widened. "The best drink of your life with the bonus of a ticket to a show you'll never forget."

NINE

In her shoes, I'd be tense, too.

THE BARKEEPER GESTURED to one of the club's bouncers, took down a full bottle of aged Scotch, a thirty-year single malt if the label was to be believed, and nodded towards the girl alone in the booth. A man with enough muscle to go toe to toe with my father approached, grunted, and gestured for me to follow him.

"You're exclusive for the night," the bouncer informed the woman, and her eyes widened. "Take him upstairs to a private booth. Someone'll bring your drinks."

Most girls I knew with blonde hair had blue eyes, but the woman I'd be spending the rest of the evening with had brown eyes touched with the faintest gleam of gold. My exposure to Dad and other werewolves gave me an appreciation for hazel eyes. I figured the color had something to do with the wild side of the lycanthropy virus, the one that blended man and beast into a whole.

She scooted out of her seat. From the bar, I hadn't noticed her slim figure had the hallmarks of a fit body. Unlike a lot of women I'd met over the years, she wasn't the kind of girl who kept her waist tiny with the goal of appealing curves. When she moved, muscles and hard lines marked her as someone who liked being active.

It didn't take long for my mind to wander to the thought of her in a pair of tight jeans riding a horse, and I was disturbed by how much I liked the idea.

Her lingerie, too skimpy to even classify as a bikini, didn't do her justice, and that annoyed me almost as much as the way she tensed when she eased her way by the bouncer. "This way, sir."

She led me to a hallway tucked at the far end of the bar and up a flight of narrow stairs, discreet enough I hadn't noticed it in my initial look around the club. My time on the force helped me recognize the woman's tension, and I could guess the cause of it.

In her shoes, I'd be tense, too, since a one-eyed man with a scarred face had just bought her time for the evening. After the past two days, I probably looked like a serial killer who lured women deep into the woods to have his way with them before tearing their bodies into little pieces and burying them.

The VIP lounge had booths with tall backs and curtains arranged in tiered rings facing an elevated stage, offering the illusion of privacy for those within.

It bothered me most likely didn't care if anyone watched what they were doing with the club's women. A pair of bouncers waited at the top of the stairs, and the woman hesitated before saying, "We're exclusive for the night."

The club had a thing for overly muscled bouncers dressed in suits, men who could probably break bones without much effort. Both regarded me with a frown. A phone rang, and I traced the sound to a nearby podium. One of the bouncers answered, "What?"

His eyes widened a moment later. "Yes, sir." After he hung up, he nodded to me and turned his attention to the woman I'd bought for the night. "Front row, Sally."

Sally? Somehow, I hid my surprise, although Sally herself had something to do with it, as she immediately headed for the steps leading down towards the front row. Following her gave me an opportunity to get a better look around the place. While the downstairs lounge had been busy, few of the booths were occupied, but a single glance convinced me to turn my attention elsewhere in a hurry.

Maybe some people enjoyed voyeurism, but I wasn't one of them. I already needed several buckets of bleach to erase the mental images my parents had painted with their un-wanted lesson on werewolf reproduction. By the time the night was over, I'd need a vaca-tion from my vacation from my first vaca-tion. In fact, I swore against ever going on another vacation ever again.

Sally led me to a booth tucked to the side and stared at the floor.

"Ladies first," I murmured, gesturing to-wards the curved bench seat.

While some of the booths were more like circular beds with end tables, Sally had brought me to a smaller booth meant for two, one with enough space between the bench and the table a determined woman could end up on her partner's lap if she really wanted.

I tried not to think about that too much when I slid onto the seat beside her. Dad had never hidden his admiration of the fairer gender, although the lycanthropy virus en-sured the vast majority of his attention re-mained on my mother.

Women were to be admired and re-spected, and he'd take my balls for a trophy if he ever caught wind of me treating a woman like I currently was, as property to be bought and sold. Would he let me off lightly since he'd sent me into the damned nightclub in the first place?

I barely had enough time to unzip my jacket before a waiter brought the bottle of Scotch and a pair of snifter glasses. "If you need anything, sir, do not hesitate to ring the bell." The man motioned towards a discreet button at the end of the booth. He left us in private—as private as a tall-backed booth could get.

A better man would have asked his company if she wanted a drink, but I poured a double and slid it to her. "I'm about as talented at small talk as the average goat, so please forgive any rudeness. It's unintentional. Sally, is it?"

"Sally," she confirmed, and the way she said her name gave me the feeling it wasn't actually her name at all. Clutching the snifter, she glanced at me before taking a sip. When I made a show of pouring my own drink, she took a longer swallow.

If she figured out I was in need of a little liquid courage, I'd probably be laughed out of the nightclub. I didn't intend to touch her any more than necessary to maintain my ruse, especially since it'd be several days before the lycanthropy virus worked its way out of my system. "Shane."

I took a sip of my Scotch, keeping an eye

on her the entire time. Most of her attention seemed focused on her drink, but she reached up and fiddled with her bra. At first, I thought she was adjusting it, although I couldn't imagine how something so insubstantial supported her breasts.

Her finger traced the black and red lace, drawing my attention to her creamy, untanned skin and a small disc attached to a tiny black wire. While I hadn't worn wires often as a cop, I'd done a stint or two undercover, and the device I'd worn looked very similar to the one attached to her bra. The way she warned me our conversation was being monitored was so subtle my jaw just about hit the floor.

To cover my astonishment, I took a swig of my drink, which burned all the way down. "You're no stranger to Scotch, are you?"

Slipping her hand out of her bra, she reached for her glass and swirled the amber fluid around. "I like it. It's complicated, a bit like you from the looks of it. To buy a bottle like this, you've got the money, but you don't dress like you come from money."

"I'm on vacation, so I thought I'd live a little." I set my glass aside and snagged the bottle, lifting it up to admire the label. "Something this nice deserves to be shared with worthwhile company."

"That leather jacket's hiding a flirt, I see."

"More like a lot of dust following a long ride on my bike." I liked I could speak the truth and nothing but the truth; while I had indulged in a long soak, Lewis's spare jacket hadn't gotten any love—or cleaning—from me, resulting in more dust and dirt on the leather than I liked. "I was looking for a nice place to unwind."

Sally drained her glass and set it aside, then she scooted a little closer to me, trailing her fingertips along the length of my arm, checking for evidence of dust, which she found in plentiful supply. "It seems you're right. You're a bit dusty from your long, hard travels. Let's get you out of that so you can be comfortable."

A trap of my own making, involving my credit card and the most expensive bottle of Scotch I'd ever touched, closed around me. With her being wired and someone likely listening in on everything we did or didn't do, I either had to play along or make a break for it.

Unfortunately for me, until I knew if hazel-eyed Sally was the alpaca I'd carted from New York, I couldn't justify escaping for the sake of my personal comfort. If they were the same, I wasn't leaving without her, although I had no idea how I'd get her out of a place with more guards than a prison.

"Let's," I agreed, shifting on the bench so I could wiggle out of my jacket.

Sally had other ideas, including grabbing hold of my jacket and sliding her hands along my sides, dipping her fingers into my pockets to relieve me of my wallet and cell, which she set on the table. "Wouldn't want to damage anything getting you out of that nice leather coat, now would we?"

"Of course not."

She took her time checking my pockets, cleaning them out, before she slid the leather off my shoulders.

While there was nothing overtly sexual about her touch, between the alcohol and my inability to keep my gaze from wandering, I was squirming by the time Sally freed me from my jacket and tossed it aside.

The waiter made an appearance and took my jacket.

"They'll bring it to you later when you're ready to leave," Sally murmured. "During the main show, they'll claim your phone, too—no devices, including cameras, are allowed. For the sake of privacy, of course. It'll be kept with your jacket."

If I hadn't had two extra phones stuck in my boots along with an extra battery, I'd be worried. "As long as it's returned, I don't mind."

Sally's brows furrowed, but she recovered

a moment later and forced a smile. "Of course."

If Sally was part of the sex trafficking ring —and a former alpaca with a spitting problem—she wouldn't be allowed to have anyone take a picture of her. Rather than asking for permission, I muted my phone, slipped it off the table, and held it on my lap, hopefully shielded from any unwanted recording devices. Her eyes widened.

"Do you like motorcycles, Sally?" I asked to cover the sound as I snapped a picture of her.

"If men like you ride them, I think I've a newfound appreciation for them."

"And you called me a flirt. You, Sally, are the real flirt here." Maybe I was a virgin and denser than a rock when it came to relationships, but I'd been around my parents enough to know how the game was played. I chuckled to cover the sound of me snapping another picture of her. "Is this when I surrender and let you do anything you want with me? I told you I wasn't all that good at small talk."

She slid her hand under the table; to anyone watching us from afar, her grip on my upper thigh probably looked far more personal. "For some reason, I doubt there's anything small about you." She paused, and her fingers dug into my leg. "Nothing small about you at all."

I somehow managed to text the pair of pictures to my parents and Lewis without dropping my phone. I also warned them not to message me, as I'd be losing the device during an upcoming show. I deleted the conversation and set the phone on the bench between us, leaving it open to a note app.

Since it'd look awkward if I did absolutely nothing, I reached up and caught hold of a loose lock of her hair, spinning it around my finger. "I never thought I'd find myself liking a blond, but you're something special, Sally."

"You're only saying that because I have my hand between your legs."

Well, technically, her hand was *on* my leg, but if she wanted to give a good show for any listeners, she was succeeding. I prayed her hand remained where it was, or I'd be more than embarrassed in a heartbeat. "It might be playing at least a minor role, yes."

Her laugh startled me. "You're an honest one. I like that."

She scooted closer and angled her body so she could rub her bare foot against my jeans, which put her left hand near my phone. I pretended not to notice, reaching across the table to retrieve our glasses and bring them closer. I refilled both and took a sip of mine, taking deep breaths to maintain my composure. "Honesty works pretty well for me. No one can catch me in a lie if I'm always telling the truth."

A few stray strands of her hair fell over her cheek, giving me a convenient excuse to shield her from any watchful eyes while she used my phone. I tucked them behind her ear, careful to keep my touch light and gentle.

"Then tell me, Mr. Honest, how did such a sweet man get trapped in such a hard, rugged body?"

I couldn't hear the click of my phone's camera, but I caught a glimpse of the screen reflecting most of my face, and to help her out a bit, I angled my head so she could get a better shot. "I'm not all that good with the wine and roses, but I like sharing my whisky with a pretty woman. I'm also a fan of sunset rides on horseback."

"A motorcycle-riding cowboy. I'm a lucky girl tonight."

Anyone listening in would think *I* was the one about to get lucky. Judging from the nature of the texts she was sending, there were going to be a lot of unhappy people in the club within a few hours, as she was furiously tapping names, addresses, and locations to a phone number.

I scooted a little closer to her, ducking my head so it looked like I was dropping kisses along the length of her neck. Hanging out with a lot of single cops, I'd heard more than my fair share of pick-up lines, although most of them were painfully awkward at best.

I couldn't afford to stay quiet, especially when she was frantically trying to pass information to someone, making the most of a bad —and recorded—situation. "How lucky do you want to be? We could make our own luck."

She broke down laughing. If I had had any pride or dignity left, I might've grimaced at her mirth, but I ended up laughing with her. Whoever was listening probably thought we were beyond drunk, although we hadn't even reached the halfway point of the bottle yet.

If she wanted to laugh, I'd give her a reason to laugh, and I ran my fingers along her bare sides, tickling her. She squealed and laughed harder, and with my head ducked, I got a good look at her typing on my phone. While she wiggled and showed every evidence of being ticklish, her left hand tapped away at the screen. When she finished, like me, she sent a message saying she was losing access to the phone and deleted the conversation and all record of her communications with the outside world.

Reaching down, I turned the screen off, put the phone in her hand, and shifted on the seat so she could reach my back pocket. Between giggles, she sucked in a breath, and her small hand worked my phone into my jeans.

When the waiter came around to claim the device, he'd see me pull it out of my back pocket, which would explain why it wasn't on the table with my wallet anymore. I intended to wipe the device on my jeans before handing it over to rub away her fingerprints in case they were smart enough to check for them.

"If you could make your own luck right now, what would you do?"

While making a run for it and taking a cold shower occupied the top two spots, I had a rather extensive list of things I wouldn't mind trying with a woman clever enough to take advantage of the opportunity I had created for her. "Some things shouldn't be said in polite company."

The last thing I expected was for her to slink her way onto my lap and straddle my legs. "Then I guess we'll have to stop talking for a while."

TEN

If you ever call me Sally again, I'll
kill you.

HAD THINGS GONE MY WAY, I would have escaped the nightclub with a few suspicious
bruises on my throat, a newfound appreciation for a woman on my lap, and the satisfaction of being involved with breaking part of a
sex trafficking operation.

The start of the show ruined my plans.

No one had told me the nightclub had an
incubus and a succubus and wasn't afraid to
use them. Every last one of my good intentions leapt out the nearest window, and my
new partner didn't seem to mind in the
slightest. The incubus and succubus had a lot
to do with that.

Fortunately, the show had ended before
the cops and FBI arrived. Somehow, I hadn't
lost my pants. Pants made facing a bust much
easier to deal with, especially when I hadn't
consumed enough Scotch to get drunk but

had drunk enough to get hungover. While I could have retrieved my shirt, which had gotten tossed out of reach, I decided fetching it wasn't worth the effort.

I had no idea where the Scotch had gone, but I needed a drink. Exhaustion weighed me down, but my worries and regrets kept me wide awake, as there was no nice way to tell a woman she needed to be tested for the lycan-thropy virus. Sally watched the raid kneeling on the bench beside me, her chin resting on her arms, completely at ease with her rather nude state. The cops and FBI agents mostly ignored us, and Sally had a lot to do with that. Every time someone approached us, she told them to deal with the rest of the club first, driving them away with snarls worthy of a werewolf.

With her lithe body built for strength and pride etched into every line of her, Sally lacked traditional beauty, but I couldn't help but stare.

She flashed me a smile. "Thanks, by the way."

"For what?" I doubted she had any reason to thank me for my part in the evening's activities. Then again, maybe she did.

I *had* prevented her from being shot in New York. That counted for something, right?

"Catching on to what I needed. This didn't

go down as I expected. I thought I'd be stuck here for a few weeks before I got my hands on a phone."

I gave the small table a shove and thumped my new boots on top of it, aware of the two spare phones and the battery jabbing my ankles. "I set that up hoping you'd message me with something I could use, but your way was even better. Honestly, I'd sent *your* picture to my parents to send to the police, hoping to hit a missing person record to justify a raid. Also, you're going to need to be tested for the lycanthropy virus, Sally. I had absolutely no intention of—"

Sally shifted her chin off her arm, reached over, and clapped her hand over my mouth. "My name's Marian, I'm an undercover FBI agent, and if you ever call me Sally again, I'll kill you."

I believed her. I wouldn't want reminded I'd spent time as an animal, carted around the United States in the back of a van, and been stuck with me the entire time. Add in the run-ins with my parents, and she would definitely have just cause to hate me. "Yes, ma'am."

"What I'd like to know is how you're here, as the last time I saw you, you were bleeding to death in a ditch. I almost had a heart attack when you came into the club tonight." Her gaze dipped to my shoulder and the two faint scars marking where I'd been shot.

"The feeling is mutual. I almost choked to death when that bouncer called you—"

Marian snarled at me.

"—by that name I'm never going to mention again if I know what's good for me."

"They thought they were being gracious by allowing me to pick a stage name. I hoped someone would notice the coincidence and take a closer look because of that horrible name. I wasn't expecting for you to show up."

"Consider this a lesson learned. My parents were involved. Actually, I'm genuinely astonished they haven't broken into the joint looking for me. They fully intended to hunt and kill the stealer of my alpaca."

"You want to die, don't you?"

Why couldn't I leave well enough alone? I blamed my mother. It had to be my mother's fault. She was always pulling my father's tail. "It's not my fault my father is a werewolf and my mother's infected. It's in their blood—literally. Shooting me was bad enough, but to take my alpaca, too? They couldn't let such an insult stand."

"*Shane!*"

I wondered what it said about me that I enjoyed the way she snarled my name. "I'm sorry. I had no idea it was even possible to transform someone like that. When my godfather informed me you were probably being transported as part of a sex trafficking operation, I had a hard time believing it."

"Well, it's true. I was sold to this club. How did you figure out to come here anyway?"

"You can thank my parents for that. They did the footwork. Dad tracked you here with his nose, and once he identified the farm you'd been taken to, they did some research and found links to clubs in the city. This was the first one we tried. So, in that regard, plain luck. When the barkeeper said you were a shy new girl, I figured you were my best bet." I pointed at my fake eye. "Since I don't look like a cop, I got volunteered to have a look around. I'm not one anymore, but my parents try to forget that. I lost my eye responding to a traffic accident and pulling a family out of the burning wreckage of their car. Since the insurance company didn't want to pay for a functional replacement, I'm retired."

Marian's eyes widened, and she trailed her fingers along the thin line of my scar. "I wondered why you had stepped in front of a gun to protect an animal. You had no way of knowing I wasn't actually an alpaca. At first, I thought you were stupid for putting your life in danger like that, but then you just, well, seemed like a nice guy. And since I had no idea when—or if—I'd become human again, sticking with you was my best option."

I thought about everything that had happened from the instant I'd seen the furry, angry alpaca in the back of the car. "I have a remarkable lack of common sense and no sense of self-preservation, as evidenced by my talking my surgeon into letting me out of the hospital the morning following major reconstruction of my shoulder. It's Dad's fault. He provided the transfusion. Would you believe they made me sign a paper acknowledging I might end up infected with the lycanthropy virus?"

"You're not going to let go of the lycanthropy infection issue, are you?"

My face warmed. "I never should have..."

Marian sighed. "I can't contract the virus, so you have nothing to worry about. And anyway, that's my problem, not yours."

"Like hell it's not my problem!" The heat across my cheeks intensified. "And it's definitely my problem if... if..." I spluttered at the thought of having a child with anyone, which was enough to rob me of my ability to speak.

"You've never been influenced by a succubus before, have you?" Marian bit her lip, cleared her throat, and giggled. "You look like you've swallowed a frog."

I groaned and slumped over the table. "No, I haven't."

"You really are Mr. Honest, aren't you? Most guys would be bragging."

"If I plead for mercy, would you just shoot me now? I'm sure you can borrow a gun from a cop."

"No. You're entertaining. You have nothing to worry about. It's a simple case of economics. It's not profitable for the women working the club to become pregnant. It's a part of the club's deal with their succubus and incubus—common practice. They're allowed to siphon energy, but in exchange, they keep the girls working the club from having unexpected kids. There's a catch to that. If a woman comes to the club and she's *not* one of the workers, she's probably leaving pregnant. Little is better for an incubus and succubus than the creation of a new life."

Great. First I'd learned more about my parents' sex life than I ever wanted to know, now I was learning about a whole new species, although I'd already known some of the details from my work in Chicago. The relief of not having to worry about becoming a father beat my discomfort over another sex talk, however. "And they knew you were one of the workers?"

Marian glared at me. "Of course. I also had birth control pills shoved down my throat before they decided I'd earn my keep tonight."

"In my defense, I had no idea I'd be running into an incubus and a succubus today." Had I known, I would have been contributing to the prevention of unexpected children, too.

"You're so shy. I never would've guessed. I've met your parents, you know. They aren't shy."

"On days like today, I want to disown them."

She laughed. "Well, you have nothing to be ashamed about. That said, the possibility you're a chronically nice guy has occurred to me. This could be a problem."

I scowled. "How is being a nice guy a problem?"

"Competition."

What the hell did she mean by that? "Competition?"

Both her eyebrows took a hike towards her hairline, and she slid down on the bench, crossing her arms over her chest. I averted my gaze to my boots. Removing my feet from the table and turning my back to Marian, I leaned over, undid the laces, and fished out my spare phones, setting them on the table along with the battery pack. Bracing for the worst, I checked for missed calls and messages.

I had a lot of each.

"Now *that's* clever. I never would've

thought to put phones in my boots as back-ups. I'm stealing that idea. This also confirms my belief there must be competition. You're considerate to the point of being disturbing, you're smart enough to keep spare phones in your boots when you're going into a ques-tionable situation, and you're kinda cute in a rugged sort of way. Also, that blue eye suits you."

Did she really think I had a bunch of women waiting in the wings for a chance at me? If so, she had a lot to learn about me. I couldn't even confess she'd been my first; if it hadn't been for the incubus and succubus showing up, I would've enjoyed a few kisses, maybe let my hand stray a little if she al-lowed, and otherwise parted ways without getting to know her intimately.

Could I get away with crawling under a table and dying? Maybe I could convince one of the cops to arrest me. I groaned and slumped in my seat, sending a text message to my godfather to confirm I was among the living.

I still struggled to accept my evening had gone from checking out a nightclub to being influenced by an incubus and succubus deter-mined to liven up the party with the added bonus of the starts of a hangover.

"There's really no competition?"

The astonishment in her tone embarrassed me almost as much as her implication I was worth competing over. "Can I get away with lying just this once?"

"No, I don't think so. I'm curious now. You look like you're about to die of embarrassment." She sucked in a breath, and I felt her hands press against my back. "Wait a second. You're the son of a lycanthrope. You weren't infected at birth, were you?"

"I'll probably be clean of the virus in two or three days unless it managed to take hold, which I doubt."

"I took your virginity," she whispered in my ear, pressing against my back. "Didn't I?"

Evil had a name, and it was Marian. Evil was also naked and far too close for my comfort, revitalizing every memory of being with her, right up until we were so exhausted we needed to stop and catch our breaths. I'd probably relive every minute in my sleep for the rest of my life.

The experience would color my future, too. She'd been everything I had dreamed of and more, and the incubus and succubus probably had something to do with that. I could easily understand how men could become hooked on the experience of being with a woman while under the influence of a sex demon.

"You're not going to let this go, are you?"

"You wouldn't let go of the lycanthropy

issue, so I'm not letting go of the virginity issue."

Turnabout was fair play, and I'd drawn the short straw. "However embarrassing, that's fair. Fine. Yes, you did."

"And there's no competition for you."

"I live in Chicago. They have a rather strong dislike of those who have been exposed to the lycanthropy virus." I shrugged.

Marian wiggled closer and rubbed my arms. "I can't wait to find out what you'll be like when you partner your enthusiasm with experience."

If I kept blushing, I'd rupture a blood vessel in my head. "You're still influenced by the incubus, aren't you?"

"Maybe a little. It's your fault."

"How is it my fault?"

"I find clever, nice men attractive."

While inexperienced with the mysterious ways of women, I knew if I ran for the hills, one of two things would happen. She would chase me down and kill me, or she would chase me down and have her way with me. For some reason, I couldn't imagine her ignoring my attempt to escape her.

The part of me responsible for enjoying her on my lap wanted her to chase me, and the conclusion of the hunt didn't matter one bit. The rest of me worried for my sanity.

"I don't suppose we can discuss this later, after you put some clothes on?"

Marian growled and bit my shoulder hard enough I bled.

NOT EVEN THE lycanthropy virus courtesy of my father could deal with Marian's bite. I suspected the succubus's influence had helped burn out the virus, but the cops called someone from the Center for Disease Control to confirm I hadn't infected the undercover agent.

We both scanned clean of the lycanthropy virus, which explained why her bite wasn't healing like I expected. I shot another glare at her, poking at the injury before an EMT slapped my hand away.

"Don't play with it," the man ordered before continuing to prepare a bandage.

I scowled. While she'd made me bleed, I didn't think the bite was worth the fuss.

Marian blushed, and I liked the way her cheeks reddened. "I'm really sorry. I don't know what came over me."

At least she had progressed from nudity to a blanket wrapped around her. Cops and FBI agents kept offering her coffee, which she guzzled as though afraid it would disappear.

I waved away her apology with my left

hand so I wouldn't earn another swat from the EMT. "If we start apologizing for every little thing, we'll be here all night and drive your FBI friends to murder."

I'd already gotten more than a few glares from various law enforcement personnel. I wasn't sure if it was because they were jealous or because I was some random civilian who happened to be in the right place at the right time. I didn't look forward to being questioned, which would happen after the EMT was convinced I wouldn't do additional harm to myself.

I sat still while he taped a bandage into place, then grimaced when he poked the gunshot wounds below her bite. "That hurts, you know."

"How long have those been healing?"

"I was shot yesterday. My surgeon is from here."

"Dr. Harting?"

"Yeah, that's her."

"That would make you the ex-cop gunned down in Lincoln." The EMT turned his attention to my back, touching the exit wounds. "And seeing the scar placement, I can understand why they flew her over. Your shoulder blade must have been a bloody mess. Why are you even here?"

Marian leaned forward and whispered in my ear, "Don't you dare."

My mother was completely to blame with my tendency to enjoy testing my luck, which contributed to ignoring the woman's hissed threats. "I was originally going to help my godfather keep my parents in line, but then they decided they wanted to sell me into slavery." I flashed Marian a grin. "And the shooter st—"

Clapping her hand over my mouth, Marian looked the EMT in the eyes and snapped, "Don't listen to a word he says."

The EMT chuckled. "Should I be concerned your parents want to sell you into slavery? Aren't your parents also police officers?"

I grabbed Marian's wrist and pulled her hand away from my mouth. "My father's a werewolf and my mother's infected. I'm pretty sure they won't sell me into slavery."

"So we have two possibly panicked lycanthropes outside?"

"I texted my godfather telling him I was fine. They've probably graduated from panicked to spitting mad."

Marian twisted, snagged my arm, and pulled me forward; the instant I was off balance, she tossed me over her shoulder and slammed me onto the floor. The air rushed out of me in a gasp, and she straddled my chest, planting her hands on my shoulders. "Shane!"

It took me a few moments to figure out I'd accidentally dropped a terrible pun about her kidnapping and deserved a beating. "Sorry," I wheezed while the room flip-flopped around me.

My introduction to the floor caught the attention of the gathered officers and agents, although I found it difficult to care what they thought. While my head hurt like hell from smacking into the floor, the view was spectacular.

"Please don't kill my patient, Agent Peterson."

"Not even a little?"

"He *is* an ex-cop. They take that sort of thing seriously." The EMT shooed Marian away, knelt beside me, and shined his pen light in my eye. "Did you happen to get a concussion when you were shot, Mr. Gibson?"

"That may have happened."

The glare the EMT shot Marian would have killed a lesser woman. "Go away and stop injuring my patient. Send someone over to make arrangements about questioning if you need something to do."

"I'm sorry, I didn't know!"

"I'm not upset with you. I deserved it." I sighed at the thought of returning to the hospital to face a scolding from my surgeon. At least I'd dodge the questioning session for a little while.

ELEVEN

In my defense, I had no idea it was
that sort of nightclub.

DR. HARTING WAS NOT happy to see me.

"You're trying to die, aren't you?" The woman prowled around the examination table armed with one of the CDC's meters, scanning me for the fifth time because she refused to believe the results of her initial tests. "I present the fact you have exhausted a large transfusion of lycanthropy-tainted blood as evidence."

"In my defense, I had no idea it was *that* sort of nightclub."

"You shouldn't have been going to any nightclub. Didn't it occur to you that alcohol would be detrimental to recovering from a concussion?"

Telling her I'd felt fine until Marian had introduced my head to the club floor hadn't impressed her the first three times I'd used it in my defense, so I kept my mouth shut. I also refrained from pointing out she hadn't told me I *couldn't* drink any alcohol. She'd mentioned refraining from sex, but no one could blame me for an unexpected encounter with a rowdy incubus and succubus.

At least she'd conceded that point; no one stood a chance against a pair of sex demons on a mission.

"Am I going to survive long enough to be questioned, Dr. Harting? The FBI and police are going to be cranky if they can't question me."

"I should make you stay for observation overnight, but even if I did, you'd probably find some way to rattle your brain in your skull just to vex me. Obviously, I made a poor judgment call. I should have been more thorough on my list of things you could and couldn't do. Let me begin. No rides on motorcycles and no driving for at least three days. Do not hit your head on anything. And I mean it, hit your head on *nothing*. I'm going to prescribe some medication to help mitigate the symptoms because you no longer have the lycanthropy virus helping you recover. When you return to Lincoln, see a local doctor for your follow-up in four days. I'll send my recommendations to the hospital." She paused long enough to wave the meter in my face. "No sex, no physical labor, no getting shot, no playing cops and robbers with your parents. You're retired, so act like it."

"So you're basically saying I'm a menace to society."

"No, you're a menace to yourself." Dr. Harting sighed. "At least you haven't undone my hard work on your shoulder. Could you explain that bite mark, though?"

"I said the wrong thing to a woman. I learned my lesson."

"Maybe I should test you for rabies." The surgeon fiddled with the meter and did another pass. The device remained silent. "Your assailant doesn't appear to have been rabid."

"Riddle me this. Why do you have to switch the settings on your meter when you test for something? Couldn't you check for everything at once?"

"I could, but it loses sensitivity doing bulk scans. By testing for one thing at a time, I can detect trace amounts. If I did bulk scans, you'd be giving me a semen sample to send to the lab to check for the lycanthropy virus. This meter cost the hospital over fifty thousand, but saves us a great deal of time and money since we don't have to use lab testing."

"So quality versus quantity."

"Correct. And since I have the damned thing out, let's do a full scan. I may as well earn my overtime pay, and I can make your insurance company weep since they can't refuse to pay for the testing." Dr. Harting chuckled, changing the settings on the device. "This beauty is also a magic rating scanner, and it can detect benchmark magic levels for all sorts of things. We'll be at this for two to three hours, but considering you've had several hard hits to the head, substantial trauma, and an infusion of highly magical blood, it's entirely possible *something* happened as a result. And frankly, burning out the lycanthropy virus as fast as you have is odd enough to warrant a second check. So far, I've tested you for lycanthropy, rabies, and a full complement of sexually transmitted diseases. I've also done a fertility scan and will be passing a recommendation to your lady friend to have a pregnancy test done."

Marian was not going to be happy, and I had no idea what I'd do if I were to become a father in nine months. "She said she was on birth control and that the incubus and succubus had an agreement with the nightclub to prevent the workers from becoming pregnant."

"You already asked?"

"Well, I mentioned the lycanthropy virus first…"

"I may have to change my opinion of you, Mr. Gibson. Good. Should there be a pregnancy, you'll have the option to transfer responsibility to the state."

I clenched my teeth and took several slow breaths to calm my nerves. "No. I'll discuss the situation with Miss Peterson should it become an issue. I'm not going to dodge responsibility."

"Well, it's my responsibility to let you know your options. With your fertility rating, you may want to consider a birth control treatment should you be anticipating any casual relationships."

"I don't do relationships, period."

"At least intentionally," my surgeon muttered.

"Point." After three lectures on sex in one day, celibacy was sounding pretty good. "One day I do want to settle down and have a family, but I don't want to engage in one-night stands or short-term relationships."

"Well, you won't have any difficulties on your end when you wish to start a family." Dr. Harting changed the setting of her scanner, pulled off a small panel from the back, and revealed a tiny needle, which she sterilized with an alcohol pad. "This specific meter can handle blood testing, which is far more sensitive than the proximity scan. This first test takes about thirty minutes and requires several blood samples."

I held out my hand. "Stab away."

"A mere prick will do, Mr. Gibson. This test is designed to scan for any diseases detectable in the blood. You should be clean, as the results of our tests in Lincoln showed nothing obvious, but this will give me a comprehensive result."

"Please tell me this test will cost my insurance company a small fortune."

Dr. Harting grinned and jabbed my thumb with the needle. "This session will cost them about five thousand dollars. Due to the nature of this examination and their approval of your exposure to the lycanthropy virus, they can't penalize you in any form. They already agreed to any treatments required. Better yet, they won't even be able to cancel your insurance on any pre-existing conditions clauses, as you've tested negative for the lycanthropy virus."

"I don't suppose I need any other fiendishly expensive tests, do I?"

"I sense a desire for some fiscal revenge."

"Well, they were cheap bastards about the eye replacement. It's the cheapest one my policy allowed."

"Typical." Dr. Harting made a thoughtful noise in her throat while she watched the meter. "Your white blood count is through the roof. Not surprising, as the lycanthropy virus classifies as a parasitic infection. Your body's response to the virus hasn't stabilized yet. Considering you were technically infected within the past twenty-four hours, it's not a cause for concern yet."

"Only if it stays elevated?"

"Correct. Your body has developed an antibody to the lycanthropy virus."

While science hadn't been my major in college, I remembered some of what I'd learned in biology. "The lycanthropy virus doesn't have a vaccine or cure, though. Couldn't antibodies be used to treat lycanthropy?"

"No, for the same reason that neutralizer and other magical treatments can't purge the virus. It's been tried—and it's still being studied. In reality, the lycanthropy virus is a pretty potent form of magic. No one knows why some people form defenses against the virus while others don't. With the high amount of exposure you've received, I'll be submitting the results to the CDC for immunity classification. That might ease your path in certain career choices in certain locations, such as Chicago."

Had I still had two eyes, the news would have left me giddy; I'd still face prejudice due to my low magic rating, but an immunity classification would erase much of the prejudice about exposure to lycanthropy. I wouldn't be a contagion risk. "What level of immunity rating?"

"Well, I can confirm it took around forty-eight hours for the virus to be eradicated by your immune system. Considering the nature of your operation and your virus levels prior to your release from the hospital, you'll rank fairly high. You'll need to go to the CDC for some basic training, but you have some good options open to you, options that don't require visual acuity minimums."

"Isn't three days the average, though?"

"Three days is the duration of the virus's survival outside the host body. Instead of waiting out the virus's lifespan, your body is actively killing the virus. In standard patients, the lycanthropy virus will attempt to replicate and take root. Even resistant patients may become infected with sufficient exposure to the virus. You have antibodies. There are no known cases of infection of people who produce antibodies."

"So there is zero chance of me becoming a werewolf?"

"Correct."

I wasn't sure what I thought about that. The possibility of contracting my father's virus, which allowed for the prized hybrid form, had never bothered me. In some ways, living beyond a standard human's lifespan intrigued me. The immunity verdict ensured I'd be old and gray while my parents remained young and healthy. "That's actually a bit disappointing," I confessed.

"Lycanthropy does have its benefits."

"As long as you're infected by someone who has all three forms."

"That is a factor." For several minutes, Dr. Harting observed the meter, which beeped whenever it finished processing one of its tests. With the exception of my elevated white blood count, my blood test revealed I was in good health for a guy with only one eye and a concussion. "These tests aren't the be-all-end-all to testing. The meter covers a lot, but only lab tests are as thorough as required for some conditions. That said, you probably don't have cancer, your organs are functioning like they're supposed to, and your immune system is doing its job."

"So no bad news?"

"No bad news. Now, the next test is where things get ugly, takes up the most time, and is the primary reason these damned things aren't the first tool of choice for examinations." Dr. Harting cleaned and sterilized the needle before stabbing my thumb again. It took all of a few seconds for the device to squeal. "Oh, look. You're a male."

A laugh burst out of me. "Are you serious?"

Turning the display to me, she pointed at the notation on the screen identifying me as a male. "I'm a male with no species?"

"It takes about an hour for the device to

completely chew through your DNA and make full sense of it. All humanoid species share a high number of DNA markers, which is why these species are compatible—it's also why a satyr and a faery usually have a human child."

I blinked. "That was not discussed in biology class."

"Of course not. I'm a doctor, and I still haven't figured out the mechanics of a faery and a satyr having intercourse. Also, do *not* ask how a faery mother gives birth to a human."

"You have no idea how uncomfortable I am with how this conversation has turned."

"You have no idea how uncomfortable it was in that delivery room."

"Why did today turn into a sex education class?"

"You're the one who decided it was a good idea to go to a shady nightclub."

"I'm pretty sure my parents were trying to sell me into slavery but forgot they had to participate in the transaction to get paid." I shook my head and sighed. "Will that test prove if I'm adopted or not? I'm starting to think maybe I'm adopted and they want to get rid of me and get back some of their investment."

The machine beeped. Dr. Harting

frowned at the display and slapped the side of the device with her hand.

"I'm pretty sure that reaction is a cause for concern."

"Hold that thought." Dr. Harting crossed the room, picked up the phone mounted on the wall, and pressed a button. "I need a general scanner and an infectious diseases meter brought to room 3406. I also need a diagnostic scan run on our comprehensive meter."

She hung up, glared at the meter in her hand, and set it on the counter.

"I broke the meter?"

"The meter is trying to tell me you're a full lycanthrope. It is also claiming there's no evidence of the lycanthropy virus present in your body."

I scratched my head. "Okay, it's obviously confused."

"It's great for mundane biologicals. It starts working with DNA and it loses its mind."

"What else is it trying to tell you?"

"It's a conflicted test, so it will be discarded. I'm unwilling to trust any of the results."

I shrugged. "They're probably entertaining."

Dr. Harting cracked a smile, retrieved the

scanner, and tapped at the screen. "According to this, you're a male lycanthrope, undetermined species, which means you aren't a common canine or feline. You're twenty-seven, AB positive, blue eyes. Your heritage is so mixed it gave up after twenty-five entries and decided to list human and lycanthrope as a heritage rather than a species. You're American Caucasian with enough Native American ancestry you might want to do a check to find out which tribe; one of your grandparents was a full Native American according to the scanner."

I frowned. "I'm pretty sure one of my grandparents isn't Native American. I've met all of them."

"If the meter is correct, one of your grandmothers wasn't honest about the father of her baby. That leads me to the second part of the test, which could support why one of your grandmothers might not have been honest about the father of her baby."

I thought about my parents, neither of whom struck me as Native American. "That would make for an awkward Christmas dinner."

"If the Native American part bothers you, wait until you hear the next part."

"What?"

"The results make a certain amount of sense. The unidentified Native American grandparent is also an incubus. That could explain your unusually high fertility rating and why your grandmother may not have wanted anyone to know her child was half incubus. And this is exactly why people don't opt for this test often. If it *is* correct, you're an anomaly."

"Because how can someone be a lycan-thrope without the lycanthropy virus?"

"Exactly."

I was glad I was already sitting down, as I doubted my legs would have kept me upright. Was it possible one of my parents was half incubus? A knock at the door prevented me from asking any of my questions. Dr. Harting opened the door and let in a man armed with a black bag stuffed with wires and devices. She handed over the main scanner. "Can you run the diagnostic tool first while I use the other scanners?"

They traded machines, and armed with a pair of new devices, my surgeon resumed scanning me. The meters remained quiet, and she narrowed her eyes. "These are reporting clean on the lycanthropy virus, too."

The technician fiddled with the primary scanner, and after about ten minutes, he un-plugged it, reset it, and held it out to Dr. Harting. "Try again. If the results are the same, it's an accurate reading. There's nothing in the diagnostics indicating an issue with the machine."

"But that result isn't even possible," she muttered.

"I'll make some phone calls about the device and find out what might give a false positive lycanthropy result," he promised before taking the devices and leaving the room. "I'll call you as soon as I have answers."

"And we're right back to square one. Well, at least I can find out if your white blood count has dropped any since the first scan."

I held out my hand so she could jab my thumb with the needle.

The second scan reported similar results to the first, although there was evidence my white blood count was dropping. Without any fanfare, Dr. Harting proceeded to the second test, and within five minutes, she was shaking her head. "Same results, Mr. Gibson. You're a lycanthrope without the lycanthropy virus. It's reporting the same heritage results, too."

"Once could be a fluke, but twice is a strong probability," I muttered.

"Exactly. I have to report these results to the CDC. They will want to do further tests to identify whether you can infect others—or figure out why their meter is reporting you're a lycanthrope despite the lack of the virus. I hope you didn't have any plans, because they were just cancelled. The other results aren't *that* uncommon. Lots of people have incubus genes. A quarter of the population is actually part incubus. I'm sure you can ask someone at the CDC for more information."

"I'm having a difficult enough time wrapping my head around the idea one of my parents is half incubus."

"It shouldn't influence your daily life. Your father or mother likely doesn't know they're half incubus. I'll leave it to your discretion whether you want to inform them so they can come in for testing."

"Christmas dinner is going to be awkward this year."

"It could be worse."

"Pray tell."

"You could be explaining to a satyr father his faery wife just gave birth to a human child."

Dr. Harting was right. Things could be worse—a lot worse.

TWELVE

Go to bed before you bite someone.

WHILE DR. HARTING was out of the examination room, I bit the bullet and called Dad.

"Where are you?" he snarled the instant the call connected.

"I'm at the hospital being tested for rabies." It wasn't a lie. Dr. Harting *had* tested me for rabies. "I'm pretty sure after they determine if I'm rabid, the FBI and local police will be questioning me. Dr. Harting wanted to do a full checkup, and she's prescribing some medications to help with the concussion. No big deal. I was just busy and couldn't give you a call until now."

"Lewis told us you'd texted him. It would have been nice if my son had texted me, too. Does my son like his godfather more than his father?"

"Dad, you're whining."

"It's six in the morning, and I've been waiting for you to call me all night long."

"Go to bed before you bite someone."

"No. I'm not going to bed until you're safe in my custody."

"I'm a grown man. I don't need to be in your custody."

While wolves couldn't roar, Dad's infuriated howl came close enough my head throbbed. "I took my eyes off you for two hours, Shane Abraham Gibson! Two hours. You were supposed to go into the nightclub, have a look around, and come back out. *Within two hours.* Did you forget that part? Then, not only do you stay in the nightclub, the FBI raids it, setting up a cordon too far away for us to see who was coming and going. The local cops couldn't get us past the cordon, and they couldn't tell us who was or wasn't in the building. What the hell happened in there?"

"Long story. It involved a fifteen hundred dollar bottle of Scotch."

"Of course it did. How old are you again? Because that's the sort of shit a teen would pull."

I lowered my voice to a whisper. "I shared it with a pretty girl named Sally, but if you call her that, she'll kill you. Good news is, she doesn't have rabies."

"You were actually tested for rabies?"

"Long story. Anyway, she used my phone

to contact someone outside of the nightclub, thus my inability to leave."

"And the concussion issue?"

"It's not a big deal. Just got a bit dizzy, so it's precautionary."

"So nothing happened?"

While a lot had happened, if Dad wanted a confession of my evening's sins, he'd have to try a lot harder to get it. "I'm fine. If anything changes, I'll let you know. After Dr. Harting is done with me, I have to be questioned, so I'm going to be really busy for a while. Don't be surprised if I don't call for at least a few hours, okay?"

"You're sure you're fine? You don't need us to come to the hospital?"

"If I need you to come, I'll call you. In fact, you can go home, and when I need you, I'll call you for a pickup."

"So you want me to drive three hours home just to turn around and come back."

"I'm going to be here longer than six hours, Dad. When I have a better idea of how long it'll be, I'll call you."

"This is punishment for sending you into the nightclub, isn't it?"

"Yes. Go away, and take Lewis with you. Tell Mom I love her, please."

"What about me? Don't I get any love?"

"You tried to sell me into slavery."

Dad laughed. "You know I wouldn't actually sell you into slavery."

"Fine. I love you, too. Go home and text me when you get in." Before he could start asking questions I couldn't answer honestly, I hung up.

A soft chuckle from the doorway warned me Dr. Harting had returned and had heard at least part of my conversation with my father. "The CDC wants you in Chicago on the next flight out. A representative will escort you to the headquarters there."

"Chicago?" I groaned. "Well, close to home, I guess."

"That factored into their selection of cities, as you have your primary residence there. The FBI has also agreed to handle your questioning there between tests."

I stared at my phone and checked the call time. "You found all that out in less than five minutes?"

"It's not hard when there's a CDC representative in the building. He wants to ask you some questions about the incubus and succubus. All I had to do was show him the meter and ask where they wanted you. Two minutes later, he had an answer. That leaves the FBI, and since they already have a pair of agents here to question you, it was trivial to ask them if they could relocate the session to Chicago."

"How long is this going to take?"

"It shouldn't take longer than a week. The representative indicated they've seen something like this before."

"All right. When do I leave?"

My surgeon checked her watch. "Five minutes. Have a safe trip, Mr. Gibson. Do try to avoid hitting your head on anything else. I'll be forwarding your file to a colleague in Chicago for any followups you need."

ALL I WANTED in life was some sleep, but I had just enough time to gather my things before two FBI agents and a CDC representative hauled me out of the hospital, dragged me to the airport in a black, unmarked car, and herded me into a small six-seater plane. I wasn't a fan of flying in the first place, and the twin-prop bucked worse than any horse I'd ever ridden.

By the time we landed in Chicago, my entire body throbbed, my head felt ready to split open, and it was a miracle I hadn't vomited.

The CDC representative narrowed his eyes and looked me over. "You've turned green."

"The last time I got any sleep, I was recovering from reconstructive surgery to my shoulder." I should have known better than to shoot venomous looks at two law enforcement officers just trying to do their job, but if anyone manhandled me one more time, I'd go ballistic. I pointed at my shoulder. "Two rounds to the shoulder."

"We're aware, Mr. Gibson," the oldest of the two FBI agents replied.

"I literally can't remember your name right now, Agent. Sorry. If you want anything useful out of me, I need sleep first. I barely know my own name at this point."

"Allowances will be made for your current state, Mr. Gibson. Bear with this as much as you can for now."

The FBI agent didn't bother giving me his name, which fueled my annoyance.

His partner snagged my right arm to direct me to an SUV waiting nearby. The motion pulled my shoulder, which agitated the healing gunshot wounds and Marian's bite, making me yelp. The pain stunned me, and I forgot how to walk, stumbling several steps before catching my balance and preventing a one-way trip to the ground.

"Sorry," the agent muttered, and while he didn't release my arm, he did adjust his hold.

I made it to the SUV without falling on my face. Sweat chilled my face, and my hands shook. I masked the tremors by flattening my palms on my legs. Others might have viewed the agent's behavior as rough handling, but I knew better. He had a job to do, which was delivering me to the CDC to confirm what sort of freak I was.

It wouldn't surprise me if the FBI agents came from a place like Chicago, a city with a healthy dislike of lycanthropes.

"Hey, Terry?" The second FBI agent, who had claimed the driver's seat, twisted around to regard his partner. "I'm pretty sure Marian said if you hurt a hair on his head she'd eat you for breakfast."

The CDC representative chuckled. "I already texted the office to make sure there was a surgeon on hand to check your shoulder, Mr. Gibson. If you have any additional problems, do let us know."

I had a lot of problems with being carted across the country, which gave me a much better understanding of Marian's reactions. Unlike her, however, resisting could land me in a lot of hot water. The government took species identification seriously, and those who could classify as public health hazards were monitored. Freedom was an illusion, a reality I understood from my work on the police force and being the son of a lycanthrope.

Even if I ended up with an immunity rating to the lycanthropy virus, I'd be tested every few years and monitored to make sure I didn't become a contagion risk.

"Sure," I replied, shrugging with my left shoulder. "Can you at least give me an idea of what to expect?"

"Ah, we haven't properly introduced ourselves, have we? I'm Daryl, and I'm an evaluator with the CDC. I live in Des Moines but volunteered to come to Chicago, as I'm specialized in the various species of lycanthropes and their mutations. Agent Lowry is our driver today, and Agent Billings is the gentleman sitting with you. They're both stationed in Des Moines, and I have the misfortune of getting stuck with them more often than I care to think about."

"If you've never been to Chicago, they hate lycanthropes here," I warned.

"They must not hate them too much. You're on file as having worked with the police here."

"They're required to hire people of certain magic ratings, and they needed a few cops with low ratings to make quota, so that's where I came in. Add in my known exposure to lycanthropy without being infected, and they got to knock two check marks off their list without having to hire two people." I shrugged. "When they figured out most lycanthropes wouldn't attack me unless seriously provoked, they used me to handle most of the lycanthrope calls."

Billings scowled, pulled out a cell phone,

and tapped away at the screen. "Our file on you shows you worked with the police, not that you were an actual cop."

"If you need my former badge number, district, and supervisor, I can provide them. I also have copies of my enrollment, scores from the academy, and work history on the force."

"So you're a legitimate ex-cop."

How many times would I have to explain how I'd lost my eye before people stopped asking—or doubt I could have been a cop? I pointed at the blue sphere provided by my cheap-ass insurer. "I was the first to arrive at a traffic accident involving a family of three and a burning car. Since police officers need to pass visual acuity tests in both eyes, I'm no longer a police officer. The insurance company evaluated my ranking in the police department and determined it wasn't worth the investment to give me a false eye capable of passing the vision tests."

"It's non-functional?" Billings frowned, his gaze fixed on my false eye. "They weren't required to give you a replacement sufficient to let you keep your job?"

"I'm technically on vacation in the form of a two-month medical leave to adapt to only having one eye. Chicago's police department isn't required to keep their employees in the field, so the best I can hope for is a lower paying desk job. That met the insurance company's requirements for securement of work. The department signed off saying they could transfer me to a non-field capacity. The department keeps their quota filled, the insurance company saves money. Worked for everyone but me." I realized I was whining about it but couldn't force myself to care. "Active field duty paid a living wage. The desk job work pays minimum wage."

I let them do the math. Daryl figured it out first and spat a few curses. "So they can force you to quit by lowering your income."

"Welcome to Chicago."

CHICAGO'S BRANCH of the CDC was located several blocks from my old station in one of the nicer parts of town. If I hadn't been so tired and grouchy, I might've helped Lowry figure out the complex puzzle that was Upper and Lower Chicago during construction season, but watching the FBI agent lose his shit when the roads split and he descended into the pits of hell when he should have risen to street level amused me.

Beneath the streets of Chicago lurked a second city, a tangled maze of underground parking, shops, and homes. Nocturnals made Lower Chicago their haven, safe from the sunlight they hated—or couldn't face without their skin burning off their bones. There was even a third level, one no one wanted to acknowledge.

Some things were best left in the dark, and we had a working arrangement with the third level dwellers. The denizens of Upper and Lower Chicago didn't bother them, so they didn't bother us. Considering I wasn't even sure what lurked down there, I rather liked the arrangement.

It took three hours for Lowry to find his way out of Lower Chicago, ending up halfway across the city before he realized he needed to take one of the up ramps to relocate civilization. Once he figured that out, he made certain to stay away from any exit ramps with a downward slope.

I managed to catch some sleep while the trio of government employees attempted to navigate through the city without asking for help. When Lowry learned he had to descend into Lower Chicago to park, his wordless cry of frustration drowned out the groans of the other two men.

"Go around the building, take the first exit into Lower Chicago, and go around the block. The entrance to the headquarters parking garage should be labeled," I said, pointing at an alley alongside the CDC's skyscraper. To alleviate some of their frustration,

I added, "Buildings like this don't have connecting streets to Lower Chicago."

"Who designed this fucking city?" Lowry
grumbled, following my directions to reach
the parking lot beneath the streets.

"A sadist with masochistic tendencies."

"I believe it."

When Lowry discovered he had to pay
thirty dollars to park for the day, he looked
ready to reach out the window and throttle
the security guard manning the entry gate. To
add insult to injury, he had to circle the lot's
five levels for thirty minutes to find a spot. "I
am never coming to this hell hole ever again."

I bit my lip so I wouldn't laugh and un-
buckled my seatbelt. The few minutes of
sleep had helped; I could walk a straight line
without assistance. Daryl scratched his head
and turned in a slow circle. "How do we get
into the building?"

I pointed at a small arrow mounted on
one of the pylons. "Follow those."

"Next time, you get to drive," Lowry
grumbled.

"No driving for me for a few days. Doctor's orders." I strolled through the maze of
parked cars, careful to watch for anyone
hunting for a spot. While the lot was packed,
there were few people in the garage. Even following the signs, it took us ten minutes to
find the elevators.

Fortunately for my sanity, we didn't have to wait long for the elevator, and Daryl tapped the sole button, which would take us to the first floor. I approved of the bottleneck; by forcing those in the garage to go through security on the first floor, the CDC could monitor anyone entering and leaving. I'd seen too many places, including hotels, which used a single elevator system, granting easy access to people who didn't belong in the building, making it simple for crooks to make a clean getaway.

Daryl endured a ten minute scolding from the receptionist on the first floor, which I spent swallowing yawns. The two FBI agents fidgeted but kept quiet during the wait. The CDC representative sighed and pointed across the lobby. "We're expected on the fifth floor, and since we're late bringing him, we're expected to help with the testing."

Agent Billings shook his head. "We're not certified with the CDC."

"You don't need to be certified. You just need to be a gopher and do what you're told. You'll still get your turn with him, but we're two hours behind schedule, and they have some specialists here who need to look at him. The looking goes faster with extra hands. I get to be a gopher, too, and I'm certified. Just deal with it. If you complain and whine, we'll be at this even longer."

"I'm not looking forward to this, either. Be happy you're not the one about to be diagnosed as a freak," I confided, strolling across the lobby. Delaying the evaluation would only draw out the misery. My goal would be to escape as quickly as possible, head home, and find out what sort of disaster waited for me at my apartment.

I'd already taken care of the majority of my bills, including paying the month's rent in advance, so I could go to New York without an eviction notice waiting my return.

"On the general freak scale, you're a minor freak at worst, Mr. Gibson."

I glanced at the FBI agents. "See? I'm not even a good freak. I'd rather be a gopher. Want to trade?"

"No," they chorused.

THIRTEEN

It keeps the prisoners from staging an
escape.

THE ONE PERSON the CDC didn't need in at-
tendance for the initial testing was me. I expected them to draw blood and do a physical
exam. That phase was completed without a
hitch. I tested above average in most categories, and except for my missing eye and injured shoulder, I classified as healthy.

Marian's bite drew a lot of unwanted attention, and since the wound wasn't healing
like the CDC wanted, they decided to give me
an injection of antibiotics. To my disgust, I
discovered the antibiotic was coupled with a
sedative, one that knocked me flat within five
minutes.

While I needed the sleep, I would have
preferred to rest on my own terms. Sedatives
always left me groggy upon waking up.

Daryl was the only one in the examination

room with me, and most of his attention was focused on the meter in his hand. "In my defense, they didn't tell me they were going to sedate you."

"It keeps the prisoners from staging an escape," I slurred. "How long have I been out?"

"Six hours. The doctors are going over your x-rays now. While you were under, you were tested with transformative substances, you were petrified twice, and you've been subjected to every single scanning machine in the building, including the MRI. You woke up following both petrifications, but they knocked you out again immediately after, so I doubt you remember that. We've pinpointed the general cause of the meter readings, but we haven't been able to refine the results."

"I was petrified?"

"Twice. Your benchmarks are below average, so a flag will be added to your medical record in case you're exposed to gorgons outside of testing."

"Below average? What do you mean by that?"

"I mean you petrify three times faster than average, and it takes twice as long for the neutralizer to do its job, even the highest grade stuff. They'll want to do a third petrification test to see if you're as susceptible to a gorgon's gaze." Daryl set aside the meter, picked up a clipboard, and grabbed a pen. "While the doctors are trying to make sense of the first batch of tests, I get to handle your initial interview."

I lurched upright, wincing at the throb in my shoulder. Marian's bite hurt even more than before, and I poked at the bandage. "Did they tell you why the hell this hurts so much?"

"We have some theories, but until we have a confirmation of the cause, I'm not at liberty to say."

"Isn't that just grand? All right. What are your questions?"

"What are your dietary habits?"

"I see food, I eat it." I shrugged. "I'm not picky."

"Any known allergies?"

"None."

"Any foods you find particularly offensive?"

"Tripe."

"Tripe?"

"Stomach lining of a cow. I'm also not a fan of haggis."

"I don't know anyone who is." Daryl chuckled. "Do you consider yourself an adventurous eater?"

"I'd say so. I know from experience I don't like tripe or haggis."

"Are there any foods you won't try?"

The questions puzzled me, and I shrugged. "I haven't thought about it."

"Have you ever had food poisoning?"

"Not that I can think of."

"Do you cook at home or eat out?"

"I'd say an equal mix."

"Do you like seafood?"

"I tried pufferfish once. Obviously, I didn't die."

"Shellfish?"

"Sometimes."

"Lobster?"

"Too expensive."

"Shrimp?"

"They're like mini lobster tails with extra legs. Also too expensive."

Daryl glanced up from his clipboard. "Would you classify yourself as a scavenger?"

"Excuse me?"

"An opportunistic eater. In short, you buy the cheapest foods with no actual preference about what you eat as long as you eat."

I would remember the question later for use on my parents if they insisted on leaving half-cooked pancakes on their kitchen ceiling. If that didn't put an end to it, nothing would. "No."

"Please try not to take offense, Mr. Gibson. It's a valid question relating to your situation."

"The answer is still no."

"So if I were to go to your house, I wouldn't find cupboards full of instant noodles, pasta, and cans of tuna fish?"

Both my eyebrows took a hike towards my hairline. "At least you didn't ask if my diet consists mostly of donuts."

"So is that a yes or a no?"

"No."

"So what would I find in your cupboards?"

"Some dust keeping my limited spice collection company. I don't keep a lot of extras on hand. I prefer to buy for a few days and freeze my leftovers."

"So you're thrifty but prefer higher quality foods?"

"I guess? If I want fast food, I either order in or go get something."

"Take lunches to work?"

"Often. That's a bit cheaper than going out every day. I usually just grab something from the freezer and let it thaw for the first half of my shift. Why?"

"Diet can give us a lot of insights on your personality, temperament, and general approach to life. How do you feel about bringing people to your home? Do you enjoy visiting others for parties? Do you rate yourself as an extrovert or an introvert?"

"I don't have company over often, no. Not a lot of people around here want to get too close to someone who has been exposed to lycanthropy. It doesn't bother me, so I suppose I'm an introvert."

"And your relationship with your family?"

"Pretty close," I admitted.

Daryl made a few thoughtful noises and jotted down some notes. He began a rapid-fire questioning session about every aspect of my life, including my depressingly dull dating life, my work with the police, and friendships. An hour later, I felt like I'd undergone an interrogation without knowing what crime I was suspected of committing. A knock at the door ended the session, and I exchanged Daryl for a pair of grumpy FBI agents determined to get their fair cut of my time.

They would be easier to handle, as all they wanted was a detailed accounting of every minute from my arrival in New York to my evening in the nightclub with Marian. I dodged some of the details, mostly because they were almost as uncomfortable discussing my intimacy with their fellow agent as I was.

I got the feeling they both wouldn't have minded being in my shoes for the evening, which only added to my discomfort. Three hours later, the CDC evicted the two FBI agents, who confessed they had everything they needed. Their dismissal indicated they found it unlikely anyone else from the FBI would contact me about the situation.

At most, I was an accidental participant, and as long as I steered clear of the area, my involvement with Marian and the sex trafficking operations was officially over.

Daryl returned to Des Moines, leaving me alone with a tired old man who regarded me with milky white eyes. "I'm Dr. Yasolovic, and I'm specialized in lycanthropes."

"Pleased to meet you, Dr. Yasolovic."

"You're interesting."

Whenever a doctor claimed I was interesting, it meant trouble. 'Interesting' was another word for 'I want to experiment on you to figure out how you tick.' "That doesn't sound promising."

He chuckled. "As you are aware, your immune system is capable of fighting off the lycanthropy virus. This occurs in approximately three percent of the population. There are several causes of this particular talent."

"Talent? You mean it's magic?"

"Yes. The ability to fight off a magical infection like lycanthropy classifies as a talent. We will need to do some additional testing to find out the nature of your talent, however."

"What sort of testing?"

"In short, we will inflict minor injuries on

you, inject you with active cultures of the lycanthropy virus, and monitor your regeneration rate. The rapid healing of your gunshot
wound indicates your body doesn't have a re-
flexive response to the lycanthropy virus. You
have an adaptable immune system. As far as
talents go, it's a useful one. Our initial theory
is that your talent uses the virus for your benefit before eliminating it, effectively granting
you temporary regeneration equal to a full
lycanthrope."

"I don't suppose you could repeat that in
English, could you?"

"Your immune system is an opportunist
capable of identifying when foreign bodies,
like the lycanthropy virus, have beneficial
qualities. Once you regenerated with the
virus's help, your immune system eliminated
it as it would a regular infection. To confirm
this, we need to inject you with the lycanthropy virus."

"So you're going to give me a transfusion
from someone with the infection?"

"Essentially. Now, due to the risks associated with lycanthropy infections, we're going
to use samples most likely to benefit you
should you become infected. We have four
samples from tri-form lycanthropes of different species: wolf, cougar, leopard, and
wolverine."

While I'd heard of wolf and cat lycanthropes before, wolverines were new. "There are wolverine lycanthropes?"

"Below ten percent of all lycanthropes are wolverines. Wolves are the most common, representing over seventy percent of the lycanthrope population. I rate your chances of contracting the lycanthropy virus at less than one percent. At the same time we do these tests, we'll be able to confirm if you have probable immunity."

I pointed at Marian's bite. "Does this count as an injury?"

"We'll be monitoring that injury at the same time we watch your regeneration of a more controlled wound. For the purpose of this experiment, we'll make a six inch incision in your arm. Should the lycanthropy virus not act as expected, a surgeon will be ready to repair the damage and minimize any scarring. There will be two tests done on identical incisions."

"Is there a reason you couldn't have done this while I was sedated?"

"Yes."

When the doctor refused to elaborate, I surrendered with a sigh. It would happen whether I consented to it or not; all fighting would do was draw out the issue and make things worse. When it came to public health, the CDC viewed personal freedoms as optional. Often, their policies benefited the country—and world—as a whole, but being the focus of their attention, I began to understand a little better why those who underwent extensive evaluations protested.

I also understood the necessity. Rules were in place for a reason, and the precautions the CDC took with public awareness, treatment, and study of diseases magical and mundane saved more lives than they hurt. I didn't have to like it. I just had to go along with it.

My grudging acceptance didn't stop me from growling, "If I lose my arm because of this, I'm beating you to death with it."

I was dead serious, too. Dr. Yasolovic chuckled at my threat. "Your arm is perfectly safe, Mr. Gibson, but I will take your warning under advisement."

TWENTY-TWO HOURS after the first incision, done without benefit of painkillers or numbing agents, the CDC ran their final test for the lycanthropy virus.

I scanned clean.

A faint pale line marked where the surgeon had inflicted a quarter-inch deep gash along the length of my forearm. According to him, it would disappear on its own within a few months. The incisions had hurt like hell, and instead of the two threatened, I'd gotten sliced six times.

"As I said, Mr. Gibson. Your arm was in no danger," Dr. Yasolovic said, leaning over me to check my shoulder. "As an additional benefit, you should notice a distinct improvement in your shoulder as well. The scars are already smaller."

Marian's bite still hurt, and I grimaced at the reminder of the woman taking a chunk out of me. I deserved it for running my mouth, but did she have to make me bleed? "I don't suppose you can explain the deal with that bite, can you? Why didn't it heal?"

If anything, my shoulder felt worse than it had before I'd been injected with various forms of the lycanthropy virus.

"I sent a swab to the lab, but it might be several days for the results to come back. I suspect there is a bacterial infection involved. For now, allow it to heal naturally. If it doesn't show improvement in a few days, I'll look into treatments for it."

"I'm surprised those meters of yours can't tell what type of infection it is."

"A single human body can contain over a hundred trillion bacteria cells. Your digestive system alone contains a thousand or more different species of bacteria. To add to the complexity, not every human has the same collection of bacteria. There are so many unique bacteria it's impossible to categorize them. For every one we learn how to scan, we discover twenty or thirty new ones, and each one has a different function in the body. Some of these bacteria are good—in limited quantity."

"So what should I do about it?"

"Keep an eye on it. If you develop a fever, give me a call." Dr. Yasolovic pulled away, took hold of my chin, and turned my head so he could get a better look at my fake eye and my scar. "I want to take a closer look at your medical file regarding the loss of your eye. Despite extensive exposure to the lycanthropy virus, there was no change to your scar. What sort of surgical work was done? Was the eye preserved?"

"Dr. Pasadena at Northwest Memorial did the operation, and yes, it was preserved."

Dr. Yasolovic dug his phone out of his pocket and dialed a number. "Get in touch with Dr. Pasadena at Northwest Memorial. I need Mr. Gibson's full medical file. His right eye should have been preserved, so put in a request to have it checked out of the vault and put into the CDC's care until further notice. Forward the necessary information to his insurance company and make certain they understand they don't have the leeway to deny coverage."

"I paid for the preservation out of pocket. It wasn't covered by my insurance company."

"Be prepared for some pushback from the insurance company," the doctor warned before hanging up. "Pop your eye out. I'd like to have a closer look at it, please."

I obeyed. I hated touching the hard, cold orb, although I'd gotten accustomed to its presence. "I didn't qualify for an enhanced replacement."

Dr. Yasolovic held the sphere up to the light, squinting as he examined it. "Glass, and not even good glass. There are bubbles. I'm going to review your file, and I'll need a copy of your employment contract and performance records."

"My employment contract and performance records? Why?"

"There's this little thing called the Species Anti-Discrimination Act, Mr. Gibson. I and three other doctors have spent a significant amount of time evaluating your health. Chicago has a serious discrimination issue, as I'm sure you're well aware. I'm willing to bet that you have a pristine performance record and you were hired to meet station quotas."

"What does that have to do with anything?"

"It wouldn't be the first time a law enforcement officer with an unwanted condition was targeted to remove them from field duty. Unfortunately, a previous mistreatment resulted in the loss of a leg. While I don't doubt your eye itself couldn't be saved, this so-called replacement is unacceptable. Consider this my thanks for your exceptional patience during a trying and exhausting test cycle. I'm going to have someone photograph and measure this for documentation. It'll take no more than half an hour. After, I'll have someone take you home."

While I doubted it would do any good, I appreciated the gesture. "Thank you, doctor."

Within five minutes, Dr. Yasolovic handed my eye to a technician with instructions. Once the woman left, the doctor opened my file and pulled out several sheets. "While we wait, we'll go over some of the results of your testing. First, you're not a lycanthrope. It's impossible for you to become one. While genetically you classify as a human, you're not. The DNA analysis is pretty clear on that front; you barely qualify as human."

"I barely qualify as human? What the hell does that mean? My parents are humans, although Dad's a lycanthrope and Mom's infected."

"It's an issue of genetics, Mr. Gibson. Your parents have non-human parentage, and there is overlap between both sides of your family. When two humans with non-human parentage have a child, if there is sufficient overlap, the child might not be fully human. This is the case with you. Certain genes are more dominant but can skip several generations before becoming active. Sometimes, specific combinations of genes can have surprising results. Magic can play a role, too. For example, as the son of a lycanthrope, if you were conceived beneath a full moon, you may have experienced alterations to your DNA."

"So if I'm only partially human, what am I?"

"How much do you know about lycanthropes?"

"Enough, I guess. Dad's one, and he has all three forms. He passed the virus to Mom, so she'll be able to access all three forms, too."

"That's because the virus is replicating itself, and the virus is the source of the magic. Because its magic is potent enough for all three forms, it's passed on. Now, it's not guaranteed. Exposure matters. As your parents are constantly in close proximity, your father is strengthening the virus in your mother's bloodstream. *That* is what will ensure your mother will have all three forms. Let's assume your father got a paper cut and someone came into contact with him, becoming infected with the virus. First, the virus is going to take a long time to incubate; there's no additional source helping the virus take root. As a result, when it has finally replicated enough for the magic to take hold and allow for shapeshifting, it's not going to be as robust. There will be a high chance the new lycanthrope will only have access to two forms."

"The full wolf and the human forms."

"Correct. Now, lycanthropes are the result of a disease—a very strong, magical disease. It has a lot of benefits for its host, but it's essentially an incurable illness. There's a second class of shapeshifter, but they're often incorrectly categorized with lycanthropes. These individuals are born capable of shapeshifting. They can't contract the lycanthropy virus. Incubi and succubi are actually capable of transforming into other shapes. Their shapeshifting, however, is unique because they become human."

"So anyone on the street could be an incubus or a succubus?"

"Exactly. Looking at the basic results of your initial DNA testing, you have a higher than normal contribution of genes from an incubus. In most humans with an incubus ancestor, the incubus genes are dormant—they're turned off. You carry the genes, but they don't do anything. This is only speculation, but I think you have active incubus

genes, but only certain markers—the ones responsible for shapeshifting."

If Dr. Yasolovic's goal was to give me a
headache, he was succeeding. "Can I get that
in English, please?"

"Because you have an incubus ancestor,
you're probably a shapeshifter of some sort.
With human DNA accounting for fifty-five
percent of your genetic makeup, you'll retain
your status as a human. Your magic rating
may be reevaluated following additional review of the test results, but if you can demonstrate the ability to shift shapes, you'll be
bumped up several categories."

"This is going to make Christmas dinner
really interesting," I predicted.

"Be glad you weren't below fifty percent
human, Mr. Gibson."

"Why?"

"If you think these tests are bad, they're
far worse if you don't classify as human.
You'd be spending the next month as a guest
of the CDC while you were evaluated, classified, studied, properly identified, and otherwise turned into a test subject until we
determined if you were a risk to public
health."

I grimaced. "Will I have to come back in
for more testing?"

"I'd recommend it, but you'll find they're
not nearly as invasive. Most of it them would

involve a talent instructor attempting to find out if you have any latent abilities. These can be scheduled later, after your shoulder finishes healing. For all intents and purposes, as soon as your artificial eye is returned, you're free to leave, Mr. Gibson."

FOURTEEN

You look like hell.

A CRUISER WAS PARKED outside my apartment building, and I recognized the pair of cops from looking at the back of their heads. In the afternoon light, Michelle Warner's red hair stood out in sharp contrast to her partner's brown, which was streaked with enough white it earned him the nickname of Stripes. I called Kayne by his real name, but only because he had a phobia of lycanthropy so intense my presence often sent him into a panic.

"Thanks for the lift," I murmured, making my escape from the SUV before the CDC thought of any other reasons to detain me. Armed with my new license, which had been shoved into my hand on my way out the door, I'd be able to wipe a lot of smirks from smug racists' faces. The license bore several new notations on it, and the lycanthropy contagion risk flag had been removed. I headed for the parked car, circled to Kayne's side, and tapped on the glass.

Kanye landed on his partner's lap on the other side of the vehicle, his scream audible through the window.

Michelle laughed her ass off, waved at me, and opened her door, wiggling from beneath her hyperventilating partner. "Shane, you look like hell."

In Michelle-speak, she was happy to see me, almost concerned about my appearance, and in a good enough mood I could likely survive the conversation without her demonstrating her martial art skills.

Of my fellow cops, I liked Michelle the most; unlike her partner, she had nothing against lycanthropes. I whipped out my brand-new license and showed it to her. "My birthday came early this year."

Michelle squinted, peered at the card, and sucked in a breath, snatching it. "No fucking way!"

"Fucking way."

"How the hell did you convince them to remove the flag? I know damn well you've been exposed at least ten times since you joined the force. There's no way this is legal, Shane."

"The CDC did it, so I hope it's legal."

"Wait, the CDC reissued your driver's license? What were you doing at the CDC?"

"Tit-for-tat. What are you doing here?"

"Waiting for you. We've been trying to track you down for days, actually."

"What? Why?"

"The captain has some questions for you about some old case, and he wanted to ask them before your medical leave expired and you got transferred." Michelle wrinkled her nose. "You have time to swing by the station for a bit?"

I groaned. "The only sleep I've had in two days has been under sedation, Michelle. Does it have to be right now?"

"We've been staking out your apartment for two days."

Something wasn't adding up, as I knew my godfather had spoken to someone in Chicago about my shooting. "The FBI or Lincoln police didn't talk to the captain?"

Who had they spoken to?

"What? About what? The FBI? Lincoln? What are you talking about?"

"I was at my parents' place and was gunned down not far from their house. Two rounds to the shoulder."

"You have got to be shitting me."

I grimaced and tugged at the collar of my shirt to show Michelle the bandage and the faint gunshot scars. "It can be easily confirmed with the Lincoln police. What's so important you'd stake out my apartment?"

"Looks like it's healing pretty damned fast to me. What's the bandage for?"

"Someone bit me during an FBI raid I unintentionally attended. I've been assured I don't have rabies."

Michelle laughed. "I've missed your weirdo sense of humor at the station. Get on in, Gibson. I doubt the captain will need you for long, and we'll drive you back when you're done."

At the rate I was going, I'd never make it to my apartment. I rubbed my forehead in a futile effort to ward off the start of a headache. My medical leave, which had given me four extra paid weeks over the state's minimum, had come with the stipulation I would go to the station whenever called. "All right."

"Good sport. Stripes, get your ass back on your side of the car and stop whimpering like a baby. Shane ain't gonna bite you. And even if he did, he's clear." Michelle waved my license in her partner's face. "Lay off the dumbass act already."

"Maybe I should bite someone. That way, I'd deserve my reputation. We could hang a sign at the station counting the number of days since the last Shane attack."

"Just get your ass in the car before I throw your ass in the car, Shane."

I obeyed before I got used as an example, and since I'd already gotten in my jab at Stripes, I kept to the other side of the vehicle. "Will the captain need me to verify my whereabouts?"

"Yep."

"Joy. I'm so excited. I suppose it could be worse. I'm not being arrested."

"Yet," Michelle muttered.

Of course. I should have known. I wondered what bullshit crime I was going to be accused of to make sure the door hit my ass on my way off the force in case minimum wage and failing a dual-eye visual acuity test didn't work. Since anything I said or did would be used against me in a court of my peers, I kept my mouth shut and waited.

LOGICALLY, I knew my desk would be cleared the next time I returned to the station, but seeing some bright-eyed new recruit in my spot annoyed me so much I refused to acknowledge anyone beyond a curt nod.

"Who pissed in your cereal this morning?" Michelle asked, nudging me in the ribs.

I didn't say a word, shrugging. Her brow furrowed, and she shot a frown my way.

Taking the most direct path to the captain's office put me in the line of fire of every officer in the station, and by the time I finished the walk, I was so tense I quivered. I rapped my knuckles on the door.

"Enter," Captain Martins barked.

I let myself in and closed the door, effectively barring my pair of escorts from joining the conversation. "You wanted to see me, sir?"

The Chicago police force mostly consisted of humans, but only individuals with a higher magic rating could rise through the ranks. With a limited pool of qualified people, the higher positions were sometimes occupied by non-humans. Lion centaurs made for intimidating officers, especially when they roared. "Where the fuck have you been? You were supposed to present yourself for duty if called."

"When, sir?"

"Two days ago."

"I was probably convincing my surgeon I could be released following the surgical reconstruction of my shoulder, sir."

Unlike many centaurs, Captain Martins had feline ears, and his turned back while his tail lashed from side to side, thumping against the wall. "And why was your shoulder being surgically reconstructed?"

"Because a man named Mark O'Conners thought it'd be a good idea to shoot me out-

side my parents' home. Furthermore, I'd notified the station I might not be available due to
traveling, sir. Anyway, I took two rounds to
the shoulder."

"That's impossible. If you'd been shot in
the shoulder, you'd still be in the hospital."

The last thing I needed was the captain
accusing me of being a liar. I sighed, pulled
out Dr. Yasolovic's card, and held it out to
him. "This is Dr. Yasolovic, who was handling
my evaluation at the CDC. You can contact
Dr. Harting in Des Moines for verification of
the operation. She was the surgeon in charge
of the procedure. You can get statements
from the Lincoln, Nebraska police if you require additional proof I was shot."

"It's impossible to recover that quickly
from being shot."

"I was given a rather large transfusion of
blood from a lycanthrope, sir. It hastens regeneration."

"Infected?"

The malicious glee in the man's voice
made me want to reach across his desk and
strangle him. "No, sir. I'm immune to the lycanthropy virus and have been given a new
designation." Since I expected Captain Martins would confiscate my new driver's license
if I showed it to him, I kept it in my pocket.
"Dr. Yasolovic can verify the details with
you."

The centaur snatched his phone off the hook and stabbed the numbers so hard I was impressed the device didn't break. "Captain Martins, CPD. I need to speak to Dr. Yasolovic, please."

At least he hadn't forgotten his manners. I wondered if the CDC would make my situation worse. Being arrested would cap off my week with a whole new level of misery—and ruin my chances of returning to the police force in any city.

I wanted to know what they thought I'd done. The clause requiring my presence at the station wasn't an arresting offense, especially since I'd notified the appropriate personnel I would be vacationing.

"Hello, Dr. Yasolovic. I have questions about a retiring office, one Shane—"

The lion's fur stood on end, and his eyes blazed gold. A low, soft growl built to a rumble, the precursor to an infuriated roar. I clasped my hands behind my back so I wouldn't succumb to the urge to cover my ears. The trick to dealing with most predators was standing one's ground, and while the lion centaur could rip me to pieces if he wanted, Dad in a fury scared me a hell of a lot more.

All I had to do was stay still and remain calm.

"I see. And is this assessment something

that can be verified through a more reliable channel?"

I really wanted to know what the CDC doctor was saying, because the captain grimaced. "I see. And—"

It took a lot of balls to interrupt Captain Martins not once but twice. I struggled to keep my expression neutral. Until I found out what was going on, I wouldn't say a word or betray my amusement at the captain's discomfort. If he lost his temper, something would be broken, and it was a coin toss whether it was me or a piece of furniture.

"And you can verify this?" Whatever Dr. Yasolovic told the captain didn't go over well; the lion centaur blanched, and his gold eyes focused on me. "And you can verify he was in your custody for the past twenty-four hours? Okay. Thank you."

Captain Martins hung up. "Considering it's impossible for you to be in two places at the same time, you can't be our suspect."

"May I ask what I was being accused of, sir?"

"Murder."

"Of?"

"Ironically, a gentleman named Mark O'-Conners."

My mouth dropped open, and I gawked at the lion centaur for so long he grunted, snapped his fingers, and pointed at the chair across his desk. I made it before my legs gave out and I thumped onto the cushion. "Mark O'Conners is dead?"

"His body was found two and a half days ago."

"And I'm being accused why?"

"Someone called in and said a man fitting your description, right down to your artificial eye, had shot someone. You had a full shoulder cast, consistent with someone with a badly injured shoulder blade."

I reached up, yanked on my collar, and pulled my shirt aside for the captain to see the pale scars. "The operation is why I was evaluated by the CDC. I scanned clean of the lycanthropy virus a full twenty-four hours ahead of schedule. They wanted to find out why."

"Your doctor confirmed you're immune to the lycanthropy virus, and that you're probably an unidentified shifter rather than a lycanthrope."

Later, I'd appreciate the captain's sour expression. "I've been asked to go in for additional talent testing as well. I have a question, sir."

"Ask."

"Were you not notified? I was informed the Lincoln police *and* the NYPD had spoken to someone here about me."

"The NYPD? What the hell have you been doing to involve the NYPD, too?"

"I witnessed a body fall from a skyscraper, land on a car, and kill the vehicle's occupants, sir. I've been notified it was a murder connected to my shooting in Lincoln—to get rid of me, an eyewitness."

Captain Martins snatched his phone and pounded the buttons. "Find out why I wasn't notified Gibson had been shot. And while you're at it, someone better have a good explanation for why I wasn't told the NYPD had inquired about him."

If he didn't start roaring soon, I'd be shocked. "If you think that's bad, it gets worse, sir."

"How could this possibly get worse?"

"The FBI is involved in the case, as there's evidence it deals with a multi-state sex trafficking operation."

"I stand corrected."

"I've already been questioned about what I know by the FBI and the Lincoln police department. How much information do you need?"

Captain Martins grabbed a pad of paper and a pencil. "Take it from the top and leave nothing out."

While tempted to request a lawyer to rain on his parade and give the centaur a taste of his own medicine, I reined in the urge and filled in him on everything that had happened from the instant I'd witnessed a corpse smashing through a car's windshield to my trip to Des Moines, omitting two important facts.

He didn't need to know my alpaca's real name was Marian, nor did he need to know the details of the show featuring an incubus and a succubus. Three modifications. He didn't need to know Marian had bitten me, either.

If he needed to know, the FBI would tell him. Or Marian. Or anyone other than me.

TRUE TO HER WORD, Michelle drove me home, and she even walked me to my door, leaving her partner to sulk in their cruiser. "Stripes is sorry he's an asshole, Shane."

Great. Michelle had slipped into guilty mode. Maybe a bit of honesty would cure her, and if she flattened me, I hoped she scored a one hit knock out. I didn't even care if I made my concussion worse if it meant I could get some rest. "Stripes can kiss my ass."

"Since when did you grow a pair?"

"Since I got confirmation I'm being bull-shitted out of my job." While I could have taken the elevator to the seventh floor of my apartment building, I took the stairs. If the hike didn't cure my agitation, nothing would.

Michelle kept stride with me the entire way. "Ah."

I wasn't surprised she was aware of the situation. Most people on the force liked Michelle. I did, too, although I suspected she pretended to like me because she had a reputation for being nice to everyone unless she was smacking them to the asphalt for pissing her off.

Considering how often she flattened people, I wondered how she had managed to trick us into believing she was nice. I needed to reevaluate my fascination with violent women capable of smacking me around. At least I knew who to blame for liking it.

Dad needed to stop influencing me.

"It's not so bad not being a cop anymore, you know."

"Then quit, if it's not so bad."

"What?"

"Put your money where your mouth is. If it's not so bad, you quit and see how you like it."

"But—"

"Get your head out of your ass, Michelle. You'd hate being forced out. You know it, I know it. You live and breathe being a cop. Maybe I did, too. Mom's a cop. Dad's a cop. Both of my grandfathers are cops. One of my grandmothers is a cop. My other grandmother's a firefighter. *Their* parents were cops."

"Okay, that's impressive. I didn't know that."

"Yeah, well, Dad's a lycanthrope. Mom's infected. Do the math."

"Point taken."

I snorted and kept on marching. "Always knew you were smart."

"I'm not disagreeing with your assessment, but why do you think you're being bullshitted out of your job?"

"I've spent more than a day being treated like a guinea pig by the CDC. When one of the doctors overseeing the evaluation calls bullshit, he's probably right. He examined my artificial eye and was very vocal about how its inferior craftsmanship, probably a deliberate attempt between the station and the insurance company to remove me from active duty. He's pursuing violations of the Species Anti-Discrimination Act. I got lucky; a new artificial eye can be made. He knows someone who lost their leg because of bullshit like that."

The first of Michelle's curses startled me. She ramped up to a shit storm of profanities so intense I gave her space to work out the worst of her fury so I didn't end up taking a trip down the stairwell. "You're fucking serious."

"When have I ever lied to you?"

"You haven't."

"Lying about something easily verified with a few phone calls is pretty stupid. So, why bother? That's the nice thing about honesty. They can check my facts themselves to learn I've spoken the truth."

"And the one time you do lie, we'll all believe it because you always tell the truth."

"There is that," I conceded. "But I have no reason to lie over something like my fake eye."

"You're right. You don't."

"What pisses me off the most is that I came to Chicago for a chance to work a different beat than my parents or their parents —to get out of a small city in the middle of nowhere. I decided I'd be a cop when I was eight. You know what I wanted to do?"

"I have no idea."

"I wanted to handle K9s or work in narcotics. You know what Chicago offers someone with my rating?"

Michelle had the decency to grimace. "Traffic patrols."

"Traffic patrols," I agreed.

"But you saved that family's life. That means a lot. You didn't even hesitate. While your partner froze, you went in, and you did what he couldn't."

"I like to think it comes from having a

grandmother who's a firefighter. She drilled it into me young to get victims out before they burned. I didn't think. I don't regret it, and if I had the choice to do it over, I wouldn't change anything. I'd still choose to lose my eye and get them out of that car, but that doesn't mean I have to like this bullshit."

"No, you're right. I'd be mad, too. Fuck mad, I'd be infuriated. I'd start busting heads together. And you're right. I wouldn't be able to quit. I'm a cop, and I'll always be one."

"Yeah. So the real question is, what do I do now?"

We finished the climb to the seventh floor in silence. A pile of mail and several boxes littered the hallway in front of my door. I frowned. Usually, the mail was left in the lobby, although deliveries were sometimes brought straight to the units.

"I'm seriously impressed it's still here. You've been gone at least a week."

"Well, it doesn't hurt the neighbors know I was a cop." I dug my keys out and unlocked my front door to discover someone, probably the building's supervisor, had left at least ten more boxes inside. "What the fuck?"

Michelle crouched by my door, pulled a pair of latex gloves from her back pocket, and slipped them on before sifting through the letters and boxes on my doorstep. "Several letters from Northwest Memorial, utility bill, some handwritten cards. Boxes are from the same sender, an M. Peterson? They're stamped yesterday."

Why would Marian send me packages? "I know an M. Peterson."

"Okay, I'll bring them in, then. Mind if I come in and look at the others?"

"Be my guest. Spares me from having to find some gloves."

"J. Gibson on this one."

"Dad." Why the hell was Dad sending me a box? "When was it dated?"

"Week and a half ago."

I sighed and shook my head. "He's a freak. It's probably fine."

"The rest look like they're from various online stores, addressed to you with gift receipts."

"So basically we just went into investigative mode for no reason whatsoever?"

"Yeah." Michelle removed her gloves and returned them to her back pocket. "A little harmless excitement never hurt anyone. Look on the bright side, you have packages to open. Call it an early birthday. I'm going to head on out before Stripes thinks we're getting real cozy up here."

"Now that would start quite the rumor around the station."

Michelle's smile made me nervous. "I like a man with scars."

Without another word, she swept out of my apartment and headed down the hall, leaving me to gawk at her back. Even I didn't need told Michelle had just flirted with me.

"What the hell?"

The boxes offered no explanations.

FIFTEEN

More insurance issues?

I DEALT with the utility bill first, making the payment using my phone before turning my attention to the dreaded letters from the hospital. One was probably to schedule a follow-up regarding my eye socket.

The other three would be disputes on the costs of the operation, more things the insurer didn't want to cover, and likely a charge for breathing air during my stay. I sat on my couch and tore into the envelopes.

My guesses weren't far off the mark, and the new bills totaled five thousand dollars in bullshit claims involving pre-existing conditions, which I had proof I didn't have. With my cheek twitching, I gave Dr. Yasolovic a call.

"Dr. Yasolovic," he answered.

"Shane Gibson. I don't suppose you can verify I don't have certain pre-existing conditions, can you?"

The doctor sighed. "More insurance issues?"

"Yes."

"Photograph and text me the documents. I'll call you back in five minutes."

I obeyed, snapping a picture of each bill and the request for a follow-up. True to his word, he called me back within five minutes. "I'll have one of the CDC secretaries file this mess with your Species Anti-Discrimination claim. It's bogus, and yes, the CDC can easily verify you have zero evidence of ever having any of these conditions—especially since we have your eye in our possession and have done a full scan of it."

"So they didn't toss it in a trash bin?"

"If they had, it would've been a five hundred thousand dollar fine."

I whistled. "How much will I owe for the CDC handling and storing it?"

"Nothing. How much did they charge you for storage and preparation fees?"

"A hundred."

"Do you have the receipt?"

"Of course."

"I'm going to send you a list of documents I will need for your case. Do not pay those bills. I will have someone draw up a letter of refusal for you and file it on your behalf."

"How much is this going to cost me?"

"Nothing. It falls under the same provisions as providing a lawyer for anyone accused of a crime. In this case, it protects patients from medical fraud. While the government would typically provide the lawyer, the CDC has the right to claim any case that falls under the Species Anti-Discrimination Act, especially if the case involves a government employee, which technically you are."

"What's the catch?"

Dr. Yasolovic laughed. "There is no catch, Mr. Gibson. Insurance companies would rather individuals weren't aware that they have recourse available to them, especially if the case involves discrimination and insurance fraud with falsified claims about someone's health. As the CDC is responsible for public health, it falls under our jurisdiction when something like this happens. Those documents you photographed support the discrimination case and the police department's failure to provide proper and adequate health care for you. I'll contact a few reputable insurance companies on your behalf. Your insurer is under contract with the CPD, correct?"

"Yes. I was set up with the insurance when I was hired by the CPD."

"Are there any circumstances you can think of that might support a claim against the CPD?"

"Someone attempted to frame me for

murdering Mark O'Conners, the individual who'd shot me in Lincoln. Someone neglected to update Captain Martins with information." I explained what had happened at the station.

"I'll contact the FBI and get someone on it."

"The CDC can do that?"

"Your shooting is directly related to the discrimination case; we wouldn't have uncovered evidence without it. Thus, the CDC has jurisdiction to request information. Since the case crossed state lines, the FBI has jurisdiction. Tell me, Mr. Gibson. How do you like the taste of just desserts?"

"I'd much prefer still having a career. I don't need to read the writing on that wall. This will just nail the coffin closed."

"Don't write off work within law enforcement quite yet. The United States is a large place, and no matter what people here think, Chicago isn't actually the center of the universe. Text me an email address where I can reach you. I'll have one of our lawyers contact you with all the documentation we need for your case."

"Thank you, Dr. Yasolovic."

"It's not often I get to actually mean this when I say it, but my pleasure."

CURIOSITY GOT the better of me, and armed with a knife and surrounded by a pile of boxes, I went to work. I targeted the package from my father first.

Big mistake.

I should have known he wanted some payback for me not coming home immediately following the loss of my eye so he could smother me with his affections. A pressurized can delivered the payload of glitter, which bloomed from the box in a mushroom cloud of tiny sparkles. Blue, pink, and silver coated me from head to toe, glimmered in the air, and settled in the carpet.

"What a dick." I shook my hands, which shined. Not only had he used glitter, he had picked varying sizes, from powder to metallic confetti. It took me several minutes to figure out how he had rigged the trap. The bastard had fixed the box so when I pulled open the flaps, the trigger depressed on the canister of compressed air, delivering the demonic craft payload. More glitter filled the box, and since he hadn't been satisfied with his initial attack, a second box waited inside the first, forcing me to dip my hands in more glitter to dig it out.

Resigned to my sparkly fate, I pulled out the second package, setting it aside. Since my father would do something evil like burying a small but important object within several

inches of glitter, I checked the bottom of the
box. Sure enough, I found another box and an
envelope.

Death would be too lenient a punishment
for Dad. Muttering curses, I shoved the
trapped package aside and went to work on
the second package.

A second cloud of glitter puffed in my
face. Luck alone spared me from getting any
of it in my eye, but I'd be picking sparkly bits
of craft herpes from my hair for the rest of
my life.

Since my apartment was permanently ruined, I dumped the contents out on the carpet. A gift-wrapped box waited for me. It was
too small for a can of compressed air, so I
tore into, tossing the wrapping paper aside.
More glitter poured to the floor, accompanying a clear plastic box with a tag indicating
my father had given me a watch.

Did I want a new watch bad enough to
deal with more glitter to retrieve it? I
scowled, and once again, curiosity got the
better of me. Glitter poured out, adding to
the disaster. Inside, safe in a plastic bag, was a
digital watch, the kind meant to link with my
phone.

I weighed the device's coolness factor
against the evils of glitter. Dad would still
pay, and he would do so for a long time. Revenge would be served when he least ex-

pected it, and I'd make sure to record every minute of my triumph. Setting the plastic baggie and the watch on my coffee table, where I hoped it would be safe from any other fiendish evils Dad had in store for me, I reached for the third box.

Continuing the sparkling theme, it contained more crap for me to clean up and directions for reaching my parents' house along with a gift card for coffee.

"Son of a bitch," I muttered, tossing the card onto the table with the watch. With my luck, the envelope would contain some sort of plea to come and visit. Part of the glitter armageddon was my fault; I hadn't told my parents I was going to New York until right before I'd left. Picking up the envelope, I tore it open. Unlike the rest of the packages, Dad hadn't contaminated it with glitter. A folded sheet of paper waited for me.

Mom's handwriting greeted me, and her note contained a list of tricks and tips on cleaning up copious amounts of glitter and a gift card so I could buy myself a new vacuum, which I would need.

I pulled out my phone, grumbled complaints over the sheen of glitter on the screen, and called my father's cell.

"If it isn't my wayward son. You're not in Des Moines," he snarled.

"Per our father and son agreement, I'm

notifying you that you and Mom deserve a fate worse than death, and I'll be coming for you. Prepare yourselves, for revenge will come when you least expect it."

"I see you've wandered your way back to Chicago."

"I see you've discovered the existence of compressed air."

"Are you shiny, my precious little boy?"

"Are you trying to provoke me into patricide?"

"You didn't tell us you were going back to Chicago."

I sighed and flopped onto the floor, staring up at my ceiling. "It was a non-optional trip. The CDC wanted to do some testing. I just got home to discover my loving mother and father had gotten bored, discovered the existence of compressed air, and somehow had gotten their hands on an obscene amount of glitter."

"You know you wanted a new vacuum cleaner. Don't deny it."

"Hey, Dad?"

"What?"

"Christmas dinner is going to be so, so fun this year. I just thought I'd give you advance warning. I'm expecting all four grandparents to attend. Don't disappoint me."

The silence assured me Dad worried because he couldn't think of any reason for there to be any surprises for the holidays. "Should I be concerned?"

"Oh, yes. Especially now that I'm covered head to toe in glitter. If I lose my security deposit because of this, you're repaying me in werewolf fur yarn. I'm sure Mom will enjoy helping me with this endeavor."

"Dare I ask?"

"The CDC did a DNA scan as part of their tests."

"Uh oh."

"Do you have anything you'd like to tell me, Dad?"

"Maybe."

"I'm listening."

"So maybe your grandpa might not be exactly human."

"May not be exactly human? You mean not human at all?"

"Basically."

"Your side or Mom's?"

"That's where it gets complicated."

"What do you mean by that?"

"Both sides."

"Say what?"

"Your mom's dad is an incubus. My grandfather's dad is also an incubus. And no, they're not the same incubus, nor are they related. I didn't even know until my great-grandfather showed up at one of the family reunions and met my father-in-law. Things got a bit awkward at that point, since your mom had no idea she's an incubus's daughter. You turned out all right, so no harm done, right? You've never demonstrated any incubus traits, so it's not a big deal. You're still human."

"Fifty-five percent human. That does classify me as a human, barely."

"You look like a human, you smell like a human, you act like a human. I say if you look, smell, and act like a human, you're a human. And that's a majority percentage, so obviously you're human. Do we get to play 'identify our son's species' over Christmas dinner? That sounds like a fun game. Make it really entertaining for us. I'm looking forward to it."

While it would've been wise to confess I was likely a shapeshifter of some form, I decided to wait. Until I shifted—if I ever shifted—it made no difference. When I thought it through, I realized if I told either of my parents, they'd take matters into their own hands.

Being glitter bombed in my apartment would only be the beginning of their evils. Under no circumstances could I let them find out I was an unidentified shifter. If startling me into shifting for the first time didn't work, they'd try to scare me. If frightening years off my life didn't do the trick, they'd

move onto something worse, like embarrassing me into shifting. If *that* didn't work, I
had no idea what they'd do, but I wouldn't
like it.

"Don't sulk, Shane. We didn't tell you because we were worried you'd be upset or
worried over how having incubus genes
might interfere with finding a wife. When
you showed no sign of having an incubus
heritage, we decided to leave it alone. Have
you developed any sudden urges to sleep with
every single woman who walks by?"

"The only urge I'm struggling with involves hunting you down and beating you for
this glitter."

"Then what's the problem?"

How was it I still managed to lose the argument despite being the one side-swiped
with surprise incubi relatives? "There's no
problem."

"Good. You sound tired. Go get some
sleep. Your mom'll call you in the morning,
I'm sure. I'll also tell her there was a good
reason you didn't pick up the phone this
morning so she stops sulking."

"Thanks, Dad."

"Anytime. Enjoy your glitter." Dad
hung up.

Instead of flinging my phone across my
apartment, I set it on the coffee table, got to
my feet, and trailed glitter all the way to my

bathroom in the futile hope I could shower the majority off.

TWELVE HOURS of undisturbed sleep did me a world of good, although it didn't make my glitter problem go away. I doubted my neighbors appreciated me vacuuming at eight in the morning, but the mess had to go. My hair sparkled. Unless I got rid of the shimmering crap, I'd never be able to leave my apartment again.

My pride could handle only so much.

Two minutes after eight, my cell rang. A better son would have stopped vacuuming before answering, but I figured since Mom had joined forces with Dad to inflict the glitter apocalypse on me, she could deal with the noise. "I'm never opening a box from you again."

Mom laughed. "Did the second box get you, too?"

"You've won this round, Mother. Expect retaliation."

"How are you doing?"

"Plotting revenge, so not too bad. Yourself?"

"Your father tells me you returned to Chicago."

"So I did, Mrs. Incubus's Daughter."

"You're not going to be letting go of that anytime soon, are you?"

"Not a chance in hell."

"Are you using your new vacuum?"

"No, I'm using my perfectly good vacuum to clean up this mess you helped make. It's everywhere. What possessed you to use so much?"

"We figured if we contaminated your apartment with enough glitter you'd come home for a visit."

"You could've warned me."

"Is there enough glitter you're ready to come back home for a visit?"

"No."

"Did we not use enough?"

"You used plenty. I have some stuff here I have to take care of. Maybe in a few weeks, assuming you keep your fridge clean and stop tossing pancakes on the ceiling. Also, tell Lewis I'll be expecting my bike delivered to your garage in perfect condition with a full tank of gas."

"Now look here, you."

"No, you look here. I cleaned that toxic wasteland. If you want me to visit in the near future, you'll keep it clean."

"Darling, you raised a clean freak," Mom called out.

"No, you raised a man with self-respect and dignity. That said, I have a lot of cleaning to do to restore what little self-respect and dignity I have left. Bye, Mom. Love you, but never again. Am I clear? Never again."

She laughed. "All right. No more glitter. For now."

"No, not for now. Never again."

"We'll see."

"Mom."

"Take care, sweetie. Call us if you need anything."

"I need this damned glitter out of my carpet!"

Instead of offering wisdom or a promise never to glitter bomb me again, she hung up. My vacuum chose that moment to give up its will to live, spluttered, and died.

I didn't blame it, not one bit.

WITH THE HELP of a lint roller and some strategically placed garbage bags, I managed to escape my apartment without trailing glitter into the hallway. I still had some in my hair, but if anyone asked, I'd blame a random toddler. My parents were essentially overgrown toddlers, so it wasn't really lying.

I almost made it to my old, beat-up car before a cruiser pulled up. Stripes refused to look me in the eye, but Michelle rolled down her window and leaned out. "Hey,

stud. Fancy meeting you here. Goin'
somewhere?"

I turned, leaned against my car, and
crossed my arms over my chest. "Stud?"

"It takes a real man to leave his home
while... is that glitter?"

"I was assaulted by a pair of toddlers."

"Toddlers? What toddlers?"

"Normal people call them parents. Me? I
have a pair of toddlers. Remember that box I
said came from my father?"

"Yes."

"Glitter bomb. Apparently, I hadn't been
paying them sufficient attention."

"Are you serious?" Michelle bit her lip,
probably to keep from laughing at me. Stripes
snickered, although he kept his gaze diverted.

"Since the glitter killed my vacuum, I'm
going to the store to buy a new one. Ironically, the toddlers planned this from the start.
Would you like a pair of parents? I'll sell you
mine for cheap."

"No thanks."

"Is there something I can do for you?"

"Not precisely. I wanted to swing over and
give you the good news."

"What good news?"

Michelle held out her fist and flung confetti in the air. "You didn't kill someone. Con-
gratulations!"

"Have you lost your mind?"

Stripes burst into a fit of laughter so intense he doubled over in his seat.

"Why would you say such a mean thing, Shane?"

"You just threw a handful of confetti at me, telling me something I already knew. But since you're here delivering the good news, how did you find out?"

"The body was a fake."

I blinked. "Excuse me?"

"The body was a fake. Since there was zero chance you could've committed the murder, the captain requested a full autopsy and evaluation done on the body, including a DNA test. It was a pig corpse transformed by a practitioner to look like the victim, who was spotted in New York City yesterday."

"That was pretty dumb of him."

"That's what we thought. But why go through the effort of framing you for murder only to show up at his regular roost? It's driving the captain mental. He wanted us to tell you to be careful, because something seems really fishy about this whole thing. You're off the hook. I thought you'd like to know."

"Thanks for letting me know. And hey, Kayne?"

Stripes canted his head. "What, Gibson?"

"You do realize I'm not going to bite you, give you any diseases, or otherwise mar your humanity, right?"

"Were you always this much of an asshole?"

"Yes. I just cared more about hiding it. Since I've got nothing to lose at this point, why not? Two-way street, buddy. Welcome to the club. It's a pissy place to be, but you know what they say. Misery loves company." Standing straight, I reached over and gave the roof of the cruiser a hearty slap.

"That was low, Shane." Michelle scowled at me.

"So is being treated like I have the plague." I dug my keys out of my pocket, tossed them in the air, and caught them. "Have a safe patrol, you two."

SIXTEEN

What started as an insurance fraud
case became a circus.

LIFE WENT on as it tended to do. It took a
week to get most of the glitter out of my carpet. During that time, the CDC investigated
my personal and professional life beginning
from my first day of college. My grades surprised the CDC almost as much as they had
my parents, who hadn't expected me to be so
damned good at classwork.

Had I been a pristine human, one without
exposure to the lycanthropy virus, my super-
visors would've promoted me within a year
despite my low magic rating.

The CDC had a field day with my case,
and they rolled my insurance company so
hard they begged for a settlement. Their
opening offer made the CDC's lawyer laugh.

Then he filed to take the case before a
judge, naming the CPD as co-defendants in
the trial. Two days later, my notice of termi-

nation arrived by courier, listing my unavail-
ability as just cause. Those documents went
to the lawyer, who added them to the
growing pile of evidence.

In a special hearing the next day, the judge
overturned the termination, declared it un-
lawful, and had it and all related reprimands
struck from my record. At the same time, I
handed in my resignation, which would at
least leave doors ajar rather than firmly
closed and locked.

Without a functioning eye, I wouldn't be
joining any branch of law enforcement soon.
I knew it, the judge knew it, the CPD knew it,
and the insurance company knew it, too. Yet,
we danced in court, and what could have
been two hundred thousand dollars in my
pocket became a circus in the Chicago courts,
one that would either nail the coffin closed
on lycanthrope rights or breathe new life
into it.

I hoped for the latter but expected the
worst. It was Chicago, after all. My initial
payout wouldn't last forever, so I looked for
some way to make a living while the rest of
my life was put on hold, at the mercy of a
bunch of lawyers and a court system rigged
against me from start to finish.

In the true American way, what started as
an insurance fraud case became a circus, one
where every last facet of my character was

put on trial in front of a jury of my peers and the media. The CDC used every resource at their disposal to shine light on the insurance frauds committed against lycanthropes and those infected—or falsely assumed to be infected.

They even did a live demonstration of my immunity, cutting my arm open deep enough one of the jurors fainted before injecting me with active wolverine lycanthropy virus serum. I had to admit the demonstration's effectiveness; the wound took less than ten minutes to close, leaving a pale scar in its wake, and within an hour, I scanned clean.

The unexpected test came when they drew a vial of my blood while I was still infected with the virus and put it under a microscope for the judge and jury to watch. Outside my body, the virus died within minutes. They performed one final test, requesting the presence of an angel for the purpose of the demonstration.

Angels creeped me out. Their lack of a head wasn't the problem; I could deal with that. It was the way they moved, silently lethal and every inch the predator, that got to me. I'd seen enough of them in my life to recognize one. What the angel hunted, I didn't know.

Judge Wellington regarded the latest witness with an arched eyebrow. "You've done a demonstration Mr. Gibson is, as you claim, immune to the lycanthropy virus. Explain to the court why the presence of an angel is necessary."

The CDC's lawyer rose from his seat and approached the judge, turning to face the crowd packed into the courtroom. "Your Honor, angels share a significant amount of biological processes with humans. They can be infected with many of the same ailments humans can, including lycanthropy. However, unlike humans, they can purge these ailments from their bodies at will. This makes them ideal for certain demonstrations, including the contraction of the lycanthropy virus. Abrahaman has generously consented to the final demonstration we wish to show the court regarding Mr. Gibson's case. This test will irrefutably prove that Mr. Gibson is— and has always been—incapable of infecting the public he served. His status as a human exposed to the lycanthropy virus led to the police and his insurance company collabo- rating in a joint effort to force him out of ac- tive duty. If he hadn't been flagged as exposed, he would have received a functional eye and been able to resume his duties as a police officer."

"Is this correct, Abrahaman?"

"It is."

I couldn't even begin to guess how the angel spoke without a mouth.

"Proceed."

"For this demonstration, we will inject Mr. Gibson with a high quantity of the lycanthropy virus, sufficient to ensure infection in a standard human. We will use a cell count of approximately half that required for a first shift. This is the equivalent of the virus incubating for an excess of ten years, which is sufficient development for the virus to spread. As angels have biological processes on par with a human's, within an hour of exposure to Mr. Gibson's blood, should Mr. Gibson be a contagious risk as claimed, Abrahaman will have detectable amounts of the lycanthropy virus in his bloodstream."

"You have the court's permission to proceed."

As the primary test subject, my job was to stand around and do as told. To either drive home the point of the case or to make the more prejudiced squirm, a cougar lycanthrope in hybrid form handled the injections. She showed her teeth to the ground while her muscles ripped under her glossy tawny fur, a not-so-subtle reminder of her inhuman strength.

The lawyer had explained to me the reasoning for the extreme experiment. First, it would establish without the shadow of a doubt I was immune to the lycanthropy virus. Second, it would establish the humanity of lycanthropes, as only humans could be infected with the virus.

Angels transcended humans, but their bodies were still human in certain ways. They could contract lycanthropy. Unlike humans, they could cure themselves of it.

The lycanthrope injected five large syringes into my arm; after the third, the fever kicked in. When I wasn't sweating, chills ran through me. Worse, it made the slow-healing bite on my shoulder throb.

"Unfortunately, such a sudden, high-level exposure to the lycanthropy virus has consequences, including general malaise and fever," the CDC's lawyer explained. "This has been recorded in susceptible humans."

I wanted to find somewhere nice, quiet, and private so I could throw up, but I clenched my teeth and waited for the cougar to finish her injections. She gripped my left shoulder, ducking her head to my ear. "You have our thanks," she growled.

Not trusting myself to speak, I acknowledged her with a nod.

"In ten minutes, we'll draw a vial of blood and inject it into Abrahaman. This will interrupt proceedings for approximately five minutes."

The judge acknowledged the lawyer with

a nod. Efficiency mattered to Judge Wellington, and he wasted no time shifting gears and
bringing up another element of my life. "You
requested for your witness to take the stand
during this phase of the trial. You have the
court's permission to call your witness to the
stand."

"Objection!" the insurer's lawyer
squeaked.

Of all the species of centaurs I'd ever met,
the rats amazed me in their variety. Most of
them were nice people, as close to angels as
humans got. Unfortunately, the ones who became lawyers gave demons, devils, and vampires a run for their money.

It said a lot the police had gone to the
worst of the worst for their defense.

"Denied," the judge barked. "You had your
chance to question the prosecution's selection of witnesses at the start of the trial. I
have the discretion to approve the prosecution's request to call their witness at this time.
Sit down, Mr. Ulsra."

"I call Carey, Francois, and Hubert
Telleman to the stand," the CDC's lawyer announced.

I only recognized the family because of a
few newspaper articles reporting on the
traffic accident that had almost claimed their
lives and had cost me my right eye. The father, Francois, carried his two year old son in

his arms. The boy was hard at work sucking on his thumb.

Carey flashed me a smile, Francois nodded, and Abrahaman startled the entire court by bringing a stool to the witness stand so all three could sit. It was a tight squeeze.

Traditionally, they would have been questioned individually. The judge, with one unusual move, had turned the questioning from the events affecting one person to those affecting involving an entire family—a family still alive because of me.

In the ten minutes before I was subjected to my blood being drawn so Abrahaman could enjoy a hefty dose of infected blood, my lawyer had transformed me from a man classified as a public health hazard to someone who'd crawled into a burning car and pulled three unconscious people from the wreckage.

At my lawyer's invitation, Carey pulled her shirt over her head to reveal her stomach and chest, which were covered in burn scars, a permanent reminder of the accident that had almost taken her life. I coughed and found somewhere else to look, as Mrs. Telleman had forgone wearing a bra so the jury could get a good look at the evidence she brought to the stand.

Only an idiot would believe she could have escaped the car on her own. Her husband shared similar scars, although he wasn't quite as dramatic about showing them off.

Hubert had escaped unscathed; I'd pulled him out first, and his mother was eager to show the jury how her little boy wouldn't carry a single mark from the accident, although he had some lingering vision problems from a hit to the head.

The CDC's lawyer to finished with his questions in forty minutes, and as though understanding he'd dig his own grave, the defense passed on his chance to ask additional questions.

On their way to their seats, Francois stopped beside my seat and set his son on my lap. "Hubert, this is the nice police officer who pulled us out of the car. Say hello."

A pair of wide blue eyes regarded me with a complete lack of fear. "Huwwo, Meester Police Officer."

Hubert put his thumb back in his mouth, staring at me while I floundered. I had swallow several times before I could force myself to reply, "Hello, Hubert. It's nice to meet you."

Taking his thumb out of his mouth, he balled his small hand into a fist and patted his chest. "Me be a meester police officer, too."

Words failed me.

TWO HOURS FOLLOWING the injection of my blood, Abrahaman scanned clean of the lycanthropy virus, as did I. Unfortunately, my fever spiked and lingered, something the CDC blamed on excessive exposure to the virus in a short period of time. My fever came with a fringe benefit.

Since the live demonstrations were complete and the Tellemans' testimonies had been given, I was no longer needed in the courtroom, which meant I could get on with my life while waiting for the verdict. The CDC compensated me for the trial time, the public testings, the risks associated with virus exposure, and the unanticipated consequences of their in-court experimentation.

If I was careful with my money, I had six months to find a new job.

For the first time since returning to Chicago, I felt good about going home, until I got in my door and faced the remnants of the glitter apocalypse. Sighing, I shook my head at the shimmering carpet, dug out my phone, and called my mother.

"Are you dead?" she asked.

"What sort of stupid question is that?"

"Just wondering, as it's early evening and you're calling me. That's a reason for concern."

"I escaped court without anyone killing me," I announced. Although I'd had the boxes for weeks, I hadn't opened any except my parents', although the one from Marian sometimes tempted me. "Let's say you received a bunch of boxes from unknown senders or distant acquaintances. Would you open them?"

"Do they tick?"

"No, Mom. They don't tick. If they ticked, I would call the bomb squad, not leave them unopened in my apartment. I'm not an idiot."

"I'd open them."

"The last time I opened a box, glitter exploded in my face. I've learned my lesson."

"Don't be a baby. Open the boxes and tell me what's inside. Your dad's working. I'm bored. This sounds like a good cure for my boredom. How long have you had them?"

"They were waiting when I came back to Chicago from Des Moines."

"That was weeks ago."

"I'm aware."

"We'll come back to the boxes. How did your court session go?"

"The jury has no idea how close I came to throwing up on them today."

"What happened? What's wrong?"

"The CDC happened. They decided to bring in an angel for an experiment involving giving me enough live lycanthropy virus to match someone who'd been infected for a decade. I have a low-grade fever. Exactly no one is surprised. At least they limited the number of times they cut open my arm. Juror Number Ten's a fainter."

My mother sighed. "Are you serious?"

"About Juror Number Ten? If she saw blood, she dropped like a rock. I'm still not sure whether it was the blood or if she's a lycanthrophobe."

"I meant about the virus injection."

"Those jurors have no idea how close I came to throwing up on them. I think the angel knew, but he was too polite to say anything. I'm pretty sure the angel was a male. His name was Abrahaman, and he found us mortals amusing."

"What angel?"

"The one they injected with my blood to demonstrate I wasn't a contagion risk."

"Have they lost their minds?"

I snorted. "That thought had occurred to me. I think they were pushing the point lycanthropes are humans, as only humans can be infected with lycanthropy. Since angels can be infected with the same diseases humans can but can purge themselves of just about anything, it was the only safe way to do the demonstration. Oh, I met a cougar lycanthrope today, too. She was about as big as Dad, and I'm pretty sure her hobby's working out."

"Are you sure you're fine?"

"It's just a fever, although I'm queasy enough I'll probably skip dinner tonight."

"Eat soup."

"Mom, I can skip dinner tonight if I want to. I'm an adult."

"So am I, and I'm a bigger, badder adult than you are. Eat your dinner, or I'm driving to Chicago. If I have to drive to Chicago, you aren't going to like it."

What sort of monster had I been in a previous life to deserve my parents? "Fine, Mom. I'll have some soup."

"When's your next court session?"

"I'm done. The judge declared they've had sufficient chance to evaluate my character and isn't entertaining any more personal questions or demonstrations. Then he mentioned something about cruel and unusual punishment while glaring at the CDC's lawyer."

"So you can come home for a visit?"

"Is the fridge clean?"

"Maybe."

"I'm going to spend the next few days looking into job prospects. If the fridge can be verified clean by a reputable source, I'll consider a drive to Nebraska to entertain you for a period up to a single week."

"I've produced a cruel and unfair human being."

While I knew Mom expected me to laugh,

I couldn't manage it. "Hey, Mom? Riddle me this."

"What's wrong, baby?"

"They had the family from the accident on the stand today." I clacked my teeth together and inhaled long and deep before exhaling through my nose to calm my fraying nerves. "Mrs. Telleman decided the best way to show what she's survived was to take off her shirt. She wasn't wearing a bra."

"Your poor virgin eyes. I bet that was not the sort of thanks you wanted, huh?"

"Well, Mr. Telleman showed off his chest, too, although his wasn't quite as…"

"Nice? Feminine? Curved? Beautiful?" My mother snickered. "Voluptuous?"

"Scarred."

"Ouch. That bad?"

"That bad. They put their son on the stand, too. I think he's two. Cute kid."

"They usually are at that age. Little devils, but cute little devils. Were you okay? No flashbacks?"

"On their way back to their seats, the kid's dad put him on my lap and introduced me as the nice police officer who pulled them out of the car. Apparently, the kid has decided he's going to be a police officer when he grows up."

"Oh, baby."

"Yeah. I handed in my resignation last

week. They tried to fire me for not responding to some bogus request for information. The judge overturned it, but the CDC lawyer had my resignation prepared so I would have a chance to return to law enforcement."

The distinct sound of my mother cracking her knuckles worried me. "Do I need to come over there and start banging heads together?"

"No."

"But I'd enjoy it."

"No, Mom."

"But I'd really enjoy it."

"No, Mom. I've already done something even worse."

She grunted and kept cracking her knuckles. "Like what?"

"I sent the CDC after them. The CDC's lawyer laughed at the insurance company's settlement offer, and the CPD has already had one smackdown in court. I'm moving on, and that doesn't mean bailing my mother out of jail for smashing heads together. And no, you can't send Dad, either. Or Lewis. Or anyone else. I don't need you or Dad coming here and ruining the CDC's chance to give other lycanthropes equal rights in Chicago and other prejudiced cities. Stay out of it."

"When did you become such a good man, Shane?"

"I'm pretty sure my parents had something to do with it. I'll talk to you later, Mom." I hung up on her, shook my head, and turned my attention to the stack of boxes waiting by my couch.

I started with the boxes Michelle had identified as gifts from an unidentified sender. The first contained a set of pot and pans, the second had a coffee maker expensive enough I searched the box top to bottom for the sender's name with no luck. Whoever had sent them had decided I needed a kitchen upgrade; by the time I'd emptied the final box, I had more stuff than I knew what to do with, including a set of dishes elegant enough even my grandmothers would approve of them.

Out of excuses to avoid them, I opened the first of Marian's packages, cautiously peeking inside.

A stuffed animal waited for me.

"What the...?" When I lifted it out, its weight startled me. At first glance, I wasn't sure what it was, but the tag informed me the animal was a badger. It was dark with two pale stripes over its head, which made it resemble a badger someone had made in the dark with two left hands. I flipped it over and discovered a zipper on its belly with another tag attached bearing Marian's signature. I set the stuffed animal on my coffee table and opened the second box.

It contained a pair of pocket holsters, several empty magazines and clips, a gun-care kit, and a thick packet stuffed with papers. My eyebrows rising, I opened the envelope and peeked inside.

Concealed carry licenses were a pain in the ass to acquire on a good day, requiring just cause, training, and an excessive amount of paperwork to be considered for the permit. Every state had different rules, but the government occasionally issued special permits allowing an individual to conceal a weapon in any state.

A laminated permit card fell onto my lap. It featured a picture of me wearing a suit; I couldn't remember the last time I'd worn a suit, making me wonder where the hell Marian had gotten the picture. It wasn't from the trial; I'd worn slacks and a dress shirt with tie and had opted against wearing a jacket. I opened my mouth, closed it, and retrieved the stuffed animal, pulling open the zipper and peeking inside.

Sure enough, inside I found a pair of handguns small enough to fit in my pockets. Both were black with white grips, matching the stuffed animal they were hidden in. Several folded sheets of paper accompanied the weapons, including the sales receipts, registration in my name, and a copy of the shipping label, which declared the package contained firearms.

A handwritten note advising ammunition was my own problem made me laugh. I picked up my phone and called my mother back.

"You're such a brat. What do you want now?"

I laughed. "I want to run a scenario by you."

"What sort of scenario?"

"Pretend you're Dad or some macho man for a minute. Let's say you're single, you go to a bar, and you meet a girl. You part ways, but later she sends you a gift. What would you do?"

"Depends on what the gift is?"

"A pair of Ruger LCRx compact handguns and a nationwide concealed carry permit."

"Marry her."

SEVENTEEN

Someone likes you a lot, buddy.

SINCE CARRYING two guns around in my pocket would inevitably lead to disaster, I acquired an ankle holster and hid the second one in my boot. Carrying them would take a while to get used to, but I appreciated having a backup plan in case something went wrong. With no way to contact Marian to thank her —or make an idiot of myself and follow my mother's blurted advice—I kept the mutant deformed badger stuffed animal on my bed and thanked it instead.

I even obeyed the woman's orders and acquired ammunition for both guns and their spare magazines.

My next step would be going to the firing range and dumping hundreds of dollars down the drain practicing with both weapons and adjusting to shooting with only one eye. Before the accident, I'd been a good shot, but I hadn't touched a gun since.

I was able to read between the lines. If Marian thought I needed two compact handguns and a carry permit for them, she was worried. Instead of a thank you, I would repay her by honing my shooting skills.

Bright and early the next morning, I took both guns to the range. My resignation from the force meant the range had been notified I was no longer a police officer, which earned me skeptical looks from the range's manager and the handful of cops getting in their mandatory hours.

"Thought you resigned, Gibson," Porter barked at me.

I tried not to take offense at his tone. The idiot had taken his mufflers off too often at the range, impairing his hearing, so he barked at everyone because he couldn't hear himself. I dug out my wallet, pulled out my concealed carry card, and dropped it on the counter in front of him. "I'm looking to get in a couple of hours. I'll need ammunition for a pair of .45s."

"Someone likes you a lot, buddy. How the hell did you get one of these?"

"Christmas came early for me this year." I pulled my Ruger from my pocket and slid it across the counter. "It's got live ammo in it, safety on. A gift from a friend."

The man's bushy eyebrows rose. "Your friend really likes you a lot. That gun's tiny but fierce. You're going to like it, Gibson. Your second?"

"Matched set."

"All right. I can fit you in for two hours. That permit puts you in the rotation with the cops, so play nice with your former buddies, all right?"

"I intend to work on my shooting, get my slips showing my hours, and keep to myself. Don't worry about it, Porter. I can handle myself."

"You know how these girls gossip."

I snorted, glancing in the direction of the loitering cops, most of whom I recognized though didn't know by name. "Don't let the actual girls hear you say that. Most of the ones I know might hesitate before they teach you what it feels like to be punched in the kidney. After the first few times, you learn to stay quiet."

"It did only take me three or four times to teach you," Michelle agreed from directly behind me, giving my side a gentle tap.

"Hi, Michelle."

"What are you doing here, Gibson?"

Porter chuckled and waved my nation-wide permit. "Gibson got himself a nation-wide concealed carry permit."

"No way!" Snatching my card out of Porter's hand, she looked it over and presented her hand for a high-five. "Well done, sir."

I gave her palm a gentle slap and reclaimed my card with a flick of my wrist. "I should have made you open the box from Dad."

"Oh? The glitter incident?"

"Rigged compressed air can for maximum spray."

My former co-worker threw her head back and laughed. "That's so wrong."

"I know, right?"

"Who did you have to hold for ransom to get that permit? That's going to open some doors for you even short an eye."

"Amazingly, no one was held ransom."

"Getting in your hours?"

I nodded. "Going to start with two and see how it goes."

"First time back to the range since the accident?"

Thinking about the whole mess from the loss of my eye to the CDC's case soured my mood, but I forced myself to nod and smile. "Yeah. Got a new pair of guns I want to put through their paces."

"What kind?"

"Rugers." I reclaimed my gun from Porter, cleared the chamber and popped the magazine before handing it over to Michelle. "They were a gift."

"Nice gift. Hook me up. I need a boyfriend."

I glanced over my shoulder but didn't spot Michelle's partner anywhere. "What, not going to hook up with Stripes?"

"You're joking, right? The guy jumps at his own shadow. If you think his reaction to lycanthropes is bad, you should see him face off against a spider. He's nice enough, don't get me wrong about that, but he has issues."

Where there was smoke, there was fire, and judging from Michelle's tone and expression, she had an inferno blazing away over something her partner had done. "Going to get in your hours while blowing off steam?"

"Fucking straight I'm going to fucking get in my goddamned hours while blowing off some fucking steam."

When Michelle lost her temper, someone got hurt, and the other cops cleared out so fast I expected a vacuum where they'd been standing. I dug out my credit card and offered it to Porter. "All right. Hook us both up for two hours, and perhaps you should give Michelle the far stall. I'll cover the ammo today if you solemnly swear not to shoot me."

Michelle slapped her hand to the counter. "You've got a deal, Gibson."

I already regretted my decision to haunt my old roost to begin getting my mandatory hours, but I hid my discomfort and went

through the process of checking in my
weapons.

MICHELLE'S AIM left a lot to be desired. I
couldn't tell if she was bothering to pick a
target before dumping her magazines. I was
grateful her gun of choice wasn't an auto-
matic; within two hours, she'd cost me a
small fortune.

Unlike her, I took my time, picked my
mark, and fired. Most of my shots hit the paper, although it took longer than I liked to
adapt to the changes in my vision. By the end
of the first hour, I'd found a new appreciation
for the Ruger. Its small size hid a big payload
while being large enough to grip reliably. It
also packed enough of a punch to remind me
I wasn't playing with a toy.

Michelle gave up before I did, and I was
aware of her behind me while I took my final
shots, systematically targeting the kill zones
before refilling my magazines and cleaning
the sill.

Since I wasn't quite ready to announce to
the world I was hiding a spare gun in my
boot, I kept the second Ruger unloaded and
slipped it into my other pocket. The
woman's frustrated sigh worried me. "What's
wrong?"

"How the hell can a man with one eye and new guns shoot better than me?"

"It doesn't hurt I wasn't a bad shot before I lost my eye."

"Come to think about it, I've never watched you shoot before."

"Few have." I shrugged, tucked the spent ammunition boxes under my arm, and headed towards the lobby. "If you need to sharpen your skills, talk to Ed Housin on the east side of town. He operates a gun shop in Lower Chicago and gives lessons. He's good, and he won't cost you a fortune."

"We've been trying to bust Ed for years on illegal gun trafficking."

I snorted. "I wish you the best of luck with that. You're going to need it."

"Why?"

"Because Ed's Ed. He's obsessive compulsive, knows the rules and regs better than anyone I know, and likes his guns more than his children or his wife. Could he be trafficking? Hell if I know. I needed to improve my skills, so I bought lessons, and there's nothing illegal about taking lessons from a certified instructor. But if you want to learn how to handle a gun better, he's a good teacher."

She frowned. "How good?"

"I'll show you. Let me ask Porter a question." I headed to the counter and handed over the spent ammunition boxes. "Hey. You happen to have a real gun I can rent for fifteen minutes and some ammo? I want to show Michelle something."

Porter straightened. "Are you going to try a demo?"

"May as well."

"Beretta, Glock, S&W, or other?"

"Hook me up with a semi that has some punch."

"I love it when you talk dirty, Gibson."

My shoulder wouldn't appreciate trick shots, but I'd work my left hand more than I had. Playing a game of oneupmanship against Michelle wouldn't earn me her friendship, but maybe it'd motivate her—or get through the skulls of the other cops loitering around the range that a low magic rating or lycanthropy wasn't a euphemism for useless. In a way, I hoped I had an audience.

Unlike some, an audience made me better, honing my focus and raising my awareness of everyone and everything around me, which made hitting my mark easier. I'd surprised Ed, which I considered my crowning achievement with the instructor.

Ed didn't surprise easy.

Porter loaned me a Smith & Wesson, a popular gun among the CPD, and a weapon I'd used before. Instead of using the closed range, he led Michelle and me to the auxiliary range, which lacked stalls and featured a

single target, serving as a classroom for larger
groups before they went to the main range
for individual shooting time. The auxiliary
range was also a place to practice shooting on
the move, which was what I'd be doing.

Sure enough, the loitering cops followed,
and I ignored their presence, checking the
pistol. "All right, Porter. I'm going to want
five magazines for this."

Five magazines would let me do a full run
of the common trick shots Ed had taught me
and still leave me with a few tricks tucked up
my sleeve. Porter's grin widened; he loaded
the magazines and set them on the range's
single table near the entry. "Want me to toss
them to you when you're ready?"

"Sure. I'm not responsible if they break."

"If you break them, I buy them."

"Just don't throw like a toddler today. If I
wanted a lob, I'd go play softball."

My small audience chuckled.

"I've missed your nasty mouth, Gibson."

I snickered. "You've just missed my
money."

"That, too. Go set up your playground
while I get these kindergarteners their mufflers so they don't end up as hard of hearing
as I am."

In the back of the range were stands for
mounting targets, allowing for paper, steel, or
clay targets. I preferred the clays, as I'd seen

too many trick shots ricochet off steel targets for my comfort. The box of clays would add an extra forty to my range adventures, but I didn't care.

I didn't mind spending a little money to prove a point, although I might regret my choice in a few months if I didn't find a new job. Twenty minutes later, I had set up a line of fifty targets ranging from six inches to six feet in height. To hit them all, I'd have to jump, roll, duck and slide while firing. I'd regret my close acquaintance with the concrete floor long before I crossed from one side of the range to the other.

Porter handed me a pair of mufflers and chuckled at my handiwork. "Feel like you need some exercise?"

"Yeah."

"Ten says you miss ten or more before you run out of ammo."

"And if I don't miss ten or more, you're paying me ten bucks *and* you're covering the ammo, targets, and rental fee."

"You're on."

We slapped hands to seal the deal, and I left my Rugers on the table in Porter's keeping. The M&P22 had a twelve round capacity, which gave me very little wiggle room in my accuracy.

If I hit forty, I'd be more than satisfied with the run—and prove my point, making it well worth the investment to give Michelle a taste of what someone could do with time, effort, and determination. My demonstration would also remind the other cops minimum hours and minimum qualifications didn't necessarily mean someone was good with a firearm. I'd poured enough sweat, tears, and blood into my shooting skills to pass muster with Ed, and I'd never be as good as him.

He lived and breathed guns; I'd plateaued at good enough to be sure of my shot so I wouldn't hurt someone unintentionally.

The real trick was balancing speed and accuracy. The faster I went, the lower my accuracy, but if I could control my body, keep my eye on my target, and be aware of my every movement, from my breaths to the quiver of tired muscles, magic would happen.

It wasn't magic like most thought of it; I couldn't whisper flame into being, knit bones back together, or do anything most viewed as magical. For a brief period of time, when my world narrowed to the feel of a gun in my hand, my target, and the resistance of the trigger on my finger, I understood Ed and his adoration for firearms.

My limited field of vision didn't hamper me as much as I feared, even in motion. My hand and eye still worked together, I could still judge distances, and from my first step and first shot, I forgot about Michelle, Porter, and the other cops. The feel of the concrete on my back when I rolled, the sting on my knees when I found my balance and surged to my feet, and the recoil of the gun in my hand consumed all my attention, my rhythm broken only when I dumped an empty magazine and caught a fresh one with my left hand.

I had missed eleven targets after forty-nine shots. When I rolled to a halt on one knee, I twisted and closed my right eye out of habit rather than necessity. I emptied the magazine behind my back, one of Ed's favorite tricks, which he'd taught me to force an awareness of the gun in my hand. My grip on the weapon and the way I pulled the trigger factored into my aim, and when I kept my hold proper and true, I simply needed to see my mark to hit the target.

The first two rounds went wide, but the rest of the clay targets shattered, leaving behind shards and little else. Rising to my feet, I checked the chamber was clear and strolled to Porter, picking up the four magazines I'd abandoned on my run from one end of the range to the other. I removed my mufflers and held out my hand. "Pay up, buttercup."

"Aren't you supposed to be crippled and rusty?" Porter complained, digging out his wallet and slapping a ten dollar bill onto my hand. "I was sure two months off the range would have put an end to that nonsense."

I chuckled and pocketed my prize, handing over Porter's gun so I could retrieve my Rugers. "It's only nonsense because you can't figure out how I do it."

"You weren't extending all the way, and you were slow."

Maybe instead of buttercup, I should have addressed him as Petty Porter. "You said nothing about timing me for the bet."

He glared at me. "You're a smug bastard sometimes, you know that?"

"Only when he's earned it," Marian said from right behind me, close enough her breath tickled my neck.

I headed for orbit, landed several feet away, tripped on the turnaround, and hit the concrete hard. At least I didn't smack my head into the floor, although my shoulder was rather unhappy with me. "Jesus Christ!"

"That was some nice shooting, Mr. Gibson." While FBI agents didn't have specific uniforms, I recognized the slacks and suit jacket as something they often favored on duty. Marian canted her head and smirked. "You're a bit flighty."

Porter turned on the woman, straightened to his full height, and barked, "Who let you back here?"

Marian flipped open her badge and

shoved it in Porter's face. "FBI. The gentleman at the counter pointed me in this direction. I need a few minutes with Mr. Gibson."

Too many questions rattled in my head, with wondering how Marian had found me topping the list. I got to my feet, dusted off, and checked to make sure my wallet, keys, and both of my new guns were in my pockets where they belonged. I glanced at Michelle, who was targetting Marian with her worst glare.

"Thanks for the company," I said, nodding to Michelle. "Give Ed a call. If he can't teach you how to do that, no one can."

Michelle scowled, and I tensed, expecting to hit the floor again. Instead of indulging in one of her usual tosses, she clapped her hand to my upper arm. "I think I'll do that. I've learned one very valuable lesson today."

"Which is?"

"Don't underestimate the quiet guy in the back of the class."

I snorted. My low rank in the police department had been the equivalent of being stuck in the back of the class with no way to advance. I chose against sighing over the confirmation Michelle had misjudged me along with everyone else and gave her shoulder a gentle bump with my fist before giving

Marian my full attention. "I'm parked in the back."

"Conveniently, so am I. After you."

Marian fell in step with me and waited until we were outside the building to say, "With accuracy like that, you should've been bumped up to SWAT or put on a specialist team."

"Porter was right; I am slow and rusty, and my field of vision is a lot less than it used to be."

"I'm going to book you an appointment with one of the FBI qualifiers and see what you can actually do. I see you found your presents."

"You should've seen Porter's expression when I showed him the nationwide concealed carry permit. He's been after one for years. It seems I owe you a great deal of thanks for that."

"With your professional record, your filed qualification records, and the fact you've already been targeted once for your unintentional involvement in a dangerous case, it wasn't hard to get the approval. I thought it would be a decent start to showing my thanks for the assist."

"And the Rugers?"

"I didn't know if you had any concealed carry guns, so I thought I'd nudge you in the right direction."

"I do like them. Thank you."

"You're welcome. You've been making some waves since we last saw each other. Was that your girlfriend?"

"No. Former co-worker."

"Ah. Cop, then?"

"Yep, and she's pretty pissed I'm a better shot than she is."

"Shane, you're a better shot than half the members of the FBI. That was some seriously nice shooting, and you're no slacker in the footwork department. That course was set up to force you to move and take shots from all angles. That's not easy."

Coming from an undercover FBI agent, the complement meant a lot. "It was nothing, really."

"Nothing except hard work and a lot of dedication to learning how to use a gun. That wasn't your gun."

"We use the M&P22s on the force, so I've fired them before."

"Still." When we reached my car, I wished I'd gotten something at least a decade newer and with fewer rust spots. "Ah, you're one of those."

Even I recognized when something didn't sound promising. I guessed what she meant. "The 'my main car is a cruiser' type?"

"Yep. My main car is an FBI marked SUV. It's like that one," she said, pointing at the black vehicle parked several spots away. "However, mine's blue."

"Is there someone hiding in there, or did you drive yourself here?"

"Unlike my colleagues, I didn't get lost. I learned from their mistakes. I wisely asked someone for very detailed directions on how to get here. I'll be following you out of here, and if you ditch me in Lower Chicago, I'll hunt you down and kill you."

Why did I find cranky women threatening to end my life so damned attractive? While Michelle would flatten me given half a chance, her temper made her more dangerous. When Marian delivered her ultimatums, the hint of a smile lowered her lethality rating significantly. "Where am I taking you?"

"FBI headquarters downtown."

"I'll cut you a better deal. I'll take you to my apartment, ditch my car, and drive you there myself. Fastest way is through the alleys of Lower Chicago, and I'll lose you in the maze for sure." With morning rush hour over, I might even be able to get her there in an hour, assuming construction cooperated. "In exchange, tell me how you found me."

Marian's smile widened, and she pulled out her phone and showed me the display. "I tapped into the tracking software on your phones. I figured the two stationary signals were the spares, so I got the address and came here."

I wrinkled my nose. "I forgot about that."

"I rather like it. That said, you should uninstall it. Convenient for me means potentially convenient for others. Will I be interrupting anything important if I borrow you for a few hours?"

Marian didn't seem bothered by my long silence. If my luck held out, she thought I was thinking over my schedule rather than remembering her on my lap. "Nothing important, just submitting my resume. No appointments I can think of, and I'm no longer required to appear in court."

"I've been following the trial, and I did confirm with the CDC you weren't going to be in court before flying in. I'll try not to take up too much of your time."

I hid my disappointment with a smile, recognizing professionalism when I saw it. "It's no problem. If I lose you, I'll pull over so you can catch up. I presume you have my number."

"You presume correctly. Let's go."

EIGHTEEN

They're supposed to start?

IF I INVITED Marian up to my apartment, would she take it the wrong way and murder me?

I needed to grab something from my fridge to keep me from melting into a starved puddle at her feet. While I had no problem getting on my knees and begging, I'd rather do it for something more pleasant, like a repeat of the evening in the nightclub, except in my bed. The idea of her hair on my pillow did unfair things to me.

So did the thought of her in a pair of jeans.

I spent the entire drive to my apartment attempting to exorcise the memory of her naked body warming mine. Despite popular belief, thinking about puppies and kittens didn't help. Sports didn't help, either, although I made progress analyzing my performance at the shooting range.

Michelle's behavior bothered me enough to distract me from Marian, but not in a good way. Before the court case, she'd been a little standoffish although friendly, but she had changed, and I wasn't sure if it was for the better. Upsetting the status quo wouldn't earn me any friends among the prejudiced, and the CDC was presenting me as a victim of unfair discrimination—discrimination she'd participated in.

Learning I could shoot better than her, essentially rubbing her ignorance in her face, wouldn't earn me any points with Michelle. At least Stripes hadn't been there; I scared him enough without him realizing how good of a shot I was. Rumors spread fast around the station. It wouldn't be long until everyone learned I knew my way around a gun beyond standard qualification.

I hadn't hidden my shooting skills on purpose, but I hadn't boasted about them, either.

At the end of the day, my marksmanship skill mattered jack shit, although the CDC could have used it in my case if I'd bothered mentioning it. Then again, it hadn't occurred to me to mention it. What did it matter?

A dead end was a dead end, and maybe I'd reached my goal of being a police officer in a big city, but it had been a dead end no matter how I looked at it. A graveyard of discrimination littered my career as a cop. I parked my car in my spot, snarled a few curses, and got out. Several deep breaths later, I straightened, locked my car, and turned.

Marian tossed her keys to me, and I caught them. "My rust bucket has a flat. I'm too lazy to fix it."

The random comment got a laugh out of me. "At least mine starts on most days."

"They're supposed to start?"

"Most of the time."

"Huh. Maybe I should look into that."

Shaking my head, I circled the SUV and climbed in. "Some might call you crazy for willingly getting into a vehicle with me as the driver."

"I'm willing to accept the risk. You driving through this hellhole seems a lot safer than me driving through this hellhole."

"Bad trip getting to the range?"

"It's a good thing the so-called engineers who designed this city are dead, because I seriously wanted to kill them."

I laughed. When I'd first moved to Chicago, killing the city's designers had crossed my mind many a time. It had taken me several years to understand the layout of the streets, the way some dipped into Lower Chicago and re-emerged several blocks later, and the incessant construction involved with making sure the whole place didn't collapse in on itself. The city still didn't make sense,

but I could find my way around without contemplating homicide most days.

"How do you people stand the traffic? Is
driving in this city the number one cause of
homicides here? I could easily believe that."

"Did   you   get   detoured   from
construction?"

"I did *not* get lost." Marian shot me a glare,
buckled her seatbelt, and wrinkled her nose.

"Did they reroute you through Lower
Chicago, up to the surface, then back a few
times before dropping you two blocks from
where you started?"

She grumbled curses, which I interpreted
as confirmation. I buckled up before starting
the SUV's engine. My car rumbled, but it was
more due to the whole thing trying to rattle
apart rather than the purr of a tuned, road-
worthy vehicle. "You didn't get lost. That puts
you ahead of half of Chicago. Even locals can
get turned around during unexpected construction."

"That's something."

"Can I get a preview of the questioning?"

"We're investigating your imposter. They
called me in since I'd witnessed your
shooting and saw you in the days following
your recovery. We're both going to be questioned, but beyond that, I can only speculate."

"Sounds like a great time, especially since
the CDC is using the circumstances sur-

rounding my shooting to support the discrimination case."

"We're aware. The CDC brought in the FBI to testify. I'll tell you this much, someone in the CPD must have pissed off the CDC, because it's a slaughterhouse. The defense is being thoroughly spanked. That rat's trying, but he just can't get anything on you. It's actually impressive. Your record is so clean it squeaks when you rub it. We can't even get dirt on you from elementary school. The only remotely questionable thing we have is something that happened when you were six."

There was only one incident I could think of when I'd been six that might catch the FBI's notice, and it involved a kidnapping attempt. I had declined the invitation using a baseball bat. Running had seemed like a good idea at the time. Unfortunately, six year old me had had the attention span of a gnat and decided to play hide and seek with the entirety of the Lincoln police force.

"I'm pretty sure I can't be held responsible in a court of law for playing hide and seek at age six."

"I was more thinking about you shattering your would-be kidnapper's knee with a baseball bat."

"Self-defense. No court would convict me."

"We were wondering how you managed to

beat up your would-be kidnapper so effectively. On top of that, you avoided capture for a full thirty-six hours." The amusement in her voice warned me of trouble. "The details of your capture are being analyzed, but the initial verdict is that it was the cutest bust of that year."

I sighed. "Why do I worry someone is going to include that in the discrimination trial?"

"I hope not."

To worry or not to worry, that was the question. I went with worry. "Oh?"

"Should the general public learn how wretchedly adorable you were as a child, you'll be the target of many single women hoping to have equally cute babies. If my co-workers are to be believed, what's a little lycanthropy when someone has a child *that* cute? You grew up to become a cop with a startlingly good record and the sort of ethics that make even lycanthrophobes think twice before criticizing you."

Yep, I was right to worry. What did I want with *many* single women? I'd be happy with one—a nice one who didn't mind I wasn't entirely human, had a father who hated fleas, and a mother who would one day hate fleas as much as Dad. I seemed to have no problems with single women who bit, although I hoped Marian's bite would finish healing soon.

"That's disturbing."

"Sources inform me you're the conservative, traditional type who would probably like being pursued by women a lot."

"Your sources are clueless."

"Your parents."

"Definitely clueless." I paused. "Wait. You were talking to my parents?"

Was that a good sign or a bad sign? Did I need to update my will or buy an engagement ring? If I ran away with an FBI agent, how long would the prison term be? Did it count as kidnapping if I asked before running off with her? Maybe I could just ask her to run off with me. That would solve a lot of problems.

It also had the potential to cause a lot of problems. I didn't even know if she was single.

"They were very useful in giving us information about you. Between the FBI and the CDC, I'm fairly certain the Gibsons have no desire to be questioned ever again."

"You grilled them."

"Not me specifically, although I did enjoy listening to the recordings."

I sighed at the thought of my parents dishing out all my dirty secrets, which probably meant they were aware I'd had sex with an undercover FBI agent in the nightclub while under the influence of an incubus. "If I move to Alaska and hide in a cave, do you think anyone will notice?"

"Probably."

Descending into Lower Chicago, I dodged the worst of the construction by detouring off the beaten path, easing the FBI's SUV through a maze of narrow alleys, stall markets set up in abandoned, gutted lots, and residential areas most in Upper Chicago pretended didn't exist.

"While I'd heard Chicago had some pretty unsavory parts of town, this is even worse than I thought."

"We're not even in the slums."

"Are you serious?"

"Very. This isn't a fun patrol, but most of the residents are nocturnals who have their own form of law enforcement. They don't bother us, we keep our noses out of their business. There are a few laws the CPD doesn't ignore, but a lot of them? Forget it. In good news, your nice little FBI sticker means no one in their right mind will bother us."

"And if I didn't have a nice little FBI sticker?"

I drove several more blocks, waited until we passed the first brothel, and pointed at it. "You'd probably end up there being sucked off by a vampire while an incubus had his way with you. The gentlemen get the vampire and a succubus. If they spot your badge, they'll dump you in Upper Chicago, place an anonymous call for a pickup, and leave you alive—they'll even give you basic first aid, but you'd need a transfusion."

"And without a badge?"

"They'll keep you for a couple of days to get you good and addicted, then they'll dump you on the surface to be found later."

"I take it you haven't been assigned to this patrol?"

Looking at her from the corner of my eye, I decided to add a few extra minutes to our trip by taking a detour to show her the heart of the nocturnals' hunting grounds. Newcomers found the odd combination of brick veneers, glass, and steel intriguing and comforting; by resembling a safe haven, the buildings lured in the ignorant.

"This is a lot nicer. That's weird."

"Kinda cozy, right?"

"Sure, if you're a mad scientist with an architecture hobby."

"Nice building and clean streets make victims unwary. They're grabbed here, taken through tunnels under the street, and sent to the various brothels."

"You know a lot about this area, don't you?"

"I'm probably the only one who's been on

this patrol without spending some time serving as a vampire's snack."

"Why? Aren't virgins special treats to succubi? How did you prevent it from happening?"

I shifted on the seat so I could reach the Ruger in my pocket, waited until I hit a stop sign, and pulled the gun fast enough Marian sucked in a breath. "After I kneecapped a few vampires, they stopped thinking of me as dinner."

"That's not on your record."

"The vampires were rather embarrassed and politely begged me not to tattle on them." I smirked. "That was with my first partner. Let's just say he washed out."

"You don't seem too upset about that."

"He requested patrols for this area." I returned the Ruger to its holster and resumed my slow drive through Lower Chicago, taking the first larger street headed downtown. "After a few months of shit shifts thanks to him, I asked for a favor."

"A favor?"

"Yeah, from one of the local vampires. Nice guy, if you don't mind someone looking at your neck like you're a tasty treat. You'd be surprised how considerate the nocturnals can be if you make it clear you're not interested. Casey never did find out why the locals stopped grabbing him for a fun time during his patrols. I really got tired of hunting his ass down in Upper Chicago and taking him to the ER. Ultimately, I *was* the reason he got fired, since I may have asked that vamp friend of mine to take notes on Casey's activities."

"Public endangerment?"

"Bingo. Since I was flagged as contaminated with lycanthropy, no one really cared if he got me into trouble, but when our patrols are interrupted because he's deliberately trying to get with a succubus, it causes problems."

"And you didn't get into any shit over it?"

"No. I had a few close calls. When the vamps decided to sink Casey, I got a concussion during his grab. If Casey had been reassigned, all that would've happened was the other cop would've been sucked into the same cycle."

"Not so squeaky clean as I thought, then."

"Nothing I did was illegal."

"You realize I'm going to verify that, right?"

I chuckled. "Would you like me to provide an exact timeline of my dastardly deeds so you can verify my pristine record?"

"That guy at the range was right. You are a smug bastard, aren't you?"

"That's the name of the game here, Marian. Some cops can get away with bending the rules. Me? They were looking for an excuse to get rid of me all along. I was just too stubborn to quit."

"So you made the most of it."

Making a thoughtful noise in my throat, I considered my situation. "Do we have time for a detour?"

"A detour? What sort of detour?"

"There's someone I want you to meet."

"I'm game. I told them it might take me a while to find you. I'd like to be there by five."

"We'll be done by five," I promised. Once she figured out what I had in store for her, she'd probably kill me, but there was no better way of learning someone's mettle and intentions than exposing them to the worst Chicago had to offer and watching the fireworks.

NINETEEN

*You're taking me into a brothel,
aren't you?*

MOST PEOPLE WERE FOOLED into believing I
was as good a person as my record implied,
but in reality, I had a mean streak, and I had
no problem dipping my toes into the cesspool
of Chicago if it meant I could get the advantage. Taking Marian to a prime hunting spot
for nocturnals put me firmly in the bad cop
category.

Taking her in the middle of the afternoon,
when the nocturnals' hunger peaked, went
beyond bad to ruthless. My favorite parking
spot, tucked between a brothel and a court-
house, would keep the FBI's vehicle safe. I got
out, sat on the hood, and waited.

Marian stood on the sidewalk with her
hands planted on her hips. "What are we
doing here?"

Instead of answering her, I smiled,
watching the third-story window of the

brothel. After a few minutes, the curtains shifted, and a dusky hand pressed to the glass. Without seeing the rest of the feminine arm, I couldn't tell which succubus was in the shop, but with a single gesture, she beckoned me to pay a visit.

I really hoped it was Amy. Amy had the best control over her powers, played a mean game of chess, and liked guns almost as much as Ed. Unlike her fellow succubi, Amy always gave me a call with where she and her partner dumped Casey, which had made my life so much simpler.

"All right. There are a few rules for this, Marian."

"What?"

"I recommend you stick close to me."

"Okay. I can do that."

I considered pushing my luck to find out how close I could get her but decided against it. She'd be getting an eyeful of one of Chicago's greater sins as it was. "I wouldn't stray more than a couple of feet away. That makes you fair game."

With narrowed eyes, Marian looked me over. "You're taking me into a brothel, aren't you?"

"Was it that obvious?"

"The sweaty hand smear on the third floor gave me a bit of a clue. How did you last as a virgin for so long if you go to brothels?"

"Didn't we already discuss the kneecapping thing?"

"You seriously kneecapped a few vamps so you could stay a virgin?"

"I like to think I have done a pretty good job of protecting myself."

Marian grimaced. "Then I came around."

While her tone and expression informed me she was being serious, I laughed. I had enough embarrassment to share, but I did my best to hide it. "I only take issue when the participants involved are unwilling. If it makes you feel any better, I didn't need much convincing, and you might have seduced me without the help of a pair of demons. If you have no regrets, I have no regrets. Anyway, I could have found a woman if I'd really wanted one. Here, it's all about the quick flings and moving on to new waters. Not my thing."

I toed the honesty line. I regretted the night had ended and that my chances of a repeat plummeted every time I opened my mouth.

"You're the marrying kind. I gathered that much from the interview recordings."

I pretended I hadn't noticed Marian's neutral tone. "Initially, my game plan was to get settled into my career, meet some nice cop, and marry her. I misjudged how hard of a line Chicagoans drew against lycanthropes. I figured I'd have some hiccups along the way, not that I'd be stonewalled."

"That Michelle woman seemed to like you."

I snorted, shook my head, and headed for the discreet door hidden in the alleyway, slowing to make sure Marian followed me and stayed close. "Michelle's pissed I can shoot better than her. I also suggested she learn from someone she's been trying to bust for years. Add in Stripes, who has enough pride, self-esteem, and phobia issues to keep the entire staff of a mental institution busy, and it wouldn't surprise me if one or both of them danced on my grave and pissed on it."

"How charming."

"I like Michelle, but she's almost as petty as Porter when it comes to being outclassed by someone she views as inferior. Her friendship is a bit like stepping on a horse chestnut."

"Hurts like hell and prone to sticking in your foot?"

"I see you have experienced horse chestnuts."

"Unfortunately." Marian sighed. "And in Chicago, lycanthropes, their kin, and those infected take what they can get, huh?"

I shrugged. "It is what it is."

"This has been so educational, and I haven't even gone into the brothel yet."

"Try not to make me kneecap someone

while we're in here. It's a mess to clean up, the vamps get cranky, and then I have to ask them really nicely to drop it, which would inevitably lead to another kneecapping. I don't like kneecapping people."

"You make it sound like this is a common occurrence."

"A kneecap a day keeps the vamps at bay," I muttered.

"Seriously?" she squeaked.

I laughed. "It's been a while since I've had to have a talk with any of them."

Marian slipped her hand into her blazer, and a quick glance revealed a holstered Ruger the match for mine. Chuckling, I pushed through the door and stepped into one of my least favorite places in Chicago. Magic kept the stench of marijuana and cigarettes inside, and when we left, the same magic would strip it off us, something I found amusing, as they made no effort to disguise the scents of sex and sweat.

"Charming."

The hostess caught sight of me, shrieked, and pounced. Marian sucked in a breath and had her gun out in the time it took me to catch the girl by her waist, spin with her momentum, and set her out of harm's way. "Don't startle the FBI agent, Kelly. She's a bit jumpy."

At first glance, Kelly looked no older than

fifteen, although I knew to add a couple of zeros to the end of the number to get closer to her actual age. Over the years, the perky brunette had refused to tell me her species, but she had a fondness for physical contact, which made me think she was a young succubus who hadn't grown into her powers yet.

"You've been gone *forever*, Gibson."

I pulled out my phone and made a show of checking the date. "So this visit, forever is quantified by six months, two weeks, and three days?"

"Why are you being mean?"

I needed all my self-restraint to keep from smiling at her whining tone. "I'm certain it's because I'm an insufferable busybody and an asshole, Miss Kelly. This is Marian, and she's with me."

Kelly glanced in Marian's direction. "Your broad's pretty slick with that gun, but she's not as good on the draw. If she wants to start kneecapping people around here, she's going to have to do better than that."

"It seems there's a theme at this establishment, and it involves crippling sentients."

"Oh, no. Gibby doesn't cripple them. He just makes them wish he had. He's a sourpuss. Hey, we've been taking bets. Is he as good of a lay as he looks? He won't play with us."

I amended my guess about Kelly to her being a young succubus who had just grown into her powers, enabling her to catch glimpses of the love and lust of mere mortals —and somehow detect who had slept with who last. The idea Marian hadn't been with anyone else appealed to me.

Marian's eyes widened. "You're a succubus?"

"I haven't gotten my wings yet, but it'll be soon. I was hoping Gibby here would be my first, but you beat me to him. Not fair."

The round went to the perky little brat playing hostess, and I sighed my defeat. "I suppose it was a bit much to expect a bunch of demons to pretend my sex life was a private matter."

"Darling, six months ago you didn't have a sex life. You had a dry well, an emaciated libido, a—"

I covered Kelly's mouth with my hand. "Thank you, Kelly. Marian didn't need to know that."

"Already knew, Shane. He may not be experienced, but he's really enthusiastic."

Grabbing my hand, Kelly uncovered her mouth. "Are you going to keep him? I wanted a virgin for my first time, but I might make an exception."

"She's not a virgin, Marian. She's got at least a hundred years of roleplaying a sexy schoolgirl for the brothels here. Don't let her trick you."

"Shane, why are you being a spoilsport?"

"You know full well your first time will be with an incubus, so don't play that sad card on me, missy."

Kelly pouted. "Spoilsport."

"Thumb sucker."

"Old man trapped in a young body."

I chuckled. "I resemble that remark. Now that we've had our fun, I've got some questions for the boss, and a tip for him."

"Bad?"

"Got me shot twice bad."

Kelly hissed, and her eyes flashed red. "Who did it?"

"Nice fellow named Mark O'Conners with the New York City Italian mafia, probably running a sex trafficking ring taking girls off the streets."

"Naughty, naughty, naughty. You don't seem undead to me, so you weren't killed. Are you going to play nice and show me the scars, or am I going to have to strip you here in the entry?"

Marian's eyes widened, and she eased her finger away from the trigger guard and reengaged the safety of her Ruger. "Shane, what's going on?"

Since Kelly wouldn't leave me alone until I showed her, I grabbed my shirt and pulled it over my head. "Right shoulder."

"Damn, Miss Marian, you bite hard. What

were you trying to do to the poor guy? Brand him for the next hundred years?"

I sighed. "No one said she was the one who did it."

"She totally did it. She branded you like a stallion up for auction. That's totally a brand. I'm so jealous. Why couldn't you find your own incubus? You had to go and take mine, Marian!"

If Marian's eyes widened any further, I worried they'd pop out of her head. "I'm sorry, did you say incubus?"

"Kelly," I hissed.

"Oh! You found out? Damn it, I was really hoping I'd nail you with that one. So not fair. Who told you? Did you find out who your incubus relative is?"

"Relatives," I corrected.

"You're part incubus?" Marian squeaked.

"This is not how I was hoping this visit would go."

"He's incubus enough I can tell." Kelly sniffed. "Between his kneecapping the boss a few times and his off-limits attitude, we were sure he was dormant."

I should have known succubi could tell at a glance if someone had incubus blood. Groaning, I pinched the bridge of my nose. "Fine. I'll tell you some details, but not only do you get me in to see the boss, Marian's not to be touched. No tricks, no influencing her,

no groping, no nothing. I expect perfect angels from the lot of you troublemakers."

"Now you're just being mean, Gibby.
Come on, she's kinda cute. I wouldn't mind a
turn with her."

"No."

"Gibby!"

"Do you want the details or not?"

"Yes," she whined.

"Then you make sure everyone leaves her
alone."

"You're being jealous and possessive.
That's not fair."

"I'll toss in a hug, but no funny business."

At first, I thought she'd refuse my offer,
but then she wrinkled her nose and sighed.
"Fine. It better be a good hug."

I paid up, giving her a tight squeeze, and
because I did like her when she wasn't trying
to turn me into succubus bait, I kissed her
forehead. "I'm sure you'll land a good incubus
for your first time. As agreed, incubus relative
number one is one of my grandfathers, and
incubus relative number two is one of my
great-grandfathers, other side of the family."

"*Two?* Two? That's *so* unfair. Not a pure-
bred, but that's better than most. Which one
of your parents is the half?"

"Mother."

"That explains so much," Marian muttered.

"Bummer. So she won't be getting her wings?"

"She's infected with lycanthropy, Kelly. I've told you this before."

The young succubus dismissed me with a wave. "Lycanthropes are amazing lays. You should try one sometime. Right, Marian?"

"Why are you asking me? Shane's not a lycanthrope."

"His daddy is. That's close enough. They're supposed to be real beasts in bed, but I'm not allowed to have my rounds with them —not until I get my wings."

"I can verify he's a real beast, but I've yet to try his performance in an actual bed." Marian smirked.

My face burned. "She didn't need to know that."

"Did he take you in an alley against the wall? That'd be hot. That scar gives him a real bad boy appeal."

"No, I did no such thing. Damn it, Kelly!"

With her smirk widening to a full grin, Marian whispered something in Kelly's ear, which made the unfledged succubus's mouth drop open. "Oh hot damn, do I wish I'd gotten a piece of that. No wonder you branded him. Screw branding him, I would've chained him up and never let him out from under me again."

I closed my eyes and wished I could disappear. "The boss?"

"Hold your horses. This is serious girl business we're attending to."

Expecting a succubus working a brothel to have restraint made me unreasonable, especially when gossiping about sex was involved. While I waited for her and Marian to finish their giggle-punctuated discussion, I faced the nearest wall and banged my forehead against it.

Turning my back to the entry of a brothel ranked among the dumbest things I could have done, so when a strong tail coiled around my leg and a silk-clad pair of breasts pressed against my back, I clacked my teeth and grumbled curses. "Hello, Amy."

"Am I so obvious, Gibby?" the succubus purred.

"Yes. You're the only one of your demonic sisters to put on clothes before rubbing up against me."

"You brought a female into my domain."

"She's off limits."

"I heard. I'm jealous. The boss sent me down to bring you both upstairs, and he asked me to tell you to leave the shirt off. He likes it."

Of course he did. Vampires enjoyed naked flesh almost as much as succubi, and Ernesto had been trying to get a sip from me for years. "All right. Get off, and at least try to keep some control over that tail."

"Kelly's right. You are a spoilsport."

I heard the click of Marian's little Ruger. "That one's mine. Get your hands off."

"Ah, I love them when they're so jealous. So delicious. You should take her for another ride, Gibson. She'd like it."

One day, maybe I'd be able to tell if the succubus was being serious.

TWENTY

Do I need to shoot you in the
kneecap again, Ernesto?

ONE OF CHICAGO'S five crime lords, a vampire the CPD hunted daily, seemed like someone I'd want for an uncle if I could ignore his record and tendency to view humans as prey. As far as arch nemeses went, Ernesto Saven numbered among the better ones, tempering cunning, ruthlessness, and greed with humility enough to put humans to shame.

Old long before Christ's birth, Ernesto possessed a Middle Eastern flair, eyes darker than sin, and a smile promising hell to any who got in his way. "Shane, dear boy, it's been too long since you've paid this old soul a visit. And to bring a lady with you? There's hope for you after all."

"Do I need to shoot you in the kneecap again, Ernesto?"

"Do I get that sip I've long desired?"

My next words would condemn me. Some

sins were worth committing, and if making a deal with a vampire sold my soul to the devil, the cause was worth the price. "I'm open to negotiations."

Ernesto rose from his seat to perch on the edge of his dark desk, and a flicker of red light burned in his eyes. "You have my undivided attention. But first, your eye. That worthless bauble is buying justice for many. I've been watching the news. Humans." Disgust dripped from his tone, intense enough Marian grimaced. "It is not often I find pride in having an enemy who has morals and integrity. If only they knew what they wasted."

"I'm confused. Are you trying to flatter me so I shoot you or don't shoot you?"

"It's been so long since I've enjoyed evidence of your love."

"Oh for fuck's sake." I whipped out my new Ruger and shot the vampire in the knee. Unlike humans, Ernesto didn't bleed, but I hated the crunch of dried, brittle bone in the wake of the gun's concussive blast. Since I knew he'd beg until I shot the other one, I shifted my aim and fired again. "I swear. You meet with me only so I'll do that to you, don't you?"

"You're the only cop with the balls to actually do it."

"Ex-cop."

"Your breed never quits. That's why you're here, isn't it? And with a badge bunny?"

"She's the badge."

"So you're the badge bunny, then?"

I grunted to acknowledge the vampire's successful baiting and wrinkled my nose.

"Say it," Ernesto ordered.

One day I would learn from my mistakes. One day. "I'm the badge bunny."

"She's a pretty cute badge. Is she tasty?"

Marian pulled out her gun and blasted Ernesto in the ankle. "I'm revising my opinion of coming here, Shane. This is great. You should take me more places."

"You're a feisty little ankle biter, aren't you?" The vamp's gaze turned to the slow-healing bite on my shoulder. "Shoulder biter as well, if these old eyes don't deceive me."

A faint hint of red spread across Marian's cheeks.

Maybe I shouldn't have stopped covering the healing wound. A bandage would have kept the vamp from eyeing the scab like it was the main course of his dinner. "See the two dimes beneath it?"

"Someone tried to rob me of my most de-sired dessert."

"Riddle me this, and I'll think about letting you have a taste."

"Ask."

"Are you involved in any sex trafficking operations anywhere in the United States?"

"No."

"Know of a man named Mark O'Conners?"

Ernesto hissed. "I know of him."

"He was the one who tried to rob you of your most desired dessert."

"Do you want him gone, dear boy?"

I smiled, holstered my Ruger, and stepped to Ernesto's leather couch. I sank onto its sinfully comfortable cushion, stretching out my legs and weaving my fingers behind my head. Goading the vamp ranked high on my list of reckless things I'd done in my life, but if I wanted him to do my bidding, I needed to play his game.

As long as I didn't behave like prey, I wouldn't become prey.

"I want to know your thoughts on this ring."

"Then let's talk. Dear lady, do sit. Make yourself comfortable. I would escort you to a seat, but it seems I'm taking a break right now."

Marian opened her mouth, her expression puzzled. She glanced in my direction, stowed her Ruger, and came to sit beside me. "I was just punned by a vampire I shot, Shane."

"You'll get used to it. Just don't shoot him in the chest. He likes it."

"It tickles nicely."

"What have you gotten me into?" she hissed.

"I suppose introductions are in order. Ernesto, this is Marian Peterson, an FBI agent investigating a sex-trafficking operation. Her last assignment went sour in New York City, resulting in a rather memorable evening in a nightclub in Des Moines. Marian, this is Ernesto Saven."

"Shane?" Marian nudged me with her elbow.

"Yes?"

"Are you friends with one of the FBI's most wanted?"

"Friends? That's far too small a word for what we share," Ernesto replied, flashing his pointy pearly teeth.

"I think you have a lot of explaining to do."

"It's simple. The CPD can't get anything on Ernesto. They try, as do the local feds. Ernesto likes the game. Few in the CPD are smart enough to figure out how to play it."

"And you are?"

"Oh, dear girl, he was the first. Chicago has been my home since its birth, and he waltzed into my domain like he owned it, kneecapped me, and demanded the location of his partner. He didn't even knock. He let himself in right under my demons' noses. It was poetry in motion. I would call him son if he let me."

"Breaking and entering plus assault?" Marian demanded. "Him? He wouldn't."

"Oh, he would. My dear boy is such a charmer. He speaks my language."

If I let Ernesto continue, Marian would leave thinking I was as much of a crook as the vampire. "He left me an invitation in my partner's blood on the hood of our cruiser, so it's not breaking and entering. As for the assault, is it really assault if he likes it?"

Ernesto threw back his head and laughed. "You've stayed away for too long. I'm a vampire, Agent Peterson. I'm old. Of course, at the time, he was his mother's son, and my ladies had had their way with his partner. I think of it as justifiable aggression."

"I'm not sure I understand."

"The first step to wisdom is acknowledging one's ignorance."

"He likes thinking he's clever. Essentially, Mom gets really pissy when someone fucks with her partner. I do, too. I might not have liked the bastard, but toothy here sent a few of his children and one of his succubi out to play catch the cop, and I took offense."

"And he knows of your mother?"

"Of course he does. He can't be a big bad scary vampire without doing his homework, and after I kneecapped him the first time, he decided to learn more about the cop the other cops shunned. I wouldn't be surprised if he knows more about me than the FBI does." I shrugged. "That's what vamps with too much time on their hands do. They annoy me, toy with the local police force, and otherwise play a complicated game of cat and mouse. Haven't played much with the vamps?"

"No. I tend to take sex trafficking cases."

"Well, in Chicago, if there's organized crime, it's usually run by a vamp or a rat. The vamps do a better job of it since the rats like to gloat. So while the rats gloat, the vamps cover their tracks and make it look like they haven't broken any laws, when in reality, they are among the worst offenders. To them, finding loopholes in the law is almost as satisfying a hunt as getting a good drink from a human. If the vamps aren't involved in the crime rings, they're lawyers or judges, playing the game from the other side of the field. Ernesto prefers to be a solo player against many, so he prefers the illegal side of the fence."

"You flatter me, dear boy."

"Do you want your elbows shot out next?"

"Yes, please."

Marian giggled. "How many laws am I breaking by just sitting on this couch?"

Ernesto rested his elbow on one of his ruined knees and feigned a heavy sigh. "None, and it disgusts me."

Shifting to get to my Ruger, I drew it and made a show of checking it over and popping the magazine in and out while eyeing Ernesto's elbow. "You're bored, aren't you?"

"Deathly. Terribly. Morbidly. It's been so boring since they shifted you to traffic patrols on the surface. Then to give you that awful bauble instead of a proper eye so you can't come play with me again? I'm offended. I hope your lawyer eats that rat and his client for breakfast."

"The clients are the CPD and my former insurance company."

"Crooks, both of them."

Marian's frowned. "Did I just hear a vampire crime lord call someone else a crook?"

"Weird, isn't it? Maybe later when we don't have a time limit, he'll give you some of his colorful commentary. If you want to know the inner workings of the government, crime, and crime's influence on local economies, talk to Ernesto. There's a reason the feds have wanted him for years."

"There you go flattering me again. If you keep this up, I might think you like me."

Vampires didn't need their elbows, so I shot out both of Ernesto's. It might challenge him when he fed, but he'd manage—probably. "Hardly."

"You love me. You truly love me. If only you were the son of my loins instead of my heart."

Shooting out the vampire's shoulders was rude in addition to cruel and unusual punishment, but I figured if he were bored enough to push my buttons, he'd enjoy overcoming his temporary handicaps. "Hell no. I already have a psycho werewolf for a father and a half-incubus mother. I don't need a vampire added to the mix."

"Why is no one coming to investigate all this gunfire?" Marian muttered.

I pointed my Ruger at the corners of the room and the tiny cameras mounted near the ceiling. "He's got his goons watching and listening to the whole thing, that's why. They might get worried if I go for headshots, but this is nothing."

"I thought you said you kneecapped vampires."

"I just like starting with their knees. It's a violent, wholesome way to say hello."

"Violence isn't exactly wholesome. Wholesome implies you leave them whole after you're done saying hello."

I looked over Ernesto's mangled joints. "But I like it, Marian."

"Obviously I'm talking to the wrong person in this room. Better question. Why don't you beat the snot out of him for shooting you, Mr. Saven?"

"Do call me Ernesto, dear girl. It's quite simple. He asked me not to."

"Pardon? He… asked you not to?"

"Exactly so. He's human enough it takes him a long time to heal, so I have to play with him in other ways. Last time, I sent Amy to his apartment to rearranged his furniture while he slept, and she rather enjoyed cuddling up to him for the evening. It's the satin sheets. She loves satin sheets and a quiet, warm man to snooze beside. Also, he panics when he wakes up and he's not alone in bed when he expects to be, which is so very entertaining."

I holstered my Ruger so I wouldn't be tempted to put a bullet in Ernesto's throat. "You sent Amy over twenty-seven times last April. I got to the point I left the door un-locked so she wouldn't have to waste time picking it. What I don't understand is why she decided to clean the place from top to bottom."

"Boredom."

"Well, yes. That does tend to happen when you send her to my apartment twenty-seven times in one month."

"Once for each time you shot me, and Amy is the only succubus I have on staff you won't shoot on sight."

I scowled. "Still. Twenty-seven times in one month."

"You got me back for that, I'll remind you."

Marian sucked in a breath through clenched teeth. "Shane, are you seriously telling me you're in a prank war with a pre-dominant crime lord?"

"She's such a flatterer, dear boy. I like her."

No matter what I said, I'd lose. I'd either give Ernesto more ammunition against me or offend Marian. "Then that might work in my favor. Mark O'Conners was involved with her kidnapping and subsequent sale to a sex club in Des Moines. She was initially taken in New York City, recovered, then taken again."

"Is this related to the corpse that fell on you?"

I should have known Ernesto already knew about the murder in New York. "If the corpse had fallen on me, I'd be dead, but yes. Marian was transformed into a rather angry alpaca for shipment."

"Alpaca? Like a llama?"

"A cute, small version of a llama, yes."

"My, my. I'd pick up my phone and call someone, but it seems my elbows are out of commission. Do be a dear boy and lend me a hand, would you?"

I nodded in the direction of the cameras. "No. Ask one of them. They like it when you boss them around."

"But you're more entertaining to boss around."

"For fuck's sake." I got up, went to his desk, snatched the phone from its cradle, and activated the speaker phone. "Who am I calling?"

He gave me a number, which I dialed for him before returning to my cozy seat on the couch. On the third ring, a gravelly voice answered, "It is early for you to be calling me, Saven."

"Pierce, you owe me a favor."

Oh great. Ernesto had called his brother, a vampire living in Georgia who really enjoyed being kneecapped.

"I hate when you say that."

"Stop asking me for favors then. A ring in New York City has overstepped its boundaries. I'm going to make them disappear. You're going to help me do it."

Marian's mouth opened, and I clapped my hand to her lips so she wouldn't say anything. The glare she shot me promised retribution later, but until she learned the rules of Ernesto's games, I couldn't let her interfere, especially when her job would become a lot easier.

"This sounds interesting. What's going on?"

"My darling boy has two dimes on his shoulder, given to him by Mark O'Conners."

"That idiot shot a cop?"

"Pierce."

"Let me correct myself. That idiot shot your cop?"

"Better. Yes."

Vampires. Whenever they found someone interesting, they forgot slavery had been outlawed decades ago. Instead of correcting him, I sighed and shook my head, lowering my hand from Marian's mouth and signaling for her to remain quiet. She nodded.

"How did you find out who shot him?"

Ernesto faked a sniffle. "He took out my kneecaps and my elbows and my shoulders. I'm so happy."

"He's there, isn't he?"

"He finally came home to visit me, Pierce."

"Gibson, do I need to rescue you?"

I laughed. "I think I'm all right for now. I'll let you know if that changes."

"I changed my phone number. I'll text you my new one. You still using that decrepit piece of shit you claim is a cell?"

"My number hasn't changed. Also, stop hacking into the police databases to steal phone numbers."

"Don't be a spoilsport, Gibson. Rumor mill says you retired?"

"Forced out."

"Morons. How'd they do it? I was convinced you'd never come to the dark side."

Ernesto shot me a look I translated to mean 'shut up.' I obeyed, holding my hands up in surrender. "You heard about the accident, yes?"

"Of course. You called me, wailing your cop had gotten hurt in the line of duty. What about it?"

"They gave him a glass eye. Plain glass, blue, with bubbles. That's what they gave him. It's an offense."

"I'm pretty sure that's what started the court fiasco I keep hearing about. Isn't the goal to get him something better?"

After snorting loud enough I jumped, Ernesto bared his teeth and hissed. Marian squeaked, her gaze locked on his pronounced, jagged teeth, evidence the vampire's hunger was on the rise.

"Is there a woman with you, Ernie?"

"She branded my cop with her teeth. So far, she's quite entertaining and a quick study for a fed. I'm considering giving him my approval."

Pierce remained silent for a long moment. "Approval for *what*?"

"Stealing his virginity. My succubi are all wailing because they didn't have a chance to have him first."

I slapped my forehead. "I don't need your approval, Ernesto."

"Yes, you do."

"Just let him have his fun, Gibson. So who is this little lady of yours? Introduce us already."

I hoped Marian would forgive me for involving her with another vampire crime lord. "Marian, Pierce is Ernesto's brother. Pierce, Marian Peterson. She's an FBI agent."

"Finally found yourself a badge babe, huh?"

I glanced at Marian, wondering how I could answer without getting into more trouble.

"Just say yes so they shut up," she suggested.

"Yes," I obediently replied.

"I like her. So what's this about Mark O'-Conners taking a shot at you?"

"I accidentally acquired one of the women they were selling in their sex trafficking ring. To get her back, O'Conners gunned me down while I was hoofin' it back to my parents' place."

Pierce snickered. "Your Nebraska is showing. And the girl?"

"My badge babe undercover."

Marian scowled and drummed her fingers on the grip of her Ruger.

"You have my attention. The FBI actually got a girl into one of the rings? That's better than they usually do. Well done, Miss Peterson. That said, as you're Gibson's badge babe now, I'm not sure you should continue with that specific line of work. He's the jealous type and will kill anyone who touches you. Though if you want to bust up every ring in the United States, that would be a good way to do it." Pierce chuckled, and the sound made my skin crawl. "You've asked a fun thing of me, Ernie. Are we really joining forces with an ex-cop and an FBI agent?"

"I'm fairly certain they'll be unwilling participants in our activities. You know how these cute law enforcement types get."

"All right. Lay it out for me from the beginning. How did you get involved? Walk us through it from the top. I'm taking notes. Ernie, I'll send you a copy later so you have them, as I'm sure your cop isn't done putting holes in you."

"He said he might even let me have a taste if I'm really good."

"One of these days he's going to snap and kill you."

"That day is not today. Now, to business. Tell us everything you know. It's been too long since I've had a good hunt."

TWENTY-ONE

I can't believe you're friends with
them.

I MANAGED to keep my word to Marian. We escaped from Ernesto's brothel a little after four, blitzing through Lower Chicago to reach the FBI headquarters with five minutes to spare. Since I drove one of the FBI's vehicles, the gate guard didn't charge me an arm or leg to park although he directed me to Lower Chicago to reach the employee lot. Marian kept flexing her hands at every delay, which I interpreted as the woman finally reaching her limit.

I waited until I was on the road before attempting to soothe her nerves. "The questioning probably won't be any worse than what we dealt with earlier. I can handle most of the talking if you'd like."

"I can't believe you're friends with them."

Right. Most people in law enforcement hated crooks—or worse, they were a crook pretending they weren't. "Who else is going to let me shoot them as many times as I want?"

"What truly disturbs me is that I can't blame you for that reasoning."

I grinned, got out of her SUV, and tossed her the keys. "As far as vamps go, they're not that bad."

"Are you ever going to let him get a taste?"

"I told him I'd think about it. If I thought about it until the day I died, he'd be happy knowing it's hanging over my head."

"So he's playing you."

"Of course he's playing me. He's a vampire. That's what they do. I'd be worried if he wasn't trying to play me."

Marian frowned, locked the car, and headed across the parking lot. I made sure both my guns were unloaded and the chambers were clear so I could turn the weapons over to security. Her clamming up didn't surprise me; if the FBI found out she'd just spent several hours keeping a wanted criminal company, they'd start taking a closer look at her professional and personal life.

I wondered if they'd find anything.

Some cops kept their noses clean, some turned out like Casey, putting their desires ahead of the job. Some, like me, took advantage of the loopholes hidden in the system to stay on the right side of the law. My relationships with Ed and Ernesto probably put me on the wrong side of the line for the good cops, those who couldn't tolerate even the whiff of injustice or crime.

Justice came in many forms, and some officers took the hard line, believing justice belonged to those who followed the letter of the law rather than its spirit. Loopholes, such as the one indemnifying people under the influence of a demon, allowed Ernesto to continue his operations.

A talented incubus or succubus could influence a vampire, thus clearing the vampire of wrongdoing. The demons took minimal risks, as most wouldn't dream of pressing charges. Few on the receiving end of the night of their lives did. The vampire got a legal drink, the victim got government-funded health care insurance companies couldn't touch, and the demons got the energy they needed to survive.

Marian put herself in danger to catch the worst criminals, those abhorrent even to the operators of the tolerated underground crime networks. Within the CPD, women like her washed out like Casey, addicted to what only a demon could provide, sacrificing far more than their bodies in the pursuit of justice.

The thought sickened me.

When Marian reached the elevator and

pressed the up button, she asked, "Penny for your thoughts?"

Courage came in different forms, and I braced for the answer I feared. "How long have you been in the business?"

"Investigating trafficking operations?"

I nodded.

"A lot longer than I care to think about. This was my first really bad run, though. They've gotten a lot sneakier. Why?"

"Call it curiosity."

"You don't approve."

The annoyance in her voice startled a laugh out of me. "It has nothing to do with approval."

The elevator dinged. I stepped through the opening doors, holding my hand out so they wouldn't close. She hesitated, watching me before joining me inside and pressing the button for the lobby. "Then what does it have to do with?"

I shrugged. "My first two partners got addicted and washed out, putting the public at risk because they wanted sex when they should've been doing their job. You tell me."

"You've been burned."

"You could say that. Maybe I don't want to see that happen to you."

"Unlike many police forces, the FBI requires all agents working in the field who have had exposure to a sex demon go through therapy. It's a two week session designed to prevent addiction. Your partners weren't treated?"

"No."

"That explains a lot. Good way to get rid of unwanted cops on the force. What I don't understand is why those brothel operators hadn't gotten rid of you in the same way."

"I amuse them."

"But you could threaten their position."

"That's part of what amuses them. Casey had ambition, but he didn't have the wits to do anything about it."

"And your other partner?"

"Had the brains but not the ambition."

"And you?"

"I recognize when removing certain individuals would leave a vacuum someone far worse might fill. That's the name of the game. What kind of enemy do you want to fight? One with rules, or the unknown quantity who might turn my home into a place like Des Moines, buying and selling people for profit and sex?"

"If Ernesto doesn't deal in human trafficking and sex slaves, what does he deal in?"

"Death. What else? He's a vampire after all. Then you need to think about the kind of people he kills—and who pays him to do it. Don't get me wrong. The vamp runs a brothel as a front for feeding his vampire children.

He lures people in with his demons and takes them off the streets, sometimes midday with witnesses around."

"Which is a disgusting practice."

"Ah, but is it? According to Chicago law, insurers must pay for all care associated with the kidnapping, even if it results in someone being treated for cancer, organ failure, or another severe disease. Vamps know when they're drinking from a healthy human, so when they take someone sick off the street and dump them on the surface after a bite…"

"You're serious."

"Deathly serious. He's no knight in shining armor, but I'd rather share my bed with a devil with questionable morals than one with no morals at all."

THE FBI TOOK TWICE AS LONG to get half as much information, a practice I found annoying but tolerable. Marian kept quiet, allowing me to do most of the talking, although I could hear the anger in her voice whenever she needed to speak. We learned nothing new, which didn't surprise me.

The human-dominated FBI could never match vampires with thousands of years of experience. While the FBI investigators wanted all the pieces of the puzzle, Ernesto and Pierce hunted specifics, the details they could use to begin their hunt. I couldn't guess who would crack the ring first, but if I were to place bets, I'd be siding with the vampires.

Discord between members of the FBI wouldn't help. They treated Marian as though she wasn't one of them, something I'd experienced often enough in the CPD. She handled their behavior with the cool calm of someone who'd been subjected to questioning before, limiting her displays of temper to a frigid tone and occasional scowl.

After the first few hours watching the FBI agents spar, I decided to place my trust with the vampires. Violating a vampire's territory stirred their ire and spurred them into action, and once they decided to take matters into their own hands, they wouldn't quit. The FBI spread itself too thin through no fault of its own. Vampires spent decades—or centuries—building their alliances, gathering favors, and honing their skills.

In their eyes, humans could never compare. I was beginning to wonder if the vampires had it right.

We escaped at midnight; the pair of agents questioning us decided it was time to go home, and my stomach growled complaints about being mistreated. We delayed leaving the building long enough to retrieve my Rugers. The FBI reclaimed their vehicle, so I had to call a cab. Marian's expression soured, and I suspected the agency had neglected to provide accommodations for her.

"I can't promise haut cuisine, but I can make us something at my apartment plus there's enough space for two. You look ready to kill anyone who comes between you and a place to crash."

"And shower."

"You could even soak if you want. It's not the greatest tub on Earth, but it works."

"Sold."

The cab took twenty minutes to show up, and I regarded the driver, one of Ernesto's vampire children, with a resigned sigh. Complaining about capturing too much of Ernesto's attention wouldn't do any good, so I held the door open for Marian and slid into the back beside her. "Hey, Larry. Small world."

"Papa said your broad was a pretty picture, so I wanted to see for myself. It seems he was right. Where'd an ugly mug like you get a lovely thing like her? Once you get tired of him, lady, you should pay me a visit."

"Can I kneecap this one?" Marian grumbled.

I was pleased I didn't have to tell her our cabbie was a vamp. "No. Larry's one of Ernesto's younger children. It's considered rude to kneecap one of his younger children without also kneecapping him at the same time."

"But we had our way with him earlier. Doesn't that count?"

I was amused Marian shared a few similarities with my mother; both women leaned towards acts of violence when stressed, although Mom targeted Dad, who could handle her at her worst. While I'd gotten lucky when I'd been shot, compared to him, I classified as fragile. "Afraid not."

"Papa wanted me to tell you he's had dinner brought to your apartment. He suspected you wouldn't have had time, and our sources tell us those idiot feds gave you nothing but coffee."

Marian sucked in a breath. Larry's words redefined the battlefield, and the real target of his ploy sat beside me. Only a fool would think Ernesto didn't have people on the inside. Information won wars in the crime world, and the best information came directly from the source.

"He played that card early," I observed.

"He thought your lady might need a nudge or two in the right direction to understand she no longer swims in shallow waters. That, plus he's learned not to underestimate your stupidity, you who will starve yourself in the pursuit of justice. Papa wanted me to remind you humans require multiple feedings each day. Do try to have breakfast, lunch, and dinner tomorrow."

"And how did you know Marian would be with me?"

"It's midnight, she's a lady, and you have opinions about escorting ladies to safe locations after midnight." Larry chuckled. "You ruin so much of Papa's fun with your rules. Had you not been with her after midnight, my cousin and his partner would have been relocating her, and she would have been presented to you as a gift. Papa's disappointed he couldn't surprise you tonight."

I sighed. Larry's human cousin liked to pretend he belonged in the crime world but couldn't quite get the hang of breaking laws. Of all the people I'd cuffed during my career, Al was the most amusing and pathetic, and I'd nailed him on a questionable misdemeanor so he'd stop pestering me for a while. No charges had been pressed, and I'd gotten away with it because Al had made a nuisance of himself to most of the station. "Who's your cousin partnered with now?"

"Donovan."

I groaned. Some troublemakers wanted to have fun. Others, like Donovan, wanted to have fun at the expense of others. The prankster enjoyed a good laugh, and he liked his schemes as elaborate as possible. Most of the time, his ideas didn't work, but when they did, the CPD ended up climbing the oddest places retrieving the oddest things. His last heist before I'd lost my eye, he'd robbed an entire department store of lingerie and decorated the Franklin Street Bridge with the laciest garments he could get his hands on.

"Admit it, Gibby. You love Donovan. He makes you laugh."

"Just because I laughed over his creative use of panties on the Franklin Street Bridge doesn't mean I love him."

"You're merely upset because you wished you could have been involved with the case."

Conceding Larry's point with a shrug and a grunt, I wondered about that old case. The panties part of the stunt I'd found hilarious until a closer look revealed the body of a murdered stripper along with a bag of evidence implicating her killer, a note from Ernesto, and photographs sufficient to pin the murder on a rival crime lord who'd overstepped his bounds. Without the tip-off and creative dumping of her body, I doubted anyone would have found her.

Larry knew me too well. I'd wanted to be involved.

"What case?" Marian asked.

"You want me to explain, Gibby?"

I'd have to thank Larry later for sparing me from describing the details. "Sure."

"A street girl got knocked up during a

rape, and someone close to the rapist didn't want anyone to find out about it. She refused an abortion, so he took matters in his own hands. Killed her, left her to rot—tried to make an example of her to other street girls. Papa took offense; wasn't one of our girls, but our girls got scared, and that's bad for business. So, once Papa found out who did it, he made an example out of him. Papa needed to get the CPD's attention since they don't care about the girls; they blame them for any trouble, trying to make it look like they deserve it. Best way to get the CPD's attention is to embarrass them. Add in a threat or two to go public with some information the CPD would rather stay private, and the girl got some justice."

Marian straightened in her seat. "And the rapist?'

"Papa ruined him in the business. After he made sure his name was shamed, he encased all but his head in concrete and dumped him in the drink, deep enough the sunlight won't get to him. I figure he's got a few more years before he starves to death. The old vamps take their time dying when they aren't exposed to sunlight—and even then, he's old enough he can get away with a few walks under the sun."

"But doesn't your lot work the market, too?"

"Won't lie to you, babe. We take people off the street for a good sip and a ride, too, but we handle it better. We make it worth their while, we don't get the girls pregnant, and if something goes wrong, they get a good pay-out, right? No unexpected daddies, either. Papa's a stickler for that. We mark our prey, learn about them, draw them in, get them hooked, and take care of them. We want our vics healthy and happy. They taste better that way. I like the sick ones, because they bring a tasty amount of gratitude to the table once they've been fixed up in the body shop. Papa prefers the cops, but he's gotta team up with one of my sisters for a drink on those nights."

I remained quiet, staring out the window while Larry kept to Upper Chicago and took the long way home. For the next few hundred years, exposure to sunlight would spell his death, so he settled like most nocturnals did, hoping for a glimpse of the sun's reflection on the moon.

"So you pick your targets carefully?"

"Usually. Keeps the accidents down, but if a vamp goes into the frenzy, it gets ugly. Happens when we're young. It's part of why we team up with demons; the demons can help control the frenzy and keep things pleasant for our donors. Haven't had anyone drained dry in over a year."

"And what makes you different from other

rapists?" Marian growled through clenched teeth.

"We leave our victims better off for having met us. The demons ensure they like it, they receive the health care they can't afford because we helped make sure the laws favor them, and we funnel donations to them for the inconvenience of having been selected. We lure them in and get them hooked so they come back without us picking new targets. It works out for everyone. What's a little anemia a couple of times a month when, because of us, they've got the treatments they otherwise couldn't afford because the system views them as worthless?"

Marian didn't say a word, and when I glanced in her direction, her cheek was twitching. I hadn't reacted well to the discovery, either, but it hadn't taken me long to realize the truth of Donovan's words. "In the eyes of the law and society, the way Ernesto's children hunt isn't considered rape. They're influenced first, drawn in, and the vamps feed alongside their demon partner. When the pairs go after a street girl, she's paid double what she'd get for taking a human to bed, but there aren't enough of them to feed all of Chicago's vampires."

Marian sucked in a breath. "And Ernesto doesn't buy girls."

Smiling over her understanding of the situation probably made me a monster right along with the vamps and sex demons preying on the city. "It's all a matter of perspective. Which kind of monster do you want lurking beneath your streets? The one who takes the street girls and gives them a better chance for a future, or the one who takes the street girls and sell them for profit? In the eyes of most, the girls get used either way, but there's more to the story than what first meets the eye. One devil at least tries to toe the line. The other devil ignores the line completely. Both are devils, but at least I can live with the one. The other…"

"Don't judge Gibby too harshly, babe. Papa tried to make sure Gibby was the one who picked up our girls and got them to the hospital, so he's seen more than most. He's seen the girls before and after, and he knows what we do for them. We aren't perfect, but at least we're doing something."

"And that's more than I can say for us humans," Marian muttered.

None of us said a word the rest of the way to my apartment, although I caught Marian staring at me more than once, her expression thoughtful.

TWENTY-TWO

Let me count the number of
speeding tickets I've written you over
the years.

DEBTS AND FAVORS ruled a vampire's world,
which meant I spent twenty minutes haggling
with Larry. Ultimately, I paid more than I
would have to any other cabbie to make sure
I won the round; Larry got a big tip along
with the owed fare.

I'd lost the previous round to Ernesto and
his preemptive strike of arranging for dinner,
which made us even. Larry chuckled and
took my money, shaking his head. "Will you
and Papa ever learn?"

"Probably not," I admitted, sliding out of
the cab, closing the door, and thumping my
palm to the roof. "Drive safe."

"When do I not?"

"Let me count the number of speeding
tickets I've written you over the years…"

"Please don't. Papa counts them for me, and he laughs when he does so."

Chuckling, I headed for the entry, where Marian waited, her eyes narrowed to slits. "What was that all about?"

"I forced Larry into accepting his fare plus a twenty dollar tip. Ernesto wanted the ride on the house. If I'm going to owe a vamp, it's going to be for something more than cab fare."

"What about our dinner?"

"I kneecapped Ernesto and gave him some extra love taps. We're even there." I chuckled, shook my head, and guided Marian upstairs to my unit. "More accurately, by kneecapping him and shooting him with a few extra rounds, he'll need to feed extra tonight to repair the damage, which will let him work with his youngest fledglings more than usual. He'll probably take Kelly and an incubus out in case she grows her wings."

"You're serious."

"Don't let Kelly fool you. She just looks young. I've always suspected she was a succubus, but I wasn't certain until today. He'll probably go to a bar, let the incubus go to town, and have a few drinks during the festivities. No one should get hooked. If he's feeling charitable because he likes you, he'll pick a strip club over a random dive. It could go either way with him."

"So he'd be causing a party like the one at the nightclub."

"Except public and everyone gets to play. He'll pay a fine of a thousand per person for his incubus losing control. Everyone will know he did it on purpose, but since everyone walks away a bit wealthier and a bit happier, everyone will turn a blind eye. Kelly's a bleeding heart, so there'll be some celebrations in the next few weeks."

Marian had no trouble keeping up with me as I climbed the steps, taking them two at a time, although we were both breathing hard by the time we reached my door. "What do you mean?"

"She's an empath, and I'm pretty sure she's attuned to sexual relationships, so she can tell at a glance if a couple is having trouble conceiving. She'll cry to the incubus, and the incubus will take matters into his own hands."

"You already knew incubi could control reproduction! You're seriously telling me I didn't have to explain that?"

I held my hands up. "In my defense, I didn't know how that club operated and had no idea what to think."

"You sly bastard."

Testing my door, I discovered it was unlocked, which warned me I still had company. I peeked inside to find Amy sprawled on my couch wearing my satin sheets and a smile. "Oh, look. It's trouble. Good evening, Amy."

"You're not even surprised. How unfair," the succubus complained.

"Larry told me Ernesto sent over dinner."

"That tattler. You've turned gray. What were you two doing to be panting so hard? Making out in the stairwell without me?"

"Running up the steps," I corrected, heading for my kitchen to see what sort of dinner Ernesto thought was appropriate for two starved humans. Enough sushi for six waited on my counter, a treat I never would have bought for myself. The round went to the vampire, and I'd have to pay him back later. "You like sushi, Marian?"

"Love it."

"He must think we're going to die of malnutrition. Are you having any, Amy?"

"No, it's for you love birds. He thought it would be an appropriate snack for you to feed each other when you're catching your breath in bed."

Of course the succubus would assume I'd sleep with Marian. While the idea appealed a great deal, I couldn't see myself begging for a repeat, at least not until I got a better idea of how she'd react to having her basic principles tested by Ernesto and his extended family of vampires and demons. "There's easily enough sushi here for six people."

"That means you can spend an entire day keeping your badge babe occupied. You can thank us later."

My face heated. "Amy!"

"He's very shy, Marian. You'll have to get aggressive with him. I recommend you feed him first. Human males get so weak when they haven't been fed. Wouldn't want his performance to suffer because he's hungry."

I sighed and hung my head, my face burning even hotter at Amy's complete disregard for my privacy. "Thanks, Amy. Do you have any other gems of wisdom?"

"Of course. Since his daddy's a werewolf, you won't have to let him rest for long, though I do recommend taking a few minutes to let him get a drink. Reward him with tidbits of sushi; he loves seafood and is too cheap to buy it for himself, as he views it as a special occasion food. Have fun, kids. Stay up as late as you want. Ernie made certain a few friends in high places are aware you'll both be unavailable tomorrow, so you have all the time in the world. The general word down the line is you both had a long day, traffic was terrible, and you didn't get in until late. There was also a mysterious overbooking at the first few hotels you tried, resulting in you both coming here. If I come back here tomorrow and you two haven't exhausted each other to a coma-like state, I'll have to help. A certain prude named Shane wouldn't like that, as he's a werewolf's son."

I whirled around in time to watch Amy slither off the couch, my sheets pooling to the floor around her. Striding towards the door, the succubus paused beside Marian, whispered something in the FBI agent's ear, and swept out of my apartment, laughing merrily as she closed the door behind her.

"Do I want to know?"

"Probably not." Marian joined me in the kitchen, her brows rising at the excessive selection of sushi waiting for us. She grabbed a piece and popped it into her mouth. "Well, we certainly aren't going to starve."

"I'll say." Shrimp waiting on perfect beds of rice lured me into grabbing one and savoring every nibble. Maybe Ernesto had been wise to send so much, because the first bite reminded my stomach it hadn't been fed anything in almost a day. "I feel like I should set the table and pretend to be a civilized adult."

"Food is here, table is over there. Why waste the effort?"

Too tired and hungry to argue, I grabbed another piece and went to work appeasing my appetite with Marian matching me bite for bite. Though we were both ravenous, by the time I couldn't handle the thought of eating anymore, the amount of leftovers intimidated me. "If you want to take a shower, the bathroom's the door on the right. I'll take care of cleaning up and getting out the spare bedding."

The leftovers went into the fridge, and I spent a few minutes tidying my kitchen so my unexpected guest wouldn't view me as a complete slob. Once done, I considered the problem of sleeping arrangements. Would it be more gentlemanly to give her my bed, or would that send the wrong message?

I'd rather take the couch so she could have the more comfortable spot. I frowned, drumming my fingers on the counter while I thought it through. Later—long after Marian returned home—I'd have to ask Mom about the proper protocol for inviting a lady to my place for the night.

Dad's solution would involve me and the lady sharing my bed and forgoing sleep altogether. On second thought, I decided I'd find someone reasonable to ask instead of my mother. My mother would begin planning a wedding. My godfather would side with Dad, as would everyone else I knew in Lincoln.

I had no trouble figuring out what Ernesto would advise, although I was astonished Amy hadn't influenced either one of us. I wouldn't last long if the succubus influenced Marian. One experience with a sex demon had taught me I didn't have a chance in hell of resisting a demon's influence, and if

I didn't end up with Marian, I'd end up with
Amy, and Amy would love every second of it.
Knowing Amy, I'd sleep with both of them at
the same time.

That thought stopped me dead in my
tracks, and I suspected my entire body
blushed at the idea of them together. I took
deep breaths and forced myself to think
about something—anything—else.

Sheets. I needed to find sheets, and a blanket, and a pillow, and I needed to find them
before Marian finished her shower. The satin
sheets Amy had been snuggling went in the
hamper. I had spares, which I dug out of the
closet. Marian had an overnight bag, so I
wouldn't have to dig through my clothes to
find her something to wear. The idea of her
in my clothes bothered me so much I doubted
I'd be getting any sleep, which would fulfill
Amy's requirement for me to be in a co-
matose state, although Amy wouldn't appreciate the real reason for my exhaustion.

Absorbed by my task of matching sheets
with my spare blankets, I didn't hear Marian
come out of the bathroom until she cleared
her throat behind me. "Hey, Shane?"

I turned.

"Which do you like better?" Traditionally,
upon finishing with a shower, people got
dressed. In one hand, Marian held some red
scraps of cloth tied together with some

threads masquerading as lace. In the other, she held a satin nightgown. The garments would have done a lot more good had she put them on before asking for my opinion.

I recognized a trick question when I heard one, but for the life of me, I couldn't figure out which answer benefited me the most. Was I supposed to dislike one of them? A better man wouldn't have taken his time admiring the outfits presented or stared so openly at the woman holding them. What would happen if I picked the lingerie? What would happen if I picked the nightgown?

No matter what I said, I was in a lot of trouble. Was neither an acceptable answer? I decided to find out. "I like you just as you are."

Marian smirked and dropped her clothes to the floor. "Good answer, Mr. Gibson."

WOMEN MADE my common sense dribble out my ears. More accurately, a specific woman, Marian, did. A sensible man would have remembered he needed sleep, but what Marian wanted, she got, and she had a ravenous appetite for things besides food. When she finally finished with me, birds were singing outside of my window, sunlight was streaming through the curtains I needed to replace with a darker, heavier material, and I barely had enough energy to burrow beneath my blanket before I passed out.

Amy's snickers woke me. "You didn't kill him, did you? I haven't seen a man so worn out in years, and it's my job to make sure they're too tuckered out to run away."

I groped for a pillow, found one, and crammed it over my head. "What do you want, Amy?"

"I came to take away the leftovers. I also brought you fresh food—food that wasn't helpfully laced with Ernesto's favorite aphrodisiac. He thought you deserved a nice reward for helping that family out at such a high personal cost, and he thought your badge babe should be able to enjoy you at your finest without the interference of my brothers or sisters. Marian, consider it Shane's application for a long-term relationship."

I should've known Ernesto would stoop to drugging our food. "When I get a hold of him, I'm going to sever his legs at the kneecaps so his children have to stitch him back together and help him feed for a week."

Since I couldn't decide between punishing him and thanking him, doing both at the same time seemed like a good idea.

"Oh, you must have enjoyed your evening

a lot. I'll make sure he knows to look forward to it."

"I call dibs on his elbows," Marian grumbled. "Damn it. Will this show on a drug test?"

"Of course not. It would be a very quick way for Ernie to earn a very angry enemy, and he wouldn't want his precious cop hating him over something like that. If you were tested right now, you would show higher than normal endorphin levels unless they used a magic scanner, which would register demonic influences. Isn't it lovely? I helped with its development. It wears off after six to eight hours, is non-addictive, and the only side effect is an understandable amount of exhaustion. Did he leave a bite for you, Marian? We're happy to provide another dose for this evening should you need to give him a little extra encouragement to start using his teeth."

"Amy!" Marian squealed.

I stretched, groaning at the ache of tired, sore muscles. "It's too early in the morning for this, Amy."

"Don't be so shy. It's an important question. Ernie gave his approval and put me in charge of the consummation of your relationship. He's expecting wedding invitations."

"Amy!" I protested.

"She already branded you, Shane. Don't be a whiner."

"Will you stop it with the brand stuff already? It's really too early in the morning."

"Lycanthropes don't brand, do they, Marian? This is an unexpected hurdle. Would you like to explain it to him, or should I?"

Marian groaned, rolled over, and stole my pillow, smashing it over her head. "Go away, please."

"I guess that means I get to do it. Your badge babe is a shifter of some sort, and shifters like leaving visible marks of their claim on their chosen partner. You've been wisely selected by your badge babe. A bite like hers is called a brand, as it's essentially a mark of ownership. They heal slowly, and when it does heal, you'll have a very permanent scar, one other shifters will recognize as a brand. I'm surprised the CDC didn't tell you. But then again, Ernie had to do some research to figure out what it is. Once he started poking at your medical records and figured out your new status as an unidentified shifter, it made sense. Normally, branding is done as part of a wedding ceremony, but demonic influences are known to drive excited females into staking their claim early. Of course, some shifter species have temporary brands—a mark to make it clear a female has reserved a male for breeding season."

Since stealing my pillow back from the

woman doing her best to hide would be rude, I groaned and draped my arm over my eyes. "Did I bite you, Marian? Wait. Didn't you say you can tell if there's a bite, Amy?"

"We do have to see the bite." Amy snickered, and before I could stop her, she yanked the blankets off us. Marian shrieked, and I grabbed the sheet, spitting curses at the succubus.

"My, my. You are a lovely woman. Do you think if I ask Shane nicely he'll share? We'd have a great time. I promise."

There was only one way to deal with a nosy succubus, and it involved my pillow and her face. I armed myself, whipping the pillow at Amy. "Are you trying to get her to kill me?" It took several swats to drive the succubus out of my bedroom. "Go away, and lock the damned door behind you, you she-devil!"

Laughing, Amy retreated, caressing my cheek with the tip of her tail. "Don't forget you humans need breakfast, lunch, and dinner, and it's already well past noon. Up, up. You wouldn't want to still be in bed when company comes calling, and trust me when I tell you that company will be calling soon enough."

"Company? What company?"

Amy didn't reply, but the front door closed with a thump and a click, muffling the succubus's laughter.

TWENTY-THREE

Can't a man visit his son?

ON THE THIRD SIP, I realized I hadn't put coffee grinds in the filter. I regarded my steaming mug of water with a frown, sighed, and dumped it in the sink.

"That took you two swallows longer than I expected," Marian murmured from my couch. Sometime between me staggering out of the bedroom to make sure Amy was really gone and beginning my morning routine in an exhausted daze, she'd dressed in a black skirt and white blouse with a black tie. "Start over. Put some pants on and go splash some water on your face. Actually, take a cold shower. That might wake you up. I'll make the coffee."

I regarded the carafe with a mixture of self-loathing, disdain, and resignation. Then it hit me I wasn't wearing pants—or anything else for that matter. Unable to think of a single thing I could say without making the situation worse, I grunted, abandoned ship, and retreated to my bedroom to fetch clean clothes.

A cold shower didn't help as much as I'd hoped, but I managed to get dressed without putting any of my clothes on inside out or backwards. I staggered into my living room, discovered my parents on the couch, and reversed course for my bedroom to sleep off what I hoped was a hallucination.

Within three steps, sickeningly familiar werewolf breath washed over the back of my neck. "Shane," my father growled.

Fights between hybrid-form werewolves and humans usually ended with the human being beaten senseless, sat upon, or otherwise immobilized. If I hadn't been so tired, I might have gotten in a punch before Dad smacked me to the floor, rolled me onto my stomach, and sat on me.

Then he grabbed the collar of my shirt and tugged to get an up close and personal look at Marian's bite.

Someone was going to die, and I needed to think long and hard about how to best kill Ernesto so he'd never bother me again. "Can't I have coffee before you start this shit, Dad?"

"No."

"What are you doing here?"

"Can't a man visit his son?"

"No."

"Don't be cruel."

"You filled a box with glitter and armed it with a can of compressed air. You have no grounds to complain about cruelty."

"But we bought you a new vacuum."

Still on the couch, my mother laughed. "You even got most of it out of your carpet. I'm impressed, Shane."

"Why are you here?"

"We received an interesting phone call last night and were offered a pair of plane tickets. We thought we'd accept the invitation, as you've neglected us horribly. Also, you've been cheating on us, and we demand to know what exactly is going on."

On second thought, murder was far too nice a fate for Ernesto. I couldn't think of anyone else in Chicago bold or evil enough to contact my parents and inflict them on me—or to have the audacity to compete with a werewolf over his son. "Escape while you can, Marian."

"It's too late. We already handcuffed your woman to your kitchen chair," Dad growled.

"They really did, Shane. They caught me by surprise. They thought I was a burgular. I decided not to fight against the cranky hybrid werewolf and accept my handcuffing with dignity. Have you considered having your father checked for rabies? He was frothing."

How had I missed hearing that nonsense

during my shower? The pipes weren't that noisy. I was still on the wrong side of barely conscious. "Did you knock on the door, Dad?"

"We did. She answered it."

"Why would a burgular answer the door when someone knocked?"

Dad snorted. "Don't get smart with me, boy."

"You handcuffed an FBI agent to my chair. Are you trying to get me arrested?"

"It's your fault you didn't notify us there'd be a woman inhabiting your space."

No matter what I said, I was doomed. "How have you not figured out I'm a grown man? I may have invited her over to spare her from trying to find a hotel after midnight in Chicago. I can invite a lady over to my apartment if I want to."

Marian giggled. "Sorry, Shane. I knew better and still opened the door."

I couldn't get mad at her if I wanted to. My parents had a tendency to worm their way into their victim's affections, and Marian would become their prey soon enough. A better man would've suggested she run, but it was too late. When my parents hunted, nothing stopped them. Anyway, it served me well.

I intended to keep her for a long time, and

if she couldn't escape my busybody parents, she couldn't escape me, either.

I grunted and squirmed beneath my father. "Why are you here?"

"Why did one of Chicago's most notorious crime lords call me at eight in the evening to thank me for siring the beautiful man he is honored to call his dear boy?" Dad snarled in my ear.

"Don't forget the part about being tricked into eating drugged food so he'd lose his virginity," Mom added.

"He'd already lost his virginity, Mrs. Gibson. We were merely getting in some practice."

Practice? For what? Testing the limits of endurance and inducing a coma-like state? If that was the goal, we'd succeeded. I sighed and regarded the doorway to my bedroom longingly. Between Ernesto and Marian, I had no hope of escaping my situation with my dignity intact. Marian didn't sound too bothered by my parents or being handcuffed. If anything, she sounded amused at my expense.

I found her ability to handle my parents at their worst promising.

"And how would you know that?" Mom growled.

"Let's just say you have just cause to be

very proud of your son. I look forward to future practice sessions with him."

Any other time, I would have savored the sound of stunned silence.

"Please kill me, Dad. If you've ever loved me, please kill me now," I whispered.

"Oh no, kiddo. I don't think so. This is far too entertaining. It seems you've been busy." Dad jabbed the healing bite with his thumb. "Were you planning on sending us a wedding invitation or introducing us to your future bride?"

"I thought I'd give him an opportunity to date me properly first. We're taking the backward approach. After sampling the wares, I thought a long-term investment was appropriate." Marian chuckled, and I heard the rattle of chain. "I don't suppose you could take these off, could you? My badge bunny hasn't had his coffee yet, and he's tired. I second Mr. Saven. Thank you for siring such a lovely man."

"I'm going to be a badge bunny until the day I die, aren't I?"

Marian laughed. "If you get a badge, we'll take turns being the bunny. Until then, deal with it, badge bunny."

"Hey, Dad? All women are she-devils, aren't they?" I whispered.

"That didn't take you long to figure out." Dad sighed, and his weight shifted off me. A moment later, he grabbed me by the back of my shirt and hauled me to my feet. "March."

Until I drank a lot of coffee and got more sleep, resisting Dad was impossible. He escorted me to my couch and shoved me down beside my mother. Since I'd already lost the battle and the war, I abandoned what remained of my self-respect and used Mom's lap as a pillow. "Good night."

"Poor child." Mom laughed and ruffled my hair. "I suppose I should apologize, Marian. It's probably my father's fault."

"Hey, my grandfather contributed, too." Dad pulled his keys from his pocket and released Marian, who stayed seated but rubbed her wrists. "I take it I'll no longer be able to get the best market price for my son. Pity."

I reached up, removed my fake eye, cleared my throat to catch my father's attention, and rolled the sapphire sphere across the carpet. I pointed at it. "That's my opinion of your current behavior."

"Damn it, Shane. Will you stop doing that?" Dad retrieved my eye and carried it to the kitchen. "What the hell do you use to clean this damned thing off? That's disgusting."

"Water works. Stop being a baby. It's not like it hurts if there's dirt on it. Just put it on the counter. I'll deal with it later. It's just glass."

"But then I have to look at you with an empty eye socket, and that's creepy."

"Why did you marry such a whiner, Mom?"

"Because I needed his services to have you, dear. Then I learned there were no refunds or exchanges. He has a certain amusement value. I do find it very entertaining you're now a badge bunny. How do you like it?"

I sighed, wondering if there was a correct answer to her question. "I'm very tired right now. Give me coffee or give me death."

Mom echoed my sigh. "Dear, stop playing with his eye and make your poor child a cup of coffee before he dies."

"To be fair, Mrs. Gibson, he tried to make the first pot and drank three sips of hot water before figuring out he forgot to add the coffee grinds. The vampire used his weakness for seafood against him."

"What did they use against you?"

"I was easy. Just look at him. If I hadn't laid claim, someone else would have. It doesn't hurt I also like seafood. It was eat the food or starve, and neither one of us had had anything to eat."

Laughing, Mom patted my shoulder. "Hear that, Shane? Finding a nice girl wasn't nearly as hard as you thought."

"She bit me."

"You probably deserved it."

She was right. No matter what I said, I couldn't win. "It was a succubus's fault."

"The incubus helped, too," Marian reminded me. "But you're right. If that succubus hadn't been there, I probably wouldn't have bitten you at that moment. That, plus you deserved it."

Unfortunately for me, I could barely remember my own name, so the full details of the night, morning, and anything prior to passing out in bed were a bit blurred. "Yeah, I opened my mouth and said the wrong thing. I deserved a bite. Did I get sufficient payback yet?"

Marian's chuckle promised either retribution or something better, but I wasn't sure which. "I'm satisfied."

Laughing, Mom patted my shoulder, worked her way out from under me, and smacked me with one of my throw pillows. "I'll remember this the next time you decide to sleep in a stall with one of our animals because you're too embarrassed to stay in the house."

"Some animals are—"

"Shane," Marian growled.

"I'm about to get bit again, aren't I?"

"You're learning."

"When do I get to bite back?"

"You did last night."

I really wished I remembered that.

"Shane, you didn't!" Mom smacked me with a pillow again. "I taught you better than that."

"He was supposed to. It was a completely provoked biting." Marian chuckled. "It'll heal eventually, I'm sure. What do I have to do to embarrass your parents enough they leave, Shane?"

"Not sure it can be done." I waited for Mom to beat me with my pillow again, grabbed it out of her hand, and shoved it over my head. "We should go to bed. Maybe they'll get bored and leave. Boredom sometimes makes them go away."

"They came all the way to Chicago. I'm not sure that'll work."

"We could run away together." I thought about it, liking the idea more and more. Quiet time in a nice hotel room sounded appealing. "I'm sure Ernesto can keep my parents busy for a few hours."

"We could probably reach the airport before they escaped. But that presents a problem."

"What?"

"If we leave, we can't kneecap him."

I had, with one visit to the brothel, created a monster. "That's true."

Dad coughed to catch my attention, and when I didn't acknowledge him, he cleared his throat several times. "I think you have some explaining to do, Shane. Get your ass off the couch, sit at the table with your woman, and have your coffee."

"I have a name, you know."

"I'm sure you do. It might even be a nice one. When I'm interested in knowing your name, I'll ask for it."

I grabbed the pillow, aimed, and fired at my father. It fell short a few feet; I blamed the combination of my half-blind state and exhaustion. "Be nice to Marian. If you drive her away, so help me, I'll shear you for your fur every day for the rest of my life."

Giggling, my mother clapped her hands. "Fur grows back, and if you're going to do that, you'll have to live nearby."

"After your first shift, you'll be joining him."

"I just said fur grows back."

No matter what I did, I couldn't win. Sighing, I rolled off the couch and dragged my ass to the table, slumping onto the second seat with a tired groan. Dad passed me a mug and headed for the couch, probably to ensure I couldn't escape out the front door. Leveling an accusatory stare at Marian, I took my first sip.

Coffee tasted so much better than hot water.

"Go ahead and say it," she invited.

"How are you so damned awake?"

She laughed. "I'm pretty sure it's because I ate less of the sushi than you. If I'd known they'd spiked the sushi, I wouldn't have kept giving it to you. I really should've figured it out. Logically, there's no way either one of us should've been that energetic."

"Point," I conceded.

A knock at the door made me sigh. Mom and Dad seeing me so damned tired and rumpled was bad, but I really didn't want to entertain any other unwelcome guests. Instead of reading my mind and ignoring the door, Mom got up and cracked it open. "Who're you?"

"CPD," Michelle said. "Is Shane in?"

"Come on in," my mother replied. Michelle wasn't alone, and the instant Stripes spotted my father, still in his hybrid form, he yelped and bolted.

Marian bit her lip.

"Oh, dear." My mother leaned out the doorway of my apartment. "Sir? It's okay. He doesn't bite, nor does he have rabies. I assure you he's mostly housebroken, too."

To Michelle and Stripes, Mom sounded reasonable, but I knew better. Mockery came in many forms, and I admired her subtle jabs at the cop's cowardice. The instant my parents got home, she'd be telling the tale of the flighty CPD officer who took one look at Dad and ran away like a coward.

"I didn't kill anyone, if that's what you're wondering. You can verify my whereabouts with the FBI, since they were interrogating me last night."

Marian kicked me under the table.

"Questioning," I corrected. "Questioning me about the incident in Des Moines."

"Okay. That's not why I'm here. The captain wanted to to check the legality of your new permit, so he asked us to swing by and get your permit number."

Maybe I hadn't known Marian long, but I recognized the instant her good humor faded to something more intense and less friendly. "Do you have the search and seizure warrant for the permit number?"

Michelle's eyes widened. "It's in regards to his past employment."

"Irrelevant. He was no longer employed by the CPD when the permit was processed, verified, and issued."

"Excuse me?" Michelle straightened.

With a flick of her wrist, Marian pulled out her FBI badge and displayed it. "FBI. If your captain wants the permit number, he needs a search and seizure warrant for it, along with a valid, official accusation justifying the warrant, signed by a judge. Mr. Gibson has been fully vetted, his performance and visual acuity has been verified post-surgical procedure by an authorized firearms instructor, and his permit legalized in all fifty states. If your captain wants the permit number, he needs to either have a search and seizure warrant issued or a legal request passed through the FBI."

"He hadn't touched a gun until yesterday, and we both know it," Michelle snapped.

"I'm an authorized firearms instructor and watched the complete demonstration. Instructors may opt for untraditional qualifications, and the course Mr. Gibson completed exceeds the basic minimum requirements for the permit. I could also request the surveillance videos from the range."

Mom was right. I needed to marry Marian in a hurry. Between getting me a nationwide concealed carry permit, buying me a pair of guns, and probably being a better shot than me, if other men figured out how amazing she was, I'd have no hope at all. Add in her determination and ability to go toe to toe with Michelle, and I doubted I'd ever find someone like her again.

I kept my mouth shut, had another sip of my coffee, and watched the fireworks between the two women.

Michelle's cheek twitched. "I see."

Wiggling in her seat, Marian pulled a wallet from her pocket, retrieved a card, and offered it to Michelle. "If your captain would like to follow protocol regarding Mr. Gibson's permit, you can contact the FBI's firearm and permit registrar at this number. They'll be able to give you the appropriate forms. Also, as the CPD is involved in a court case against Mr. Gibson, the judge in charge of the trial will also have to sign an approval for any warrants, as such action could be viewed as obstruction of the trial. Someone at the registrar's office will be able to assist your captain with the legalities."

While Michelle took the card, she looked like she'd swallowed something sour. "I'll make sure he's aware of this. Thank you, Agent."

"You're welcome." Marian smiled, but I was aware of the tension in her body and her less-than-pleased tone.

Without another word, Michelle nodded, spun on a heel, and stormed out of my apartment, closing the door behind her with so much care I almost pitied the explosion Stripes would endure soon enough. "Well, that was fun."

Marian picked up her cell and dialed a number. "It now becomes a great deal more fun for me and a great deal less fun for them." Putting the phone to her ear, she waited for several moments before saying, "Agent Peterson. Transfer me to the person in charge of police investigations. I need to report an incident involving the Chicago Police Department regarding Mr. Shane Gibson's nationwide concealed carry permit. It may be relevant to an insurance fraud case currently being handled in Chicago."

TWENTY-FOUR

She loves me almost as much as you
do, dear boy.

SINCE WHEN HAD my home become a general assembly? I could understand Michelle and her partner showing up; the CPD would be actively looking for ways to sink me, but had the captain really believed sending four different pairs of officers with the same request would do any good?

Marian looked ready to blow a gasket while Mom and Dad were enjoying the fireworks.

The sixth time someone knocked at the door, Marian answered it, her hand on her holster. She cracked open the door, sucked in a breath, pulled out her gun, and fired so fast I reached for mine, which was locked up where it did me no good. A moment later, she opened the door, grabbed her victim by his hair, and dragged him into my apartment.

Ernesto giggled. "She loves me almost as much as you do, dear boy."

I hated vampires old enough to survive exposure to sunlight, capable of visiting my apartment during daylight hours. "We've had five pairs of CPD officers trying to get their mitts on my concealed carry permit. Know anything about that?"

"Trying to bust you on a fake permit. They're idiots. Did you enjoy your evening?"

I hated trick questions almost as much as I hated old vampires. "I drank hot water instead of coffee this morning, Ernesto."

"Oh! You must have had a very nice evening then. You're welcome."

Digging her toe into the vampire's ribcage, Marian leaned over, waved her gun in his face, and snarled, "Did you spike the rest of the food?"

"Maybe with a minor amount of a completely legal stimulant to help your badge bunny get through today without being a risk to himself. Completely legal. I even have a scanner in my pocket for you to confirm it."

Frisking the vampire, Marian located the meter and handed it to my father. "Check the fridge while I deal with him."

Dad chuckled and, in what I classified as a miracle, obeyed without question.

Amy peeked into my apartment. "It's a real party in here."

Mom's eyes widened. "Shane, there's a succubus here."

"I'm aware. Her name's Amy. Amy, this is my mother. Fluffy checking out the fridge is my father. I'm disappointed, Amy. The vampire survived the journey."

Laughing, Amy strolled into my apartment, stepped over her boss, and smacked him with her tail. "There were two cops staked out in front of your building. I left them playing together in their cruiser. I thought you would like to know, in case you wanted to report them unable to complete their duty. You're always such a stickler for that sort of thing."

I groaned and went to look out the window. Sure enough, there was a cruiser parked across the street with a good view of my apartment building's front door. "Please tell me it wasn't Michelle."

"One day, I'm going to have to find out what happens to the gentlemen officers I do that to. Do they stay partners afterwards? You never tell me, Shane. So cruel."

The CPD trying to get dirt on me didn't surprise me in the slightest. When they figured out Ernesto had paid me a personal visit, they'd take a closer look at my activities. "Did they see you or Ernesto?"

"Of course not. I'm no amateur. I made sure their party was in full swing; their win-

dows were nice and steamy before I brought
him in. I started a few extra parties around
your block and several other blocks nearby.
Actually, we spent the past two hours starting
all sorts of parties for everyone to enjoy. It
was fun. I enjoyed it very much. In our personal investigation of your neighbors, we've
uncovered this cute little couple on the first
floor who wants a child. They'll be very successful today. I thought you'd appreciate me
keeping your neighbors happy. The poor girl
was rather barren. I fixed the problem for her
tonight. I hope she'll forgive me, as I expect
her incoming triplets will cure her any desire
for additional children, but should she want a
few extra, let me know. It's always nice when
I can play doctor without the real doctors
getting pissy at me for taking their cut of the
financial pie."

Amy on the prowl meant a lot of trouble,
and I tried to imagine how much trouble she
could start given two hours and free rein.
"How many blocks did you visit in the past
few hours, Amy?"

"A few. My sisters helped. There were several patrols on other nearby streets. They're
busy, too."

"Dear lord." I shook my head and
stretched out across my kitchen table, wag-
gling my fingers in Ernesto's direction.
"Ernesto gave you all pixie dust, didn't he?"

"Maybe a little."

"And there goes loophole number one. And how did Ernesto give it to you so he can't be held accountable this time?"

"Tainted sugar packets. In a tragic mishap, a local warehouse mixed unmarked packets of sugar and sweetened pixie dust, thus resulting in a widespread accidental distribution of tainted sugar. To make sure it was a city-wide event, these sugar packets have been distributed to many of the city's restaurant supply chains. C grade pixie dust, so it isn't classified as a health risk, but it has resulted in us demons spreading the joy a little more than usual. The culprit was an overturned container during shipment. So tragic, right?"

I chuckled and waved my hand at Marian. "This is why they can't prosecute Ernesto. Welcome to hell. It's populated by smug vampires and their demon partners. Amy, if you want a pair of victims for later, take my parents. Maybe you can keep them out of my hair for a few hours."

"Hybrid-form werewolves are a delicacy, but it's so difficult to get them to play. It's not fair. That one's been with his mate too long. You brought me a treat I can't enjoy."

The succubus pouted, and if Dad had managed to keep his tail still, I might've been fooled by the nonchalant way he browsed through my refrigerator. "Your fridge is clean of illegals, pup. I even reset the meter and cleared its settings to ensure they didn't tamper with it."

"Dad, stop wagging your tail. You're not a dog."

"But your guest said nice things about me. It's an expression of happiness. Allow me to express my happiness without your prude rules getting in the way."

Werewolves. I sighed. "Mom's hopeless, too, Amy. Sorry. She's been infected for too long."

"I noticed. That's also unfair."

I turned my attention to Ernesto. "Why are you here in the middle of the day, and what possessed you to invite my parents to town?"

"Could you ask your blushing bride to leave me with at least one leg and both arms today? It's so difficult finding a donor this time of day, especially when I have to behave myself for the first time in my life."

"Hey, Dad. Remember how you were expressing curiosity about meeting a bloodsucker, and how you were bragging your virus is so robust not even an ancient vamp could knock you out for more than an hour?" The bragging had happened back home, but I rarely got to call my father out on something.

Mom cackled. "You're an awful child."

"It's not against the law if he consents, and Amy can make sure Ernesto doesn't hurt him."

"But I can't play with him. That's not fair," Amy whined.

I was going to regret the next words out of my mouth, but how often would I have a vampire indebted to me? Since I had made the offer, it was my favor, and it also served to add a few protections to my parents while they were in Chicago. "Show my parents the sights, take them down to Lower Chicago. Marian and I will slip out a little later to run some errands in my rust bucket. We'll swing by to make sure they're okay. Then we can talk, as I expect that's what why you bothered to visit. And since you came here to talk in person, you probably think my phone has been tapped."

Ernesto faked a sniffle. "You have bred such a beautiful child."

Dad's eyes widened. "You're seriously calling me out on that old bet, Shane?"

"Have fun, Dad. And if you ask really nicely, Ernesto can give Mom's virus a boost while he's at it." I arched a brow at the vampire. "You are that good, aren't you? It'd be a shame if I thought you were this amazing vamp for no reason."

"My dear boy, you flatter me."

"Get out of my house and take these two

cops with you. Remember, Ernesto. Cops. Both of them. Visiting cops. Don't dump them anywhere."

"Don't ruin all my fun!"

"Amy?"

The succubus purred. "Don't worry, Shane. I'll make sure he behaves—mostly."

"No siblings this visit."

Her purr shifted to a pout. "Why not?"

"Because I don't want to wait twelve hours."

"And if I speed things along a bit for them?"

"If both of my parents don't consent, you will not help them. Understood?"

"Not fair!"

"Stop whining. You're almost as bad as my father."

Mom turned to Dad. "This is payback for the joking we did about selling him to a sex trafficking ring. I hope you know this. This is your fault. March, dear. We will be talking about this later, Shane."

Surrendering with a sigh, Dad set the meter on my table, snagged Ernesto by the waist, tucked the vampire under his arm, and headed for the door. "I'll remember this, you rotten manipulative brat."

"Remember the glitter. This is only the beginning, dear father. Have fun." I waved, shooed the quartet from my apartment, and closed the door. I waited until I heard the stairwell door slam before turning to Marian. "And that is how you legally sell your parents to a vampire and a succubus for the afternoon and evening. What's for lunch?"

"A lot of cold Italian food, an appetizer tray, and a gift card for a sushi restaurant, which I presume is the supplier of last night's dinner. There were written instructions with the card, which I hid in your drawer after the cops came over. I figured you wouldn't want your sexual exploits public."

"What did I do to deserve you?"

"Standing in front of a gun pointed at me was a good start."

"I guess that would support my case."

"Considering the circumstances, a man brave enough to defend someone who'd just spit on him…"

"I thought we weren't supposed to discuss that."

"I'm making an exception this once. I haven't had a chance to properly thank you yet."

I dismissed the thought with a wave of my hand and poked around in my fridge in search of cold Italian food, discovering a myriad of single-serving portions taking up most of the space inside. "Spaghetti and meatballs?"

"Sounds good."

I grabbed a pair of the clear-covered aluminum pans and set them on my counter. "I'm having mine cold. Want me to warm yours up?"

"Nope. We need to eat in a hurry, then I need to properly thank you."

"But you already did. You just said thank you."

"In bed. We need to let them get a head start on us, don't we? And since you'll fall asleep if you don't eat, which wouldn't be good for either of us, lunch comes first. We'll take the appetizer tray to the bedroom, if you don't mind."

Did she really think I was going to argue with her? "Don't mind at all, ma'am."

Marian smiled.

DID I really need to retrieve my parents from Ernesto's clutches? I was enjoying dozing in bed with Marian nestled against me enough I wouldn't complain if I stayed there for the rest of my life. Amy could keep Mom and Dad occupied for a long time. Succubi enjoyed the sort of challenge a bonded pair of lycanthropes provided.

"We should go rescue your parents before someone notices they're gone." Marian wiggled against me, and I tucked her closer, my nose buried in her hair. She smelled like my shampoo, and I indulged in several deep breaths. "Your phone keeps ringing. You should answer it."

"They'll survive until tomorrow. Probably."

She laughed. "Let me go. I'll fetch your eye and bring your phone in while you laze for a few more minutes."

Although I sighed my disappointment, I released her and stretched, wiggling my toes against the sheets. "It's probably my parents, some pests from the CPD, the lawyer trying to bother me with updates about the trial, and probably your friends from the FBI."

"You're popular."

"Too popular. Unfortunately, I'm not popular for positive reasons. I was serious about running away. We could."

Marian chuckled and sauntered out of my bedroom, returning with my cell phone, which she tossed onto the bed beside me. "I'll take a shower while you sort that out."

I took a nap instead, and my phone and Marian's laughter woke me. "Shane Gibson's phone. Marian speaking. Oh, Larry. Sorry, he conked out, and I didn't have the heart to wake him. He left one of his cards in your cab? Hey, since I have you on the phone anyway, we're going to need a cab in about an hour. We need to run some errands, and I have to do a bit of shopping. You free? Great. See you then. Yes, same place."

A moment later, Marian poked me. "Wake up, sleepy. You can't stay there all day. We have a date with Larry."

I grumbled something incoherent and groped for my pillow, which Marian stole before I could get a good hold on it. "What does everyone have against sleep?"

"You had a five-hour nap. Up! Go take a quick shower. We have an hour."

"I was out for that long?"

"You needed it. I was down for three hours. Your phone woke me up."

"Sorry about that."

"Not your fault. Now, up! Take a shower, make yourself presentable. Larry dropped a hint or two I translated to mean you should dress up."

"I don't even know if my suit fits anymore."

"Do what you can. I'll make sure everything's cleaned up while you're getting ready." Marian shooed me out of my bedroom and into the bathroom, tapping her foot until I cooperated with her demands. "I'll warm up a quick snack while you're showering."

"What do I have to do to make sure you never leave?"

Marian laughed. "Should you find yourself being kidnapped, as long as I'm with your kidnappers, don't be too alarmed. You should be more worried about me deciding to take you with me. I have resources, and I'm not afraid to use them."

"Challenge accepted."

"That wasn't a challenge, Shane."

"I just made it one."

"How is that supposed to work?"

"Whoever performs the first successful kidnapping wins."

Marian giggled. "And what does the loser have to do?"

"Whatever the winner wants?"

"You sound so hopeful, Mr. Gibson. I'm sure I'll think of something appropriate when I win."

"I already know exactly what I'm demanding when I win." Later, I'd thank Mom for the idea. I'd even try to be a gentleman about it—mostly. "Prepare yourself, Miss Peterson."

"You have no hope of winning. You haven't met my family yet."

"No, you have no hope of winning, and you should know this, since you have met my family."

Marian hesitated, then she narrowed her eyes. "Pussy cats. What sort of big bad werewolf lets his offspring shave him?"

"You'll find out soon enough."

"Keep dreaming."

TWENTY-FIVE

You're going to make me wear suits
for the rest of my life, aren't you?

MY SUIT STILL FIT, barely. It took more wiggling than I liked to get into the slacks, but the shirt and jacket were still within the realm of socially acceptable. Then again, the way Marian kept looking at my ass made me think the dark material was doing something right.

Having been guilty of sneaking peeks at women in tight jeans many times in the past, I pretended not to notice, making a point of adjusting my cufflinks, straightening my tie, and otherwise doing all the fiddly things Dad insisted were necessary to play the part of a well-dressed man. "Why am I wearing a suit again?"

"I'm burning the rest of your clothes, and you're wearing the suit so you don't have to leave home naked."

"If you win our bet, you're going to make

me wear suits for the rest of my life, aren't you?"

"Yes. Or uniforms, should you return to law enforcement. Uniforms are like casual suits, so that's okay."

"I'm obviously going to have to get a good job to pay for all these suits." I held up a single finger. "This is how many of these things I own."

"I don't mind providing clothing for my badge bunny."

With my slacks still the appropriate length, just shy of reaching the floor, I could get away with wearing my ankle holster and hiding my second Ruger in the interior pocket of my jacket. I braced my foot on my chair and made sure I could reach the gun with minimal effort. "Cute thought, badge babe, but face reality: you're going to be saving all those pennies for a nice white dress. Then you're going to be fitting that cute ass of yours into tight jeans."

"Is that so?" Marian's brows rose.

"I might even take pity on you and dress up, too. My mother has opinions about what a man should do with a girl who buys him a gun and gets him a permit. It'd be a pity if I didn't look the part of a gentleman." I grinned, settled my slacks over my Ruger, and straightened, checking my leg for evidence of the weapon. "That worked better than I thought it would."

"Don't even notice it. Good. Your other one?"

I opened my jacket and slipped the holstered Ruger into the interior pocket, but after a check, the bulge was too obvious, so I relocated it to my pants pocket instead. "I should get a shoulder holster and a good jacket."

"And what is your mother's opinion about what a man should do with a girl who buys him a gun and gets him a permit?"

"It involves the white dress you'll be wearing upon my successful kidnapping of your person. Never underestimate a werewolf's determination to plan a wedding, Miss Peterson. Maybe I haven't met your family, but mine's already here."

Her eyes widened. "Oh."

"I'm sure Ernesto wouldn't mind helping me."

"You wouldn't dare."

"All's fair in love and war, badge babe. Since we're doing this backwards, maybe you should keep some form of white dress in your carry bag, so when I kidnap you, you'll be ready."

"I'm starting to think I may have miscalculated."

"I think it's a fair wager. If I win, you

might get what you want just because I like the way you can't seem to remember my face is up here." I smirked, did a final smoothing of my suit, and pocketed my wallet. I shut off my phone before slipping it inside my jacket. "One of our errands will be getting me a new phone and a new number and trashing this one. I don't like people tapping my lines."

"Better take the spares you have, too."

"Good idea." Armed with all three of my phones, I went to my front door and opened it to discover Michelle lifting her hand to knock. "How many cops is the captain going to send over today?" I complained.

"As many as it takes to get your permit number out of you, apparently." Michelle sighed. "Just tell me no so I can go back to work."

"Okay. No. When he presents the court-authorized warrant, he can have the permit number."

"You're really going to be a pain in the ass over this, aren't you?"

I sighed. "Hasn't it occurred to you if he'd just call the FBI and ask, he'd get the proof he wanted that the permit is legitimate?"

The way Michelle blinked and gaped at me led me to believe the thought hadn't crossed her mind.

Marian set her hand on my lower back and peeked around me. "Is he trying to give the prosecution of the discrimination case legitimate grounds to file an addendum for harassment? If that's his intention, could you plan your harassments for tomorrow? Our cab is going to be here soon."

"Where are you going?" Michelle refused to look at Marian, and the woman's rudeness both bothered and amused me.

"Errands."

"Dressed up like that? That's odd."

"The loser of our bet isn't going to like posing in white dresses all night long, either. I just thought I'd pretend to be a gentleman and wear a suit so she didn't feel completely ridiculous while modeling a selection of white dresses for me."

I deserved the pinch Marian gave me, although I suspected her choice of location had something to do with the snug fit of my pants.

"White dresses? What white dresses?"

I allowed myself a smile. "Take a wild guess." In a move Dad would've liked, I escaped my apartment, locked the door, and tucked Marian close to my side, resting my hand on her back, guiding her with a gentle push towards the stairwell. "Don't wait up for us, Michelle."

LARRY WAITED OUTSIDE MY BUILDING, and before Michelle could find her wits, I herded Marian into the cab and slid in after her. "I need a new phone, and Marian needs to try on a few white dresses in case someone is following us."

With the number of unwanted visitors to my apartment, I'd be surprised if no one checked our activities.

"White dresses?"

"I'm hearing that question a lot tonight," I muttered.

"Apparently, if I plan a successful kidnapping of his person before he can plan a successful kidnapping of my person, he has to wear suits for me every day for the rest of his life. Should he win, which he thinks he will, he's putting me in a wedding dress before making me wear tight jeans all the time. I suspect he's trying to prove some point, although I'll have to do additional investigation to learn more. Since he was rather territorial when she came calling, he dropped hints he was taking me dress shopping."

"You do look sharp in a suit, Gibby. You should just give the woman what she wants. You'll be rolling with ladies if you dress like that all the time."

"I don't want to roll with all the ladies. I want to roll with a single lady, and for some reason I can't fathom, the one I like seems willing to put up with me. I might humor her on the suits, though—or a uniform if I can convince some law enforcement agency I'm worth hiring."

Larry chuckled. "Papa is going to be so happy. I'm sure he would be delighted to assist you with your endeavor."

Marian nudged me in the ribs. "That Michelle woman looked like you'd punched her in the gut, Shane. How long has she liked you?"

"She doesn't. Part of the whole lycanthrope in Chicago issue. I think she tolerates me because I didn't give her extra work."

"That was not the expression of a woman who tolerates you. That was the expression of a woman who just had her territory violated and is pissed off about it. She was too stupid to bite you first, so she's just going to have to live with it."

"Don't I get a say in this?"

Marian glared at me. "You already did your talking with your teeth."

I really wished I remembered that. I also wished I knew how badly I'd bitten her, what her general opinion of my biting her was, and if she'd let me do a very thorough examination of her person to investigate any bites I may or may not have inflicted. While I'd already been given a very good opportunity to investigate potential bite sites, she'd distracted me from the thought of checking for teeth marks on her tanned skin. Until she offered me a better selection of clues, I'd assume I'd bitten her and she liked it. "She can't shoot worth a shit, Marian. That's a deal breaker. And she didn't give me a pair of guns and a really nice concealed carry permit. I've been informed that the appropriate response to that sort of gift is marriage."

"You asked someone for advice, didn't you?" The amusement in Marian's voice would've stung if I hadn't cheerfully accepted my ineptitude years ago. "Who did you ask?"

"I asked my mother to pretend she was Dad, then gave her the model of the guns. She didn't even think about it before informing me the correct response was marriage."

Snickering, Larry drove us away from my apartment and into the depths of Lower Chicago. "Papa is going to be so amused to hear about this."

"I'm expecting his assistance with the kidnapping. It can be partial payment for making off with my parents earlier."

"Papa did find it rather humorous you ditched them so effectively. I've been asked to assure you he is taking good care of them. They're sleeping off his feeding until you get in."

"Still recovering from the earlier kneecapping?"

"A little."

"And Marian's shot today?"

"Healed. Werewolf blood is very potent. Would you like to handle the phone or the dress first?"

"Phone. It's faster. Leave the meter running while I'm inside getting a new one."

"That will cost Papa dearly." Larry made a thoughtful sound in his throat. "If you shop at the canal, you can take care of both your errands at the same time in a rather public place. I'll leave you my card, so when you need to call me on your new phone, you'll have my direct number. I'll run the meter the entire time and be at your service."

"That will cost Ernesto dearly. I like it." Chuckling, I settled into the seat and stared out the window at Chicago's gloomy underworld. In a way, I appreciated the place's harsh honesty. The dim lighting told the truth about the place and its nature, especially far from where the roads rose to the city above. The denizens of the shadows made no efforts to hide what they were and that they lived in darkness.

In Upper Chicago, looks deceived; I'd been on the force long enough to understand the truth of human nature. I liked to think I was one of the better humans, but in reality, I had survived in the city by making friends with unsavory people and consorting with demons.

Had I become as shady as those who lived beneath the streets while masquerading as a good person? I no longer knew with certainty I was one of the good guys.

"That's a troubled expression if I ever saw one," Marian murmured. "What's bothering you?"

"What isn't bothering me might be an easier question to answer." The confession was easier than I expected.

"Walk me through it."

"I'll only tell Papa the juiciest bits," Larry promised, his tone so playful he got a laugh out of me.

"Why would the captain send that many cops to my place with the bogus excuse of wanting my concealed carry permit number? He could pick up the phone, dial a number, and have it in less than five minutes. There's no reason to send patrols to my apartment since he knew I wasn't going to relinquish the number without a legitimate reason."

Marian sighed. "Or why didn't he have a cop ask for it while you were outside your apartment? Then he would've had legal grounds to check it. He set those visits up so you wouldn't be forced to provide the number unless you wanted to. The whole thing stinks. I have two theories. How many can you come up with?"

"I could think of a few."

"Humor me."

I replied, "One. He caught wind of a death threat against me and decided one of his ex-cops being killed during a discrimination trial would look really bad for the CPD. Two. He's looking for an excuse to nail me and thinks if he does a lot of visits, he might catch me in the act. Three. He wants to forge a copy of the permit and use it to frame me for something. Four. Someone tipped him off about Ernesto coming to my place, and he hoped to make an arrest. Five. He hates me. I could go on."

The look Marian shot me worried me. "The first one was on my list. That last one should have been on my list. The others are viable, which disturbs me more than I care to think about. What type of hellhole town is this, Shane?"

"Yeah, things would have been different if I'd poked a little deeper into the discrimination issue *before* being hired by the CPD and moving here. I underestimated what it meant to be a quota filler."

"With your education, grades, and academy performance, why did you pick Chicago, anyway?"

"I thought it'd be a challenge. I wanted to

work with the dogs or one of the more active teams and thought if I had experience in a good force, that would simplify things for me."

"On paper, you'd be right. Chicago does have a reputation for producing good cops."

"Unfortunately, that reputation is founded on crap politics. Here's how the CPD actually works. If your dad is a cop, your resume gets bumped up the list to be looked at. If both of your parents are cops, you get kicked to the front of the line. I'm pretty sure that's the only reason my resume got looked at; it's simple to check someone's pedigree, and the first thing they look at here is who you're re-lated to. If your pedigree is good enough, then they look at your background and species. I had an instant flag as someone who'd been exposed to lycanthropy; it was part of the application. After that, they look at experience, magic rating, and education. I filled two quota boxes, so I got hired. When my stints in Lower Chicago didn't wash me out, I got shit patrols, usually in the more dangerous parts of town—or places where run-ins with lycanthropes were more likely. And that's how the story ends."

"You were on patrol and got called to the traffic accident. Your insurance company and the CPD worked together to screw you out of your career." Marian inhaled, and when she sighed, she shook her head. "I'm amazed the CDC is actually taking it this far."

"Unlike the other victims they've had as potential trial fodder, I might actually get somewhere." I tapped my fake eye. "From my understanding, the last guy lost a whole limb. Eyes can be replaced if you have the money."

"Prosthetics will never be equal to the real thing, especially in a field like law enforcement. We've had a few exceptions in the FBI, but the prosthetics cost a lot."

Larry cleared his throat. "Tell the lady how much that eye of yours will cost."

Since popping my eye out and tossing it at Ernesto's vampire spawn child would probably cause a wreck, I settled for a grunt. I couldn't remember if I'd told Marian the cost of the eye I couldn't afford. "Two mil."

"Ernesto could pay it without missing a beat. You should let that vampire actually be useful."

"Doesn't work that way, badge babe. The good guys don't become indebted to the bad guys for a two million dollar eyeball. It would end my career as everyone would question why someone like Ernesto would help someone like me with something like that."

"There's nothing illegal about charitable donations to a good cause. Giving a cop an eyeball is a good cause. I bet he could legally write it off his taxes, too, if he established a charity fund to help those injured or crippled in the line of duty."

"Where *did* you find this lady, Gibby? Think she'd come work for Papa?"

"FBI agent," I reminded him.

"But she's smart and pretty. Papa would love to have her batting for him."

"No."

"Gibby, don't be so cruel. Papa would owe you more than two mil with a broad like her batting for our team."

"No."

"You are as Papa says, mean and cruel. What has he ever done to you to deserve such treatment from you?"

"He exists."

"Evil!"

If I banged my head against the window hard enough, would I render myself unconscious for the remainder of the thirty-minute drive to the underground mall skirting the canal? "I think you're confused. Vampires are evil. Cops are good. She's the cop, I'm the ex-cop. You and Ernesto are vampires. What does that make you?"

"Misunderstood."

TWENTY-SIX

Do yourself a favor. Don't fall in.

DEEP beneath the heart of Chicago, the storm drains emptied into a canal, which cut across most of the city before disappearing into the depths of the third level. Magic darkened the water to hide what lurked beneath the surface, and that same magic hid the smell, something my nose appreciated. I'd been to Lower Chicago once when the magic had failed, and the experience had taught me one very important lesson.

If anyone dredged the canal, they'd find bodies—a lot of bodies. Not a week went by without a body turning up in the Chicago river, and I had no doubt corpses gave the underground water its distinctive stench. I still wasn't sure who maintained the spells that kept the canal's smell from driving everyone away, but I appreciated their work.

Most people had no idea what the dark water hid. While I got a card from Larry so he could come and pick us up later, Marian stared at the rippling surface with wide eyes. "Shane, the water's black."

Larry grinned and winked at me, flicked a salute, and drove off, leaving me alone with the FBI agent who'd turned my world upside down and made me like it. "Do yourself a favor. Don't fall in."

"Why not? It doesn't look that bad, just weird. Why's the water black?"

Capturing her wrist in my hand, I pulled her a safe distance from the canal. "Magic. It's an illusion—a good one. It's also hiding the smell."

"Smell? What smell?"

"Do you want the pretty version or the truth?"

"Truth."

I pointed at the canal. "Corpse stew."

She blanched. "And no one has pulled them out?"

"Welcome to Chicago. The CPD looks the other way because it would cost more than they're willing to spend to get the bodies out of there. They only interfere if a witness sees someone dumped in, and even then, they only check the grates for the body. All part of the whole 'you mind your business, we mind our business' mentality shared by Upper and Lower Chicago. Anyway, the current is pretty strong, so the CPD assumes if the body doesn't wash up there, it's gone."

"My opinion of Chicago gets worse every time you open your mouth."

I thought about it and shrugged. "It is what it is. I visited New York, and a corpse fell on the car I was standing next to. A few bodies in the canal doesn't seem so bad after that."

"That was gruesome. I was surprised by how nonchalant you were. You didn't even grimace when you put the car in park. You were blinking rather like an owl, though—a bloody owl."

"I was more concerned about preventing the vehicle from taking out some pedestrians than getting more blood on me. I'd already gotten splattered, so a little more didn't matter. Not the first time I've seen someone killed because they decided to improvise on their windshield."

"Is that what happened? I'd thought the windshield had buckled in a bit easy, but I wasn't sure since the body had fallen so far. I wasn't really in a position to get a good look."

"Window glass shatters into large lethal shards, where safety glass, the kind used in cars, either pebbles or sticks together. When the vic hit the windshield, it broke into shards, which is pretty damning evidence someone had put the wrong type of glass in the windshield. You don't deal with a lot of traffic incidents in the FBI?"

"Not in my division, though I'll be transferring to violent crimes soon. That's part of why I'm here; I get paid leave because of the botched operation plus they're figuring out where I'll best fit. When I go back, I'll train for my new division."

"You're being pushed out?"

Marian snorted. "No. I volunteered for transfer. I may have done some additional research into lycanthropy and decided I didn't want to find out if you had inherited a lycanthrope's base tendency to slaughter threats to people close to them. There's surprisingly little research on what happens when a shifter bites a lycanthrope."

"Well, I'm not a lycanthrope."

"I didn't know that then."

"So what does happen when a shifter bites another shifter? I can tell you exactly what happens when a lycanthrope gets someone in their sights." Sliding my hand along her back, I propelled her towards the underground mall.

Marian's cheeks turned pink. "I should have asked before biting you."

"I didn't ask before I bit you, so I think that makes us even."

"But I knew what biting does!"

When an opportunity presented itself, a

wise man took advantage of it. "And you had a double dose of sex demon. So what? I'm assuming you laid some sort of claim on me, which means I get watch you model white dresses and openly indulge in admiring a woman I find very pretty. Since I'm a lycanthrope's son, I'm well aware of what happens when a boy lycanthrope meets a girl human and is a pushy bastard until she says yes and is stuck with him until the day they die. Now, if I wanted to be a pushy bastard about it, I'd just tell my mother you were the one who gave me the guns and the permit and let her worry about the details. She'd have us married within a day, and knowing her, she would resort to cruel and unusual methods to accomplish her goals. As I'm a gentleman, I gave you sufficient chances to escape. I'm afraid you failed to escape, so now I'm going to enjoy hunting you."

"You're enjoying this, aren't you?"

Grinning, I nudged her in the direction of the nearest mobility store. "Immensely. First, you gave me a pair of guns, then you tricked your way into my apartment. I think I'll just have to keep you, since you warm my bed and make it more comfortable. Your sales pitch was successful. You'll just have to deal with it. I'm not sure I bit you hard enough, so I'll have to do a very thorough investigation of your person later. But first, you'll have to model white dresses for me. It seems fair, because you've seen me in a suit before the completion of the bet."

"Most of the time you're shy, but then you make it clear you're not nearly as dense or oblivious as you appear to be."

"I'm pretty sure I'm dense, but your hands-on approach makes it pretty clear what I'm supposed to be doing. It doesn't hurt my parents and the rest of society are very vocal about what I should be doing. You didn't have to work very hard to convince me, and my only problem with you biting me is how long it's taking to heal. It's still sore."

"Well, it's my turn to deal with it for a few weeks, so you've gotten your revenge. Magic works in mysterious ways."

"Excellent. I'm pretty sure you owe me an apology for biting. You can apologize the same way you thanked me. I enjoyed that."

Marian laughed and elbowed me in the ribs. "You don't need to catch up for lost time."

"What sort of nonsense is that? Of course I need to catch up for lost time. Right now, however, I need to buy a phone and get you to model some dresses for me. Once I'm certain I've run the cab bill to horrific levels, we'll go rescue my parents, and since I'm a considerate gentleman, I won't tell them your biting has more significance than rough foreplay."

"You sneaky, manipulative bastard."

I laughed.

THE EASIEST WAY TO get rid of unwanted tracked cell phones was to toss them into the canal, which I did with a certain amount of glee. Marian watched me, her arms crossed over her chest. "Is there any reason you didn't toss them *before* we hiked to other side the mall and back?"

"More time on Larry's meter."

"Do you like or hate Ernesto? I'm really not sure."

"Neither is he, and it drives him insane." Smirking, I linked my arm with hers and pulled her back towards the mall. "I believe it's time to find a clothing store. You don't have to model wedding dresses. The dresses just have to be white. I can also live with skirts, if you find a white one you like. But I think showing off your legs should be mandatory."

"I should be complaining, you know."

"You've pinched my ass at least five times since we arrived at the mall."

"It's not my fault it's so tempting and

those pants fit you so well. It's begging to be touched."

"So we're even. You can keep stealing pinches as long as I can openly admire your legs. We're sexist pigs in equal proportions. It works out for everyone. You can even up-grade from pinching to gentle caresses if you like."

"How about a solid slap?"

"Two-way street. If you slap, I slap. If we start slapping, I might have to leave my par-ents with Ernesto and take you home." I paused. "I'm not sure that's a bad thing."

"We should rescue your parents."

"I suppose we should, shouldn't we? I'll be happy if you try on one white dress before our daring rescue of my parents from a vam-pire's clutches."

"And what if I want to try on a black dress?"

"You can try on as many dresses as you like. I'm a patient man. All I ask is that I get to see you in them."

"You just want to see what I look like in a dress so you know how much effort to put into winning the bet."

"Either way, I win the bet. If you can't keep your hands off me when I'm wearing a suit, I win. Since I have no doubt you're gor-geous in a dress, I win. No matter the out-come, I'm a winner."

Marian stared at me, her mouth ajar and her eyes wide. "I'm pretty sure that's cheating."

"How is it cheating?"

"I'm supposed to enjoy you wearing suits."

"You do, don't you? Just because you can't keep your hands off me when I'm wearing one doesn't invalidate the bet. If my goal is to have you eager to come home with me, then it works in my favor to dress appropriately."

"I see. You're willing to make sacrifices for sex."

"You only have yourself to blame for this one. I have a sample size of one." I gestured to the mall. "Pick your poison."

"Most women would kill for a man willing to take her shopping without complaint."

"I'll even buy the first dress, but if you bankrupt me, you'll have to move in with me and pay half my rent."

She laughed. "Or you'll have to move in with me and beg for scraps and work off your rent with manual labor. Emphasis on the man part of manual."

"I'm out of my league in this discussion, but I'm pretty sure my answer is supposed to be okay. Where do you live and will I need clothes for my work?"

"You need clothes to leave the bedroom. It's a rule. Inside my bedroom, you may dress however you like. View it as gift wrapping yourself for my pleasure."

"You know, a month ago, I was destined to be alone for the rest of my life, dying a virgin."

"Why would you think that?"

I pointed at my false eye and scar. "I wasn't pretty before the scar. Add in the lycanthropy issue, my decision to become a cop in a city that hates lycanthropes, and general inability to figure out what women are thinking, and I was pretty sure I was going to be alone for the rest of my life."

Marian hopped a few steps ahead of me and pressed her hand to my chest. I halted, loving the way she scowled at me. "Listen here, you."

When Dad smiled at Mom's annoyance, she found ways to get back at him, but I understood him. For the moment, Marian gifted me with her undivided attention, and that alone was worth smiling about. "I'm listening."

She poked my cheek where the scar faded away to nothing. "If I wanted a dainty model, I'd have bitten one. If I wanted a man who preened in front of a mirror and thought himself God's gift to women, they're a dime a dozen. Maybe I want a man who has the guts to stand in front of a gun for another living being, sentient or not. Maybe

I want a man who understands the value of life. Maybe I want a man who puts his money where his mouth is and has the scars to show for it. And if you never get a functional eye because we can't afford it, then I'll happily be your badge babe while you serve as my badge bunny. I'll even listen when you bitch and moan about missing being on duty, because that's what the good retired cops do."

Mom was right. I needed to marry Marian before she got away. "Since we're going out of order anyway, maybe we should skip the white dress part and go straight to the marriage part, then we can do the white dress part later?"

"I'm going to put my foot down and say a wedding is non-negotiable. It's the only day I'm legitimately allowed to pretend I'm a pretty princess. For the clueless man in this relationship, it's the one day you get to pretend to be the handsome prince. The white dress part is happening."

"You won't have to pretend. You're already pretty. Maybe I should take courses on how to act. I may need them. Handsome prince is going to be a stretch for me."

"Shane!" Marian thumped my chest and her scowl deepened. "You're plenty handsome."

"There has to be an eye doctor in this mall

somewhere. We should make you an appointment."

"You aren't the judge of your looks. I am, and I say you are. That's final."

No wonder Dad liked goading Mom so much. I enjoyed Marian bristling over something I'd accepted long ago. "I think we're going to have to investigate this matter very carefully."

Marian put her hands on her hips and glowered, then she sucked in a breath. "You're trying to get me to prove it by wearing sexy dresses for you, aren't you?"

In reality, I was testing her temper to see how far I could push her, but I liked her idea a lot more. "Yes, that's exactly what I'm trying to do. I'm trying to get you to try on every sexy dress I see so I can buy the one I like best for you. And if it's sexy enough, I may have to win the bet so you're forced to wear it often when you aren't wiggling into tight jeans."

I ruined my ploy by laughing, which earned me a solid smack to the chest.

"You have everyone fooled, don't you? You play this shy, good cop who doesn't bother anyone, when in reality, you're a clever little weasel who prefers halos over horns."

While I would have preferred to be called a wolf, I liked weasels. "Most people would be offended if you called them a weasel."

"Are you?"

"Don't tell anyone I said this, but weasels are rather cute, and most people wouldn't think to accuse me of being clever."

"Weasels are also vicious."

"I don't have much of a reputation for being vicious," I confessed. "I obviously wouldn't be a very good weasel."

"You're a hell of a shot, though. That makes up for it."

"I should introduce you to Ed. He helped me go from being a passable shot to a decent one. My godfather taught me the basics growing up, though."

"Not your parents?" Marian made a thoughtful noise in her throat and pointed down one of the hallways. "I think I saw a clothing store that way."

I'd never understand why other men found shopping such a chore. I didn't want to be the one trying on the clothes, but I appreciated the inclusion. I blamed Mom for my opinion; if a woman took a man shopping, she wanted to spend time with him doing something she enjoyed.

I'd make the most of it and enjoy the view the entire time, even though I wasn't much of a shopper.

"Lewis is a better shot than they are, and he liked his godfather duties. I think it's because his wife isn't ready to put up with the hassle of conception with a werewolf."

"I'll admit I don't know why it's a hassle."

"Trust me, that was a sex education lesson I didn't want. If you really want to know, research wolves. I've been informed lycanthropes share certain characteristics with real wolves, and they don't stop until they're certain of pregnancy, which isn't not a short process." My face flushed. "I was informed it was twelve uncomfortable hours for my mother, something she's not in any hurry to repeat."

Marian's eyebrows shot up. "Twelve hours."

"Apparently."

"Should I be worried?"

"I don't know. Do you want kids?"

"Eventually."

I thought about that. Then I thought about it some more. I got so distracted thinking about it I almost plowed over a couple standing in the hallway.

Laughing, Marian tugged me out of the way. "I seem to have fried your circuits. Which part got you? The idea of kids, knowing I'm interested in having kids with you, or the practice involved in making kids a reality?"

The idea of woman wanting kids wanting kids with *me* stumped me almost as much as me having kids with anyone. "I never got past finding a nice woman who might want to settle down with me to think about kids."

"I'm not nice. I'm actually a bit mean. I also bite."

"When I get a few minutes, I'm going to research that biting habit so I know if I should be encouraging you to bite me more often or if I need to get better at dodging your teeth. I'm sure I can amuse myself with this research at a later time. Right now, we have more important business to attend to."

"I'm not sure me trying on dresses is more important business."

"Sure it is. You in a dress directly influences how elaborate my plans to kidnap you become. Choose your dresses wisely, Marian Peterson. I'll be watching you."

"Most women would be seriously creeped out by that statement."

"Says the woman who keeps pinching my ass."

She shot me a glare, scanned the mall, and pointed at a shop I suspected contained the most expensive dresses in the mall. "I hope you can live with your regrets, of which there will be many." Grabbing my hand so I couldn't escape, she dragged me into the store.

She had no idea how wrong she was, and I'd enjoy her finding out.

TWENTY-SEVEN

My eyes are up here, Shane.

SOME WOMEN COULD WEAR red well, but Marian wasn't one of them. While the dress fit her athletic body, hugged the curves she had, and made it clear a strong woman stood before me, the color didn't do her justice. Such a vibrant shade should have been stunning on her, but it distracted instead of complemented.

"No." I handed down my verdict with an exaggerated wave of my hand.

"My, my. Aren't you a bossy badge bunny today," Marian murmured, putting her hands on her hips, lifting her chin, and staring down her nose at me.

I changed my mind about the dress the instant she shifted her shoulders and the fabric clung to her chest. "Do you think they have that dress in black?"

"My eyes are up here, Shane."

I grinned. "But you're not wearing the dress over your eyes."

Marian shifted her weight and stuck out her leg, which caught my attention and held it rather well. "It's not covering my legs, either."

"Thank God for that."

"They might have it in black." Marian spun on her heel and marched in the direction of the dressing room, leaving me with one of the two amused store clerks. I had no idea what it was about the black heels she'd partnered with the red dress, but I needed to see her in them again.

"How much are those shoes? I think I'll buy them."

"Six hundred and forty, and of course, sir. I'll grab them when she tries on a different pair of heels." The woman flashed me a smile and went off to do my bidding.

I didn't know much about women's clothing, but I hoped black heels went with more than a red dress. And if they didn't, maybe I could talk her into wearing them with a pair of jeans. The wait bored me, but when she returned, I had no regrets.

The store did have the dress in black, and I forgot how words worked when she sauntered my way. "Is this better?"

Unable to think anything coherent to say, I bobbed my head. She did a slow turn that showcased her legs, which did terrible yet wonderful things to me. "I don't need my parents anymore, right?"

Taking her home and unwrapping that dress from her body became my highest priority. Ernesto could keep my parents occupied for another day or two.

"I'm pretty sure you'd miss your parents after a while."

I flagged the clerk down. "I'm buying that dress, I don't care what it costs, and if she could just wear it out, that'd be great."

"Shane!" Marian laughed. "Don't be crazy."

"There's nothing crazy about you in that dress." I turned to the clerks for help, and the women grinned. "I'm right, right? She's stunning in that dress."

"You are, ma'am. The red was nice, but the black is perfect on you."

"These aren't my shoes, Shane."

"I'm buying the shoes, too."

"What?"

"I'm buying the shoes."

"But, Shane, they're—"

"Worth every penny. Can you get a bag for her regular clothes and a jacket that suits that dress for her, please?"

The clerks knew a sucker when they saw one, and both women darted off to do as I asked.

"It's not white."

"I've changed my mind about the color requirement. There will be one white dress I'll want to see you in, but you get to pick that one."

"You're weird."

"I'm going to blame my parents for that."

She laughed. "All right. I'll wear the dress out, but only because you wore the suit like a champ and didn't complain about it. Why the jacket?"

"You need somewhere to hide your gun."

"So practical."

"I try. We should go have dinner before we call the cab. Preferably somewhere that will take several hours." I grinned and checked my new phone for the time. "Two hours should do it. That'll give them enough time to be a little less snarly when we go over."

"And where would you suggest we go for dinner?"

I looked up the number of a restaurant on the canal, owned and operated by one of Ernesto's vampire daughters. Dialing the number, I tapped my foot while waiting for someone to answer.

"Michietti's," a man barked before stifling a yawn, which made him one of Ernesto's many children. I thought about the candidates and assumed I was speaking to Quinton, one of Ernesto's older sons, a vampire able to handle daylight without frying to a crisp.

"Quinton, it's Shane Gibson. Is there any chance Pierina she can fit me in with a lady friend?"

"Since when do you have a lady friend?"

"She's a recent development. I'm even wearing a suit, so I shouldn't embarrass you fine folks too much this time."

"A private table for two?"

"If you could. Oh, by the way, your father is paying, so make it extravagant."

"He is?"

"He borrowed my parents, so he owes me."

Laughter rang out, loud enough I winced. "Give me a minute, Gibby. I'll ask the boss, but I bet she'll fit you in. I think the balcony is free."

The balcony was private for two and hung over the canal where it fell into the abyss of Chicago's third level, making the view one of the most spectacular in the lower city—and the most dangerous. I waited, wondering if Marian had any issues with heights. No one had fallen from the balcony at Michietti's since I'd been in the city. It was over the Lower Chicago side of the canal, so if someone did fall in, there was a chance they could be peeled from the grate before they drowned.

"When do you want to come in, Gibby? I

translated the boss's shrill squeal as an affirmative."

"We're at the mall, so it'll take us twenty or thirty minutes to walk there. Can I get one more favor?"

"What do you need?"

"Tell Larry. He's running his meter while he waits for us."

"Our Papa did something to annoy you, didn't he?"

"When doesn't he?"

"Good point. Your table will be ready for you when you arrive."

I hung up, chuckled, and headed for the cash registers so I could make my credit card weep from the amount I'd be spending on Marian's new dress. We lost ten minutes picking the perfect jacket, but it hid Marian's gun and had space for her wallet, keys, and phone, making it a win across the board.

The shoes cost more than the dress, and the jacket cost more than the shoes and the dress combined, which confirmed I understood nothing about women's clothing. I slipped the receipt into my wallet before Marian could get her hands on it, grinned, and grabbed the bag filled with her other clothes.

"Michietti's is one of the better restaurants in Lower Chicago. It usually serves nocturnals, but it caters to humans, too. It's also one of the few places that doesn't discriminate against lycanthropes, so it's a popular spot for them."

Marian waited until we left the store to say, "And it's run by Ernesto."

"One of his daughters."

"Biologic or vampiric?"

"Both."

"I thought vampires couldn't have children."

"I believe Ernesto and several of his children were all turned at the same time. Ernesto's sire turned him, and then Ernesto turned his children during his first feeding. It's a sore point, so don't mention it around them. I don't know why, but it makes Ernesto unhappy, which in turn makes his children unhappy, and when all of them are unhappy, it causes trouble."

"Noted. And this restaurant? Is it any good?"

"Considering Pierina has been cooking for several thousand years, yeah, it's good. It'll be different, though."

"Why?"

"Let's just say the Etruscans had a slightly different opinion about what counts as food. They tend to use *everything*, and Pierina is no exception. I've done some of my more adventurous dining at Michietti's, but she does feed those with more modern interests, too. If in doubt, let me order for you."

"I'm not a squeamish eater."

"If you get a bleeding heart on your plate, it's not my fault."

MICHIETTI'S EMBRACED the glory days of the Roman Empire, breaking free from Lower Chicago's doom and gloom to offer diners a step through time and a glimpse of the luxury enjoyed long ago. Most people believed the decor, from the ancient busts on podiums lining the walls to the gold leafing patterning the crowning near the domed ceiling, were reproductions, but I knew better. The rare times I caught the older staff staring, the weight of long memories dampened their expressions, especially when their attention turned to the frescos on the ceilings.

The entry featured a painting depicting the Garden of Eden and the dawn of humanity. Every room in the restaurant presented a different fresco on its ceiling, each one capturing a glimpse of history—or a variant of it.

Marian inhaled, her gaze locked overhead while Ernesto's daughter swept across the room, stood on her toes, and kissed my cheeks. Pierina brushed her fingers against my scar but said nothing of the crippling injury. "It's been too long since you've visited, and looking so handsome for your lady. Introduce us this instant, Gibby."

"Pierina, this is Marian. She's in the FBI."

Marian smiled and held out her hand. "Pleased to meet you."

"Finally found yourself a badge, did you? If she leaves you heartbroken, come to me. I'll cheer you up."

I bet Pierina would, and she'd bring a succubus friend with her. "I'm really hoping that won't be necessary."

Pierina's eyes widened. "That serious?"

"He's hinting very hard he'd like me in a white dress." Marian chuckled. "I've already bitten him."

Clapping her hands together, Pierina spun and snapped her fingers at one of her vampire brothers. "This calls for a bottle of our best, and charge it to Papa. It's a miracle."

I was tempted to pop my fake eye out and roll it across the marble floor. "I wouldn't go that far, Pieri."

"I would. Come, come. I'll take you to your table, darlings. Don't mind Gibby, Miss Marian. If he gives you any problems, smack him around a bit. He likes it. You're lucky he let you bite him. He shoots us in the knees when we think about it. So unfair."

"He bit me back."

Marian's four words widened Pierina's

eyes and her smile. "Wonderful. There are many reasons to celebrate. I would love to get to know you better—and share with you some tidbits that may help you unravel the mystery that is our Gibby."

I didn't look forward to Marian joining forces with Ernesto's daughter, who ran crime rings right under her father's nose and made him like it. No matter what happened, it would cause trouble for me. Too wise to voice my concerns, I slid my arm behind Marian's back and guided her across the restaurant.

The main dining room's fresco of Noah's Flood intrigued me the most; there was no ark, only craggy mountain peaks covered in snow and surrounded by churning water, where the remnants of Earth's life clung to tenacious survival. Only after several visits and unashamed staring had I realized unicorns lurked within the waves, fighting back the waters, while on the bitterly cold peaks, a phoenix and another unicorn, blacker than night with flames in its eyes, protected the survivors from winter's cold embrace.

When the lights were turned off, the fresco revealed its true secrets, and I hoped I would get a chance to show Marian a special sort of magic—and draw her attention to a few of the figures huddled on the slopes of the mighty mountains withstanding the raging sea.

The lights were on and the place was packed, forcing us to navigate through a sea of tables, chairs, busy waiters and waitresses, and diners to the staircase tucked in the far corner. It spiraled upwards to my second favorite room, which featured a fresco of the eruption of Vesuvius over Pompeii and the destruction of Herculaneum. After dark, it replayed the final days of the cities, and at the end, a phoenix rose from the mountain's heart and took to the skies, raining cinders and ash on the ground below.

Pushing aside the dark curtain separating the main dining room from the wall-to-wall window, Pierina gestured to the opened door, and I waited for Marian to go first. Instead of the white tablecloths used in the rest of the restaurant, Pierina had brought out the black cloth embroidered with gold thread, which depicted dragons in flight chasing phoenixes while unicorns galloped beneath them, whinnying their dismay they too couldn't fly. Long red candles, surrounded with an olive and laurel wreath, served as the center piece.

I was pretty sure the silverware was made of white and yellow gold.

"You've outdone yourself as always, Pierina."

The vampire smiled at me. "It's our plea-

sure to bring you our finest at our papa's expense. Please, sit. Enjoy the view. My
brothers will bring you your wine and serve
you tonight while I attend to matters in the
kitchen."

I took advantage of Marian's hesitance to
pull out her chair. "Now try to imagine me in
either a cop uniform or a pair of jeans doing
this. I've seen the entire secondary dining
room stop and stare at me for sitting on the
balcony fresh off duty."

She giggled and sat, and I nudged her
chair closer to the table. "I never would have
taken you for the type to know proper
etiquette."

"I'm a man of many surprises. Usually,
Pierina sets the table with the white cloth, but
she's feeling extravagant today for some reason." I smiled and sat across from Marian.
"It's definitely nicer when I'm not dining
alone."

My choice of seat for Marian gave her the
best view of Lower Chicago's drop into the
abyss, and the rumble of the canal's waterfall
drowned out the conversation inside the
building. While we'd be able to hear each
other, the noise meant others couldn't, not
easily.

The waterfall's noise made the balcony
one of the best places to do business, and if

secrecy mattered, the curtains could be drawn for absolute privacy.

Marian leaned to the side, her gaze fixed on the black waters tumbling into the darkness below. "It didn't seem so loud on the street!"

"Magic. Pierina likes the ambiance of the falls but doesn't want it disturbing the diners in the restaurant, so she had a practitioner muffle the sound to only be heard in certain locations in the restaurant. The balcony is one of them."

"That's amazing. What happens if you fall in?"

I turned and pointed to where the canal washed over the edge. "There's a grate down there. If you fall in, it's possible to get your head above the surface; the current's really strong, but every now and then someone survives. It's one of the jobs the CPD has; if someone falls into the canal, we're the S&R team for the grate. I've pulled a few people off the grate in my time. Some of them survived. If you go over, survival is a coin toss. It's a manmade waterway. If you go over, it's a violent water slide to the bottom into a deep pool. The denizens below send the survivors back up and call for a patrol and ambulance. The city pays them for the live bodies."

"How many survive each year?"

I thought about my years patrolling the

area. "For every five or six who get pinned to the grate, one goes through or over, and I'd say maybe fifty-fifty odds of living to tell the story."

"And the denizens below don't mind the water is so disgusting down there?"

"I think they like it."

Marian stared at the canal and the darkness beyond. "Well, isn't that charming?"

I smiled. "Even in darkness there's beauty. If you're lucky, you'll see something really special."

"What?"

"While many of the denizens are unknown, some come up from time to time. Among them are the lampad."

"Lampad?"

I smiled. "Nymphs, believed to be the daughters of Nyx, the constant companion of Hecate."

Marian's eyes widened. "Hecate? The Greek goddess?"

"Roman, too."

"Is she real?"

I held my hands up in a gesture of both surrender and ignorance. "Who am I to say? All I know is that sometimes, if you're on the balcony, you might see lights in the distance, and no one is ever really sure what they saw, except it's never the same."

Marian leaned towards me and asked in a hushed voice, "Have you seen them?"

"I haven't, but I think I've heard them," I confessed in a conspiratorial whisper. "It is said Hecate favors dogs, for they help her to guide the spirits of the dead. Once, I thought I heard the braying of dogs in the distance, but no one else heard it."

"You have to be pulling my leg."

"Would I do that?"

"Yes."

I laughed. "I did think I heard the dogs. As for the rest, it's just a story—a really interesting story, one close to the heart of Ernesto's daughter."

"Just when I start to think I understand you, you surprise me again, Shane."

I smiled and was saved from having to answer by Quinton, who came bearing a bottle of wine so encrusted with dust I couldn't imagine how it had survived the ages. Then again, I could.

At Michietti's, anything was possible.

TWENTY-EIGHT

I'm supposed to drink this?

IF I'D READ the Roman numerals on the label correctly, we were drinking a two thousand year old bottle of wine. The rest of the label made no sense to me; ancient Latin looked like gibberish to me. I hadn't even realized the Romans had fashioned anything out of glass.

The bottle's long, fluted neck and short, bulbous bottom were unusual, and I wasn't sure I wanted to know what the label itself was made of, but it was tied to the glass rather than glued. Quinton pulled the stopper and poured the wine into my glass then waited for me to taste it and discover if it had somehow survived the millenniums since its making. I lifted the glass, holding it up so I could get a good look at the liquid in the light streaming in behind the old vampire.

The ruby wine looked okay, and when I

gave it a swirl and sniffed it, its sweetness surprised me. I took a cautious sip.

I'd tasted a lot of wines over the years, from the earthy ones Ernesto favored to the sweeter, aged ports. Fruity sweetness, spice, and earth mingled on my tongue in a delicate balance, no flavor overpowering the other until I couldn't quite tell where one ended and the other began.

"It's exquisite." I had no other word for the vintage, and I doubted I'd ever taste the wine's equal again.

Quinton smiled and filled Marian's glass before topping mine off. "My sister will be so pleased. It was her very first, and it holds a special place in her heart."

Thousands of years had left Pierina's heart shriveled, renewed only when she fed from a human. "She honors us."

Marian tried a sip and sucked in a breath. "It's so different."

"Grapes have survived thousands of years, but these were not the same grapes that grow now. You'll not taste its like again. A pity, really." Quinton restored the stopper to the bottle. "I'll take the bottle inside and bring it back when you're ready for more. When you leave, my dear sister would like you to take the bottle home with you so it might become a cherished memory. I'll bring your appetizers shortly."

I should have known Pierina would take matters into her own hands. Knowing her, we'd sample everything on the menu before she finished feeding us.

"Thank you." The two words seemed insignificant compared to what the vampires offered, but Quinton bowed and left us.

"How old is this wine, Shane?"

"At least two thousand years old. I'm pretty sure the label was written in ancient Latin, and the numerals were in the single digits. I'm not sure if it's from AD or BC, though."

"Oh my god." She stared at her glass. "I'm supposed to drink this? Me? How was it preserved for so long?"

"I'm going to guess magic, which is why Quinton took the bottle back inside."

"But why are the vampires giving it to us?"

"What's the average lifespan of a shifter?"

"No one told you?"

"No. To be fair, I didn't ask."

"Longer than lycanthropes. We aren't reliant on the virus to stay alive. We're a lot less common than lycanthropes, but we can live longer. If their virus dies, they die. But they have advantages we lack."

Relief I wouldn't die of old age long before my parents washed through me. I needed to do a lot of research, but I could work with what I'd learned. "Like enhanced regeneration?"

"Right. We heal faster than regular humans, and we have a much higher ability to withstand lethal damage, but we'll never match a lycanthrope's regenerative ability."

"And the lycanthrope virus in other shifters? That doesn't help their regeneration?"

"No. If I'm exposed to lycanthropy, I get a fever for a few days. I suppose it might help a little, but I've never tried it. I've only had accidental exposure."

I wasn't sure what I thought about that, and to cover my uncertainty, I took another sip of wine. "Ernesto knows I'm an unidentified shifter by now, and once he knew, he would've told his children. To them, humans live such short lives, like brightly burning flames that wink out too quickly. As soon as they begin to truly witness the complexity of a human, the human dies. He probably knows a lot more about shifters than I do, so he'd know my lifespan—barring death from unnatural causes—has been greatly lengthened."

"So he's celebrating that you'll be around a lot longer to bother him?"

"That would be my first guess."

"But it's Pierina's wine."

"She's cut from the same cloth as her father, and she loves feeding her favorite people."

"The Italian food he brought over. It's from here, isn't it?"

"Wouldn't surprise me. Pierina loves cooking. She can't eat much beyond a taste, but little makes her happier than feeding living things."

"That seems so weird. She's undead."

"I'm no expert on vampires, but I've come to the conclusion they value life even more after undeath, because they can no longer experience it in the same way." I took another sip of my wine.

"If he likes you so much, why doesn't he just turn you?"

"Because he likes me—that's why. If he hated me, he'd turn me and get his revenge by making me into the type of person he wanted. But death is a part of undeath, and when someone is turned, everything that person used to be dies with them. Vampires become new people. Who they used to be is truly gone."

"You've known someone who became a vampire, haven't you?"

I shrugged. "Hard not to around here. Chicago has a high population of vamps and demons."

"Yet they can't stand werewolves."

"I never said it made sense."

"That's true." Marian drank her wine, her gaze focusing on the canal behind me. "Whenever I start thinking I have you figured out, you surprise me."

"Isn't that a good thing?"

"Well, I won't get bored." She grinned and turned her attention back to me.

"Good."

PIERINA MUST HAVE BELIEVED Marian and I were at risk of starvation, because she served us a sampling of everything on her menu. The vampire retained some of her common sense, limiting the serving sizes to something in the realm of sane—if we were lycanthropes fresh off a rampage and in dire need of sustenance.

We weren't, but I couldn't resist the challenge, and neither could Marian. While I'd warned her about the vampire's tendency to use every bit of an animal to enter her kitchen, I doubted Marian believed me until the heart arrived. At least Pierina had cooked it, which was better than the first time I'd sampled one of her more unique dishes.

"Dare I ask what other organs are going to end up on my plate tonight?"

I laughed, and because Pierina was pulling out all the stops, I played the game and tasted her offerings. Despite the ick factor, I actually liked heart—even when it wasn't cooked as thoroughly as I'd preferred. "The CDC asked if I considered myself an adventurous eater. I pointed out I knew from experience I disliked tripe and haggis. The second time I got sick on tripe, Pierina took pity on me and stopped making me eat it."

"You got sick on it?"

"Nothing is quite as undignified as throwing up over the balcony railing. The first time, I think she was taken by surprise. The second time, she laughed. Vampires have terrible senses of humor. Ever since, she threatens to feed it to me if I've been bad."

"When aren't you bad?"

I grinned. "But my record is so clean it squeaks."

"I still haven't figured out how you pulled that off."

"There's nothing illegal about being nice to people, even hardened criminals. If you know the rules, it's surprisingly easy to obey them. It just takes creativity."

"That's still impressive. There weren't any mentions in your file that you have a relationship with any of the people you actually know."

"That was easy; every cop who's done a traffic patrol in Lower Chicago has met Ernesto and his brood. It's not worth putting

on the records, since everyone's been involved at some level or another. If you really
wanted to connect the dots, you'd look at my
busts and realize I've been waging a quiet war
with Ernesto for years."

"What do you mean?"

"Speeding tickets, parking violations, anything a patrol officer might be able to nail
him or his children on. When I'd catch him,
he'd find some way to prank me, usually at
my apartment."

"Like with Amy."

"Exactly."

"That's absurd."

I grinned and toasted her with my wine
glass. "It made my dead-end career a little
more fun."

"Would you be willing to move away from
Chicago?"

"If it means I might have another stab at
law enforcement? Definitely."

"How do you feel about—"

The crack-bang of something detonating
nearby drowned out Marian's question, and
the balcony lurched. The concrete, steel, and
stone groaned, and before I could do more
than rise to my feet, the entire structure collapsed beneath us. I hit the canal back first,
and the air rushed out of my lungs.

Water flooded into my mouth, and while
every instinct I had screamed at me to do

something, my body refused to move. The current sucked me under, and I hit the grate hard enough to knock what little breath I had left out of me along with the water I'd swallowed on impact.

Somehow, I wasn't dead from the fall, but unless I wanted to change my status from living to dead, I needed to move. The first few seconds, my stunned body refused to obey me. I twitched, remembered how my arms and legs were supposed to work, and struggled to orient myself. Which way was up? Which way was down?

At a depth of fifteen feet, if I went the wrong way, I'd be able to change directions. If I found the wall, that would be even better; I'd be able to climb out on my own. I twisted until my chest touched the bars and reached over my head, groping for the metal crossing the end of the canal.

Everything went according to plan until a flash penetrated the murky waters, and the grate shuddered from the force of a blow. I froze, aware of the burn in my chest, the strain of my oxygen-deprived lungs, and the quivering in my muscles.

The metal shuddered again before dumping me into the abyss.

TWENTY-NINE

I rode a demented slinky with an
attitude problem.

DURING MY INITIAL training with the CPD, I'd
been told the canal drained over a concrete
spillway, one designed to mimic a waterslide
for any sentients unfortunate enough to go
over the grate meant to keep them from tumbling to Chicago's third level. While my instructors hadn't exactly lied, they hadn't been
speaking the complete truth.

Madmen on a pixie dust high might call
the twisting, turning concrete monstrosity a
waterslide. Either through magic or clever
engineering, the water spread out and slicked
the whole thing, and I plummeted through
six slimy inches of fluid I hesitated to think of
as water.

I could have dealt with a flat slope, but no.
I rode a demented slinky with an attitude
problem determined to tenderize me before
dumping my bruised and battered body at the

bottom. At least the creators understood a human wouldn't be in any condition to swim after such a fall; instead of plunging into water, I landed on a net. Water still pounded me from above, but I could breathe.

I liked breathing. Breathing meant I was alive and had some chance of making my way back to Lower Chicago. First, I needed to find Marian. She'd been closer to the restaurant's wall, and I worried she'd landed on the sidewalk instead of in the canal. The water had helped break my fall, and I didn't want to think about her landing on broken rubble.

After blinking several times and realizing how dark it was in Chicago's third level, I modified my game plan. First, I would figure out where I was, find a source of light, and then I'd find Marian. If she'd fallen nearby, she might need my help.

Instead of calling her name, I squeaked.

All right. I didn't need a manual to figure out part of my problem. In lycanthropes, injury or stress could force shifting; the virus took over to give its host the best chance for survival, and I had no reason to believe other shifters were different. It was logical. I could deal with logical.

Falling from a balcony into corpse stew before slamming into a grate and then taking a plummet into the abyss could easily kill someone. Had I not been warned I was some form of shifter, I would've panicked when I started squeaking when I tried to call Marian's name.

Whatever I was, I squeaked, which eliminated a wolf, much to my disappointment. Wolves didn't usually squeak. Squirrels squeaked. Mice squeaked. Great. Instead of a fierce predator, was I some sort of rodent? I didn't want to be a rodent.

I sighed.

Grousing over what I couldn't change wouldn't help. I needed to escape the net and find my way to the surface before something from Chicago's third level decided to have a tasty treat of shifter rodent. My curses emerged as short, high-pitched yaps.

What sort of rodent yapped? Until I escaped to where I could see, I'd have to live with the mystery of what I'd become. In a way, I envied my mother; when she shifted, she'd know exactly what she was, and Dad would help her get the hang of her two new forms. Me? I didn't even know how many legs I had.

I hoped it was four, or I'd classify as a mutant rodent, and the CDC would love a chance to study a mutant rodent. Assuming I was a rodent did simplify things for me; two arms and two legs easily translated to four paws, and it didn't take long for me to figure

out I did, indeed, have four paws of some
sort.

The ease with which I grasped the net's
ropes gave credibility to my rodent assump-
tion, although something about the way my
toes moved gave me pause. I secured a hold
on my precarious perch with my hind feet
and fumbled in the dark to rub my forepaws
together.

I discovered I had webbing linking my
digits. What sort of mutant rodent had
webbed paws? My fingers—if I could call the
digits fingers—seemed a lot longer than I expected for a rodent, too.

Did the presence of webbing disqualify
me as a rodent?

I rubbed my forepaws together, and after
several minutes of rubbing, I determined not
only were my fingers webbed, I had opposable thumbs. Life seemed a little better with
opposable thumbs, although I wondered what
sort of critter I had become.

Armed with the knowledge I had thumbs
and four paws, I began the tedious process of
climbing the net. Maybe I wasn't human, but
my body seemed well equipped to handle the
ropes, which were large enough I had to
stretch my paws to get a good grip on them.
Without any ability to see in the dark, I relied
on the net to guide me, following one rope
across while the water beat down from above.

Whatever I was, the water didn't bother me. I kept warm, and even the constant barrage over my face—muzzle?—wasn't a problem. As a human, I probably would have been flailing and falling without making any progress.

I hated nets, especially ones I was expected to climb.

I could check one mark on the advantage column for being whatever I was; a werewolf in hybrid form would've torn right through the net and fallen into the water below. Dad's claws could do serious damage to steel. Rope didn't stand a chance. If I could find the spillway's ledge, I'd be in good shape. I'd never gone into Chicago's third level, but I'd helped retrieve victims often and knew there was a way up on both sides of the canal, a way blocked with magic to keep people from wandering to places they shouldn't.

If memory served, the magic was a one-way barrier, allowing people to escape the third level, although I'd heard of one person making it out without help from Chicago's more questionable denizens.

With a little luck, I'd be person—critter—number two.

I LOVED SOLID GROUND, and to express my love for it, I rolled around and made a complete fool of myself, not caring if anyone saw me. Without the canal's magic helping, I stank, and the rocks surrounding the spillway smelled of moss, which I preferred over the malodorous water.

Someone really needed to do something about the canal. No one deserved to have to put up with the stench. The smell was bad enough I contemplated beating those in charge of Chicago's infrastructure to a near-death state for being too cheap and lazy to deal with the disgusting problem.

A faint glimmer of light from above oriented me so I could start the long journey back to where I belonged. I didn't look forward to the hike, but I fumbled my way over the rocks in search of a ramp, stairwell, or something I could use to reach Lower Chicago.

It took a lot longer than I liked to locate a staircase by feel. The steps were so tall I had to stand on my hind legs and jump to climb them, which supported my theory I was some sort of rodent-sized critter with thumbs, webbing, and a nice fur coat able to keep me warm and dry. I settled into a pattern of hopping up two stairs and stopping to catch my breath, my body aching from my tumble down the spillway.

Maybe I couldn't take stubborn pride and sell it, but it got me from the bottom of the spillway to the top, although I trembled and longed for a nap by the time I spotted where the canal emptied onto the concrete slide. The water churned, and I suspected magic was responsible for how evenly the water spread out and thinned.

Twisted metal jutted from the water falling from the canal, marking where something had busted the grate. From what I could tell, only a five-foot section of the grate had come loose, offering hope if Marian had ended up in the water, she might've been able to escape to the safety of the sidewalk.

In Lower Chicago, a wall surrounded the canal, but from my side of it, the wall had a rather translucent quality. A careful poke with a paw revealed it was insubstantial. I bounced through, squeaking as the brighter lights stabbed at my eyes.

Next time, I'd remember to avoid stepping from dim illumination into a spotlight. I shook my head, blinking to erase the spots dancing in my vision. The culprit—actual spotlights—focused on the blown-out portion of the canal grate and Michietti's, leaving me in a brightly lit but rather empty spot.

Shaking the water out of my coat, I took in the flashing red and blue lights of patrol cars, the blur of motion around the building, and the black-stained, gaping hole where the balcony had once been. Soot marred the stone veneer still clinging to the wall, and I grimaced at the amount of damage done to Pierina's beloved restaurant.

Once my eyes stopped aching, I took a good look at my paws, which resembled furry, webbed human hands. I twisted around, discovering I had a long, brown body with a long tail tipped in black.

Whatever I was, I didn't think I was a rodent. I'd seen enough rats, mice, and squirrels to recognize I wasn't one of them. Without getting a good look at my head, I wasn't really sure what I was, but I was satisfied I'd escaped the humiliation of being a rat.

I blamed the CPD's lawyer for my reaction to the thought of becoming a species Dad would happily eat given an opportunity.

Satisfied with my brief examination, I turned my attention back to the chaos around Michietti's. I spotted Pierina in the entry, her arms crossed over her chest, every inch of her stiff. She faced off against a member of the CPD, a man I didn't know, and her elongated fangs peeked out between her lips whenever she spoke.

Maybe Pierina wouldn't recognize my body, but her heightened senses as a vampire might help her recognize my smell since the canal stench still clung to my fur. After several strides, I figured out how to run without tripping over my own paws, although I bounced more than I ran. When I reached her, I panted to catch my breath, eyeing her legs. I decided to give climbing a shot, and I clawed at her clothes so I could reach her shoulder.

The vampire jumped, squealed, and made it halfway to Upper Chicago before landing in a crouch, which made it easier to reach my goal. Stretched out, I was long enough to span her shoulders, and I clung to her jacket with my paws. Instead of questions, she got an earful of squeaks.

The cops pulled their guns, and I stiffened, watching them while wondering if they'd be bold—or stupid—enough to fire a weapon at Ernesto's daughter.

"Put those away," Pierina snapped, lifting her hand to touch my head. "Haven't there been enough loud bangs at my establishment today?"

I supposed an explosion counted as a loud bang.

"That animal—"

"Does it look like he's biting me? Does it look like he's attacking me? Don't be an idiot. He just came up to say hello. He's been a very naughty little child." Pierina flicked me with her finger. "Bad. Ask before you jump up."

At an utter loss of what game Pierina was

playing, I did the first thing to come to mind. I bit the hell out of her hand. The vampire hissed at me.

I squeaked around a mouthful of her dry, leathery skin.

"Yes, it does look like he's biting you, ma'am," the cop replied.

Pierina snagged me by the scruff of my neck with her other hand and peeled me off her shoulders. I dangled in her grip. With two firm but gentle shakes, she forced me to release my hold on her hand. "I tire of this. Where are the werewolves?"

The cops flinched but pointed along the canal. Pierina huffed and strode away, leaving them spluttering in her wake. When we were out of earshot, she looked me in the eye. "You've scared your mother into her first shift. I hope you're satisfied with yourself. I'm certain you scared at least a decade off my lifespan. How is it you managed to not only fall into the canal but also slip through the one section that didn't hold? I was certain I'd be delivering the news of your demise to my father, thus breaking his shriveled heart."

Since I had one mode of communication open to me, I squeaked.

"Your lady friend wasn't quite as lucky as you, but she's tough and emerged with only a broken wrist. She protested, but they carted her away to the hospital. I sent my brother with her as a guard. We thought you'd be rather angry if we left her alone."

I clapped my paws together to sign my approval.

"For your sake, I'm grateful you seem to be aquatic. Your father has your mother mostly contained, although if she starts howling again, I'll lose my temper."

Almost two blocks away beyond a curve effectively blocking their view of Michietti's, my father in his hybrid form loomed over a smaller red wolf. He held my mother in place with one of his clawed hands on the scruff of her neck while she whined and struggled in his grip.

"I come bearing a gift," Pierina announced, holding me out in front of her. "It seems this youngling has a lucky horseshoe crammed somewhere. If you can get your lady wolf somewhat restrained—or preferably back to human—I recommend you take him to his lady friend so she might educate him on how to shift back. First shifts are so troublesome."

Dad reared back, released my mother, and snatched me out of Pierina's hand so fast I squeaked my alarm and struggled in his grip. He breathed wolf breath all over me and, with a croon, stroked his tongue over my face.

I wasn't sure which was worse: corpse stew or wolf slobber.

Either unwilling or incapable of speaking

English, my father snarled, jumped back to my mother, and dropped me between her front paws. I squeaked and stood, but not in time to prevent Dad from pinning me in place so my mother could have a turn bathing me with her tongue.

Enduring a tongue bath from Dad when I was human was bad enough, but Mom's head was bigger than I was. I let out a displeased yip, twisting around so I could glare at Dad for daring to hold me hostage. Dad bared his teeth and snarled.

Okay, then. Letting the werewolf win seemed the wisest course of action, since at a fraction of their size, they could gulp me down in one or two bites. They wouldn't—probably—but I'd already tested my luck enough for one day, so I shut up and suffered through wolf slobber in silence.

THIRTY

Don't you lecture me, you scrawny
pipsqueak!

DESPITE A HEFTY DOSE of xenophobia when
lycanthropes were involved, the CPD didn't
need long to clue in the two raving werewolves had quieted their snarls and gone
from infuriated to calm and deceptively
docile. Fortunately, Pierina understood my
parents' nature and intervened before any of
the cops could get too close to me.

Explaining to idiots why it was stupid to
come between a mated pair of lycanthropes
and their child took the vampire several minutes, but the cops stayed back, my parents
stayed calm, and Mom finally decided she'd
had enough of licking me and decided to use
me as a pillow.

It hurt. Lacking the ability to speak, I vo-
calized my discomfort with a whine.

"He's probably bruised," Pierina interpreted. "It's a long way down the slide to the

bottom, and since he didn't have an escort with him when he climbed out, he made the trip alone. You may want to be gentle with him—and call in someone from the CDC to have a look at him."

"The CDC?" Dad snarled the question and dug his claws into the sidewalk. The cops flinched at the sound of stone breaking due to the abuse of an angry werewolf. "Why the CDC?"

"They'll treat him better." Pierina leveled a glare at the nearby cops. "These fools wouldn't care if he lost his other eye due to their negligence. Nor would they care about you, despite your record as cops of good standing within your department. Racist, elitist wastes of good blood and air."

I lifted my head and gaped at the vampire, stunned she'd said what I'd thought on more than one occasion.

Dad snarled and stood over me and Mom, growling with every breath. "We have a word for cops like those where we're from."

If Dad lost his temper and went for the cops, the cops *might* survive—maybe. I wiggled free of Mom's hold on me, climbed onto her back, and jumped on my father's chest, digging my paws into his fur and clinging to him, squeaking rebukes at him for a crime he hadn't committed—yet. He straightened, plucking me off him and holding me at eye level. "Don't you lecture me, you scrawny pipsqueak!"

I yipped at him to make it clear he wasn't my boss and paddled my paws trying to swat his nose. When that didn't do the trick, I sucked in a deep breath and made the loudest, shrillest noise I could.

Flattening his ears, Dad glared at me. "What's your problem, pup?"

"He probably doesn't want you ripping his former co-workers to shreds, no matter how much they might deserve it for their lack of loyalty," Ernesto's daughter contributed.

I really needed to have a long talk with her about fanning the flames because she thought it was fun watching people lose their tempers. Since she was turning two sets of cops against each other, she was probably having the time of her life. Sighing, I hung my head and groaned.

"He's probably eager to check on his lady friend. He's very fond of her—fond enough to wear a suit for her." Pierina pouted. "He never wears suits for me."

"We need to ask him questions," one of the cops blurted.

Dad turned me around and held me out, keeping a firm grip on me from behind, the tips of his claws pressing against my belly. "Ask."

"As a human."

"Well, start talking, then. Do *you* know how to get him to shift back? I do not. I am a lycanthrope. He is not."

When Dad started talking at his most formal in his hybrid shape, it meant one of two things: he really liked the person he was talking to, or he was holding onto his temper by the barest of threads. Were the cops *trying* to provoke him into leaving a trail of cop bodies? If so, they were close to succeeding.

"I thought—"

"You thought what? That he should somehow magically know how to shift back? Your ignorance is showing. Did you come out of the womb knowing how to fire a gun? No. Were you born capable of walking? No. The only shifter I know of around here *you* ordered off to the hospital, which is where I will be taking my son. I do not recommend getting in my way. You will not enjoy the consequences." Dad tucked me close to his chest and growled. "Read up on your species exemption laws. They're in the Federal code, in case you haven't done your reading. You touch my puppy while he is hurt, and I will rip you into tiny little shreds—legally. And when I am done, I will gather your blood and offer it to the vampire you have been menacing with your pitiable excuse of an investigation. You do not care who tried to kill my pup and his mate. You are only here because you have to be."

"You're most considerate, Mr. Gibson," Pierina murmured.

"Where's my pup's woman? If you want to ask questions, send someone there—*after* I make sure they're both all right."

In what I deemed a miracle, the cops co-operated and informed my father where they'd sent Marian.

WHILE DAD DIDN'T MANAGE to coax Mom into assuming a human form, he did convince her to take the hybrid form by using the simple and effective argument she would be better equipped to slaughter anyone who touched me if she had nice, big, lethal claws and several hundred extra pounds to work with.

Like her wolf form, my mother's hybrid coat was red, tipped black with a splash of white across her nose. Pierina insisted on re-trieving her SUV from the nearby parking garage and driving us to the hospital—the same one I'd gone to when I'd lost my eye. The vampire had the presence of mind to warn me, and I appreciated the courtesy.

Had the news been sprung on me, I doubted I would keep my cool. I found it odd the worst of my anxiety over losing my eye manifested at the hospital. The post-operation appointments made me clammy and shaky before and after.

With two tense werewolves to worry about, I found it a lot easier to control my nerves. I was too busy convincing my parents I was alive and mostly well to think about how my career had come to an abrupt end. Mom cradled me in one arm and waggled her claws in front of my nose, an invitation to play I failed to resist.

"He's otterly adorable, isn't he?" Mom cooed.

Of all the tricks for my mother to grasp without lessons, why did it have to be mastery of English in her hybrid form? While I was still dealing with the realization I wouldn't be spared from her tongue, everyone else in the vehicle groaned.

Why did my mother's first words as a full lycanthrope have to be a pun? It also explained a few things; I'd become something disgustingly cute, an otter, instead of a vicious and feared lion, tiger, or bear. I tried my best to glare at her, but she was unimpressed. She grinned a toothy, werewolf grin and waggled her claws at me.

A more dignified man would have protested his mother's affections, but I was too tired to fight her, and I enjoyed the attention—and the certainty if I did land a bite, her virus would take care of the injury in short order. I wondered if Ernesto had meant to bolster my mother's virus enough to trigger her first shift.

Knowing him, it could go either way.

Hospitals were a terrible place for lycanthropes, especially one still riding the high of her first shift. Since holding me would keep Mom out of trouble, Dad put her in charge of making sure no one thought about touching me.

Dad annoyed me sometimes. The arrangement kept me and Mom from doing anything Dad didn't want us doing, leaving him to play guard and lead the way. Two hybrid werewolves in the same place were more than most Chicagoans could readily handle, and they gave us plenty of room. A single snarl terrified the woman behind the glass at the ER's entry.

"Let me," Pierina murmured, patting my father's arm and sliding between him and the nurse. "We're here to see Marian Peterson. She is with my brother, Quinton Saven, and has a broken wrist. We're family." The vampire twisted around so she could point at me. "He is her partner, which can be verified by the CDC or through an incubus or succubus."

The nurse paled enough I was worried

she'd faint. "The CDC arrived ten minutes ago," she squeaked.

"Good. Where are they?"

Pierina took several minutes to cajole the information out of the nurse, who tried to protest we had no proof of our relationship with Marian. Dad looked the other way when the vampire resorted to using her preternatural charms. Mom followed Dad's lead, but I squirmed in my mother's hold to watch.

I wasn't sure what Pierina did, but she stared the nurse in the eyes. Within a minute, the nurse's posture relaxed, and a dreamy smile spread across her lips. Within two minutes, she was answering the vampire's questions in a murmur too soft for me to hear.

"They were going to operate on her wrist, but someone intervened; they've taken her to a recovery room on the fifth floor. The CDC has a few people here, so they can check your wife's virus levels and make sure everything's going well with her shift, Mr. Gibson." Pierina dared to approach my mother, which made my parents growl. "They'll also be able to check Gibby."

My father huffed, and after a few moments, I realized he laughed. "Gibby?"

"Blame my brother. He started it."

Turning to me, Dad poked my nose with a claw. "We will have a long talk over your choice of friends, pup. And once we are done

talking about that, we are going to have another long talk about why you were dining at
an exclusive restaurant with your woman instead of coming to visit us."

While Mom was smart enough to keep
her hands out of my reach, cranky, formal-
mode Dad either thought I wouldn't bite or
didn't care if I did. I latched onto his finger
behind his claw, clamped down, and held on.
He flattened his ears and bared his teeth
at me.

I bit him harder.

Pierina cleared her throat. "Perhaps if you
wouldn't poke him, he wouldn't bite you?"

"He needs to learn to control his teeth,"
Dad growled.

"But he's otterly adorable, Justin. Look at
him! How can you resist that face?" Mom
lifted me up, forcing me to choose between
clinging to Dad's hand or being the rope in a
game of tug-of-war. I released Dad and
sighed while my mother rubbed her muzzle
against mine. "We should take him and his
woman home with us."

"We can't take home an FBI agent because
we feel like it." Dad sounded rather disappointed, which worried me—and might benefit me later when I told them I intended to
kidnap her so she'd have to marry me and
wear tight jeans whenever I wanted.

Then again, if they found out my side of

the bet, they might join forces with her. I'd have to be careful about how I presented my case.

"We'll see about that," my mother swore.

IT TOOK HALF an hour to cross the hospital; every security guard we met believed they could take on a pair of lycanthropes and win. Any other day, I would've found the situation amusing. However, my mother's hold on me was the only thing between the well-meaning but prejudiced idiots and a very messy death, so I really hoped they got their shit sorted out before someone got hurt.

Dad handled their behavior better than I expected. He didn't bite a single person. The first security guard to seriously challenge him was a woman who didn't hide the fact she knew was pretty and thought she could charm my father into leaving until she got a good look down his throat. Brandishing a gun at a cop was stupid in my opinion, and she deserved to have her weapon crushed into a useless hunk of scrap metal.

A lot of bystanders learned a valuable lesson about cranky werewolves: they didn't need a gun to be dangerous.

"It's not my fault she pointed a gun at me,"

Dad growled. I'd lost count of the number of times he'd presented the same argument.

"It's probably better she pointed it at him and not you, Mrs. Gibson. We'd be picking bits of security guard out of our hair for months," Pierina said, grinning at my mother. "I haven't had this much fun in centuries."

Another pair of security guards approached us as we neared Marian's room, both men, both old enough they should have known better, and neither looking happy to see us. "Excuse me, but you're not supposed to be here."

Dad twitched and turned to Pierina. "Is everyone in this city stupid?"

"Yes. I'll handle this." Pierina opened her mouth, showed her fangs, and hissed. "You're in the way of a man visiting his future daughter-in-law. He's very protective and has violent tendencies when provoked. You're provoking him. He's also a visiting cop from a different city. Unless you *want* to be ripped to pieces, remember you have no right to bar visitation based on species alone. I recommend you move, or you will be moved."

"This is a hospital, not a zoo."

If I'd been human and able to speak I would've begun giving the old man his last rites. Pierina lunged forward, captured the man's throat in her hands, and squeezed until he choked and gasped to breathe. "Fortunately for you, this is a hospital. If I'm delayed one more moment, you'll be occupying the ICU ward for much of your remaining lifespan. Should I drag you with me so others might remember lycanthropes aren't the only dangerous species in this city, *human?*"

If I'd been human rather than an otter shifter, I would have been a lot more insulted by the way she spat the word, as though every last one of Earth's problems began and ended with my species. Then again, she made a good point. Humans caused problems for everyone, especially themselves.

Maybe the guards had an issue with werewolves, but messing with a vampire was enough to break the second one's nerve, and he held his hands up in a gesture of surrender. "It's dangerous for the other patients…"

The last sound I wanted to hear was Ernesto's rumbling chuckles directly behind me. "If you want your patients to be in danger, you're going about it the right way. Dear daughter, do put the nice man down. It wouldn't do to crush his windpipe. The doctors here would be oh so inconvenienced should something tragic happen. It would sting their pride if they had to send one of their employees to a different hospital."

Ouch.

"Papa," Pierina complained, although she

eased her hold on the guard. "But I was just starting to have fun with him."

"It's rude to play with your dinner. If you're going to have a drink, drag him off and have a drink, but don't do it in the hallway. I taught you better than that. If you need bail money, call me. I'd also like to point out I received a call that not one, but *two* of my beloved children were in the hospital after someone bombed my daughter's restaurant, where my dear boy and his lovely lady were dining. Do you know what that might be about, Pierina?"

If the guards could have paled any further, they would have.

"Papa!"

"Pierina," her father replied in a perfect mockery of her complaint. "Put the human down. Wouldn't it be much faster if you let them show us to Miss Peterson's room? Then you can tell me why I received such a phone call."

I enjoyed knowing I wasn't the only one stuck with a parent able to go from reasonable to bat-shit crazy and scary in less than ten seconds flat.

After shooting a glare at her father, Pierina turned to the guard. "Miss Peterson's room. Take us there."

"Politely," Ernesto chided.

"Please."

The ancient vampire sighed as though his daughter tested every last iota of his patience. "Please forgive my daughter. If you wouldn't mind, sirs, could you please show us to Miss Peterson's room?"

"Suck up," Pierina muttered.

Ernesto grabbed his daughter in a head lock and tucked her close to his side. "Now would be nice."

The security guard rubbed his throat and exchanged a long look with his partner, who gulped and gestured down the hall. "This way, sir."

THIRTY-ONE

Is there a reason you threw our son
across the room?

DAD TOOK ME FROM MOM, and before
anyone thought to stop him, he chucked me
through the doorway into Marian's room. I
squealed, hit the bed, and bounced off,
smacking into the floor and sprawling in a
stunned heap.

Aiming me towards the head of the bed
rather than the foot would have increased the
probability of an intervention. Then again, I
probably deserved to be tenderized a little,
but did Dad have to make it hurt so much?
Groaning, I struggled to remember which
end was up.

"Is there a reason you threw our son
across the room?" Mom asked, her tone deceptively calm.

I would miss Dad if Mom decided to
murder him over my short flight across Marian's hospital room.

"That won't kill him."

I'd remember those words when I planned my revenge for being tossed around like a toy. Getting up was too much work, so I stretched out, sighed, and indulged in feeling sorry for myself.

"I believe Mr. Gibson meant for you to catch him, Miss Peterson," Ernesto said. "I believe his judgment regarding your current ability to intercept flying otters is impaired."

The bed squeaked, and Marian giggled. "Flying otter."

A man cleared his throat, and I recognized Dr. Yasolovic's voice. "Please forgive Miss Peterson. She was recently given painkillers so one of my colleagues can properly fuse the bones in her wrist. The CDC doesn't want her to suffer any impairment. This hospital has an unfortunate reputation concerning the care of humans with talents others perceive as inconvenient or unwanted."

No kidding.

"Tiny flying otter," the FBI agent contributed, still giggling.

Hands—human hands—grabbed me around my middle and lifted me up. I blinked at Dr. Yasolovic. He made a thoughtful noise and set me on the bed at Marian's feet, poking and prodding at me. "Perhaps throwing the otter was not the wisest of choices, Mister...?"

"Gibson," Ernesto answered. "The otter's father. The red werewolf is his mother, and it's her first shift."

"I trust you'll keep your mate contained, Mr. Gibson. Should you need sedatives to keep her calm, I can prescribe them. I'll have to call in someone else to handle Shane's examination. I wouldn't know what a healthy otter looked like if you slapped me in the face with one."

"I'm fine," my mother growled.

"Oh! Communicative already? That's excellent. You may as well come in. There's no reason to lurk in the doorway. Make yourselves comfortable, procure some chairs, have a seat." Dr. Yasolovic pulled out his cell and made a call, requesting for a vet able to do a full physical on an otter of unknown species, adding I was probably injured in some fashion or another. When finished, he pocketed the device, took hold of my head, and held me in a firm grip while he examined my right eye. "I find it intriguing the glass eye shifted with him."

Everyone came into the room and found places to sit or hover, something done in relative quiet while Marian watched, her gaze slow and dulled from painkillers. Mom leaned over the FBI agent, sniffing with one ear pricked forward and the other twisted back. I watched, tensing but waiting to see what my mother would do.

Mom licked Marian from chin to hairline, and I sighed over the embarrassment of having two overly affectionate werewolves for parents.

"Gross," Marian complained, waving her left hand in front of her face, as though the flopping, feeble motion would somehow make the smell of wolf breath dissipate faster. She had a lot to learn about werewolves, like the fact she'd be smelling wolf breath for at least an hour.

Instead of backing off, Mom licked her again.

I sighed.

"Patsy, you're embarrassing our puppy."

Dad's words only encouraged Mom to upgrade her tokens of affections from licks to nuzzles, resulting in the oversized red hybrid werewolf half crawling onto the bed. Drugged and with her right arm in a sling, Marian was unable to fend off my mother, and her giggle-laden protests didn't help matters, either.

Of the two sane people left in the room, Ernesto would add fuel to the fire to watch it burn, so I turned to Dr. Yasolovic.

"Don't look at me. I'm not coming between a new werewolf bitch and the target of her affection. Be grateful it's not you."

"He already had a round," my father said, coming to the foot of the bed and scooping me up. "How long until Marian's wrist heals?"

"Four to seven days to be safe; she doesn't benefit from lycanthrope blood quite like your son does. While we could speed her recovery a little with the virus, it would cause high fevers and general discomfort. Your son's recovery rate is essentially a talent—a rather impressive one. There aren't many natural-born shifters around, but he's the first I've seen with the same general resilience as a werewolf. There aren't many with his parentage, either. Werewolf children are either infected at birth or are resistant to the virus. Should you two decide to have another child, I'd be interested in monitoring the pregnancy and development. We might learn more how to identify shifters who haven't undergone their first shift."

With the current chaos in my life, I didn't want anyone encouraging my parents to have another child. I squeaked and squealed, waving my paws at Dr. Yasolovic in my desperation to change the subject.

"Shane, behave," Dad growled, tapping the top of my head with a knuckle. "Should we decide to inflict a second child on our son, I'll keep that in mind."

"Please do. I look forward to visiting an area that isn't infested with overly haughty humans lacking basic common sense."

"Onto more important business. Someone tried to kill my son and his woman. How can we get involved and can the CDC help?" Dad passed me over to Pierina, who decided I was best worn draped across her shoulders.

Dr. Yasolovic smiled. "That depends on a few things, Mr. Gibson. Someone close the door."

Ernesto reached it first. "My children and I will be assisting, as will my brother. We have three theories about the attack, and I'm very interested in aiding the investigation."

Although the FBI hunted the vampire with more enthusiasm than the CDC would ever invest, I suspected the CDC had their reasons to either want Ernesto gone—or acquire his cooperation. Since vampires counted as sentients—formerly human ones —they received benefits demons and other races didn't. On a DNA level, vampires classified as human despite the magic granting them unlife and a thirst for blood.

"Once my colleague arrives and handles fusing Miss Peterson's wrist, we can get more details from her about the attack, but I don't think either one of them noticed anything. Everything she told me before I had her dosed with painkiller gave me the impression they were focused on each other and little else. Shane was seated with his back to the canal, so he wouldn't have seen anything. I believe he gave her the seat with a view of the third level; a section of the wall there is translucent so diners may see events. Is that correct, Miss Saven?"

"Correct. Gibby was seated facing the restaurant, and yes, where Marian was seated is the ideal viewing spot of the entry to the abyss. I had the table set that way in the slim hope she might see something interesting. Gibby's not really interested in that sort of thing, so whenever he's on the balcony, he's usually facing the restaurant."

Dr. Yasolovic grunted, pulled a slim book from his pocket, and jotted down a note. "How often does he go to your restaurant?"

"Every couple of months, but it's been a while; I'd say maybe five months—he hadn't been in since the accident." Pierina scratched under my chin, and I enjoyed it more than I probably should have. "It definitely looks like they were the targets; the explosive went off right beneath the balcony, destroying its supports."

Mom straightened, set her clawed, furry hand on the bed beside Marian, and twisted to face Ernesto's daughter. "You're certain?"

"Positive. I know my building like the back of my hand—I helped build it, I helped design it. I would guess some sort of grenade was used, tossed from the sidewalk. Quinton? Did you see anything from the front?"

I hadn't noticed Ernesto's son lurking in the corner of the room, standing between the window and one of the machines rolled out of the way. "I was answering a phone call about a reservation."

While my parents had more problems than they could shake a stick at, they were still cops, and the hunt for the culprit lured them both into the discussion. Dad was tense, a growl slipping out of him every now and then. Mom hopped a few steps towards Quinton and landed in a crouch, her teeth bared. "How long before the detonation?"

"No more than a minute."

"The conversation. Do you remember it? Are you normally near the door?" Mom sniffed, stretching her head towards Ernesto's son. "You smell of her blood."

"She was cut when she fell. I reached her first, and when I saw no sign of Gibby, she became my priority." Quinton shrugged. "I was outside when the second detonation occurred—the one that broke the grate for the canal. Quick job, not well planned. Had it been planned in advance, they would have gotten the entire grate rather than just a section of it. I believe Gibby was their target, however."

My mother crept forward, her ears flattening. "Why?"

"They left when he didn't surface. I could feel them watching." The vampire hissed, flexing his hands. "I recognized a predator hunting, waiting for his prey to emerge. I know the scent of satisfaction. He thought he'd won."

"He?"

"I could smell him."

Dad growled. "Close, but not too close. How sensitive is your nose?"

"Not as sensitive as yours, werewolf," Quinton replied. "Papa's nose is better."

"Is the scent still there?"

"Likely gone now. The cops do as they do, bringing too many people who have no real interest in finding the truth."

I could guess why, especially with my name on the victim list. My stunt at the shooting range wouldn't have earned me any friends, and after my resignation and the court trial, it wouldn't be surprised if they were disappointed I'd survived.

Mom clacked her teeth together, flexing her hands as though restraining herself from taking a swipe at something—or someone. "If you smelled him again, would you know him?"

"Yes. I have a long memory. I won't forget,

not until his blood flows down my throat and his life sustains mine."

I added a bloodthirsty, infuriated vampire to my list of problems. Marian burst into laughter, and I leveled a glare at the woman. If anything, when she noticed me watching her, her mirth intensified.

Ernesto glanced in my direction, and he chuckled. "What do you find so amusing, dear girl?"

"Two angry werewolves, three pissed-off vampires, the world's cutest little otter..." Instead of getting to the point and saying what exactly she found so funny about the combination, she dissolved into helpless giggles.

"I may have given her too much medication," Dr. Yasolovic admitted. "I thought I'd err on the side of caution. Young Quinton informed me the Gibsons were in town and might respond adversely to her being in pain, especially with Mrs. Gibson being so close to her first shift. Close wasn't an exaggeration, I've noticed."

Young Quinton? I twisted around on Pierina's shoulder and regarded the ancient vampire with a canted head. While I wanted to ask questions—complete ones, in English—I settled with an inquisitive chirp.

"Gibby knows roughly how old I am." Quinton laughed. "You are not as sly as you think."

Dr. Yasolovic scowled. "Vampires," he spat.

Over Marian's laughter, Pierina cleared her throat. "We need to hunt. Don't waste time. First, we need to decide who'll stay and protect Gibby's woman—and how to get Gibby to shift back to human."

"I will guard her," Dr. Yasolovic said, dismissing Pierina's concerns with a flippant wave of his hand. "As for Shane, you may wish to leave him as he is for a while, if his health checks out. He shifted for a reason, and forcing another shift may exhaust him more than necessary. With three pissed-off vampires and two angry werewolves guarding him, he should be perfectly safe. I wouldn't recommend irritating the frothing lycanthropes."

"Frothing?" Dad asked, his tone mild.

Without any evidence of fear, the doctor pointed at my mother, who had a bit of foam along her jaw, the result of her growling and gnashing her teeth at the same time. "I'm genuinely impressed she hasn't bitten anyone yet —and trusted your child with a vampire."

"I'll eat her if she hurts him," Mom growled.

She meant it, too. What would happen if my parents went up against Ernesto and his brood? I suspected a lot of bloodshed and maiming on both sides. I sighed, twisted around, and did the only thing I could. I hid my head in Pierina's hair, covered my eyes with my paws, and wished I could disappear.

No such luck. Dad chuckled, and a moment later, he plucked me from Pierina's shoulders. "And you're confident you can protect her?"

"The man I called in is an exotic species specialist, and his magic rating is in the upper tiers. The surgeon specializes in breaking people apart and putting them back together again. He has no problem breaking them apart and neglecting to put them back together again. I have a few tricks up my sleeve." Dr. Yasolovic glanced at Quinton. "Right, young Quinton?"

Vampires could move fast, and in the time it took me to blink, Quinton relocated to a safe spot conveniently behind his father. "Right."

"I think I'll be fine, Mr. Gibson. You have bigger fish to fry."

THIRTY-TWO

Whatever she was, she scared the
piss out of the staff.

THE HOSPITAL PROTESTED USING their precious CT scanner on me, an animal, starting a
second battle with the CDC, one Dr. Yasolovic had obviously planned to have
happen all along. When his colleagues arrived, they brought a suitcase, one filled with
forms—the type of forms I'd seen too many
times in the recent past. Although Ernesto
was present, I decided the doctor was the
most intimidating—and possibly dangerous
—sentient in the room.

We would have to wait an hour, but instead of an x-ray, I was scheduled for a full
MRI since the hospital's CT scanner was already booked for use. That pleased Dr. Yasolovic enough he put away his forms,
although he kept the briefcase handy and left
me in the care of the exotic species specialist,
Dr. Valentine. She took no shit from anyone,

and only had to snap a single clipboard in half to teach the obstinate hospital staff the meaning of fear.

She wasn't a werewolf or a shifter, which I deduced from the conversations around me. Whatever she was, she scared the piss out of the staff, who bolted from the room as though the devil himself chased them. The resulting smell offended my sensitive nose so much I yipped curses at them.

Dad sighed, pinched his nostrils closed, and breathed out of his mouth. "It might be more efficient if we flew him to Lincoln, called in Dr. Harting, and asked her to handle this."

"Patience," Dr. Valentine murmured, stroking her hand down my back. "An MRI is our best option. Even though he shifted, I'll be able to evaluate his injuries from the attack, which I can record for a trial, should there be one."

Mom canted her head to the side, crouched with her hands flat on the floor, a position Dad used when he wanted people to think he wasn't a threat. In reality, if my mother wanted to attack someone, she was in the best stance for a strong leap. Werewolf legs were strong, and werewolves often pretended they were demented, living springs, jumping distances normal humans could never hope to match.

From my perch on the examination table, I had a good view of Dad keeping a close watch on my mother, his ears pricked forward while his tail twitched. The tail twitching bothered me. It meant one of two things.

He could be struggling to contain his good humor, or he could be fighting his more violent tendencies. With Mom's posture and tense muscles, I bet on the latter.

Ernesto and his two children waited by the door, tense and on guard. Against whom I wasn't sure. I thought they liked my parents, but with Mom in the midst of her first shift, but I wouldn't be surprised if they considered her a threat.

I certainly did.

Dad broke the silent standoff with a huff and shook as though ridding his fur of water. His glare settled on the closed door. "This is the hospital that treated Shane."

"According to his medical file and our own research into the matter, his eye truly couldn't be saved. They did a better than average job on the scar mitigation as well, and while the false eye is inferior, the measurements were excellent."

"They'll treat his woman well?"

"Dr. Yasolovic will ensure she receives the best care. It would reflect rather poorly on the CPD if an FBI agent received anything other than the best. I expect he'll insist she be transferred to a different medical facility, one either associated with the FBI or in a different city. I'll recommend against a different city unless your son goes with her, as he wouldn't react well to separation."

Dad huffed again. "Why?"

"Because Asian small-clawed otters are a monogamous species. Miss Peterson is in for quite a surprise when she learns his bite packs a great deal more of a punch than hers. Her species is not monogamous, but I'm sure she'll readily adapt."

My mother rose, resting her hands on her knees. "What's her species?"

Laughing, Dr. Valentine shook her head. "That would ruin the fun. You'll discover it soon enough on your own, I'm sure. Most shifters are, by nature, shy about their second forms. In part, this is due to being mistaken for lycanthropes. When she wants you to know her species, she'll tell you—and she'll do so in an amusing fashion."

I thought about what Dr. Valentine had said, then sucked in a breath at the memory of the stuffed animal Marian had used to hide the Rugers. Chirping, I hopped across the table, snatched up Dr. Valentine's pen, and struggled to find the best way to hold it in my hand-like paws. With a chuckle, she flipped over a sheet of paper and held it still for me.

Badger?

I tapped the paper to indicate I wanted an answer and hoped she wouldn't judge me for my wretched scrawl. I should've been happy I could write at all since normal otters couldn't as far as I knew.

"Indeed. Now, keep that to yourself, Mr. Gibson. She'd appreciate having the chance to reveal it—or not—to the others." Dr. Valentine ripped the paper into tiny pieces, and to ensure no one cheated and taped it back together to learn Marian's secret, she ate it.

"So our son is an Asian small-clawed otter?" Mom asked.

Dr. Valentine picked me up, holding me with one hand while she gestured at my head with the other. "His species is the smallest of the otter family, although he's rather small for an adult. Interestingly, his species spends the vast majority of their time on land."

Mom flattened her ears. "Are otters even compatible with other shifter species?"

"If your motivation behind that question involves grandchildren, I assure you there will be no problems in that department. Genetically, they're human. Miss Peterson will be advised to exercise caution unless she wants to single-handedly increase the birthrate of their state of residence."

The glee in my mother's grin disgusted me. "Excellent."

"Patsy, you will not hide our future daughter-in-law's birth control, nor will you interfere in any way with their decision on when—or if—they have children."

I truly had the best father.

Pierina clucked her tongue. "At least give Gibby a chance to marry the woman first. He was trying so hard to court her, then someone went and ruined his efforts."

Ernesto leaned against the wall beside the door and crossed his arms over his chest. "How was their mood before the explosion?"

"Gibby and his woman?"

"Yes."

"High-spirited and playful. He was rather like an eager child hoping to impress his first love with the little things he treasured. Whenever I sent Quinton or one of our brothers to check on them, they were far too occupied with each other to pay attention to much else. I thought it was going well. Gibby?"

I wished Dr. Valentine would put me down. Clapping my paws together seemed like the best way to inform Pierina I was less than impressed with her analysis of my evening with Marian.

"So shy," she teased.

It turned out otters could, with a little work, flip someone the middle finger.

I THOROUGHLY ENJOYED WATCHING Dr. Valentine browbeat the doctors, MRI techs, and nurses at the hospital, as she made it clear she had no tolerance for anything less than their best. She'd made enemies of the staff within a few sentences, but at least they handled her displeasure better than their co-workers.

No one had the piss scared out of them, for which I was grateful.

Since my job during the MRI was to keep still and behave, I made the most of my situation and tried to nap. Unfortunately, the machine made thumping noises, which killed any hope of falling asleep. Fortunately, my small size meant the procedure didn't take long to finish. When Dr. Valentine came to retrieve me, I yawned and wobbled in her direction.

"You're a very lucky man, Mr. Gibson. Had you been a vanilla human or an infected lycanthrope pre-shift, you would be rather dead right now." I gaped at her, stiff with surprise, and she reached out and touched the middle of my spine. "From our limited understanding of shifters, we've come to the conclusion that most first shifts are induced by some form of trauma, which can show on medical scans as discolorations or shadows marking where the transformation process healed equivalent organs and tissue. Your spine showed these shadows, as well as most of your organs, with your lungs and kidneys suffering extensive amounts of damage. In humans, these organs are located near the spine, so I suspect the fall was the source of your injuries. Involuntary shifting typically addresses life-threatening injuries, leaving behind those shadows as evidence of trauma."

I added 'falling onto my back from a second-story balcony' to my list of experiences never to repeat.

"Here's the bad news. When you shift back to human, those life-threatening injuries will have been addressed, but you're going to be rather miserable. We'll want to handle your shift in a controlled environment, with one or more surgeons on hand in case anything goes wrong. I'm going to recommend we take advantage of your unusual response to the lycanthropy virus and do a transfusion upon your reversal and monitor your health from there. Do not misunderstand me; shifting is not a cure-all. Your first shift is the only one with any guarantee of fixing otherwise fatal injuries. There are theories on why. My favorite is that the first shift comes with a rather intense magical burst. Future shifts don't have the same potency. Shifters aren't invulnerable. Do try to keep that in mind."

I bobbed my head to acknowledge I'd received her message. Assuming I could stop getting into trouble, I might survive long enough to enjoy my lengthened lifespan.

Dr. Valentine picked me up and carried me out of the room, pausing in the hallway to dump me in my mother's arms—my mother's human arms. Someone had found her a pair of sweats, and she cuddled me while Dad hovered, still in his hybrid form.

Of the three vampires, I saw no sign.

"You can take him out. I'll handle all the paperwork. Remember what I told you. Don't try to get him to shift, let him get a lot of rest, and feed him. While otters favor seafood, he'll eat almost anything. Shifters have rather adaptable digestive systems." Dr. Valentine pulled a card from her wallet and handed it to my father. "Call me if there are any issues. And Mr. Gibson?"

"Yes?" my father replied.

"If I hear that you tossed your child across a room again, I will do a very close examination of your ass with my foot. Am I understood?"

Dad ducked his head and mumbled something.

Dr. Valentine cleared her throat.

"Yes, ma'am."

"Good. Enjoy your hunt. If you have to leave any of them alive, try to keep them in tolerable condition. Nothing leaves a bad taste in my mouth like being forced to give medical care to would-be cop killers. It's illegal to make their treatment as painful as possible." Dr. Valentine heaved a sigh, shook her head, and marched down the hall, her chin lifted just high enough she could peer down her nose at anyone stupid enough to get in her way.

"Now that's one hell of a woman," Mom muttered.

"No kidding. Let's get out of here before she finds out we've been tossing our brat around since he was old enough to bounce."

ERNESTO and his children waited outside the hospital in an SUV with windows dark enough to protect even young vampires from the sun. Fitting into the vehicle was a tight squeeze, as Dad refused to shift out of his hybrid form and insisted on sitting as close to Mom as possible. I'd had enough of my clingy parents and took the first opportunity to escape, picking Quinton as least likely to bite me, continue the cuddling trend, or otherwise do anything but serve as a seat.

Next time, I'd remember Quinton was his father's son. Since I couldn't kneecap the bloodsucker, he took advantage and treated me like a pet for his amusement. Sighing over my lot in life, I turned my glare in Ernesto's direction.

I'd have to have a long talk with the vampire about teaching his children I wasn't a toy for their amusement.

"What's the first item on our list?" I hadn't pegged Ernesto as the type to drive, but he approached Upper Chicago as though it were a challenge to overcome, viewing traffic laws as basic guidelines. I suspected he mostly avoided breaking the law to keep the peace in the vehicle. If my parents noticed his minor misdeeds, they made no mention of them, so I followed their lead.

I'd enjoy yanking Ernesto's chain about it later.

"Back to the restaurant for a better look at the crime scene. Quinton, I want you to try to pick up that scent trail again." Dad growled softly between breaths. "Until his woman's off the painkillers, we won't be able to get more info from her. I suspect she'll want to help, so we should probably keep her in the dark as much as possible."

"I trust Dr. Yasolovic to handle her."

I found that interesting; trust was an odd word when it came to vampires.

"I don't suppose you can enlighten us about those doctors, can you? Dr. Yasolovic and Dr. Valentine, no matter how human they look, don't smell like humans." As much as Dad was growling, I worried he'd lose control before Mom did.

A moment later, Dad yelped. "Behave," Mom ordered.

The more things changed, the more they stayed the same.

"They're no threat to Shane or Miss Peterson. That's all you need to know."

I missed being able to communicate in English. I yipped my annoyance, twisted on Quinton's lap, and bit his wrist.

"Something tells me Gibby's not happy," Ernesto's son reported.

Vampires tasted terrible, but I kept gnawing on him, using my paws to hold his hand steady while I took out my frustration on his wrist. If I turned my head sideways and squinted, I could pretend biting was similar to kneecapping. Vampires liked when I kneecapped them. Quinton could handle a few bites. He wouldn't even notice the marks after a few hours and some time with one of his girls and his succubus partner.

Mom laughed. "Considering how much Shane enjoys running his mouth, he's probably upset he can't contribute to the conversation or make himself useful. He's never happy unless he's doing something productive. Shane, darling, you can help investigate things at the crime scene. Stop trying to separate your friend's hand from the rest of his body. That's rude."

With a low, rumbling chuckle, Ernesto said, "You should see him with a gun. He always goes for the knees first. It's so charming. Quinton, work with your sister and keep an eye on him. I'll work with the Gibsons to thoroughly check the restaurant. Pierina, I'll be meddling in your affairs. You can suitably punish me later."

"Of course, Papa. The office computers at the restaurant weren't damaged, so you can access the call records there. You may need to take them to your office; power was out the last I heard. You'll be able to get the phone number of the caller from the system. If that takes too much time, I'll call the phone company and get the number personally."

"Good. Quinton, once we're at the restaurant, give your uncle a call and fill him in. Go on a walk around the block, get a good sniff of those who've been around, and hit the other side of the canal. If you can get a closer look at the damage to the grate, do so."

Quinton stroked my back with his free hand. "A suggestion, Papa?"

"It always worries me when you strive to

prove you're capable of independent thought."

"We should extend our apologies to our friends below for having disturbed their evening. I might be able to retrieve Gibby's things, too."

Vampires made a variety of sounds, but Ernesto's growl came close to a werewolf's in its intensity. "You want an excuse to go down the slide."

"I thought Gibby might appreciate a chance to experience it in a more controlled fashion."

Ernesto sighed. "Talk the cranky werewolves into it. I don't care. Maybe you can bribe those below for help. I might forgive you for being capable of independent thought if you do something useful for a change instead of causing me problems."

I was glad I wasn't the only one with a crazy family.

THIRTY-THREE

You're as bad as a pissy cat.

QUINTON HAD no trouble convincing my parents the safest place for me was the most dangerous place in all of Chicago. Instead of making a break for freedom and finding a good place to hide, I went along with the stupid plan to take a swim in the canal's fetid waters and descend into the abyss.

Of course, my parents didn't know monsters lurked beneath the streets of Lower Chicago, and I couldn't make my uncooperative tongue speak English. Quinton presented our venture as exploring a rather large cave most people avoided because they were afraid of the dark.

Dad fell for it hook, line, and sinker. I doubted he'd ever confess a single fear to vampires—or anyone else for that matter.

Before our side trip into the abyss, Quinton and I took a long walk around Pierina's restaurant, crossed to the other side of the canal, and investigated every spot with a view of the balcony. We weren't able to access two possible locations, second story balcony and several third story windows and another balcony, which Quinton regarded with a frown.

So many scents clogged my nose I couldn't make sense of them, and I lashed my tail instead of squealing my frustration, which would draw unwanted attention to us.

"You're as bad as a pissy cat, Gibby. The balconies up there are possibilities, but I doubt it. I'm betting it was a one-person job. There's enough foot traffic if he used a sticker and a short-delay fuse, no one would have noticed, and if he used a long enough fuse, he'd have plenty of time to get in position to drop the grenade against the grate after you fell in the water. On this side, he would've been able to judge where you'd fall in and hit the grate. One easy toss and all his problems are solved."

I hated stickers; the adhesive clung to just about everything, and bomb makers loved being able to set their devices anywhere they wanted. Someone with good aim could plant a grenade and walk off without worrying their explosive would come loose.

Stickers had one saving grace. The

damned things were expensive, which deterred the hacks, and the pros preferred more sophisticated methods. The nastiest pros enjoyed playing lethal games of cat and mouse with the police, using innocent lives as the prize.

I'd never qualified to serve on the bomb squad, but I'd done my research. If someone had used a sticker, he was better than an amateur but not as good as a pro, or he'd been paid enough to ignore his professional pride and take on a quick, dirty job.

Most of the real professionals wouldn't touch ex-cops, not without leaving their mark.

I could only nod in agreement with Quinton's assessment.

"Papa would have my head on a platter if I did such an inelegant job."

Of course Ernesto would. When Ernesto made people disappear, he went to extremes —or had Donovan go to extremes. If he found out who'd been responsible for the destruction of his daughter's precious restaurant, the panty incident on the Franklin Street bridge would pale in comparison. The bodies of all involved would be found, and their guilt would be made known in as humiliating a fashion as possible.

I wanted to find the bomber myself. I

could deal with someone coming after me, but he'd hurt Marian. Her choice of career told me she could take care of herself.

I didn't care.

Someone had hurt her trying to get me, and I couldn't forgive that. In that, I was my father's son. It began to truly sink in that someone hadn't just tried to kill me—they had succeeded. Without the magic of my first shift, I would have died.

If the grate hadn't broken, I probably would have drowned. Even if it hadn't, I'd heard Dr. Valentine's assessment.

Magic had kept me breathing, and I wouldn't get so lucky a second time.

"All right, Gibby. You'll want to hold your breath for a moment. I'd rather not have to explain to Papa you drowned. Since someone conveniently left the grate open, I see no need to take the harder way."

Curiosity consumed me as the vampire's words confirmed there was a way to the third level without going through the canal. I supposed it was better I didn't learn what it was.

I had a rather bad habit of poking my nose in places I didn't belong.

Quinton strolled along the canal to the hole in the grate. While the police had set up a tape cordon, but no one guarded it. I found their negligence both tiresome and amusing.

No one in their right mind deliberately went into the abyss, so why waste manpower guarding a hole in the canal's grate? The locals knew corpses rotted in the water, no one in their right mind wanted to fall in.

I suspected Quinton used some sort of vampire magic to keep people from noticing us. He held me to his chest with one hand, his grip firm enough I couldn't escape if I wanted to. "Hold your breath."

I took a deep breath and bobbed my head.

Quinton speared into the water feet first, angling for the canal's side to avoid the jagged, blasted metal. The chill water closed over us, and we emerged on the other side moments later. Smacking into the concrete slide feet first, the vampire took the full force of the landing, and his laughter rang out.

Unlike my haphazard descent, Quinton shot down the slick slope. My second trip down the spillway reinforced my initial impression a mad scientist and an engineer had gotten together to design the damned thing.

After the first loop-de-loop, I was glad Quinton had suggested I wait to eat until after our descent to the third level. The second loop left my head spinning, and by the time Quinton shot out of the third one into the air, I swore to get revenge on the entire Saven brood.

No net broke our fall, but Quinton entered the water feet first at an angle and lost his hold on me, leaving me to fend for myself in the utter darkness. I had no idea how an otter swam, but I discovered I could use my paws, tail, and long body to cut through the water after a few strokes.

I didn't go far before a hand grabbed my tail and yanked me out of the water. I yowled once and writhed before the vampire flipped me over to hold me under my forelegs. "Sorry. Didn't want to lose you in the current. Wasn't that fun?"

We bobbed in the water, and I slapped my head in the universal expression of disgust.

"You can't see a thing down here, can you?"

Flipping my middle finger might become my default mode of communication.

"All right, keep your pants on. Unless you want to take a one-way trip straight to hell, you should ride on my shoulders until I get us to shore. *I* can see down here. You'd probably find the one way to get sucked into the underground river and get killed. I can't tell if you're cursed or lucky sometimes."

Dumb vampires and their magical talents. Resenting him for his vision was ridiculous, but I couldn't help my feelings. My awareness of what I couldn't do as well hung over me every day. Grunting, I wiggled in his hold and scrambled along his arm to his shoulders, clinging to his jacket with my claws.

Quinton reached the shore and walked out of the water, one hand pressed to my back to keep me from falling from my perch. "We're close to the end of the darkness zone, so you may want to shut your eyes. It's rather bright on the other side."

I closed my left eye since the light wouldn't bother my fake one.

"It's really creepy when you do that. Have I told you that? While the color is rather interesting, knowing you can't see with it makes my skin crawl when it's the only one open. Have a little mercy."

I stuck my tongue out at him and left my right eye open.

"No wonder Papa likes you so much. You're an irreverent fellow sometimes. Ah, well. It's good for Papa to remember there are those who don't fear him as they probably should—and that there is someone who can beat him at his own game. I haven't had this much fun in a long time. Papa thinks men like you are catalysts. You bring people together. You divide them. Wherever you go, things change. Papa enjoys the challenge you create for him. You changed the nature of our game with the CPD. You changed the nature of our hunt for prey. Papa gets bored."

Of course Ernesto got bored. He'd been

alive since the dawn of humanity, dead long before anyone had thought to write their history down in words rather than pictures. I didn't know exactly how old he and his children were, but they played at being Etruscans, as the world had moved on without them, erasing their existence from the history books.

Pierina's restaurant, her bewitched ceilings, and the stories they told were their true history, the one forgotten by everyone else. Maybe one day I'd ask for more of their truth, but part of me hoped Ernesto would share it on his own.

I liked to think he understood me; he'd been a vampire long before humans had believed in magic.

Quinton was careful to keep his stride smooth, which made it easy for me to hold onto his shoulder so I wouldn't fall and add to my collection of bruises. "Papa will be angry, but I'll warn you now. I won't be surprised if our hosts ask for you to become human. It's their nature to be curious. They possess the skill to force you to shift. They also possess the skill to help you heal better than those hospitals."

The vampire spat the word as he would a curse, something I found interesting. I borrowed from my father's silent language and bumped my nose to Quinton's neck, giving him a brisk rub to indicate my approval. He laughed. "Your whiskers tickle. We're almost to the barrier. You will feel strange. Most humans claim it tingles. For me, it burns as though I've stepped beneath the noon sun; it doesn't harm me, but it's uncomfortable. Don't be alarmed at my hissing."

One day soon, I needed to have a long talk alone with Quinton. Vampires didn't drink alcohol, but I thought he'd be the sort I'd enjoy taking to a bar for a good bottle of Scotch.

I'd never think of Scotch the same ever again. It had brought Marian into my life.

Before I pulled a Dad and ripped Marian's kidnapper to pieces, I'd thank him for bringing her into my life, although I'd have to fight with Marian for the right and privilege of shredding the participants in the sex trafficking operation.

"Here we go," Quinton warned.

Lightning zapped me, and I yowled at the unexpected pain. I jerked so hard I toppled off Quinton's shoulder, and the vampire caught me with a hissed curse. I shuddered, my body twitching. Light pierced my eyelid, and I cracked it open.

Golden crystals jutted from beds of blue and black opal, reflecting the light of chandeliers swaying from the cavern's domed ceiling. The whisper of wind and tinkling of chimes teased my ears.

Quinton straightened, placed me on his shoulder, and lifted his chin, making no effort to disguise the pride and arrogance of someone who'd withstood thousands of years. "Welcome to Babylon, the City of Gardens."

Gripping his shoulder with my hind paws, I stood, stretching so I could get a better look at the vast cavern, so vast I couldn't imagine how it fit beneath Chicago—or how it had gone unnoticed. The ceiling peaked at a hundred feet, which put it near the surface.

"It has been long since you have darkened our doorway, Shepherd." The grind of stone on stone accompanied each word, and I twisted around in search of the voice. I dropped to all fours on the vampire's shoulder.

We were alone.

As though aware of my unease, Quinton rested his hand on my head. "I see you, Abil Ili. Please forgive my companion. He is still learning his second nature."

"I see you and yours. I would welcome you, but you always welcome yourself, so I will welcome yours instead. May you walk in peace in our gardens, friend I've yet to have the pleasure of meeting."

At a complete loss, I looked to Quinton for guidance.

"Abil Ili, this is Shane Gibson. Perhaps when he decides to stop being clever, Abil Ili will properly introduce himself. You know full well you can't hide from me with your trickery, but it's unfair to play such games with a youngling with but one eye and not yet taught to see you."

"So I am rebuked." Abil Ili chuckled, and one of the golden crystals moved. At first, I thought him human, but his similarities to a human began and ended with his pair of arms and legs. With the slow fade of a chameleon exposing itself, the golden crystal dissolved away to reveal a tall figure.

A mosaic of rainbow mirrors separated by thin bands of silver formed a carapace over an almost human chest. What I had initially mistaken to be arms were tentacles, tentacles that branched into seven curved claws, each one tipped with a glistening black hook. Fluid dripped off one, fell to the floor, and was absorbed by the stone at its feet, ridged with scales and taloned like a bird of prey's.

The crystals nearby glowed, and the sweet scent of flowers filled my nose. For a long time, I couldn't tear my gaze from the ground, which shimmered as though granted life.

"What has happened for you to darken our doorway, Shepherd?"

I jerked my head up and yipped at the close proximity of a mouth full of sharp fangs, the largest at least six inches long. A curved beak promised a quick death if Abil Ili decided he wanted an otter snack. I figured I'd be two decent bites. A crest of feathers rose from his head and, like his carapace, they were covered in prismatic mosaics.

"First, I wanted to notify you that the grate to the spillway has been damaged."

"Damaged?" Abil Ili reared his head back and hissed. "Who damaged it? Why?"

"It's a long story, and most of its telling belongs to our friend, but I think the intrigue of his words may be worth the price of his shifting and the soothing only the Babylonians can provide. I think you'll find him an even more intriguing patient, for he's a human who is nearly not."

If Quinton kept speaking in riddles, I'd have a headache in no time, but I wouldn't complain. For the moment, the pair spoke in English, allowing me to follow their conversation.

"What else do you desire from us?"

"I'd rather wait to discuss that until you've heard his story. It'll influence your decision, and I don't want you to make a decision in ignorance. But, I will say this. Someone has tried to murder him twice for the sin of helping another."

"It has been long since we have been amused by a human—especially one who is almost not. Very well. A bargain made and struck. Our soothing for your story." Abil Ili paused. "And I shall invite you to partake of our gardens, only because it will chafe your sire's nerves he cannot taste the flavors of his youth."

THIRTY-FOUR

Humans—even ones who are almost
not—are so curious.

THIRTY CHAMELEON-LIKE BABYLONIANS
emerged from their crystalline hiding places
and overwhelmed my ability to handle the
new and strange. Burrowing into Quinton's
jacket was rude, but hiding in a soggy vampire's clothing seemed a lot safer than facing
a group of predators as dangerous as
werewolves.

"I think we have distressed our new
friend," Abil Ili murmured.

"He's had a long day. Someone essentially
murdered him earlier today. That's hard on a
man."

"You would know this well, vampire."

"Maybe a more private audience with one
or two of your soothers might be wise. While
Shane is adaptable, I think he's at his limit.
His beloved was injured while he was

courting her, and we had to leave her with a capable guard."

I bit Quinton on basic principle. Why was he telling people Marian was my beloved when I hadn't said three most important words to her yet?

I hadn't had a chance to get to know her, but I recognized the truth of his words, which was why I bit him a second time and ripped his shirt in the process. The vampire laughed, subtly mocking my impotence and acknowledging he had bested me with his words.

"Who is this capable guard?"

Quinton switched to a fluid language, and his voice chimed from the golden crystals and rang in the air. The conversation didn't last long, but when they finished speaking, everything had quieted, even the whispering of the wind.

"It seems this story will be more intriguing than I believed. Humans—even ones who are almost not—are so curious."

"That's part of why I brought him. That, and I thought you might enjoy a hunt worthy of you."

"A hunt," Abil Ili echoed, and in his melodic voice, I could hear his longing.

"It's been a long time since we've hunted together, old friend."

"So it has. At least two millennia, when

the world was a much different place. This story. It will lead to the reason for this hunt?"

"Indeed."

"Very well. We will deal with this in the sapphire garden. That should be private enough, and I think it will suit our friend better than the others. Tell me what has befallen him, so we might best soothe him."

"Based on the tests done in the hospital, we believe an explosion collapsed the balcony he shared with his beloved, and he fell onto his back into the canal, went under, and hit the grate. The attacker blew out the grate with more explosives, sending him onto the spillway. What we don't know when he shifted; he may have shifted after he hit the water and went under. He's an otter, and they're aquatic by nature, so it's possible he shifted and slipped through the grate before it was damaged. Unfortunately, we have no way of knowing—and he may not remember. I've been informed most people don't remember their first shift, and there was evidence of a concussion."

"His chances of survival had the grate held?"

"Not quite zero but not good. The balcony was twenty feet above the canal surface—maybe a bit higher. I didn't check the water level. Between the spinal damage and the organ damage, Dr. Valentine didn't think he would've made it to a hospital even if someone had pulled him out right away."

"It intrigues me that it so often takes humans facing death to realize their full potential. I find it curious you have called our friend a child of your father's heart when he is so fragile." Abil Ili paused and sighed. "What other wisdom did San Valentina Gula impart?"

"She was worried and didn't want him to shift again until he was in her care. The human healers dislike him, for he took their evils and made them known."

"Coming from you, darkener of doorways, that is impressive."

Quinton laughed. "You're never going to let that go, are you?"

"Perhaps in a few decades. Come, then. You will be useful for this. I need you to hold him in thrall while we work."

"Papa will hang me from the highest tower if I bite him."

"I would not call it a bite, but rather a delicate nibbling—just enough to keep him from struggling, yes? If San Valentina Gula worries, then we worry, and so it goes."

"So it goes," the vampire agreed with a sigh. "Sorry, Gibby. If Abil Ili thinks it's necessary, then it's necessary."

Great. I found nothing soothing about the situation, but without a way to vocalize my misgivings, I was forced to accept my fate with a heavy sigh.

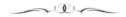

QUINTON PULLED me out of his jacket, looked me in the eye, and did something—something that made me a prisoner in my own body. Abil Ili reached out, and his claw pierced my shoulder near my spine. Pain flashed through my body, blinding in its intensity. When my vision cleared, I was human, sprawled on blue crystal with Quinton straddling my chest, his gaze locked on mine.

My right arm hung limp in his hand, and without breaking our eye contact, he brought my wrist to his mouth and bit down.

I understood why Ernesto and his brood partnered with demons; sharp but jagged teeth tearing through my skin hurt far worse than I could've imagined. Any other time, I would've screamed.

The vampire's bite woke every nerve in my body, and the agony in my back and chest exploded, searing away all other thought.

"San Valentina Gula did not exaggerate," Abil Ili murmured, and one of his hook-tipped claws traced the scar running from my brow down to my chin. With a twist of his tentacle, he stole my right eye, pulling it from the scarred socket with a soft pop. "This—

now this is a disgrace. This marble. They would inflict this thing upon one of their own? It is not art, it is not magic, it is nothing —*glass*."

Quinton released my wrist; my blood stained his lips and dripped down his chin. "More soothing, less yapping."

Then he bit me again, latching onto my wrist, and heat flared up my arm to my head. I expected fire but got ice deep in my skull, and what started as a shiver ended as a shuddering convulsion. My world narrowed to my chest and the stabbing pain each time I struggled to draw a breath.

I remembered the sensation; the instant I'd smacked into the canal, the air had rushed out of me, and with my next choked, gasping breath, I'd tasted blood. The water had flowed into my mouth, and I'd gone under.

Abil Ili stroked the back of his tentacle along my jaw to my throat. The moment he hooked his claw into my neck, my entire body jerked, and my head went numb. The edges of my vision grew hazy, but I saw several more of the mosaic-skinned Babylonians approaching with their claws dripping black fluid.

One by one, they pierced my skin with their hooks, and numbness spread from their touch.

Quinton's eyes remained locked on mine until I sank into a cold, dark void.

MY PHONE RANG. If I could get my hands on the wretched device, I'd fling it as hard as I could in the hope it'd shatter into a thousand pieces.

Wait. How could my phone be ringing? I remembered changing the ringtone on the new device to a shrill, evil sound meant to wake the dead, but I'd lost it when I'd fallen into the canal, hadn't I? Confusion paralyzed me until I remembered I needed to breathe, and I sucked in a breath.

"Have I ever told you that you're the worst example of false advertising I've ever met, Abil Ili?" Quinton grumbled. After the third ring, my phone fell silent. "Can you explain the clothes thing?"

"A rather useful talent for a shifter. He will enjoy not destroying his wardrobe whenever he desires to wear a fur coat," the Babylonian murmured. "The phone woke him."

Great, the tentacled, clawed terror knew I was awake. "That hurt," I rasped.

Quinton sighed. "Well, dying typically is painful. Sorry about the bite, Gibby. There's no way to make it hurt less without help. I didn't want to do it like that, but you thrashing around wouldn't have been good."

I shuddered at the memory of claws tearing through my skin. "That should classify as cruel and unusual punishment."

"You can kneecap me later as many times as you want."

"You don't have enough kneecaps for me to do that."

"I volunteer Papa's."

"Better." I groaned, cracked open my eye, and stared up at countless sapphire crystals encrusting the distant ceiling. "What was that about clothes?"

"When you shifted, your clothes shifted with you. I'm afraid your suit's ruined; we had to cut it off you. Your phone seems to have survived, along with your wallet. Cute guns."

"When a lady gives you cute guns, you carry them." I braced for pain and lurched upright, but beyond the pull of sore, aching muscles, I didn't hurt. They'd cut my suit off, but someone had found a replacement, and it fit better than the original. "I only own one suit, so who'd you mug for this one?"

"The determination of the Babylonians to be good hosts is unmatched. While Abil Ili and his soothers were tending to you, others decided to replace your attire."

"Thank you. How long have I been out?"

"Twelve hours. All things considered, not bad. I called Papa and told him we were occupied and you were safe. I didn't tell him what we were doing. He would've stormed the castle and fidgeted. It's so very annoying when he fidgets."

"No kidding," I muttered, shaking my head in the futile effort of clearing away the foggy feeling, as though my skull was stuffed full of cotton balls. Turning until I could see Abil Ili out of my left eye, I said, "Thank you."

"The honor is mine, my friend." The Babylonian's gaze shifted to Quinton. "You should tell him."

"Well, now I have to. And you call me a darkener of doorways."

"Tell me what?"

Sighing, Quinton reclined beside me, stretching his legs and wiggling his bare toes. "I haven't told Papa, but he'll find out soon enough. Pierina called."

My phone rang again, and with my eyes narrowing in suspicion, I reached over, grabbed it, and checked the display. Although I no longer hurt, my hands shook when I fumbled with the device, and it took two attempts to answer the call. "Gibson."

"*Shane!*" Marian shrieked in my ear. "Where are you? What happened?"

Ouch. Grimacing, I resisted the urge to toss the device away. "Give me a sec," I requested, turning my glare to Quinton. "By any chance, did Pierina call about Marian?"

"Maybe."

"Okay. Sorry about that. I'm planning how best to make an entire brood of bloodsuckers suffer. Would you care to join me?"

"Yes," Marian snarled. "Where the hell are you?"

"I'm fine."

"That's not what the doctors said. You're not supposed to be human. You need to be at the hospital if you're human."

"Marian, I'm fine. Really." I hesitated, listening for the telltale beeps and noises I expected from a hospital. Wherever she was, it wasn't a hospital. Distant horns honked, accompanying the familiar sounds of the city. "Where are *you*?"

"Lower Chicago, contemplating killing some civic engineers. I *think* I'm near the canal—god, the smell."

The smell? "Wait, the smell?"

Quinton flinched. "It's not my fault."

With a soft, chiming laugh, Abil Ili waved his claws to claim the credit. "They broke our grate. When they restore our grate, we will restore our illusion."

"I see. Yes, I've been told the spell over the canal is down. If you follow the smell, you should find it."

"It makes me want to throw up."

I didn't blame her. The first time I'd smelled the canal, I'd thrown up. "Head to Michietti's. Dare I ask how you escaped the hospital?"

"Out the window."

"Are you naked?"

"No, Shane, I'm not running around Lower Chicago naked. How about you? Are *you* naked? Because from my understanding of the situation, you have no clothes. I'm amazed your phone survived. How'd you find it?"

"I'm wearing clothes! A suit, for that matter."

Quinton snickered. "Give me the phone, Gibby."

"The bloodsucker wants to talk to you." Wrinkling my nose, I handed Quinton the device. "She's wandering Lower Chicago, probably alone, and possibly wearing nothing but a hospital gown."

Abil Ili's laughter echoed in the cavern, chiming off the crystals. "I will make certain she finds her way here."

"If you make her feel like she's been kidnapped, I win a bet."

Quinton jabbed me with his elbow. "Marian, it's Quinton. Gibby's quite fine, so don't worry. What are you wearing?"

Before I had a chance to lunge for Quinton and take my phone back, Abil Ili's tentacles wrapped around my chest, pinned my arms to my sides, and held me in place. I was aware of the pressure of all fourteen of his claws against my skin. "Be at ease. While you are healed, you still suffer from blood loss from his bite. Be calm. We will make sure no harm comes to your beloved."

Since screaming 'get it off!' wouldn't do me any good, I sat utterly still, aware of each pinprick of Abil Ili's claws. Numbness spread through me, and I unwillingly relaxed into his hold.

"Ah. I see. Yes, he had a few bad minutes, but he was perfectly safe. It was a controlled shift, supervised by those well equipped to handle all of his problems. You'll get him back as good as new. Please keep calm. Someone is going to come get you and bring you to us. If you can get to Michietti's, stay there with someone from my family. Until we learn who was behind the attack, you might still be a target. Yes, I understand you're worried. Of course you are. He's your beloved, and you're his. That's how it should be. Can you shift? It might be wise for you to travel with more discretion."

The vampire's emphasis on his final word made me think Marian's hospital gown was the paper kind and hadn't survived her slinking through alleys in Lower Chicago trying to make her way across the city without being seen. I sighed.

Abil Ili released me, and I had to concentrate to remain upright.

"Very well. The fastest way to reach us is through the canal. Slip through where the grate is damaged. The way down is safe. When you hit the bottom, tread water. Someone will retrieve you. It's very dark, but don't worry. It won't take long for someone to reach you." Heaving a sigh, Quinton hung up and pointed my phone at me. "I'm certain this is your fault."

"How is it my fault?"

"Only you would pick the most stubborn female alive outside my family for a mate."

I couldn't help it; I laughed until I cried, which earned me the disgust of the ancient vampire.

THIRTY-FIVE

Is that what they call it nowadays?

WITHIN TEN MINUTES, the numbness faded, and Abil Ili left with another Babylonian to handle preparations. He planned to take me closer to the entry to Lower Chicago, because he felt I'd be the best person to keep Marian calm so he wouldn't have to use his claws.

I appreciated that, since I doubted I'd be able to contain my rage if I saw them pierce her skin with their talons. I owed the Babylonians my thanks, which would make my harming them in a fit of fury even worse. Some things would never change, and I was my father's son.

Curling up and passing out wasn't an option, so I got to my feet with Quinton's help, needing his grip on my arm to stay there. "This is obviously not going to work well."

"It's the blood loss. You'll be hungry in an hour or two, but that stuff on their claws does a number on humans, and you've had a lot of it."

"What *is* that stuff?"

"Hell if I know. It's a secretion, and its effects change depending on their mood. Abil Ili is rather versatile. He can adapt his secretions within minutes. His favorite is a sedative to slow his prey—or aid in healing. You're feeling fuzzyheaded, right?"

"Understatement."

"That's what I thought. That's part of why you were down for so long. It takes a bit of time to work out of your system, and you got a huge dose of it. All my biting did was give them time to dose you so they could fix the real damage."

"Do I want to know how they did that?"

"No. And I trust you understand you can't tell anyone they helped you."

I understood. "Considering I thought the Babylonians were human, I'm pretty sure they don't want humanity knowing they're still around, or they wouldn't have disappeared in the first place."

"Good."

"Could you explain the whole story in exchange for not dying thing? Aren't I walking away the winner on that one? Not that I'm not grateful—I am. It just doesn't seem like an equivalent exchange."

"To those like Abil Ili, stories are worth

more than gold, especially interesting stories. When they retreated from the surface, they left behind myth and legend, a puzzle and challenge to those who might seek them out. So here they are, waiting."

"In Chicago."

"They're not the only denizens of the so-called abyss. They're just the friendlier ones— well, friendlier if you happen to be interesting." Quinton smirked at me. "I, of course, am very interesting."

"Is that what they call it nowadays?" I muttered.

Quinton sighed. "Just stay near me. I'd rather you not fall and give yourself another concussion, and you'll be unstable on your feet for a while yet. Once we fetch your lady, you'll pay your part of the bargain. Then the true fun begins."

"Dare I ask?"

"The Babylonians are a polyamorous colony with a very limited genetic pool; it's so limited they're essentially identical beyond certain markers, including gender and specific magical talents. They don't reproduce anymore, either. Think of their community as a hive mind. If you hurt one, you hurt them all. They have no tolerance for in-fighting and disloyalty. Acts of sexual violence are exceptionally offensive to them for this reason. The instant they find out what happened to your woman, they'll be ready to hunt. They aren't the only Babylonians, either. Most cities have a crystal hive. They gather where there are people."

"I don't understand. Why would they do that? Don't they want to hide?"

"I'm certain you've heard the legend of the Tower of Babel." Quinton pointed at the gap in the blue crystal spears jutting from the walls. "Watch your step. The floors are a bit slick, and you're going to be a wobbly for a while."

Wobbly was an understatement. I needed to lean on the vampire to walk in a straight line. "I walk better than this when drunk," I complained.

He laughed and patted my back. "You'll be all right. We'll wait for her in the sun room; she'll be blind until she gets there, anyway. They'll be careful with her, but I'm worried about how she'll react. She seems quite feisty. You need to keep her from trying to take them on barehanded."

"I think they'd win."

"They would. Now, the Tower of Babel. What do you know of it?"

"I'm not exactly religious," I warned, shrugging. "It was in the Bible. It fell—destroyed by God—if I remember correctly."

"Yes and no. The Bible's really good at taking bits of history and twisting them. The tower existed, it did fall, but God didn't destroy it. The Babylonians got bored, so they abandoned it, leaving their wealth of knowledge for humanity to find. As do all good intentions, it backfired. They'd been distant from humans to begin with; the humans had enough trouble with infighting. The Babylonians are not human, nor do they understand what it means to be human."

"I noticed. I also noticed the different representations of the Bible's history in the restaurant."

Quinton smiled. "We noticed you noticing. We could lose you for hours if we put you in Noah's room with a good view of the ceiling. It wasn't damaged, in case you were worried—none of the frescos were."

"Good. You were alive before the Tower of Babel fell, weren't you?"

The vampire sighed, dodged around a sapphire protruding from the floor, and guided me to the gap in the cavern wall. "We're old, our family."

"Are you going to bite me if I ask a question?"

"No, but I may choose not to answer."

"Fair. Were you already a vampire during the flood?"

Quinton glanced at me, looked away the instant he realized how closely I was watching him, and guided me to the next room, one made of emerald green, cubic crystals. He pointed at one nearby, large enough to serve as a seat for both of us. "Catch your breath. You really have studied that fresco, haven't you?"

"Or I know you and your family well."

"When people tell me that, I laugh at their arrogance. In your case, the sentiment may be correct. No, we were still alive then but not for much longer."

Vampires couldn't remember their old lives; when their souls died, the memories of who they'd once been died with them. I sucked in a breath. Someone had made that fresco for them—someone who remembered, someone older. "Were you still alive when you first met Abil Ili?"

Quinton's smile carried a sharp, predatory edge and showed me his teeth. "You ask hard but good questions. My father still lived. I did not."

Sinking onto the stone, I stared at him, a chill running through me. "But your father sired you, didn't he?"

"I was the reason for Papa's fall. Papa was, in life, a wiseman—an elder of a tribe. We don't remember which one. That's something Abil Ili refuses to tell us. Some secrets are best left in the grave, he says. He's probably right. The Babylonians can do many things, but they can't bring back the dead. Knowl-

edge is power, Gibby. Magic is power. Together, they're a dangerous, terrible,
wonderful thing. Abil Ili's love for Papa is the
love he shares with his hive. They shared
their grief. No one says so, but we were a
mistake—a beloved mistake, a cherished mistake, but a mistake all the same. It was not
God who destroyed the Tower of Babel, but
the Babylonians themselves. From their li-
braries, they stole the secrets of magic and
left the mundane teachings for humans.
Then, it was a concept. Theory. They'd never
risen someone from the dead before, but they
knew the law; one life for another. Papa laid
down his for mine, but instead of my resur-
rection, it became his, and the man Papa had
once been died, gone during the turning, his
soul forever lost. But Abil Ili remembered,
and he refused to let Papa's sacrifice be in
vain. Thus, we all died, but we rose with the
dying sun, made new by Papa's fangs." The
vampire paused. "I'd been dead for several
days by then."

I thought about the Saven brood's odd respect for the Bible and the stories it told.
"Three days?"

"Three is a funny number. It's the pro-
claimed sacred number, the time the Christ
spent dead before he rose. Before the Babylonians, magic had been a more common, accepted thing. Then it disappeared with them

—and a good thing that was, too. Their time became a time of myth and legend. But three days is the limit for a lot of things, including the rise of a vampire. Had Papa not risen me from my grave before the rising of the sun on the fourth day, I wouldn't have risen at all."

"Abil Ili recreated your family after your deaths."

"We owe him much for that. It's why we are like we are. Newly risen vampires are driven by instinct and the need to hunt. We must be taught. We were born anew." Quinton touched his chest. "This soul is not the soul of my birth."

I wasn't brave enough to ask whose soul gave the vampire his unlife.

A NEWBORN KITTEN could've outpaced me, but I didn't whine about my exhaustion or trembling. Quinton knew; he kept licking his fangs, displaying a hint of his hunger in the presence of weakened prey.

"If you bite me again, I'm shoving my Rugers up your ass and firing," I informed him in my most cheerful voice, picking a slanted yellow crystal to lounge on until Marian arrived. If someone wanted me to move, they'd have to move me. "I feel like I could sleep for a week."

"You'll feel better after you have something to eat. It's been a long time since they've made something palatable for humans, so I expect they're challenged finding something you'll enjoy—and being careful about what they bring up from the gardens. I'll get them to give you a tour before we leave. I think Abil Ili underestimated how badly you were injured at the restaurant."

"I think I underestimated how badly I was injured," I confessed.

Quinton straightened, tilting his head to the side to listen. "Ah, she's here."

I thought about getting up. I spent so long thinking about it I missed my chance. Two Babylonians shoved Marian through a crack in the yellow crystals, and she squeaked, stumbling to a halt. Silver, shimmering cloth swaddled her, and she held it in place with a hand, her brown eyes wide. Her wet hair was plastered to her head.

With preternatural speed, Quinton stepped to her, tucked her under his arm, and guided her through the cavern while the pair of Babylonians melted into the stone. If I looked carefully, I could find the outline of their bodies. They crept away from where they'd disappeared, the faint, rare reflection of light on their carapaces betrayed their presence.

Marian's eyes widened when she saw me. "Shane."

I liked the way she breathed my name. "You all right?"

"I threw up."

The confession motivated me to get to my feet, and I closed the distance between us, aware Quinton was ready to catch me if I fell. I tucked her wet hair behind her ears and smiled at her. "Pity party for two later?"

"I'm in. I broke my wrist." She struggled to free her other hand from the fabric wrapped around her and revealed a brace covering most of her hand and extending to her elbow. "I think a tentacle touched me."

After exchanging a worried glance with the vampire, I nudged Marian to the nearest crystal large enough to support our weight. When I thought of towels, shimmery and silky didn't come to mind, but the fabric the Babylonians had wrapped her in seemed to be drying her and keeping her warm. "I won't talk about the tentacles if you don't."

"I jumped in corpse stew, Shane." She lifted her injured arm and sniffed the brace. "Why don't I smell bad?"

"Shock," Quinton whispered in my ear.

"Magic," I answered, grateful the Babylonians had spared us from the canal's stench. "What were you thinking, escaping from the hospital?"

"You were hurt," she hissed at me, clutching the towel closer. "Of course I escaped from the hospital. I needed to find you. Who did it?"

I laughed, knowing I could get Quinton into a world of trouble with the woman if I wanted. I sat close and shamelessly leaned my weight against her. She leaned against me, too, which made me think everything was right in the world, at least for the moment. "I'm sorry I worried you. I wasn't being hurt. I was being helped. It was just a bit painful is all."

"I thought you were dying."

Later, I'd need to ask her how she'd known. Instead of denying the truth, I kissed her cheek. "Quinton took care of me, so don't worry. I'll be fine."

"You're shaking."

"I've been told that'll stop after I eat and get some rest. I owe our hosts an accounting of everything, so please don't kill me when I say the S-word and the A-word?"

"This once," she replied, gracing me with a smile. "You're all right?"

I hooked the top of her towel with a finger and peeked, discovering a lovely, unimpeded view of bare skin. "Hospital gown didn't survive the slide?"

"That was not a slide. It was a torture device. Then tentacles grabbed me, Shane.

There were tentacles in the water. You didn't tell me there were tentacles in the water."

I laughed, wrapped my arms around her, and hugged her close. Whatever magic the Babylonians had used had erased the evidence of her trip, for which I was grateful. "Sorry, Marian."

"You're going to be sorry. *Tentacles.*"

Unable to blame her in the slightest for her crankiness, I wondered if I'd discovered one of her fears. I wasn't a fan of tentacles, especially ones tipped in poisoned claws and hooks, but at the same time, those claws and hooks had helped me remain among the living. "I'd be unnerved by tentacles in the dark, too. The owners of the tentacles are the ones who helped me. And I needed the help. Right, Quinton?"

Maybe if I dumped the whole problem on the vampire's lap, he could better prepare Marian to accept the Babylonians, especially since I still had trouble with their hooks and claws and secretions.

"I'm sorry, Miss Peterson. Part of what you sensed was likely my fault. He couldn't be sedated until after he'd shifted back to human, and it was a painful process. I bit him so I could hold him in thrall long enough for him to be treated."

Marian stiffened. "You bit him."

"Out of necessity. Had I not, it would have

been difficult to treat his injuries. I saw the MRI scans, and they were rather dire. He needed help the human hospitals here are unable to provide. Down here, they aren't prejudiced—they aren't human, nor are they anything like humans. His wrist will bear the evidence of my bite for a few days, but it'll heal without scarring."

I tightened my grip on Marian, holding her close. "I consented to it. If I'd known you would know, I would've done it differently. I had no idea you'd be aware."

Marian frowned, her attention fixed on the vampire. "Really necessary?"

"Unless you wanted him in ICU for a few weeks, yes."

I flinched, as did Marian.

"These people who helped him have tentacles?"

Quinton chuckled. "Yes. They're the residents of these caves. They're also the ones who help maintain the illusions over the canal and help the survivors get back into Lower Chicago. They're friends with Papa."

"All right. And he doesn't need to go to the ER?"

"I'm fine, Marian. Tired, but fine."

She shot a glare at me but sighed and touched the scar above my right eye. "You lost your eye."

"Oh, the Babylonians took it." I shrugged. "It's all right."

With wide eyes and her mouth gaping open, Marian stared at me. "Babylonians?"

"Well, I suppose there's no use hiding it from her now." Quinton scowled at me and sighed. "Abil Ili?"

Although I'd been able to spot the pair of Babylonians near the entry, I hadn't noticed Abil Ili until he separated from the crystals beside us, dipping into a bow, his crest rustling while the rest of his body gleamed in rainbow hues. "I'm honored."

Marian made a strangled noise in her throat and went limp against me. My eyes widened, and I held onto her. "Marian?"

Quinton covered his mouth with a hand, but I could hear him snickering.

"Oh dear. We were right to worry. She reacted rather poorly when we grabbed her in the water. She screamed loud enough to stir the ire of the dead below." Abil Ili crouched in front of Marian, and the fluid covering his claws faded from black to a pale blue. The Babylonian watched his hands, waiting until the last of the black dripped away before reaching up and touching Marian's shoulder, pricking her with a single claw. "This will help her stay calm when she awakens. It suppresses emotions—all emotions—making fear easier to handle. The effect will only last an hour or two, but long enough for her to adapt to our presence, yes? Quinton?"

"She's tough. I don't think she would have had a problem if she hadn't been stressed worrying about Gibby. Gibby, I'll carry her. Abil Ili, he's still unsteady on his feet."

"I will make sure he does not fall. Let's go inside, then we will feed our guests so the storytelling may begin."

THIRTY-SIX

This woman sure knows how to pack
on the muscle, doesn't she?

DEEP within the crystal cavern complex, I
discovered the glory of Rome blended with
the exotic splendor of Ancient Egypt. A ziggurat, carved of shining gemstone and embraced by a sparkling river, rose from an opal
floor. Most wouldn't view its seven stories as
impressive, but something about it gave the
sense of looming majesty.

"A few cultures did learn from us," Abil Ili
murmured, gesturing to the archway leading
into the structure. A path of pale crystal
spanned the still, clear waters. "Within, you
will find comforts appropriate for the humans we had once longed to teach, food to
nourish your body, and peace to soothe your
soul."

Quinton sighed, shifting Marian's weight
in his arms. "She looks dainty, but this

woman sure knows how to pack on the muscle, doesn't she? She's no wilting lily."

"Trust me, I noticed." I liked it, too. I appreciated that Marian was a capable woman who could protect herself—and do anything she set her mind to. "What can I say? I'm my father's son."

"And werewolf males get off on their women beating the snot out of them." Throwing back his head, Quinton laughed. "She's tough enough to handle you. You're perfect together."

"To handle *me*?"

"Gibby, you shoot innocent vampires in the kneecaps because you can."

"Innocent?"

I had to concentrate to walk a straight line, but I didn't need Abil Ili's help to reach the ziggurat. The instant I stepped across the threshold, I held my breath. I knew the room; I'd stepped through it countless times in Michietti's. The entries were identical, including the mosaic on the ceiling. "Quinton?"

"A reminder of who and what we were and who and what we've become," the vampire murmured, and in his tone, I heard a plea to drop the subject.

I did, shutting my mouth with a clack of my teeth.

Abil Ili led us through an archway off the foyer to a sea of cushions awaiting us. Dipping into a bow, he gestured to the room, a riot of brilliant colors cradled in golden crystals peeking between Roman columns. "Nest to your comfort, and I shall bring sustenance for us."

Unlike the two Babylonians I'd spotted, when Abil Ili disappeared, I couldn't spot any sign of his presence. I stepped into the room, stepped onto a thick layer of cushions instead of solid floor, and fell on my face with a startled squawk.

Quinton laughed, took more care descending into the cushions, and lowered Marian onto them. "I should have warned you. You all right?"

"My pride may never recover."

"You'll live. Make yourself comfortable, cuddle with your lady, and relax. You'll tell Abil Ili everything that's happened from your first meeting with Marian. Then we'll decide how to deal with the people who've brought murder onto the Babylonian's doorstep. It'll be interesting."

I worried when a vampire thousands of years old thought something was interesting. "All right."

Wading through the pillows to Marian, I slid beneath her until her head rested on my chest. I cradled her on my lap and, with a little help from Quinton, propped myself up with cushions. To make sure I was the only one to see every perfect inch of Marian, I tucked her towel around her securely.

"Why don't you wake her up? That way, we can get her acclimated to Abil Ili before bringing in the others—or more accurately, having them reveal themselves." Quinton nodded towards a column, and I caught a faint shimmer near a golden crystal sticking out of the wall.

A few gentle slaps against her cheek roused her, and when she snuggled close to me, I decided I wasn't in any hurry for her to wake up. Smiling at her warmth and the way she wiggled, I wrapped my arms around her and hugged her. Still, the vampire was right. She needed to be alert—and calm. "Marian?"

"The tentacles have claws," she mumbled.

"His name is Abil Ili, and he's a Babylonian." I rubbed her back and leaned over so I could kiss her forehead. "He startled me, too, when I first saw him. I hid in Quinton's jacket."

"It's true, he did."

"Where are we?" she lifted her head from my chest, her eyes dull and glazed. Anxious about her lethargy, I turned to Quinton in silent inquiry.

"It's from his claw," the vampire whispered in my ear. "She'll be fine, so don't *you* panic on me."

Sighing my relief, I rested my cheek

against Marian's hair. "We're in part of the third level of Chicago. There's no sign of Hecate and her lampad companions, but it turns out there are Babylonians and crystal caves."

"Oh, the lampad are real. They don't come out often. They aren't a threat, not usually." Chuckling, Quinton lounged beside us. "And be grateful Hecate isn't a frequent visitor. Nothing good happens when the gods walk the Earth. Sometimes they come and go with us none the wiser, but they usually leave trouble in their wake."

If Quinton's goal was to distract me and Marian, he succeeded. Marian squirmed on my lap and turned to face the vampire. "What sort of trouble?"

"If you ignore the death, doom, and destruction, their children are the problem. When a goddess takes a mortal to her bed, sometimes said mortal finds himself the unexpected caretaker of a human infant, a mostly vanilla one. The real trouble starts after several generations, when the bloodline is thinned. A little like you, Gibby. No one knows why the children of gods tend to be pure human while *their* children are ticking bombs."

"Think gods are good lays, Shane?" Marian murmured, and she rubbed her brace-entrapped hand over my shoulder, resting her palm over her bite on my shoulder. "Never mind. I'm not sharing."

"I find that promising."

"Hey, Quinton? What if Shane had been forty-nine percent human?"

"You'd still be in his apartment having sex."

I was disappointed I wasn't at my apartment with Marian. "If you're trying to embarrass me, it's working."

"You wouldn't be embarrassed about having sex, either. You'd be a slut. You'd also be a very long-lived slut likely to grow a pair of wings and a tail in a thousand years if you're a slow bloomer like Kelly."

"So no incubus for me?" Marian complained.

"You got Gibby instead. He's better."

"Indeed," Abil Ili said from the doorway, carrying a silver tray in his clawed tentacles. "Honored guest, I am Abil Ili, and it is my pleasure and the highest privilege to serve you. May you find peace and shelter within our hive and home."

Marian's gaze locked on the Babylonian, and her body tensed against me. I pulled her closer to offer the illusion of safety and comfort. "Thank you, Abil Ili. I owe you much for your help."

With far more grace than I'd ever manage, the Babylonian descended into the cushions, wading his way closer. Offering the tray to Quinton, he crouched barely out of reach. Marian took long, deep breaths. "You helped Shane."

"I did."

Although she trembled, she jerked her head in a nod. "Thank you. I was scared for him."

"Of course you were. He has given you the rest of his life, but you have only given him your firstborn."

Marian shook her head, and only the brace kept her from clutching my shoulder painfully tight. As it was, she dug her fingertips into me. "No. I'll brand him again, over and over, if I must to keep him."

"How odd." The Babylonian tilted his bird-like head, the paneled feathers of his crest rising. "But your kind is not like that."

"Forgive him, Marian," Quinton said, setting the tray on his lap, which was burdened with fruits and vegetables. I recognized none of them, although a bright orange bunch reminded me of grapes. "Abil Ili is accustomed to when human men had many wives and loyalty was... not common. By nature, humans are polyamorous, but they now sometimes choose to bind themselves to only one partner, much like werewolves."

Abil Ili tilted his head the other way. "It is

the nature of humans to change things, isn't it? I can fix that."

"Fix what?" Marian growled.

"Your bite. To make it like his. Permanent, until the end of your days. It is not difficult for me to do, this binding. His magic already touches you. I will merely reflect it back on him and tie it with yours, so you will never worry someone might infringe on your territory. It would repay the hurt and fear we caused you, however accidental."

"Mine, forever?"

If Marian had had claws like the Babylonians, she would've shredded my shoulder with her grip. "I'm not going anywhere, Marian."

"You will not have to renew your bite whenever he blesses you with children," the Babylonian cooed.

Me, bless *her* with children? I was of the opinion it would be the other way around; the thought of us having children stole my breath.

"You're giving him ideas," Quinton said with laughter in his voice. "I thought you wanted to hear their story first. Aren't you doing this backwards?"

"Every part of our relationship has been backwards," I muttered.

"Not my fault." Marian sniffed.

"I enjoyed the results, so it is your fault."

"Shane!"

Quinton laughed, popped one of the orange grapes off its stem, and popped it in his mouth. "They're perfect for each other. He'll spend his time making certain she's happy enough to bite him again, and she'll spend her time making him happy enough to give her many children, which he'll insist on raising with her, because that's how he is. Since she won't be able to get rid of him until all their children are grown and have moved on, she'll inevitably brand him again, until they're both too old and tired to have more children, and then she won't be in any hurry to drive him from her territory, because she'll have no interest in breeding due to her age. You could let nature run its merry course without any intervention on your part, Abil Ili, and they would persist. Shane is stubborn, as is Marian."

"If it makes her happy, give her what she wants." I didn't want any other woman, and I was glad to do the work in reverse, learning about her and learning to love her properly for the rest of my life. Maybe she'd been beautiful before I'd begun to love her, but I didn't love her because she was beautiful. I loved her because she was the kind of woman who would sacrifice a great deal to do the right thing.

Before I'd met her, she'd sacrificed her body to put an end to sex trafficking rings. I'd take over her mission to protect her from becoming a victim again, no matter what the cost. I'd be selfish and keep Marian for myself, but at the same time, I'd work to make sure other women didn't fall prey to traffickers.

When she had been busy elsewhere, she had given me the tools to protect myself, trusting in me to put them to good use.

She had so much courage and stubborn pride I'd spend the rest of my life worrying about her and toeing the line between protecting her no matter what and trusting her to protect herself.

I still hadn't told her I loved her, but I looked forward to spending the rest of my life showing her how much I cared. The words would come eventually, but when I said them, she wouldn't doubt my feelings for her.

Abil Ili's laugher chimed, and the crystals sang echoes of the cheerful sound. "Is that what you want, Marian?"

"My bite hurts him and takes a long time to heal. I won't have to bite him like that again?"

"Never again. Your mark will remain, untouched by time, as his will on you."

"Shifters call it a brand," Quinton supplied.

"Your brand. Would you like me to make it permanent?"

"Yes," she whispered.

Abil Ili crept closer. "Show me where you bit him."

I stifled my laughter over how fast she moved, squirming on my lap so she could shove my jacket off my shoulder. The buttons of my shirt somehow survived her rough handling, and she shoved the material away from where she'd bitten me, revealing the scabbed wound. "Here."

I was so amused by her possessiveness and resemblance to my mother whenever another woman looked at my father, I made the mistake of ignoring Abil Ili. He whipped his tentacle around Marian and stabbed me with a talon in the heart of her bite.

The pain didn't last long. Passing out helped. I groggily became aware I was slumped against Marian, and she had her towel pressed to my shoulder. I blinked at her.

The towel would have been more useful wrapped around her instead of serving as a bandage. "You're naked," I slurred.

Abil Ili must have done something to his secretions, something that made my tongue feel thick and unwieldy in my mouth. Or, perhaps not. It might've been the blood loss. How much blood did I have to spare? If I kept losing it, I'd end up in the hospital again for sure.

"Shane," she complained, her tone so exasperated I laughed.

"Warning him would have made it hurt more." The Babylonian offered no apology in word or tone, which amused me even more.

"How long was I out?"

"About twenty minutes." Marian glared at Abil Ili. "Quinton, stop eating those oranges and, for fuck's sake, stop laughing."

"They're grapes."

"Grapes aren't orange. Those—"

Quinton popped an orange grape in Marian's mouth. "Grapes."

She chewed, her eyes widening. "It tastes like a peach."

Setting the tray next to me, the vampire picked up a fresh cluster of the fruit and handed it to her. "Feed those to your man. They're loaded full of things good for him."

"He is right. For vampires, it is as nourishing as a blood meal. For humans, it is nutritious and filling." Abil Ili picked up a fruit that looked like a kiwi but was deep red, snapping the tip of his beak into it to slice open the skin. Between his claws and his beak, he made short work of the peel to get to the pale pink flesh within. "After you eat, you can tell me the story of what brought you to here and why someone would want to kill you, a child of Ernesto's heart."

While I could have fed myself, I wouldn't

complain if Marian wanted to feed me. I
showed my appreciation for her attentions
with a careful application of teeth on her
fingers and a smile. She was right. The orange grapes tasted like peach, so juicy they
burst in my mouth. If I'd been alone, I
would have spent a great deal of time
playing with them, amused by the contra-
dictions in its appearance, its taste, and its
texture.

The Babylonian spoke the truth; eating
only a few eased my hunger and soothed the
dryness in my mouth.

"They're so cute together it's disgusting,
isn't it?" Quinton muttered.

"He seems to be enjoying himself despite
his recent inconveniences."

"There's a naked woman feeding him
grapes while she's lounging on top of him. Of
course he's enjoying himself. Had I known
her clothes were hiding such a lovely lady, I
might've been less eager to support their
pairing. Now I'll never have a chance with
her. The universe is an unfair place."

Marian's left hand slithered down my
chest, probably to retrieve one of my Rugers.

"You can't kneecap him today, Marian. I
already told him you'd get a turn with him
later."

She sighed and fed me another grape-or-
ange-peach which I'd call a delicious devil

berry for the rest of my life. "So you owe Abil Ili a story?"

"Yes. I promised to tell him everything that happened since New York."

"I should start, then." Rolling off me, she stretched beside me, oblivious to her nudity, keeping her right hand and her towel pressed to my shoulder. "My name is Marian Peterson, and I'm an FBI agent. My work, until recently, involved infiltrating sex trafficking operations so they could be dismantled. I was undercover as a young, vulnerable woman driven to prostitution—someone with no friends or family to miss her, out on the streets."

The thought of her alone that way made me growl like my father, but before I could say a word, Marian shoved a handful of the delicious devil berries in my mouth and pressed her palm to my lips.

"In her hands, anything is a weapon, I'm convinced of it," Quinton whispered.

"Anyway, our plan worked a little too well. We hadn't expected the sex traffickers to have practitioners capable of non-permanent full-body transformative magic. Instead of a woman, they were transporting an alpaca and could cross state lines without permit or quarantine. I'd been in their custody for three days. They bound me with duct tape, put me in a car, and planned to drive me out of New

York. That's when the body fell off the sky-scraper and hit the car I was in."

Lowering her hand from my mouth, she kissed me, and I made an appreciative sound in my throat. "Your turn," she murmured. "And I won't bite you for saying that name for the rest of this conversation."

"So merciful." Laughing, I stole one of the berries and fed it to her. "I suppose my part of the story starts a little earlier, when I lost my right eye. I was a cop, mostly working traffic and foot patrols, when the call came re-porting a bad accident. My partner and I ar-rived first. He froze. I didn't. The car was burning with three people inside, one a child. I pulled him out first, then I got his parents out. It cost me my eye." I paused to pop an-other berry into my mouth, chewing to buy myself a few moments. "I knew the injury would end my career, so I decided to go away for a while—see other cities, maybe find somewhere I might like to live. Somewhere a little cheaper, a little less prejudiced against lycanthropes. Somewhere I might be able to get something better than minimum wage."

"It's worse than he makes it sound," Quinton helpfully supplied.

I missed my false eye; without it, I couldn't shoot him my worst glare. "Thanks, Quinton. I was trying to look on the bright side."

"Do not do so on my account. The unvarnished truth allows full understanding."

"Unvarnished truth it is. It's simple. The police didn't want a no-talent lycanthrope's son on the force—not in the public eye at least. They used me to tick two boxes off their anti-discrimination list, but they wanted me out of the way and to work at cheapest price bracket possible. When I lost my eye, the department worked with my insurance company to screw me over. They made sure I didn't qualify for a functional eye —or even a realistic imitation. Now, granted, I rather like the all-blue one. It's different enough to be interesting, but I'll be honest with you. It's a piece of shit. I'm pretty sure a mass produced marble would be higher quality, but they don't fit my socket."

I had tried.

"I see. I have heard they do not like the moon swayed in the above world, but it is not a concern of my hive. It is a pity humans have not changed their ways."

Moon swayed made lycanthropes sound nicer, gentler somehow, although I knew the truth of the infected and those transformed by the virus's magic. Dad could—did—rip metal apart with his claws, and on the hunt, he frightened everyone, myself included. But he was still my father, and he was always welcome to guard my back.

"Lycanthropy has its disadvantages, but there's no one more loyal than a werewolf. My father is one. He'd infected my mother before I was born. I grew up believing I was resistant to the virus. In Chicago, exposure to lycanthropy flags you for life as a possible contagion risk—a danger to the public. There was a mark on my badge declaring my exposure status. Add in my magic rating, and I remained at the lowest tier of the department, and only luck got me on the streets at all."

"And this led you to New York, where you met your mate."

"I was standing beside the car when the body fell on it, close enough to get sprayed with a lot of blood. While I called 911, I put the car in park. The white, fluffy alpaca in the back seat didn't like me and showed her dislike for me by spitting. She hit three of the cops that came to the scene and annoyed one into pulling a gun on her. I got in the way, stopped them from shooting her, and claimed custody so she wouldn't be put down."

Abil Ili hissed, but I waved his anger away with a hand. "They had no way of knowing she was human. To them, she was just an animal. To me, too, but I was brought up better than them. I figured I could take her to my parents' place, keep her for the mandatory time, find her a good home. So, that's what I did. I went home to Lincoln, Nebraska, and I took her with me. By the time I got there three days later, I'd decided I was going to keep her. She was soft, warm, devilishly cute, and had better manners than my father most days, especially once she stopped spitting on me. My mother decided to name her Sally."

Talking was more tiring than I expected; I pilfered some more of the berries to give myself a chance to catch my breath. Marian made a soft sound in her throat and pressed the back of her left hand to my forehead. "Do you want me to take a turn?"

I waved my hand and let her decide what I meant.

"His parents have two horses, and they had made a stall for me. I... hadn't expected a lycanthrope, especially not one as rambunctious as Shane's father. I thought we were both going to get eaten before I realized he was just excited to see his puppy. After an evening of watching Shane wage war against his parents—a fun war, involving the shearing of a lycanthrope male who overstepped his boundaries—Shane slept in the barn with me. Unbeknownst to Shane, his parents camped in the barn after he'd fallen asleep."

I should have known. Sighing, I shook my head. "Damn them, terrorizing you like that."

"I played dead. It seemed to work. They

weren't willing to wake you up, but they weren't willing to leave you alone, either. I thought it was sweet."

Of course Marian would. She was a tricky woman.

"Anyway, the next day, Shane's parents went to work. They're both police officers, though they have different partners. Shane decided to return the rental van and took me with him. The rental place wasn't too far from his parents' home, so we were going to walk back."

"We were hoofin' it back," I corrected in my gravest tone.

Quinton laughed and tossed a second bunch of the devil berries at me. "Your Nebraska is showing."

"Fine. We were hoofin' it back when Mark O'Conners, a member of the New York Italian mafia, pulled up, shot Shane twice, and took me. I thought Shane had been killed, since he'd been caught completely flat-footed and wasn't armed. He dropped hard and fast, and there was a lot of blood."

"My turn," I murmured, picking up the berries the vampire had thrown and handing them to Marian. "I woke up in the ER, where I was treated by a surgeon they brought in from Des Moines. My father donated blood, which gave me regeneration on par with a lycanthrope—not the expected result. I think they expected some help with recovery, but not anything to the level I got. So, instead of spending several weeks in the hospital, between Dr. Harting and Dad's blood, I escaped the next day. I headed home where my godfather intercepted me. A neighbor had gotten it into his head I shouldn't be left alone."

Marian snickered, but she didn't elaborate, much to my relief.

"Lewis, my godfather, decided to chase down my parents, because he was worried they would begin mass murdering anyone involved in my shooting if they got a hold of them. Which is true, because it's essentially suicide to hurt a werewolf's puppy. We followed them to Des Moines, and after a bit of planning, I was designated the sacrificial lamb to check out the nightclubs to see if any of them looked like they could be a part of a sex trafficking operation. I struck gold on my first try, and with a little help of fifteen hundred dollars, a good bottle of Scotch, and proof I wasn't from the area, I got a front row seat to a sex party and a beautiful blond named Sally on my lap for the show."

"Lucky man," Quinton muttered.

I grabbed a devil berry and tossed it at him. "Quiet, you."

"I took his virginity in a show hosted by a succubus and an incubus. He was very enthusiastic, and I appreciated his performance and wanted to keep him—permanently, especially since he'd already stepped in front of a gun for me, gotten shot twice for me, and was this disgustingly nice guy. Disgustingly nice guys are very rare on the singles market. Not only had I claimed his virginity, I had a chance to claim his firstborn as well. Wasn't letting *that* chance go by." Marian sniffled.

"You bit me because I got mouthy with you," I reminded her.

"All the more reason to keep you around. I like your mouth."

"So, she bit me, I was worried I'd infected her with lycanthropy, only to discover I'd already burned out the virus. That oddity earned me a trip straight to Chicago, courtesy of the CDC, for testing. The tests ate up a solid day, after which I went home. Life happened for a while, then I learned I was a suspect in Mark O'Conners' murder. However, as I couldn't be at the CDC being tested at the same time I was killing the guy who shot me near my parents' place, I was exonerated. That whole mess led to the CDC and the CPD and my insurance company getting into a court battle over the replacement of my eye and medical care."

"I can give you reports and recordings of the entire trial," Quinton offered. "It's a pleasure to watch, and I think you'll learn a lot from it. Anyway, the trial kept him busy for a few weeks, during which Shane was closely monitored by Papa, the CPD, and the CDC. Papa and the CDC wanted to make sure nothing happened to him while the CPD wanted him to dig a grave for himself."

"Yeah, they tried to nail me on the nation-wide concealed carry permit Marian arranged for me. That tactic didn't work."

"It did, however, present an interesting issue." The vampire sat up, grabbing one of the red kiwis from the tray. "After Gibby returned to his home with Marian, Papa visited him, and the CPD kept showing up. What was it, six pairs of officers over several hours?"

"That's right," Marian confirmed. "The department kept trying to get his permit number. We ran into the last pair as we were leaving to replace Shane's phones and visit the mall."

"White dresses," I murmured, although I appreciated how comfortable she was with her nudity.

"I recall you lost your mind over the little black dress. It's a shame it was ruined."

Quinton sighed. "I'll see that it's replaced. You were in our care when it happened. Papa will insist. Gibby brought her to my sister's restaurant in his best clothes, and he dressed her like a queen. He isn't a romantic man by nature—I feared he'd never find a woman sufficiently interesting for him to pursue—but there they were, together as though born to be side by side. My sister had me bring out her wine, Abil Ili."

"The last?" the Babylonian asked, quiet and still.

"The last." The vampire lifted up a bunch of the devil berries. "These are the grapes that made that wine, Gibby. When fermented, they turn blood red. It's old magic that kept that bottle preserved."

"Tell me what happened," Abil Ili demanded.

I sighed. "We were on the balcony having dinner. Pierina had made everything for us, sending out in small portions so we could try everything. I had my back to the canal so Marian could look into the abyss."

"The abyss." The Babylonian chuckled. "Yes, that is a suitable name for our home. An abyss, which leads to treasures unsurpassed by humans, beyond the comprehension of mere mortals."

Since I couldn't argue with the truth, I acknowledged him with a nod. "I heard the bang before the balcony collapsed and had time to stand before I fell into the water."

"We think they used a grenade with a delayed detonation, stuck to the wall beneath the balcony to knock out the supports. Gibby fell into the water. Marian fell onto the sidewalk. I had to choose, and he never would have forgiven me if I'd chosen him over her, so I helped her. By the time Pierina had made it outside, someone had tossed another grenade onto the grate, breaking it. Gibby was gone, washed away. I thought he'd drowned—or died when he fell."

"He had," Abil Ili confirmed with a clack of his beak. "Saved only because he had not yet had his first shift. I was challenged healing his body. Do you know who did it?"

"No. His parents and my family seek the culprits."

Abil Ili rose from his crouch, standing to his full, intimidating height. "I have heard all I need to know. Rest. When I return, we will have work to do. Sleep for a while, even you, my favored darkener of doorways. We will be busy soon enough."

His body shimmered, and he vanished, although the movement of the cushions betrayed his presence until he reached the ledge. With a few clicks of his talons on the crystal floor, he was gone.

"Busy? Busy doing what?" Marian demanded.

Quinton smiled, and a red gleam washed over his dark eyes. "Those who tried to kill you have issued a grave insult without knowing it."

Frowning, I turned my head to better see the vampire. "What insult?"

"Never mistake Abil Ili for human. He doesn't have human emotions, nor does he understand emotions the way humans do, but there are a few that overlap. He is very fond of Papa, and the people Papa cherishes, he cherishes. Someone ruined something my sister loves. Someone hurt someone Papa loves. These things he understands. When he heard Pierina had shared the last of her most prized wines, the last bottle of that specific vintage, a treasure to her, he knew where we stand. He isn't a vampire. He isn't part of our brood. But he's family all the same, and that Abil Ili understands, and so he will hunt." Quinton's smile turned cold and calculating. "He's angry enough he means to take us with him. Tomorrow will be a bloody day, one I plan to enjoy."

THIRTY-SEVEN

You love me. You truly love me.

I WAS PRETTY certain I'd gone from wide awake to sound asleep in a heartbeat—and mid sentence. A hazy memory of discussing potential suspects played through my head, but I could barely make sense of it, except Marian kept wanting to blame Michelle. Why would Michelle want to kill me?

"Why Michelle?" I blurted.

Marian rolled over to sprawl over my chest, her hands resting on my shoulders. Though I had no recollection of taking off my jacket and shirt, our bare skin touched. At least she'd left me with my pants, else I would've fallen prey to her for something entirely inappropriate for the situation. "I'd be offended, except Quinton already warned me you'd pick up right where you left off after fainting. Stop fainting. I don't like it."

"It's not his fault. He needed the rest," the vampire said, emerging from beneath the cushions. "If you two are going to get hot and heavy, you should let me join in for a light snack. I'd like it a lot."

Instead of kneecapping the bastard, I twisted under Marian and kicked him in the face. "No."

"You love me. You truly love me." Quinton backed away and rubbed his nose. "But I'd like it a lot."

"You're not getting a drink from either one of us, so forget it. I might consider selling my parents to you for a fair price."

Marian laughed. "You can't keep selling your parents to vampires, Shane."

"Why the hell not?"

"You love them, despite appearances. Selling them once as payback for trying to sell you was fair. Selling them twice would be mean."

"Do I want to know how long I was out this time?"

Marian stuck her hand in my pants pocket, located my phone, and checked the time. "Eight and a half hours. We both needed sleep, so don't worry about it. I was just worried because you conked out fast. Quinton said it didn't count as a faint because you were tired and needed sleep. I'm counting it as a faint."

"All right. Did I miss anything important?"

The look Marian and Quinton exchanged warned me I had, but neither spoke.

"What did I miss?" Since Quinton would be a harder mark, I snagged Marian by her waist, pulled her to me, and pressed my lips to her throat. "If you want more of this later, you'll talk, Miss Peterson."

She giggled, wrapping her arms around me. "You're bad."

"So are you, lounging around without any clothes. I'm just a man, and I can't take you home yet. When I get you home, you only have yourself to blame for all the ravishing of your person I intend to do."

"I like the sound of that."

"But you have to tell me what I missed first."

"You're a tough negotiator, Mr. Gibson."

"You're also going to have to marry me. That's non-negotiable."

She chuckled, settled herself on my lap, and rested her chin on my shoulder. "I think we may have slightly miscalculated."

"We did?"

"It's less we miscalculated and more that we underestimated how enthusiastically the Babylonians would join the hunt. Someone here talked to someone from a different hive, and that someone talked to someone from yet another hive, and it may have spiraled out of control."

I made myself comfortable holding Marian, something I'd have no problem getting used to, as she was warm and fit against me just right, even though she did make my legs fall asleep. "How out of control are we talking?"

"Well, this hive has a hundred and thirty Babylonians, all adults, all with mounts, and eager to make a few forays to the surface. There's another hive across the city with another twenty adults. They don't have mounts, but they're quadrupeds to begin with, so they don't need them."

I had a difficult time imagining a talon-footed, carapace-covered, tentacle-armed, clawed-handed Babylonian became a quadruped. "I'm becoming concerned."

"That's because you're as wise as you are smart. Detroit's hive mobilized about five hours ago, so they're probably reaching the outskirts of the city now. They're a mixed hive, so the bipeds are likely riding the quadrupeds, because if they brought *their* mounts, Chicago's fucked."

"Come again?"

"They have, in their infinite wisdom, convinced a herd of shedu to partner with them. The quadrupeds are the hive's warrior maidens, and they partner with their shedu to protect each other in battle. In their hive, the bipeds are all males, and they ride their shedu to better slaughter their foes. Where the shedu roam, blood flows. Unfortunately, the shedu associated with this hive are more violent than their brethren." Quinton grimaced.

"What the hell is a shedu?"

"The shedu of Detroit's hive have the head of a man, the body of a lion, the wings of a great eagle, and the hooves of a bull. They're tall, and when they look upon a man, their eyes see into his heart and know his worth. Sin is made clear, virtues are known, and justice is delivered. When they speak, only the truth falls from their lips, and when they hear a lie, their fury burns hotter than the sun. A wise man bows his head in the presence of the shedu, for the eyes are the mirrors of the soul, and only through the eyes may a man's worth be known." Quinton shuddered and shook his head. "I'll pray they don't bring their shedu, for should they, the canal will run red with blood."

Okay, when *Quinton* feared something, it meant bad news. "Right. If I see any winged bulls, I won't look up."

"That's a good start, except they are accompanied by the Babylonians. You won't see them until it's too late."

"The Babylonians are chameleons."

"There's a reason you haven't seen or heard of them before, except in myth and legend. They aren't just chameleons. They're masters of illusion. One could walk right by you on the street, and you'd never know he was there. Some are loners, separated from the hive, wandering the Earth gathering knowledge, returning only to share the wealth they have gathered. You'll never meet the son or daughter of one; they can't reproduce with humans—they can't even reproduce with each other. There are always exactly one hundred and forty-four thousand of them. When one dies, rebirth is immediate, and they rise on the morning of the fourth day."

An unsettled feeling started in my chest and swept through me. I remembered the vampire telling me the significance of the sunrise of the fourth day. "They're immortal."

"They're immortal with long memories, and should you make enemies of them, the best you can hope for is a four-day respite from their fury before they rise again and re-sume the hunt. Something has stirred their ire beyond what I anticipated. I don't know what, and that frightens me most of all. I'd hoped for one or two to aid us in the hunt for the people who tried to kill you, to learn their names and their goals. Something tells me they know, and the corruption they've found is more extensive that I believed."

The vampires I knew rarely showed fear; they'd already faced death, choosing to respect and control it rather than allow it to control them. I'd heard of other vampires of different broods, every bit the monster legend and lore made them out to be. But Ernesto and his children?

They were still scary, but they were a familiar fear, one I could respect and understand.

The Babylonians were beyond anything I could've imagine.

I swallowed and ran my hands along Marian's spine before holding her closer. "It gets worse, doesn't it?"

"See, this is why you were smart to lay permanent claim, Marian. You need to convince him to let you go so you can get dressed. Abil Ili brought you clothes hours ago."

"I'm comfortable as I am," she replied.

"Of course you are. I think you like making me nervous. I'm waiting for Gibby to tire of me seeing your beauty and take one of my eyes to replace his."

"Now that's a thought. I'd look strange with a vampire eye, Quinton. You're safe for now, assuming the Babylonians give mine back. If they don't, I may have to consider taking yours. Also, stop looking at her. I saw her first. You can't have her."

Marian laughed. "You can't take his eye, Shane. That's just rude."

"Do vampires even use their eyes?"

"Yes, Gibby, I need my eyes. Both of them."

"Is there anything else I should be worried about? The shedu are the biggest concern, right?"

"Depends on what you view as a problem. If the Babylonians stick to the people involved with your attempted murder and any connected sex trafficking operations in Chicago, it won't be wholesale slaughter—just a bit messy. There are so many factors to consider. Who's involved? How far does the corruption go? How many of the other crime lords have gotten their hands unforgivably dirty? *If* there's a ring here, it's possible the attack was intended to get rid of both of you. If that's the case, you'll be targeted again."

"I'm worried there are police officers involved," Marian confessed. "They had you heavily monitored. Six pairs of officers visiting for bogus information would be a good way to track you. You ditched your phones in the canal, but if someone had been using the phones to track you, they could have followed us there. They had the time to hack the software. Anyone with a little knowledge and skill could do it."

"Okay. You're worried the CPD is involved. That's fair. They have no reason to like me right now, and making me disappear would benefit them in more ways than one. I hadn't exactly made a lot of friends on the force. The sex trafficking ring is more likely, though."

"Unless the CPD is involved in the ring," Marian whispered.

The suggestion horrified me and went against everything I'd ever believed in as a cop. Worse, I couldn't deny the possibility. A substantial sum could be made buying and selling of people, and the more exotic the person, the higher the pay off. I'd never been involved with busting any of the rings, but I'd heard rumors.

A single corrupt cop inside the system could clear the way for the masterminds behind a ring to get away with murder—or worse.

"Someone on the inside is always a possibility," I conceded.

Quinton looked grim. "And if there's someone on the inside, and they were afraid you were getting too close to them, they might try to get rid of you. It doesn't take a genius to see you're dedicated. You have connections to the FBI now, a permit that shows you're far more of a threat than anyone believed. You've done a masterful job of avoiding attention. That's no longer the case. You were shot twice, and within a day, you were back on the move. Someone knew you'd been shot, heard you'd been released, and tried to get you locked away for a crime you didn't commit—someone in Chicago."

"Why do you think it's someone in Chicago?"

"Because there's no record of the so-called case anywhere else. The crime only exists in the CPD's database—I know because Uncle Pierce looked. The accusation was never fully filed."

Marian sucked in a breath. "When a law enforcement officer, past or current, commits a crime, it's supposed to be reported to the FBI for monitoring. Exonerated cases are re-viewed, and an investigation of the accusa-tion is conducted. But if the case is never submitted to the FBI, that investigation can't take place."

"Someone inside the system was setting Gibby up. Gibby, do you know who was be-hind it?"

"No. Captain Martins explained the accu-sation to me, I informed him where I'd been, and that was that."

"So he knew you were in Des Moines." Marian wiggled free of my hold, planted a kiss on my cheek, and waded through the cushions towards the archway. She threw my jacket and shirt at me, and the jacket's weight betrayed the presence of my Ruger and wal-let. "What species is this Martins fellow?"

"Lion centaur."

"Racist?"

"Yeah, he is. If we were alone on a bridge, he might think twice before tossing me off. I was a body to fill a quota to him. I don't think that opinion has changed even with my new status as a shifter. The trial won't have helped matters much. That said, I don't think he's the type. He takes his job seriously, and when he found out the NYPD had called about me, he flipped his lid because he hadn't been informed."

"Well, if he's behind the attack, of course he'd flip his lid," Marian countered, bending over to pick up a bundle of dark clothing. "It's information he didn't have but needed to keep tabs on you. The nationwide concealed carry permit number he wants would be a convenient excuse to keep an eye on you."

"Or he wants to make sure I continue breathing, since a former CPD officer being killed by a mafia hitman would be a publicity nightmare." While my shoulder still ached where Abil Ili had stabbed me to make Marian's bite permanent, I shrugged into my shirt and jacket with minimal discomfort. "He probably doesn't care what happens to Marian. He's not a fan of the feds."

"We do have a reputation of stomping all over their territory when working a case. I've done it, and since I don't take bullshit from uppity police officers, they don't like me all that much."

I didn't hide my admiration while Marian wiggled into a pair of jeans and a form-fitting blouse. "I don't know who the Babylonians stole those jeans from, but remind me to thank them later."

"You're welcome," Quinton replied, laughing. "I left while you were napping. Your lady needed some space, so I went up top for a few minutes. I could have asked Abil Ili, but I thought his time was better spent elsewhere. You need to loan her one of your cute pocket toys, though. It was one thing to duck into a store. Getting firearms would've drawn too much attention."

"I'm running light on ammo," I warned.

"Then I suggest you make every shot count."

"It would help to know who we'll be shooting." Checking my pockets revealed someone had stuffed a tie inside, which somehow hadn't wrinkled. At Dad's insistence, I'd mastered the art of tying my ties without using a mirror on the grounds if a woman spent hours looking pretty for, I needed to put in the few extra minutes to make myself pretty for her, too.

We both agreed I needed all the help I could get.

"I'm sure we'll find out soon."

"Very soon," Abil Ili announced, separating from the crystals near Marian. She launched towards the ceiling and almost reached me before she touched down. With a soft laugh, I caught her and pulled her to me as Abil Ili announced, "We are ready. I have a list of names, locations, and information. Follow, and I will tell you all I have learned—and the role you three will play in the hours to come."

THIRTY-EIGHT

Someone had watched too many
war movies.

THE BABYLONIANS DIDN'T APPEAR to be technologically inclined until Abil Ili guided us several floors beneath the ziggurat to their server room. My first glimpse into the cavernous chamber took my ignorance, bashed me over the head with it, and made my fingers itch for a chance to play with the countless systems packed inside. The computers needed a lot of electricity, but I couldn't fathom where they got it from; I hadn't seen a single power outlet anywhere in the caverns, nor sign of anything modern, not even a lightbulb.

Yet computers surrounded me, installed into countless racks forming aisles, fans buzzing while thousands of lights blinked. Abil Ili marched ahead, and Marian shoved me to spur me into motion.

"That's a lot of computers," I stammered.

"While we still have our traditional library, knowledge has evolved, much like humans. There is a certain amount of wisdom in making knowledge accessible."

"It's my fault," Quinton admitted, flashing me a grin. "About a decade ago, I made the mistake of showing them my new cell phone. They'd been rather reclusive and missed the dawning of the technological era. They rectified the situation with their typical determination. When they discovered a wealth of information could be at the tips of their claws in an instant, they embraced computers. Now, many of them fill their hours separating truth from lies, taking news and hearsay and distilling them to truth and fact. They even have a library dedicated to the study of human fallacies. It's interesting. Perhaps they'll show you one day."

"One day," Abil Ili murmured, turning at an intersection. "We have more important things to do now. Follow, else we will be late, and the other hives will be displeased with us for being poor hosts."

At the end of the aisle, an archway waited, which Abil Ili ducked through, vanishing beyond a shimmering curtain of light. Quinton waited for us, gesturing for us to precede him. "This blocks the sound of the fans so those beyond can work. It's quieter than normal; they're shutting down many of the systems since no one will be here to maintain them."

Marian and I exchanged worried glances. I stepped through first, uncertain of what to expect. A cool breeze washed over me. I blinked at the dim illumination, squinting to adjust to the unexpected darkness.

Someone had watched too many war movies, basing their construction on the White House Situation Room. Counting chairs, I wondered why anyone would build a table big enough for thirty people—and whether Babylonians even bothered with chairs. The ten in the room were all standing, their attention focused on the largest digital screen I'd ever seen.

I added television crime dramas to the list of programs someone spent too much time watching. The CPD station where I'd worked had exactly one digital crime board, an ancient model less effective than a standard white board and markers.

Captain Martins used it as a status symbol.

Since patrol officers didn't get to use any type of crime board, I thought my drooling over the ten foot wide, clear-backed display was justified. Laughing, Marian wrapped her arm around me and squeezed. "If you want to play with a murder board, arrangements can be made. I have one at home."

First she gives me two guns, and then she tells me she has a murder board I can play with? Ah, heaven. I'd found it at last. "Take me home with you."

"I can't tie you to my bed and have my way with you if I don't take you home with me, so I suppose I must."

"Well, that got his attention. You'd already talked him into going home with you with the murder board." Quinton snickered. "I don't think he needs extra encouragement, Marian."

"I'm making sure he understands there is no point in resisting." Turning her attention away from me, she stepped to the gathered Babylonians with no evidence of her earlier fear, planting her hands on her hips while she regarded the panel and its data. "Nice board, terrible organization. You're going to have to start over. Make it snappy. Also, your board privileges are revoked, so after we're done, that board is coming home with me, where it will be used properly."

I laughed. "I see she wants it, too."

"Who doesn't? That damned thing's state of the art and cost a pretty penny. That woman's going to tire you out, Gibby. Anytime you need rescued, you let me know. I'll take you over to Papa's, and he'll keep you until she comes storming the castle to retrieve you."

"I'll remember that."

The Babylonians made space for Marian, and not to be outdone by the FBI agent, I came up behind her, wrapped my arms around her waist, and rested my chin on her shoulder. A grid of faces and names appeared, and the one in the upper left corner caught my attention. "Surprise, surprise, Mark O'-Conners."

"New York City, Italian Mafia," Abil Ili confirmed, pointing at the man who'd shot me. "He is our linchpin. He and those he knows that tie them all together, an intricate tangle of the red threads of death."

The poetic side of the Babylonian startled me. "He's the one who got me involved with all this."

Mark O'Conners had taken Marian—who known as Sally at the time—away from me. He'd try again, and he'd keep trying until he succeeded, either by taking her, killing me, or killing us both. For men like him, there'd be no other choices, not ones they'd be willing to make.

"Yes. This is why we started with him. His master is Luca Ricci, a vampire—a traditional one."

Quinton sighed. "We know of Ricci. He's a young fool who wishes to own the world so he might drink it to dust."

Abil Ili flicked his hook-tipped claws at

Ernesto's son. "Tell them of traditional vampires, the ones like this Ricci. They only know of your brood. It shows in their lack of true fear, their respect, and their friendship. If you demonstrate, take his jacket and shirt off, and try not to leave a mess on my floor. They should know what they face. Ricci is here, and he is prepared to hunt."

His entire body tensed, and Quinton stared at me. "Traditional vampires aren't kind when they feed."

"I'd say your fangs weren't so kind to my wrist. Your bite hurt."

"A forced feeding is much worse. Although my bite hurt, I had your consent. You knew I was hurting you to help. You didn't fight me. If Ricci fed on you, you would fight, and you would lose. A vampire's sway becomes easier to fight with subsequent bites. It's why Papa insists we feed as we do. We don't need to prey on an entire city, only a few. The violence of Ricci's feeding grows with every bite because the will of his prey strengthens. He's a weak, despicable vampire." Quinton hissed, flexing his hands. "You believe it's necessary?"

"For both of them. If you take him first, you won't have to fight both of them. His lady, I think, will understand the necessity."

Marian pressed her back against me, and

her hands covered mine. "Convince me it's necessity, perhaps."

"Vampire magic. If I bite you both, you'd fall under the protection of Papa's brood—blood magic. Your parents, freshly bitten, already have that protection. It takes roughly three days to fade. We're aware of the blood in our veins, and it binds us together. Papa will bite your parents again once he learns Ricci is coming. Papa is stronger than Ricci, and Ricci's magic cannot overwhelm Papa's. They would be immune to his enthrallment, immune to the enthrallment of Ricci's entire brood."

"So if you bite us, we enjoy that same protection?"

"The bite will hurt. There's nothing kind of how a traditional vampire feeds. Papa would use Amy to mitigate the pain—enraged lycanthropes are a force that challenges even him, but you two need to understand it in its entirety, so you can fight its effects should you be taken or they try to bite you."

Marian sighed, a frustrated, angry sound. "Explain how this Ricci is involved."

Abil Ili tapped Ricci's picture with his claw, and a map of the United States appeared. Red and gold lights marked most of the major cities, with thin lines connecting them into a network. A network of what, I wasn't sure.

"Ricci is one of three masterminds of the operation. One part feeds the sex industry, which is how you were caught in the web. With a little help from a friend, we learned the true purpose of the sex trafficking operation. Not only does it provide women, but it provides blood —last life blood, death blood. The women are used until they no longer appeal to the market, and then they are sold a final time to old vampires in need of new life. Their deaths are purchased, and they're drained of their lives, their bloodless, empty husks discarded."

The thought of Marian being killed after being sold into slavery chilled me to the bone, and I tightened my hold on her. "They're murdering the victims."

"Our research, provided to us from another source, indicates the women are killed when they are either too old to fetch a good price or become pregnant. A pregnant woman can't work." Abil Ili's claws slashed the air, and the reflective panels of his carapace turned crimson. "You got too close to their operation. Ricci must eliminate you both. He would rather the woman serve him and add to his wealth, but he has no use for a man who has thwarted his plans too many times."

"Accidentally," I muttered.

"Accidental or not, you could break the circle of his so-called eternal life. That is the problem with traditional vampires. They do not understand or care other ways exist to gather the life they need to sustain them. Sustenance is more than blood taken."

I inhaled, a sharp, hissing sound. "The Saven brood drinks blood freely given. Ricci's brood steals it."

Turning to Quinton, Abil Ili chuckled. "Intent matters. To nurture and flatter goes against a vampire's basic instinct to hunt and kill, but for the Saven brood, it is the secret to a long, life—an immortal one. Ernesto's children walk beneath the light of a noon sun hundreds of years before other vampires. Even in their youth, a glimpse of the sun isn't lethal. It hurts, and it is dangerous, but they survive long enough to seek shelter. Ricci must create new children more frequently because his are weak and die young."

"Papa is different."

"Your entire brood is different," the Babylonian corrected. "But you would be wise to show them how most vampires feed. Not only to gift them with the protection of your bite, but so they might feel what it is like to be truly dominated by a vampire."

Marian pulled free of my arms, stepping closer to the murder board to touch the map, zooming in on Des Moines. Flags marked twenty locations, and I recognized one as the farm she'd been taken to when she'd been trapped in an alpaca's body. "This is worse than I thought."

"The FBI was close to discovering the truth, too close. Mark O'Conners was not supposed to let you live. From what we have learned, framing you for his murder was an attempt to redirect resources and turn attention away from their operation to allow time to restructure, reroute, and erase evidence of their crimes." Abil Ili pointed at several of the markers in Des Moines. "Most of these are part of the sex trafficking operation, but some are part of the final sales network. The clients are almost always vampires, but demons participate, too. The demons interest me. They take the pregnant ones."

I shivered. "What happens to them?"

"They are the reason the FBI was getting close. Vampires want life to end. Demons feed on the creation of new life. The women would have been impregnated due to their influence. That creates a bond—with the mother, with the child. The bond fades within a few months of the child's birth, but it is against a demon's nature to kill those they help bring to life." The Babylonian tapped a flag, bringing up information on a butcher's shop on the outskirts of Des Moines. "This butcher works with an animal auction not far outside the city. He provides the tag numbers for the animals—transformed women and men—so the vampires can purchase them. The demons infiltrate the market, outbid the vampires on the pregnant women, and take them to safety. They have figured out the secret to reversing the transformation, so the woman is sold to new owners—owners who care for her and her infant. The mother and child are relocated, and often will rejoin the cycle, but in a more pleasant atmosphere. Incubi tend to become protective of the women in their keeping. It is not uncommon for one to settle down with a female thus procured until the end of her lifespan."

I froze, cold terror stabbing deep into my chest. "My grandfather is an incubus."

"Yes. Your grandmother may have been a victim of such an operation, and your grandfather had claimed your grandmother as his to protect her and your unborn mother. We do not know for certain, but it is possible. Incubi do not settle with lifelong partners often —not without duress being involved." The Babylonian sighed. "Or angelic influence. I have seen the results of your genetic testing. You are no angel."

I took several wobbly steps to the conference table, grabbed a chair, and sat down before I fell down. "How likely?"

"Very likely. We have uncovered some interesting facts during our research." Abil Ili tapped the screen, focusing the map on Lincoln, Nebraska. Unlike Des Moines, it was clear of flags. "This is today."

He tapped a few more times. Seven gold and two red flags appeared. "This was thirty years ago." After a few more taps, a handful of other flags appeared. "Forty years. The FBI has never investigated sex trafficking operations in Lincoln."

My grandmother fought fires, and because knowing how they ignited and burned was critical to extinguishing them, she could start them, too. I shivered as the possibilities tangled in my head and led me places I didn't want to go. "Arsons?"

"You understand."

"God," I muttered, wiping my hand over my face as though I could erase the horror of what my grandmother had endured, resulting in the birth of my mother. "You're really implying my grandparents took on one of these rings all on their own."

"The numbers do not lie. Someone did, and it wasn't the police nor was it someone within the FBI."

"And my great-grandfather? What of him?"

"Things like this have been happening for as long as humans have realized they could enslave each other for wealth. That is a question you have to ask him, but it is not an incubus's nature to remain with a human family unless they have been forced to claim responsibility for something, a life that would not otherwise exist, one made of his seed against his will. They do not form bonds easily. Is that not right, Quinton?"

"He's right. An incubus doesn't form a bond unless he has had constant and frequent exposure to a woman. Ours often bond with our donors; it's part of how we feed. That's why we take care of our donors like we do. It isn't just for us, but for them, too. A succubus won't form a bond unless she's ready to have a child, and she'll bond with the incubus or the human who'll become the father of her child. Her bond fades after her child's birth."

Marian joined me, pulling a chair close to mine, sitting with a grunt. "Against his will—as in if he didn't get her pregnant and take her out of the situation, she'd be killed?"

"That is our current theory."

Quinton hissed, glaring at the digital board, his eyes glowing a brilliant red. "It fits. We're very careful with our incubi and our donors for this reason. We prevent unwanted children, but Papa insists on being close at hand for any wanted ones. We have incubi wanting to join our brood because they want a bond—or a child. It's their nature to desire the creation of life. We try to make the arrangements in a way satisfying to everyone." The vampire relaxed and smiled. "Your neighbors are a good example. The parents of those triplets will find themselves with a mysterious donor of toys and everything they need to give their children happiness. That's a succubus's nature. Papa enjoys it, too. The important thing to understand is that in a healthy relationship, the incubus's bond fades when their child is self-sufficient or the mother is ready for another child, whichever comes first."

"And to think most people view demons as evil," I muttered, shaking my head.

"Good and evil are as much of a choice as they are nature," Abil Ili murmured, swiping a claw against the screen to return to the main map of the United States. He zoomed in on Chicago. "Chicago has two markets, one of each type. We have confirmed Ricci's involvement with them. We have also confirmed connections with members of the CPD. Some members of the CPD are covering these operations with the goal of keeping the Saven brood unaware of their presence. There are no demons involved with Ricci's operations."

I leaned back in my seat and struggled to take slow, even breaths. "How important is Chicago to their operations?"

"We do not know. Given time, we could find out." The Babylonian shrugged. "Luring Ricci here was not hard. We will eliminate Ricci's operatives and the corrupt police, and we will cleanse Chicago. It will not stop the trafficking, but for a time, it may protect the innocent. If we kill Ricci, another vampire will take his place, but he might be a younger, inexperienced vampire—one easier for mortals to hunt. Such a result would even the playing field and bring balance. This would repay our obligations to you and yours."

I shook my head. "You owe me nothing."

On a Babylonian, a smile resembled a declaration of hunger, one involving a display of sharp, flesh-rending teeth. "That is not for you to decide. This is our territory, and we have allowed it to become unbalanced. We owe you much for bringing the problem to our attention. We merely even the scales so humans might be able to wage war on a level battlefield, rather than serve as the helpless cattle of traditional vampires." Abil Ili's smile widened to a gaping grin. "We are no angels, either. This is a hunt we will enjoy. Please allow me to introduce to you our prey, so you know them for what they are."

THIRTY-NINE

It didn't feel like a scratch, did it?

ABIL ILI WENT through the list name by name, and one shocked me so much I had to sit before my legs gave out beneath me. How could cowardly Stripes number among them—or be so predominant a figure in the operation to enslave women and turn them into fodder for vampires? Although Michelle hadn't played an active part, I could read between the lines.

Turning a blind eye to Stripes's activities made her an accessory, and she'd watched me with the others. All the officers who'd come to my apartment were involved in one way or another. I found little comfort in the knowledge Captain Martins wasn't on the list.

Lions lived to protect, and lionesses were the jewels of a lion's pride. All females stirred a lion's protective instincts. I couldn't see a lion selling any female. Buying, claiming them as his own, and controlling them I could readily believe, but Martins had never seemed the type to sow terror.

I wondered if he even knew his officers had attempted to acquire my permit number —if he knew of their activities. I pulled out my phone and stared at the screen for a long time in sullen silence.

"I'm sorry," Marian whispered.

I shook my head. "It's not your fault."

"Still. You worked with a lot of these people. How do you think Ricci and his crime network got to so many of them?"

Quinton made a thoughtful sound in this throat. "Likely blackmail. Our bite can't control people—not like that. These officers acted of their own free will."

"They will not understand until they experience a traditional bite, although Shane has seen a little of your powers, for all you were gentle with him." Abil Ili clicked his talons together. "It is necessary."

"Take your shirt and jacket off, Gibby," the vampire ordered. "I'm only going to take a sip, but it'll still get messy. Marian, don't be alarmed. It's going to look a lot worse than it is. Abil Ili will stop you from interfering if he must."

Marian crossed her arms over her chest. "You better not hurt him."

"I'll be hurting him, he just won't come to any lasting harm, and should one of Ricci's vampires get a hold of him, he'll be safe from their bite—or at least capable of fighting them off. Unless you want him easy prey?"

"Fine," she snapped.

Standing, I slid out of my jacket and tossed it onto my seat, my shirt following it shortly after. I glared at Quinton. "I don't like this."

The vampire showed me his teeth, and for the first time since meeting him, I recognized his intent to bite me. I tensed, my breath catching in my throat.

Strong arms circled me from behind, pinning my arms to my sides. Fangs tore into my shoulder, but they weren't Quinton's; Ernesto's son watched, his smile vanishing behind a visage so neutral it frightened me almost as much as the stabbing, throbbing pain ripping through my shoulder, down my spine, and into my head. Unable to scream, I choked out a faint, weak cry.

Marian jumped to her feet, took one step towards me, and Quinton grabbed her, shoving her down, catching her wrists in his hands and forcing them to her sides, his legs caging hers and pushing her knees together.

I didn't see him bite; bright lights flared in my vision, and I shuddered.

Then, as quickly as it began, the stunning agony was gone, and I hung limply in a pair of iron-hard arms, which kept me from top-pling to the floor.

"And that is what makes a vampire so dan-gerous. One minute, you are alone. Safe. Fine," Abil Ili turned to face me, clasping his taloned tentacles behind his back. "The next, you are held in strong arms, too strong for a human to escape. The pain takes you, stuns you, makes you easy prey for him. With the first sip, you are his. Had he continued to drink, the second and third, you would feel your pulse weaken as he drained the life from you, your heart struggling to adapt, fighting to keep you alive. If he meant to drain you dry, he would drink for ten minutes, one hungry swallow at a time."

Quinton straightened, although he braced his hand on Marian's throat. A few drops of blood stained his mouth and splattered his chin. "Next time, the pain'll waken your prey instinct, and you'll fight, understanding death comes for you. It won't be so easy, then."

"Indeed," Ernesto agreed, his voice a purr in my ear. "Take your time and find your feet, dear boy. I've not hurt you much—hardly more than a scratch, but it didn't feel like a scratch, did it?"

Relief and fury waged a bitter war, but re-lief won. "I'll kneecap you a hundred times for this, Ernesto."

The ancient vampire laughed, adjusted his

hold on me, and gave my chest a solid thump. "You had no idea I was behind you."

"I didn't. If your goal was to scare me, you get full points. You okay, Marian?"

Marian shook her head, slapped away Quinton's hand, and touched her neck. "I think I'm fine." She checked her palm. "Yeah, I'm fine. Just a scratch. That didn't feel like a scratch. I thought you'd ripped my throat out."

Ernesto sighed, hooked my chair with his foot, and dragged it closer. Freeing an arm, he set my clothes on the table and shoved me down. "That's how traditional vampires feed. Pain is a good way to stun prey. With practice, a vampire can activate the nerves near the bite, all at the same time. The older the vampire, the easier it is. I could've knocked you out with the most intense pain you've ever felt in your life. For the next three days, if another vampire tries to bite you, he'll have to go through me first—and he won't succeed. Don't bother with kneecapping when you fight them, dear boy. Go straight for the head, and make sure you sever the spine before you're finished."

I had to take more than a few deep breaths to gather my wits enough to sit up and rub my shoulder where I'd been bitten. For the amount of pain, the damage and bloodshed was minimal. "Sever the spine. Right. With what, exactly?"

Ernesto smiled, and the viciousness of his expression repulsed me. Slipping his hand into his jacket, he pulled out a pair of bone-gripped daggers in black and gold sheaths. "These, one each. Consider them an early wedding gift. They're carved with a very special bone—the same bone for both." Setting the first blade on the table beside me, the vampire circled my chair, leaned over Marian, and kissed her cheek. "My apologies, my dear. Please accept this token of my regret for frightening you." He slipped the dagger's hilt into her braced hand, gently closing her fingers over the bone so she wouldn't drop it.

With wide eyes, Marian jerked her head in a nod.

Turning to Quinton, Ernesto canted his head to the side and crossed his arms over his chest. "Explain yourself this instant, son. I felt your bite on him."

Ernesto's son grimaced.

"Ernesto," I called, scooting the chair a few inches forward so I could retrieve the dagger and examine the black and gold sheath, fashioned in the likeness of a phoenix rising in billowing flames. "I consented." Aware of the odd way the Babylonian spoke, I did my best to mimic him. "Abil Ili honored me with his help, but to do so, he needed

Quinton's aid. He bit my wrist so I would not thrash while Abil Ili showed his expertise."

The Babylonian chimed his laughter. "Such a clever little human."

"Shane," the ancient vampire complained. "What have you done to yourself now?"

"The injuries from his fall were fatal. It was just as bad as we were warned—perhaps worse. Abil Ili and his soothers gave him care humans couldn't have provided. It was bad." Quinton shot an apologetic look Marian's way. "Worse than I anticipated when I asked to enthrall him to smooth the way for Abil Ili's work."

"I promised to kneecap him over it later."

"Boys," Ernesto spat, shaking his head. "Let this be a lesson to you, Marian. Don't have sons. Daughters grow up to become beautiful women worthy of protection. The sons? Sons grow up to be men determined to give their old men heart attacks."

"That would necessitate you having a functional heart," I shot back.

With a long-suffering sigh, Ernesto bowed his head.

"Be nice, Shane."

"He bit me. I don't need to be nice."

She laughed and smiled at me. "You're grumpy. Put your clothes back on. He's bribing us with weapons, so forgive him—for now. We can kneecap them both later. It'll be a date."

If I counted the ways I loved Marian, I would begin with her adaptability. Her smile and laughter were close to the top of the list. Add in her protectiveness, something I hadn't known I'd wanted, and I was lost and gratefully so. "All right."

"I'd have come sooner, but I had preparations of my own to make. Abil Ili, it has been too long, old friend. Where do we stand?"

"We have gone over our target list, although I fear I may have dealt a wound even I cannot heal." The Babylonian bowed to me. "For that, my apologies. It is a deep pain, knowing friends have turned to foes."

Ernesto sighed. "How bad?"

"It's bad," Marian answered. "At least a quarter of the officers Shane worked with are involved. His former captain appears to be innocent. And it gets worse; another quarter aren't actively participating, but they're aware of what's going on and have done nothing to stop it. Disgusting."

"And when it comes to something like this, being aware it's happening is no different from participating." Ernesto slammed his fist into the table, startling me so much I jumped in my seat. "They willfully ignored the slavery of others."

"Yes," Abil Ili confirmed. "The visiting

hives are getting into position now. We have confirmation Ricci has arrived, and he has brought Mark O'Conners. They are yours, should you want them."

Ernesto hissed. "I'll take O'Conners. That grudge is personal, and I'll stain my hands by showing him what a truly ancient vampire can do. He'll experience the worst pain in this world before I weaken him and leave him for the wolves to rip apart."

I had no doubt he meant my parents, who would do just that; pieces of O'Conners would be scattered over several city blocks by the time the pair of lycanthropes finished with the hitman. "Wear a poncho."

"A decent human being would be concerned for the victim."

I looked around the room. "Decent human being? Where?"

Marian scooted her chair closer and kicked me in the ankle. "Shane!"

"You're an exceptionally sexy human being, so my point stands."

I liked when Marian blushed, and I smiled at having gotten a reaction out of her.

"And that's the smug expression of a man who knows he won that round." Ernesto sat on the table and swung his legs as though he were a younger man. "If you need me for Ricci, I'll come, but I'll take out O'Conners first. He doesn't leave Chicago alive—or in pieces big enough to bother with a bodybag. I'll take the children with me while you and yours begin the purge. Once we've taken care of O'Conners, we'll rendezvous with you. Text me the location when you have him cornered. Do be careful, Abil Ili. He may be younger than me, but he's still dangerous."

"Not dangerous enough," the Babylonian replied.

I believed him.

WHILE THE CHICAGO Babylonians had mounts, they were not shedu. Instead, we got scaled demented deer with a giant curved bone horn jutting out from under their equine chins. The one nearest to us had a long, pale beard falling down to its broad chest, braided and decorated with sapphire and ruby crystals. A pair of antlers rose from its brow, each prong sharpened to a lethal point. Green, brown, and golden tufts of fur stuck up through the gaps between its scales, and it wore a bejeweled saddle but no bridle. The saddle lacked stirrups, and I could guess at why.

The Babylonians rode into battle with their talons sheathed in steel blades.

"Ernesto?" I swallowed to ease the dryness in my throat.

"What is it, dear boy?"

"What have we done?"

"Nothing yet. And anyway, they started it. We're just finishing it."

The demented deer turned its head towards me, opened its mouth, and showed off its curved teeth. Its long, tufted ears twisted back, and the fires of hell burned in its black and red eyes.

"We're really riding these?"

"These are the kirin. Yes, we are."

"Kirin?" I'd heard the name before, but it took me a minute to remember why. "Chinese unicorns?"

"No, those are qilin. Qilin are nice Chinese unicorns, guardian spirits. Qilin don't have much use for vampires. Consider the kirin a rather distant cousin of the qilin. They enjoy getting their hooves dirty for a good cause. They're tricorns, if you want to get technical about it. The lower horn is for gathering blood and cutting open prey for easier eating. This habit is the source of enmity between the qilin and the kirin; the qilin don't approve of the consumption of meat."

"They think it's blasphemy," the kirin said, a female judging from the sweetness of her voice. She laughed merrily, tossing her head, turning a bright eye to me. "I haven't gotten to eat a human in centuries. This will be delightful. I am Bai Bao Chen, for I am a jewel of the morning sea. You bring change and chaos where you go, so I look forward to carrying you into battle. Prove yourself interesting, and I may grace you with my presence longer."

I really needed to stop hanging out with beings who thought of me as food. I only knew two things about the Chinese, which were to bow when being polite and that I really liked their food, even the fake stuff made in America no one else could tolerate. I dipped in a bow, my hands clasped in front of me, careful to lower my head enough to be respectful. "I'm honored, Bai Bao Chen."

"A quick study, this child of yours," the kirin murmured, and I thought she sounded pleased. "Introduce him, Ernesto, as is your place."

"He is Shane. The lady is his mate and future bride, Marian. You honor us, Bai Bao Chen. Who would you recommend ride with us into battle?"

I raised my head, and the kirin lifted hers high, her fiery eyes scanning the herd. "Fen Guanyu Shi, for she remembers the old forests and their beauty well and honors their memory."

A deep green kirin stepped forward, and golden crystals chimed from her beard. She lowered her head, approached Ernesto, and blew her breath in his face. "You still stink, ancient one."

Ernesto's laughter rang out. "And you're as irreverent as you are beautiful, as always. I would be honored to share the hunt with you."

"Quinton, as my loathing for you will never die, I shall send Tai Wu Xiang with you, in the unlikely chance he might rid the Earth of you once and for all."

A jet black kirin separated from the herd, head held high. "Rude, Bai Bao Chen. I would not rid the Earth of such entertainment."

"Can I not dream?"

"Do not listen to her, friend Quinton. She sends me with you for I am the best equipped to protect you, for I bring good fortune in the heart of battle. Blood will flow, but it will not be ours, not this day."

Quinton smiled. "It's good to see you again, Xiang."

"And it's good to ride into battle once more. My herd sister is right. It has been too long since we have walked the Earth, far too long since we have been instruments of balance, even for a small matter such as this."

Marian leaned towards me. "Is it just me, or are we majorly outclassed here?"

"Glad I'm not the only one to have noticed that. Between the two of us, we have thirteen bullets, two guns, and a pair of daggers. I'm pretty sure we're spectators."

Bai Bao Chen turned her head to me and showed her teeth. While I was fairly certain she smiled, I got the feeling she was hungry and thought I looked tasty. Her attention turned to Marian. "My mate will carry you. He is Fang Jiahao Yi, the keeper of justice in our herd, the guardian of our virtues, and the heart of our family."

The largest of the kirin, blood red with fire blazing from his eyes, split off from the herd. The prongs of his antlers curved, sharpened to razor edges. Unlike the others, no crystals decorated his beard. Instead, they sprouted from his scales, as though he slowly transformed from flesh to gem.

Marian mimicked me, bowing with her hands clapped in front of her. "I'm honored, Fang Jiahao Yi."

"As am I. You may be small, but in you, I see a warrior's heart."

Bai Bao Chen snorted. "It is decided. We ride together. Abil Ili has named our prey and has made his face and his sins known to us. His final breath belongs to the werewolves, whom were slighted first. We may feast after they have enacted their justice with their claws. We are to leave no trace of our passage, so hunt well, hunt clever, and hunt beyond the eye of mortal man, for they are not ready to accept the truth of us."

I agreed with that readily enough; I sure as hell wasn't ready to accept any of the insanity around me, although I had no choice in the matter. The kirin all reared, lifting their heads to the crystals overhead, their hooves tucked to their chests. Silence fell, and in the still quiet, I thought they prayed, although I didn't know to whom or for what.

As one, their front hooves clicked on the crystal floor, and Bai Bao Chen turned to me. "There is one last matter we must attend to."

I frowned. "What is it?"

"Your eye. Abil Ili, do not forget your manners. My rider's eye. Return it to him. It does him no good in your hands. Really, making us look at that empty socket. Do not strip him of his dignity."

Somewhere in the crowd of Babylonians, I heard Abil Ili laugh. "Yes, I have his eye. I was merely examining it for a while."

"And you could not do this when it was in his head where it belongs?" The kirin flattened her ears. "He has lost his center without it."

Truer words had not been spoken, although I tried my best not to let it bother me. "It's all right, Bai Bao Chen. It's not like I don't take it out and roll it around to express my disgust at times. It doesn't bother me he has it."

"No, it just bothers you what is rightfully yours was taken from you due to greed. I see your heart, Shane, as well as its shadows. The wound has scarred, but it has not healed."

Not only did I need to stop hanging out with beings who thought of me as food, I *really* needed to stop hanging out with people who saw through my bullshit and called me out on it. "Guilty as charged."

"The name of your heart is Cheng, for it is an honest one. The name of your spirit is Shui, for you flow like water. In the way of our herd, you are Shane Shui Cheng, for you are as true and honest as the water's flow." Bai Bao Chen lifted her head and stared down at me, a challenge in her bright eyes.

Names seemed important to the kirin, so I accepted what I couldn't change with a bow.

"The matter of his eye, Abil Ili. My dignity demands my rider have two eyes, not one. Fix this travesty immediately."

Abil Ili approached, and like the others of his hive, he wore swords over his talons, forcing him to adopt an odd, swaying stride so he would not slice through the crystal floors. He stretched out an arm to me, and adhered to one of the suckers was a rich blue sphere.

It wasn't my eye; mine was a darker shade,

while the one Abil Ili held was the vivid blue of the purest flame.

"In my rage over that distasteful bauble, I broke yours. Thus, it was my duty to replace it. Its size should match, for I was very careful with its measurements before my fit of rage overcame me."

I translated that to mean the Babylonian had very deliberately broken my glass eye so I couldn't refuse the new one. "My thanks, Abil Ili. The old one was fragile and easily broken."

"So eloquent," Bai Bao Chen cooed.

The stone fell onto my hand, and its warmth surprised me. Marian leaned over, and her eyes widened. "What type of stone is this? The color's beautiful."

"Topaz, its color pure and untouched as the day it was pulled from the Earth. A rare stone for a rarer man. May its light shine for you in dark places. Although it will never allow you to see as you once did, it may share other secrets with you in time. While you slept, we strengthened the stone so it will endure for the rest of your days, so it can become a trusted friend. Should it be taken from you, it will return on its own, for you belong to it as much as it belongs to you. Please accept this as a token of our thanks for making us aware of what we should have already known. We are old, and we had forgotten our duty."

I didn't understand, but I decided I didn't need to. Thank you seemed too small, too insignificant, but I said the words anyway, although they stuck in my throat and took two tries to choke them out.

Marian took my hand in hers and squeezed.

Abil Ili was right; the topaz didn't restore my sight, but it warmed me all the same. The gesture was so little yet meant so much. The Babylonians saw through me, recognized me as someone deserving better than flawed glass, valued me so few others did.

"It is time," he said. "Ride well, fight better."

FORTY

Don't worry about being graceful.

I STARTLED Bai Bao Chen when I vaulted onto her back, settling in the saddle. Marian gaped at Fang Jiahao Yi's back, her expression so uncertain I smiled. "Come here, Marian."

She did, and I surprised her, too, by hauling her up onto Bai Bao Chen's back with me, sitting her sideways on the saddle, crammed between me and the horn. "Fang Jiahao Yi?"

The kirin gave a throaty laugh and trotted to Bai Bao Chen's side. "A good show of skill and strength, human. You will teach her how to mount, yes?"

"On a fence to start so your patience is not sorely tested," I agreed, securing my hold on Marian's waist. "All right. Don't worry about being graceful, just get on his back. I'll teach you as we go."

With a little help from Fang Jiahao Yi, I managed to get her leg over the kirin's broad back and place her pretty ass in the saddle. Without reins offering the illusion of security and balance, Marian clutched the horn and tufts of his mane. "If I slow us down, buck me off. You can probably do it walking."

I chuckled, reaching over and patting her leg. "You'll be fine. The horn is there for you to hold onto. Just clamp your legs to his sides. You're not going to hurt him. Riding's easier with reins, but his mane and the horn will help you balance. I'll admit balancing is a lot easier with stirrups, but we'll make do."

"We did not think of stirrups for the humans and vampires," Bai Bao Chen admitted. "We are accustomed to the Babylonians, who have no use for them, as they prefer to make use of all their weapons. We will go as slowly as we can. Should we need speed as a group, I will trust you with my rider, Yi."

"I will flow like water over the sand for her, no fear. Your rider will best serve as a watchful guard. Should she need help, I will recruit one of the vampires. They are sturdier."

"They're harder to kill than I am," I conceded. "I have a knife and six bullets. I'm not sure how much use I'll be once I'm out of rounds."

Marian snorted. "Says the man who knocked out a werewolf with two punches."

"Caught him by surprise. It usually takes a lot more than that."

"You still knocked out a werewolf with two punches. Once you had him down, you chained him to a tractor, dragged him off, and shaved off his fur." Marian grinned at me. "If you run out of bullets, just punch them in the head until they stop moving."

I scowled at Marian, who smirked unrepentantly.

One by one, the Babylonians and their kirin faded from view, although I could hear the chime of hooves on crystal. Ernesto watched for a few moments before turning to me. "Your new eye's pretty."

I faked a swoon and fluttered my hand near my face. "You're such a flirt."

Marian wrinkled her nose. "Ew."

Laughing, I flipped her a salute. "When else has he said nice things to me?"

"Every time you kneecap him, Shane."

"True." I grinned at Ernesto. "Stop flirting with me. Marian doesn't like it."

"I'm beginning to think your parents are right. You truly are an awful child. You were put on this Earth to punish us, weren't you?"

"He can punish me anytime he wants," Marian chirped.

Could I get away with stealing her, finding somewhere nice and private, and skipping the battle altogether? I could think of a lot of things I'd love to do with her. I pointed at her and smiled. "I'll remember that."

"I think he's almost as enthusiastic as you," Bai Bao Chen said, sidestepping and bumping her hindquarters against Fang Jaihao Yi's. "New love. It's a precious thing, isn't it?"

"As long as they engage in their new love somewhere other than on my back," the kirin stallion replied.

Now that was a thought. I'd never considered trying anything like that on horseback. Could it be done?

"I don't like that look, Shane. Whatever you're thinking, the answer is no."

Bai Bao Chen laughed. "We will wait a few minutes for the others to exit the caverns, then we will follow. Since you lack the ability to camouflage yourselves, we will use our magic. It is part illusion, part misdirection. They will mistake us for horses, because they don't believe creatures like us exist. The more imaginative ones will see us for what we are, but even if they told the tale, who would believe them?"

Not many, and I nodded my agreement with her wisdom. "Do we know where O'-Conners is?"

Ernesto growled. "Not far from the scene of the crime. He watches, hoping one of you will show up. He missed Marian coming down the spillway, which was luck more than anything else, but I've seen him several times since the attack. I worry he'll try for Pierina next."

"That would be the last thing he did in this life," I muttered. "She's almost as dangerous as you are."

"You flatter me, dear boy. She eclipses me daily. Daughters are amazing creatures, and she's more amazing than most."

"And my parents?"

"Waiting for O'Conners to be lured out. We'll strike in front of my daughter's restaurant. Quinton, you and I shall flush him out, and once we have him, we'll tear him apart. Don't toy with him. Make him dead. We'll get our satisfaction mutilating the body. Corpses can't hurt us. Since he's likely bound to Ricci, we'll want to make certain he can't be raised. I wouldn't want him to become one of us."

I agreed. "Violent in life, violent in unlife?"

"There's no knowing what he'd become, but there's no doubting who his master would be—Ricci. If Ricci has drunk from O'-Conners many times, we may hurt him when we make our move." Ernesto's tone and grim smile told me that was exactly what the vampire hoped for. "I don't know which one of you O'Conners will go after first. He may try to take Marian and leave you for another day, dear boy."

"Over my dead body."

"That's what he wants, so let's avoid that."

Scowling because he was right, I reined in my fraying temper. "Okay. So what do you want me to do if he tries to take Marian?"

"Shoot him, of course. In the head. Multiple times. Splatter his brains all over the sidewalk. The kirin don't care if their food touches the floor, so don't be shy. Make a mess."

"Mhmm," Bai Bao Chen agreed. "Brains. I like them scrambled."

RIDING a kirin turned out more pleasant than I expected. Bai Bao Chen's stride rolled, which made keeping my seat easy, allowing me to instruct Marian on how to ride without worrying she'd fall from Fang Jaihao Yi's back. We reached the spillway in thirty minutes, but instead of the impenetrable darkness I expected, I was able to see the outline of the stones and the concrete, although I couldn't make out any details.

From what I could tell, the spillway, rather than being simply a slope for water or a slide for unfortunate sentients swept beyond the grate, truly was a mad scientist's architectural nightmare consisting of bumps, curves, twists, and in several spots, a loop-de-loop.

I thanked my lucky stars I had missed the

loop-de-loops my first trip down the demented slide; it'd been bad enough with Quinton.

Marian made a distressed sound, and with a gentle pressure of my leg, Bai Bao Chen stepped closer to her stallion, allowing me to reach over and take her hand. "It's all right."

"It's so dark," she whispered.

I frowned at the fear in her voice and the tightness of her grip. "It won't be too hard to get to the top, not with the kirin helping, for which I'm truly grateful."

"He climbed the steps to the top as an otter." I was aware of Ernesto holding his hands apart in a rough estimation of an otter's size. "He's about this long when he shifts and cute as a button."

"A long walk indeed," Fang Jaihao Yi said. "I will not let you fall, Marian. The darkness only lasts until the top."

"And it's entirely possible we'll walk straight into a fight, especially if O'Conners got within range of your parents' teeth. They aren't going to wait for us if they get a chance to tear into the man who tried to kill their pup—twice, if our speculations are correct." Ernesto chuckled. "This doesn't bother me, as I'd rather have two happy lycanthropes than two grumpy ones robbed of the chance to rip their son's assailant to bits. I'll be satisfied with Ricci. He's decent prey."

"Should we emerge at a canter?" Bai Bao Chen asked. "I do not mind. A nice challenge, taking the steps at a canter."

Fang Jaihao Yi whinnied. "If we do that, I will take up the rear and come at a respectable, safe walk, as I do not think my rider would appreciate a trip down the spillway, however fun."

Marian tightened her grip on my hand. "Pass."

The kirin laughed while I gave Marian's hand a final squeeze and freed myself so I could pull out my Ruger. "With your wrist in a brace, you're better off guarding our backs. How's your aim with your good hand?"

"I'm good. I put in my hours on both, and I'm double qualified. I can guard the rear."

"It's been a while since I've brought a knife to a gun fight," I admitted, a little happier than I should've been at the idea of taking a knife to a gun fight. Six bullets wouldn't last long, and I regretted not having extra ammunition with me. I couldn't remember why I was one bullet short, which bothered me. We both should've had a full set of seven.

I hoped the extra bullet helped Marian.

"Have you ever taken a knife to a gun fight?"

"Yeah, every time Dad took me to the range. We played a game. He'd shoot me with blanks, I'd chase him around with a knife. Dad usually won."

"Usually? Not always?"

"His blanks hurt; not quite empty shells, not rubber, either. Don't know where he got them, but they were probably magic of some sort. Think of them as paintball rounds from a handgun. Well, I can't dodge a bullet, but it's possible to make Dad aim where I'm not. The times I got him before he got me, that's how I did it. I think after this is over, I'll have to go for a few rounds at the range to get back in shape."

Marian laughed. "I'd like to try that."

"I'll make you use a practice blade, because I'd like my father to survive to tell the tale."

"Flirt."

I smiled. "So, if you can get me close, Bai Bao Chen, I can take care of myself if I run out of ammo."

"While on my back?"

"You could buck me in the right direction, I suppose. I am happy with either. Dad's horses are old and tired, but when they could still be ridden, he liked to play another game with me."

Ernesto snickered. "I can imagine the games a werewolf would play. Toss the puppy?"

"Toss the puppy," I confirmed. "I'd ride one of the horses. He'd chase us in his hybrid form. Skunk loved it. He was still a stallion then. Since there were no stallions for him to fight, he'd fight with Dad. So I'd ride the horse, Dad would chase the horse, and if I didn't ride just like Dad wanted, he'd either toss me off or the horse would buck me off."

Bai Bao Chen pranced beneath me and snorted, tossing her head high. "I may have finally found a rider worth his weight."

"Please forgive my mare. She gets quite excitable at times, and there is a limited number of humans she actually likes and doesn't want to eat."

When *would* I learn to keep company with beings who didn't view me as food? Probably never. Oh well. I'd survive—maybe. "What's your range at a canter?"

"We could start our run now. That would give us time to clear any unwanted company before Fang Jaihao Yi catches up. The barrier and water should mask our hoofbeats. I am the fleetest, so we shall draw fire, Shane Shui Cheng. Do not get shot. I would rather not drink your blood this day."

"I don't want to be shot, either. I've already been shot, at ground zero of a detonation, and bitten by two vampires. I've reached my quota for injuries for at least a year."

"Ernesto, take the other side of the canal. Quinton, guard my rider's back. Marian, when you and Fang Jaihao Yi catch up with us, you will be the lookout. Your eyes to the sky. You never know what might come from above, especially since the shedu can fly. They are not the most fearsome of allies the Babylonians have, nor are we, and the shedu do not care for what happens to those who get in their way."

FORTY-ONE

Fancy meeting you here.

SINCE WE DIDN'T HAVE a real plan, no one could ruin it for us, although the idea of flying blind into battle worried me enough I shifted in the saddle and tensed, preparing for the worst. Bai Bao Chen snorted, pawed the step, and surged forward, hurtling upwards faster than any mere horse could hope to manage.

I somehow stayed on her back, though I suspected that had more to do with her than any skill on my part. It took several strides to adapt to her canter, which rolled as she flowed up the steps, each hoof placed with the precision gained only with practice. I believed she could've found her way even blindfolded, running with confidence I envied.

We burst through the barrier into chaos, bodies, and carnage. The dead or dying barred our way, assuming the kirin refused to trample anyone. Bai Bao Chen jumped, soared, and crashed down on a man's back, who was swinging at my father from behind; I only recognized Dad from his size.

Blood dripped from his fur, masking its color.

"Well, isn't this interesting." The kirin kept all four hooves on her prey as she took stock of the battle. Dad whirled, his claws lifted to strike.

"Hey, Dad. Fancy meeting you here." I lifted my new dagger in salute.

Gold roiled in my father's eyes, and he bared his teeth at me. "Boy. I'm tanning your hide later."

"Okay." The group Dad fought seemed to like his back, and without missing a beat, I whipped out my Ruger, aimed, and fired. I didn't remember the man being in the Babylonian's files but decided I didn't care who he was.

Another attacker approached, and without bothering to turn, Dad kicked out, catching him with his clawed feet. Blood splashed, and Bai Bao Chen whinnied her approval. Snarling curses my father whipped around and slashed, grabbing hold of his victim's arm and yanking. "My turn to go clubbing," he announced, before wading into battle with his new weapon.

"Have I ever told you my father's armed and dangerous?"

"No," the kirin replied. "You had not."

"He is. I'm quite proud of him, just don't tell him that."

"As you should be. It was a very skilled disarming of his opponent."

"Do you think we should give him a hand?"

Bai Bao Chen made a thoughtful noise in her throat, shifted her weight, and bucked, kicking her hind legs out. I twisted in time to watch a head fly into the canal while the man's body dropped lifeless to the sidewalk. "No, I think he is ahead of the game thus far, but should he need our aid, we will give him a leg up."

Having adjusted to the lack of peripheral vision on my right side, I was startled by a flash of movement. I brought my blade up, catching a vampire in the hand, her fingers curled into claws and her fangs bared. Cold fear trickled through me at the memory of Ernesto's bite.

Instead of shooting her with my Ruger like a smart man, I smashed it into her teeth before jamming the barrel into her mouth. I fired twice.

Cursing at the waste of a perfectly good bullet, I ripped the weapon free and sliced the dagger across her throat. She'd drank recently; blood sprayed from my slice, and her scream ended in a gurgle. She slashed her hands at me, her nails sharpened to dangerous little points. Kicking someone was hard without stirrups, so I reversed my dagger and smashed the pommel down on the top of her head.

She withstood the first three hits, and tired of wasting time on her, I drove the business end through the top of her skull. Bai Bao Chen snorted, twisted her head around, and grabbed the vampire's arm in her teeth. Bracing her legs, the kirin shook like a massive dog, whipping the undead woman's body side to side. Only when the gurgling screams fell silent did the kirin release the vampire, prancing over the fresh corpse.

"That was a lot harder than I expected," I confessed.

"She was old, but she was old and stupid." Plowing forward, the kirin shunted aside several Babylonians, their reflective panels larger and divided by gold rather than silver. I suspected the gold marked them as being from a different hive. She followed Dad, who shoved his makeshift club down a vampire's throat.

I'd seen Dad fight, but I'd never seen him engage in such blatant brutality. At first, I didn't understand what he was doing, but then he ripped his club out of the back of the vampire's head and resumed beating his victim with it.

The vampire, despite half its head being gone, was still alive.

"That's totally unfair. I fall off a balcony and essentially die, and that thing takes a lickin' and keeps on tickin'." With three bullets already gone, I didn't want to waste a round on a vampire who wouldn't die from it anyway. "There's gotta be a better way of killing these damned things."

"Decapitation works well." Bai Bao Chen closed the distance between Dad and his prey, lowered her head, and stabbed with the horn protruding from her jaw. With a great heave of her hind quarters, the kirin tossed the vampire in the air.

"That one was mine," Dad complained.

I waited for the vampire to fall. Instead of obeying the laws of gravity, it reached the zenith of its flight and hung there while I frowned at it. Bai Bao Chen chuckled. "Shedu. We should move." The kirin tossed her nose to the alley between Michietti's and the neighboring building.

Dad bounded over, pausing to slash his claws at someone stupid enough to get in his way. The kirin followed, and the instant we were out of the way, something slammed the vampire down on the sidewalk.

The stone cracked under the force of the impact.

I didn't catch a glimpse of the shedu, and I

wasn't sure if I was disappointed or relieved. "Where's Mom?"

"She fell."

"What?!" My eyes widened, and I sucked in a breath.

Dad shot me a look. "Into the water, pup."

I exhaled. "Oh."

"Last I checked, she'd figured out vampires don't drown but do flail in water, so she was playing with a pair of them. Since she looked like she was having a good time, I left her to it."

"Wonderful. Wolf-infested waters. What the hell is going on?"

Bai Bao Chen turned to watch the chaos on the streets, which involved a lot of vampires trying to bite other vampires, something that wasn't ending well for the vampires belonging to the rival brood, especially with the Babylonians participating in the fray. As far as I could tell, the vampires of Ernesto's brood were toying with their victims to give the Babylonians a turn with them. I twisted around in the saddle to watch our back and keep an eye on Dad.

"About fifty vampires swarmed the restaurant half an hour ago. We think they were trying to take Pierina."

When Ernesto found out, Ricci would be smeared across half of Chicago. "Really? That's pretty stupid of them. Where is she?"

"Playing volleyball with one of her brothers and someone's head in the restaurant's entry. I got the feeling she knew the guy and had a grudge, so I thought I'd leave her alone. That was right before the..." Dad held his hands up in helpless surrender. "I don't know what they are. They came and started making a mess of things."

"Babylonians," I supplied before gesturing to Bai Bao Chen. "Dad, this is Bai Bao Chen, and she's a kirin."

"Pleasure to meet you, ma'am. If my pup gives you any trouble, kick him a few times. He's tough. Try not to hurt him too badly. I'd have to take offense if you did that."

Bai Bao Chen chuckled. "The pleasure is mine."

"I think you should be aware humans are part of her diet, Dad."

"We're going to have a long talk about your life choices when this is over, pup." Settling in a crouch, Dad watched the battle, his eyes glowing gold while he panted. "Where's your woman?"

"Probably within five minutes of scaring a decade or two off my life," I confessed, wondering if it was possible to convince Fang Jiahao Yi to stay near the barrier where I could pretend she wasn't about to wade into a brawl. "Seen O'Conners?"

"He's around. I haven't gotten close to him yet."

"Bai Bao Chen?"

"We hunt. Eat well on this battlefield, werewolf."

Dad displayed his teeth in a hungry grin.

WHEN THE COPS joined the party, the battle turned into wholesale slaughter, a bloodbath the Saven brood declined to participate in. At the first sound of sirens, Bai Bao Chen had jumped the canal, taken to the alley on the other side, and stood statue still, watching Michietti's from the shadows.

"They're on the list," she said, her ears twisting back. "For that, I am sorry."

"Let's find O'Conners." I would deal with reality later—after I made sure the hitman couldn't target Marian again. "So much for being the good cop."

"It is not your fault they decided to sell other humans for profit. Do not carry guilt that does not belong to you. Their victims will not see justice in your human courts. The evil ones will face judgment from a higher power now."

I hated she was right. "If I were O'Conners, and I was looking to get rid of specific nuisances, I'd be on higher ground waiting for a good shot."

"But his position is bad else he would have taken you out already. Over the restaurant?"

"Possibly."

She shook her head. "The rooftop here. You cannot go my way."

"Fire escape?" Michietti's had one at the back of the building, facing the alley away from the canal. "Probably on the back of the building so the canal view isn't ruined."

The kirin twisted, more flexible than any horse, turning in the narrow confines of the alley. I spotted the fire escape, but someone had taken offense to the first fifteen feet, leaving scars on the brick and stone where the metal staircase had once been. A second look revealed the building's other two escapes had been likewise damaged. "He might be up here."

"If I toss you, can you grab hold without falling to your death? I would hate to explain to a werewolf I killed his puppy, who was attempting an act of unnecessary heroics."

"Unnecessary?"

"I could go up there and eat him."

I thought about that. "Someone should be there to witness you eating him."

"You doubt me?"

"No. I just doubt you'd leave any evidence

by the time you were done licking the roof clean."

She whinnied a laugh. "Try not to die. I do not want to eat you."

"I don't want you to eat me, either." I pointed at the closest fire escape. "All right. Line up under it."

Once Bai Bao Chen was in position, I stood on the saddle, eyed the few feet between me and the twisted railing dangling beneath the first intact step, and jumped. She helped with a buck, and I hit the metal chest first, hissing at the pain in my abused shoulder. I grabbed the rail, pulled my legs up, and jammed my toes against the first step. Hand over hand, I scrambled onto the intact stairs. The entire structure swayed under my weight, so I tested every step, aware if the fire escape toppled, I'd be trapped in a cage of broken, rusting metal.

When I reached the third story and the ladder to the roof, I checked to see if the kirin waited below. She was gone. I reminded myself ladders weren't nets, and I could handle one stupid little flimsy ladder, cursing to myself while I climbed.

The ladder shook more than the steps, and I was shaking by the time I peered over the roof's ledge.

Trouble came in threes, but if I multiplied by three, I was closer to the number of men and vampires hanging out on the flat roof. The din of the battle masked the creak of metal when I eased over the ledge and landed in a crouch.

I had three bullets, and I counted twelve potential targets. The math was not in my favor. My gaze locked on the most important target, Mark O'Conners, who watched the battle below with a sniper rifle in hand, although he hadn't set it up.

The weapon did him no good leaning against the roof's half foot tall ledge.

Since I'd already abandoned all semblance of playing fair, one of my rounds had his name on it, and he'd be the first one I took out. I wasn't sure who my next two targets would be, but I'd figure it out. The best I could do was lower the odds down to one against nine until Bai Bao Chen made her way to the roof—if she could.

A better man would have given a warning, started an old-fashioned duel, or announced his presence, but I took aim, steadied my grip, and pulled the trigger.

My bullet struck true, plowing into the center of the man's spine, but Mark O'Conners didn't fall. In his hissed cry, I recognized the sound of a vampire's pain. I shifted my aim to his head and drilled the last two rounds into the back of his skull.

The third round did the trick; the newly

turned vampire tumbled off the roof. Unless his head was severed or someone staked him, he'd get back up, but I had other problems to worry about. With my ammunition gone, I'd brought a knife to a gun fight against vampires, and the eleven remaining figures whirled to face me.

Stripes was one of them, but he hadn't had a cute pair of pearly fangs the last time I'd seen him.

Since an empty Ruger was useless, I wound up, took aim, and threw it as hard as I could. The handgun smacked right between Stripes's eyes, and he yelped his astonishment. While I had the element of surprise, I lunged forward, closing my fingers over my new dagger, and brought the fight to them before they remembered they had guns and I didn't.

I'D DONE some profoundly stupid things in my life, but facing off against eleven vampires —even newly fledged ones—topped the list. Maybe I was a shifter, but they had abilities I lacked, including speed, strength, and the stamina born from not needing to breathe.

The older vampires would kill me the instant they got a hold of me; the only ones I stood a chance against were the young ones.

Since wasting my breath would get me killed, I didn't bother saying a word. Stripes had made his choices. I'd made mine.

Deciding to join an organization enslaving people and turning them into cattle for vampires' wealth, profit, and sustenance made him dangerous—too dangerous to leave alive.

Some vampires did good, and I was learning those were the exception rather than the rule.

Later, I'd regret killing a cop, although his transformation from human to vampire made him like me, no longer eligible to serve on the force. Firming my grip on the dagger, I slashed it across Stripes's throat, grabbing hold of his hair with my other hand and yanking with all my strength. Beheading someone took time and a lot of effort, two things I couldn't spare, but I gave it my best shot. The edge sliced through muscle and bone with startling ease, leaving his body to fall to the ground.

An infuriated scream cut over the cacophony of battle.

I turned to go for the next vampire, and another hit me from behind, his knees slamming into my back and driving me down, my chest smacking against the rooftop. Fangs tore into the back of my shoulder.

All the warnings of a hunting vampire's

bite hadn't prepared me for the sensation of my blood being pulled from my body as my heart stuttered and skipped several beats. It hurt, but nothing like what Ernesto or Quinton had inflicted on me.

My world narrowed to the wheeze of my breath and the growing tightness in my chest. I knew I needed to fight, but more hands than I could easily count pinned me down while I thrashed.

"Don't kill him," a man's voice rumbled. "Not yet. I want Saven to watch me make this one in my image."

The pressure on my shoulder eased, but my heartbeat remained rapid, throbbing through me. My vision cleared, giving me my first look at Luca Ricci, who crouched beside me. His red suit dripped blood, and the vampire displayed his fangs.

"Luca Ricci," I ground out through clenched teeth.

"How flattering. You know my name. You've been a thorn in my side, Shane Gibson. I would kill you, but you'll be far more useful as a pawn forced to work at my side, turned against everything you believe, dead and gone, made new in my image, so I can savor the moment when those who claim to love you are forced to put you down. You'll become just another monster among many. Aren't you excited? I am. I will only regret you will be unaware of it at the end. You'll have forgotten everything. That black were-wolf is your father, is he not? I think your first task in your new life will be to kill him for me—and that red bitch of his. Your mother, right?"

I said nothing because he was right. If he turned me, I'd die and carry a new soul, one with no memory of who or what I'd once been. I should've been afraid, but there was no room for fear. I trembled, but in growing rage because I couldn't pull free from the vampires holding me down.

Leaning towards me, Ricci brushed his leathery fingertips down the line of my scar over my right eye. "It burns so beautifully, this eye. Tell me, what do you see through its flames?"

Flames? Movement and a flash of green and gold drew my attention behind Ricci. Bai Bao Chen stilled, her head held high with her fire-bright eyes staring at the vampire as though she was considering the best way to slay and devour him. At her side, his suit untouched by the carnage of war, stood Ernesto.

One by one, Abil Ili and his hive shimmered into view, and their claws dripped red and black. Several more kirin popped into being, their coats stained crimson. Towering over them all was a creature with the body of a lion, the legs of a bull, and a human head on a short, sinewy neck. Great black wings banded with white folded over the shedu's back.

I met its gaze, and it judged me with brilliant emerald eyes and found me lacking.

"Your death," I answered, although I wondered if I'd live to see it. The shedu might choose me as the one to punish first. "You've made a mistake, vampire."

Bai Bao Chen had told me she could work magic of misdirection, and I figured the kirin and the shedu were doing just that, for the vampires were behaving as though we were alone on the roof. Then again, maybe I was hallucinating. Blood loss could cause delusions, and I'd easily believe I'd conjure such an army to comfort myself.

Even if Ricci killed me, Ernesto would protect Marian. I'd already taken care of O'-Conners and Stripes. They wouldn't touch her.

That left only me. Whether I was dead or alive, if Marian stayed safe, I won.

Ricci smiled and patted my cheek. "You're such a mouthy little delight. No wonder Chicago's elite brood master calls you his own. I'll enjoy taking you from him and flaunting my victory before I send him to his final sleep. Humor an old man, one soon to be your sire. How have I made a mistake?"

I counted Babylonians and did the math.

"One to three odds, and they aren't in your favor."

"You drank too deeply, Wilhelm. His thoughts have become clouded. It's no fun for me if he doesn't fear me while I'm killing him." Ricci's gaze turned to one of the vampires pinning me from behind. "I told you when we found him to take a sip, just enough to stun him."

"He's already been bound, Father."

"Bound? To who?" Ricci's tone sharpened.

Ernesto smiled and remained quiet, watching and waiting, catching my eye and giving a slight nod.

"To Ernesto, of course. Who else? You really are as stupid as you look."

Mouthing off to a vampire always caused trouble; in Ricci's case, the sort of trouble born of a sharp kick to the collarbone. He rose, wound up, and kicked me hard. Bone cracked, and I shuddered from the pain. His second kick wasn't as hard but struck the side of my throat, stunning me, and I struggled to breathe. "Ernesto is too busy fighting to save his true children to help the likes of you. This city becomes mine tonight, and you have only yourself to blame."

Ernesto looked heavenward as though praying for patience, lifted his hand, and mimed a duck's quacking. I found his lack of concern both comforting and disturbing.

Behind Ricci, where the roof ended in an alley, something large and black slinked over the ledge and landed in a crouch. In his hybrid form, Dad inspired fear, but he seemed even more menacing than usual. While smaller and younger as a lycanthrope, Mom slinked behind him with equal grace.

"I have one thing to say to you, Ricci."

The vampire hissed at me. "What?"

"Woof."

FORTY-TWO

Just in time for the fun.

RICCI BROKE my nose with his heel, and I swore I'd never make fun of someone for crying over a broken nose again. The pain blinded me and robbed me of breath. The flow of fresh blood stirred the appetites of the vampires, and one of them sunk his fangs into my arm before Ricci could tear him off —literally.

That would leave a scar, assuming I survived to tell the tale.

In retrospect, if I had yelped from the start, Ricci never would've gotten a chance to land the second blow. My pained sound unleashed my parents' fury, and the lycanthropes abandoned their careful stalk for the sort of assault I shouldn't have attempted.

Dad hit Ricci at full throttle, and the vampire and werewolf rolled across the roof, fur and flesh flying while the pair tore into each other. With excited yips, Mom dived into the fray, lifting her claws. She snatched one of the vampires off my back, lifted him up, and threw him off the roof, taking his place with a roar worthy of a lioness.

I'd have to remind Dad he needed to teach Mom to howl.

The vampires scattered, and I went limp from relief that I might survive for a few more minutes. I concentrated on my breathing, tasting blood. Mom roared again, crouching over me, one of her clawed hands on my shoulder, her hot breath washing over the back of my neck. "Shane?"

"He lives," Ernesto reported, and he took Ricci's place, his fingertips resting on my forehead. "Broken nose, probably stunned. I'd bitten him earlier, but they've bitten him several times, which is rough even with my protection."

Bai Bao Chen stepped forward, lowered her head, and prodded my shoulder with the tip of her horn, hard enough to hurt. "Conventional wisdom states it is unwise to take on part of a brood and its master at the same time."

"Good to know," I croaked.

"See? He'll be fine. Go help your mate deal with Ricci. I'd be honored to guard your puppy and watch you toy with that vampire before you tear him limb from limb until the unlife flees his body."

Mom whined an eager whine and bounded away.

The kirin laughed and gave me another poke. "So enthusiastic. O'Conners is dead. You dropped his body on your father's head. Your father took severe offense to that for some reason. Werewolves are fast, strong predators. I should tell my kin to cohort with werewolves. They are entertaining."

"Long lived, too." Ernesto shifted his hand to my throat, pressing to check my pulse. "Weaker than I like. How is it you wander off and manage to find the worst of the trouble, my dear boy?"

"The broken fire escapes offered a clue. I didn't think O'Conners had been turned into a vampire. He had a sniper rifle." While tempted to sit up, I erred on the side of caution and stayed down, careful to breath through my mouth. "Fucker broke my nose."

"Yes, rather badly, too." Ernesto worked his arm under my chest and hauled me upright. "I'll set it, but you'll need to see a doctor to make sure it doesn't heal crooked."

A little warning would've been nice, especially since I blacked out when the vampire grasped my nose and gave a yank. When I pried open my eyes, the din of battle and the screams of the dying and the undead still filled the air. I was leaning against Ernesto, who absently patted my back.

Bai Bao Chen bumped my chin with her soft muzzle, careful to angle her horn away from me. "He's coming around."

"Just in time for the fun. Look."

I needed the vampire's help to sit upright and stay there, but I had no trouble figuring out what he meant. Before Mom's lycanthropy virus had matured, she'd enjoyed playing tug-of-war with Dad in his wolf form, battling with him over an old, frayed rope.

That game had been more playful in nature, with my mother the destined winner, since Dad refused to risk hurting her. His care and tenderness were absent in their new version of the game. My parents waged a vicious, snarling war over who'd get their new rope.

I almost pitied Ricci. Almost. I might have had more mercy if the vampire was still alive, but he hung limply in their grasp, and his open, dead eyes stared at nothing.

"I've learned a valuable lesson. I underestimated the viciousness of a pair of lycanthropes defending their puppy. It won't happen again. I thought their violence had peaked when they'd gotten their paws on O'-

Conners—nicely done, by the way. He would've died on his own soon enough. Your parents just helped him along." Ernesto chuckled, and a satisfied smile brightened his expression. "You made quite the pained sound when I set your nose. Your parents were greatly offended. Ricci did not survive to his next breath. I think they're just working out their frustrations."

"I'm surprised you don't want a piece of him."

"I don't need that satisfaction. I lured him here, and I tricked him into bringing his most vulnerable children. The ones who don't die will belong to me, and they won't be long for this world if they don't give up their old ways." Ernesto's smile turned grim. "I have lost none of my children. He has lost all of his. Some of my children are weakened and will be a long time recovering, but none have died their second death. I have won this war —and you have bought many human victims time. No, I don't need anything else from his corpse."

"Is Marian all right?"

"She's with Pierina, guarded by my other sons and daughters and by Fang Jaihao Yi as well. It would take an army to reach her. Last I saw her, she was sulking, as she only got to shoot one vampire."

"Offer your knees later."

He laughed. "I shall. We'll both enjoy it. Bai Bao Chen, I leave him to you. It may take a while to cool the temper of the lycanthropes."

The kirin slid her way between me and Ernesto until most of my weight rested against her foreleg. "An entire cow, vampire. That is what you owe me for making me miss my share of the battle's bounty."

"It'll be done." Ernesto rose to his feet and approached my parents, staying out of their reach while they fought over the dead vampire.

"I was stupid," I confessed.

Bai Bao Chen lowered her head so I could look into one of her bright eyes. "Perhaps. It will be a challenge tempering your courage with wisdom. You killed one before they caught you."

"Two."

She whinnied. "Even better than I thought. You fought well, although foolishly. You are lucky you emerged with your true life. That vampire would have turned you, given a chance. That would have been a pity. That vampire's plan was well-aimed. It would have hurt Ernesto's heart to put you to your final rest. But who knows? It is an odd thing, the nature of souls. Like attracts like, so perhaps he would have found himself the father of a new son, one with similar spirit to the one he would have lost. But it would have hurt him all the same, knowing it was not you within your body. A near thing."

"A near thing I will try to avoid." I meant it, too. Vampire bites hurt, and my chest throbbed as though my body still fought a vampire draining my blood. "I got O'Conners."

"You did."

"The Babylonians?"

"Ah, yes. They are the reason Ernesto's children still live. They accepted their deaths so Ernesto's children would not have to die. They'll rise on their own. The survivors take their fallen to their crypts to await the sunrise of the fourth day. Abil Ili lived, although he will miss his left arm for a while. It'll grow back eventually. None of the kirin, the shedu, or the others fell. Given an hour, there will be no sign of what has happened here."

"What others?"

Bai Bao Chen grinned at me. "Some things you are not ready to know. *They* are one of them. One day, when you are old and I am still young, I will introduce you."

I wondered if she meant for her words to sound like a threat. Probably. "The cops?"

"We have the word of an angel they had fallen, turned by Ricci last night, from what we understand."

I remembered Stripes, and I flinched. "The second one I killed. I knew him."

"His death hurts you. For that, I am sorry. This will not bring you peace, but perhaps a little comfort. Their disgrace will be covered up. A disgusting, pretty story will be invented to explain away their deaths, those who turned their back on the sun in their pursuit of evil."

I glanced at Ernesto, who was crouched near my snarling parents, talking to them in his calm, mellow voice. "Yet you're friends with Ernesto."

The vampire turned at the sound of his name and flashed me a toothy grin. "Of course she is. She was but a wobbly filly when I was already old. Cute as a button, all fluff and stubborn pride, prone to tumbles until she could make all four of her hooves cooperate, which took her many years."

Bai Bao Chen snapped her teeth. "I will eat you, vampire."

"No, you won't. You would miss your papa."

The kirin stomped her hoof. "Ernesto!"

"Maybe she will tell you the story, some day, of the qilin parents who could not accept their deformed, wobbly kirin filly. They had abandoned her as a living sacrifice to what they believed was a fire god. Of course, phoenixes do tend to believe themselves gods, but who am I to judge? And so the little filly came to be in my care—and in Abil Ili's care, beginning many long and happy years of partnership between our three races. In a way, you can thank Bai Bao Chen for Abil Ili's skills in the arts of healing. Before the kirin, the Babylonians had no need for or interest in the art of restoring broken bodies. Ah, do see Abil Ili before you run off, my dear boy. You need to ask him to soothe your collar-bone and return it to its proper place, although I think he should leave your nose broken as a reminder of why you should be more careful in the future."

"Ernesto," Bai Bao Chen complained.

"Bai Bao Chen," he replied, his voice a perfect match for her tone. "Don't forget I will spank you as I would any of my other children. The only shame would be in hiding the difficulties you have long overcome, difficulties that were no fault of yours."

I lifted my shaking hand and patted Bai Bao Chen's leg. "He won't stop if you argue with him."

"Papa," Bai Bao Chen spat.

"I know what you want to ask me. If you want to see the world, who am I to argue with you? You were an adult long ago. You need not haunt my doorstep and lurk beneath the streets of Chicago. You have always been free to come and go as you wish. Of course,

I'll feel better if you and your stallion keep an eye on the more delicate of my children. I'm sure they will keep things interesting for you."

Stretching out her neck, Bai Bao Chen snapped her teeth at the vampire. "Insufferable!"

"This is what you have to look forward to, my dear boy—long years of your children talking back to you. The better you raise them, the mouthier they'll be."

That caught my parents' attention; they dropped Ricci's body and turned to face us.

"We have raised the best of sons, if that's the criteria," Dad muttered, spitting out a chunk of vampire. "Your kind tastes rather unpleasant, Ernesto."

"And yours tastes rather delicious."

While Dad took a swipe at the ancient vampire, his claws ruffled Ernesto's suit rather than tearing him to shreds. "Do I need to take you to the hospital, pup?"

I waved my father off. "I'll just sit here. That's fine. If anyone bothers me, Bai Bao Chen can eat them. Right?"

The kirin chuckled. "It would be my pleasure to eat any annoyances."

Ernesto heaved one of his long-suffering sighs. "No, it's better he doesn't go to a hospital. We'll have problems explaining the violence tonight. The blood loss will heal, and once Abil Ili has a few moments, he can numb the pain and fuse his collarbone. The rest is best left to nature. Your blood won't do him much good at this point. There's too much vampiric magic at play. I've shielded him from the worst of it, but it's best for him if he fights this battle on his own. Some rest, some peace, and some quiet will do the most good."

"Very well. Let's get off this roof before the uncorrupted police arrive. We should make ourselves scarce."

"Indeed. At least an explanation for this tragedy is readily available; after all, the police did neglect to replace the grate promptly, and everyone in Chicago knows great evils lurk within the city's vast underbelly, the abyss only fools brave." Ernesto's chuckle possessed a sharp edge. "Isn't it funny how rumors spread? A little bit of mystery, a little bit of darkness, and a few unexplained lights in the deepest shadows spawn the oddest stories—and such delicious fear. Now, that said, there are worse things than Babylonians and kirin lurking in the deep places of the world... but they won't bother us as long as we don't bother them. Right, Bai Bao Chen?"

"You're a terrible being, Ernesto," the kirin muttered, shaking the blood off her coat. "Up, Shane Shiu Cheng. One more ride, then you can rest to your heart's content."

I SHOULD'VE KNOWN Bai Bao Chen meant to jump from the roof, and only luck kept me in the saddle when she thumped to the ground. As it was, excruciating pain radiated from my broken collarbone, and I slammed my nose into her neck, breaking it a second time. While I cursed and bled all over her, she laughed.

Dad sighed when reached us, grasped the back of my head in a massive paw to hold me still, and set my nose with a jerk. "Don't break it again."

"Wasn't on purpose," I grumbled, and my voice sounded strange to my ears.

To add insult to injury, Abil Ili stabbed me with one of his hooks, cutting over my broken collarbone and dripping black fluid all over me before he was satisfied with his work. It hurt like hell, but my father and Bai Bao Chen worked together to hold me still until the Babylonian finished his so-called soothing.

I'd have to explain to them torture wasn't soothing.

Shortly after Abil Ili finished treating my broken collarbone, Marian emerged from Michietti's with Pierina at her side, and she clapped her hands to her mouth. "Shane!

What have you done to yourself? Are you all right?"

"He decided to play with a vampire master and got used as a chew toy," my father announced, hauling me from Bai Bao Chen's back, grabbing me by the back of my neck, and dragging me as he had when I'd been little and prone to getting under foot and causing trouble. "He did score full points for his viciousness in eliminating a threat to you, so you shouldn't punish him too much. Just a little."

With a shove, he surrendered me to Marian's custody. Unlike my father, she wrapped her arm around my back and scooted close to me. "I saw O'Conners fall from the roof. He landed on your father. Was that your doing?"

"It was," I confirmed.

"Good. I was disappointed I didn't get a chance at him. I can live with my disappointment if you got a few hits in on my behalf."

Considering I'd killed him for her sake, I was being honest when I nodded.

"However, we'll be having a long talk about running off without me during a pitched battle."

"Why don't you try to impress upon him why it's dangerous to attack the master of a brood without assistance." Ernesto patted my shoulder. "If Ricci had been a little wiser about when to go about it, Shane would've been turned. I've learned a new lesson about this world of ours."

Marian tightened her hold on me, and I gratefully leaned against her. "What lesson?"

"I've seen many great and terrible things, but nothing quite as daunting as a pair of lycanthropes witnessing someone hurting their puppy. I'd heard rumors of what enraged werewolves could do, but I'd underestimated them. Ricci was no minor vampire, and he stood no chance. It was an honor to witness."

My parents preened, and my father shoved his muzzle in my face and licked me.

I pushed his snout away. "That hurts, Dad."

"Shouldn't have broken your nose. I taught you to ride better than that."

"She jumped from a third story roof!"

"No excuses. I taught you better than that."

I sighed. No matter what, I couldn't win. Then again, I couldn't lose, either. I turned to Marian and rested my brow on her shoulder. "You know what? Forget it. Let's just go home."

"What about the cops?" Dad growled.

"If they want to ask me questions, they'll have to come to Nebraska." I waited for Marian to relax against me, listening to her laugh softly. I caught her by surprise, and despite my exhaustion, I ducked and tossed her over my shoulder. Fortunately for me, Bai Bao Chen was close by, giving me the perfect chance to dump Marian onto the kirin's back. "We're kidnapping her. I have a bet to win. Game?"

The kirin tossed her head and whinnied her laughter. "Always. Yi? We're leaving. We're going to some place called Nebraska. Do you think they have cows in Nebraska?"

Bai Bao Chen's stallion trotted over from deeper within Michietti's, chortling when he caught sight of Marian sprawled across his mare's back. "I would not know. How interesting. I would like a cow, too. Do you think they will give us one still alive? Do cows run fast? I hope cows run fast."

Ernesto sighed and turned to my father. "I'll take care of things here. Don't worry. It's best for everyone if this remains quiet."

"Come visit. I'll even let you into the house before you burn to a crisp, vampire." Dad rose to his full height, grabbed Marian by her waist, and lifted her up, seating her in the saddle. "Boy, I expect you to teach this woman how to sit a horse without embarrassing us all. Get your ass in the saddle and take her home. We'll be along soon enough, so try not to destroy the house before we're back."

Bai Bao Chen spared me from having to vault into the saddle by stretching out her front hooves in a mimicry of a bow. Swinging my leg over the kirin's back, I slid into place behind Marian, wrapping my arms around her waist and taking a moment to enjoy the feel of her pressed against my chest. "How many pancakes do I have to peel off the ceiling?"

The way my parents refused to meet my eyes promised a mess of epic proportions for me to clean up. "You two!"

"Just take your woman home already."

Bai Bao Chen rose to her full height and canted her head to look at me with a bright eye. "How far is it to this Nebraska?"

"About five hundred miles."

The kirin turned to Ernesto and asked, "What is a mile?"

The vampire tossed his head back and laughed. "Why don't you go find out? Have a safe ride, children."

"Seriously, Ernesto. Do not make me bite you. What is a mile?"

I struggled to imagine how the kirin had lived so long under the streets of Chicago without learning what a mile was. "I'll show you," I promised. "Leave your papa to his business so he feels important. You know how he gets when he doesn't feel important."

Ernesto scowled at me. "You truly are an awful child."

"I am. This awful child is going to kidnap

his woman and spend the next few days convincing her she should marry him. If you have any problems with this, take it up with the werewolves. It's their fault I turned out this way."

My parents sighed, and Dad shook his head, giving Marian's leg a pat. "If you need rescued, give us a call. We'll come save you, eventually—maybe."

"I think I'll be all right. I need a vacation anyway, but if my boss gives me any shit for taking a few extra days off, you get to deal with him."

Dad laughed. "That's on you, Ernesto. You may as well earn your keep."

"What do I look like to you?"

I shook my head and let my parents bicker with an ancient vampire who'd lived through the rise and fall of civilizations. I was eager to find somewhere nice and quiet to take a long nap. "Sorry, Marian."

"For what? I don't know about you, but I've gotten exactly what I wanted. You have nothing to be sorry about—except bleeding all over me. You'll have to tell me what you thought you were doing on that roof, Mr. Gibson. And once you're done explaining that, keep in mind we won't be staying in Nebraska long. I may have submitted some applications on your behalf, as is my right as your mate. Unlike Chicago's police force, the

FBI doesn't have rules against partial blind-
ness or approved fraternization among officers. You're mine."

Even when I won, I lost, and even if I lost,
I still won, and the thought made me laugh.
I'd address the issue with the FBI—and any
stealthy applications she may have made on
my behalf—later, preferably when I had her
somewhere nice and private so I could thoroughly thank her. "I was being an idiot and
was busy getting my nose broken, of course.
How about I promise not to do it again? I'll be
good."

She twisted around to glare at me. "Don't
make promises you can't keep."

I smiled because it was true. "How about I
take you home with me?"

Bai Bao Chen heaved one of Ernesto's
long-suffering sighs. "Puppy love," she complained to her stallion. Fang Jaihao Yi wisely
said nothing.

Maybe one day I'd learn from him, but
today was not that day. "You're just jealous,
Bai Bao Chen."

Somehow she bucked me off without
losing Marian, and I laughed with everyone
else while I picked myself off the ground. I
had to cajole and bribe Bai Bao Chen with
every bit of meat in my fridge and freezer to
convince the kirin to forgive me and allow

me to ride instead of making me walk to my apartment.

Through it all Marian laughed, and I'd never heard a sweeter sound.

Want more? Hearth, Home, and Havoc is the next in the series.

Like vampires? Keep reading to sample Blood Bound: A Lowrance Vampires novel.

About R.J. Blain

Want to hear from the author when a new book releases? Sign up here! Please note this newsletter is operated by the Furred & Frond Management. Expect to be sassed by a cat. (With guest features of other animals, including dogs.)

For a complete list of books written by RJ and her various pen names, please click here.

RJ BLAIN suffers from a Moleskine journal obsession, a pen fixation, and a terrible tendency to pun without warning.

When she isn't playing pretend, she likes to think she's a cartographer and a sumi-e painter.

In her spare time, she daydreams about being a spy. Should that fail, her contingency plan involves tying her best of enemies to spinning wheels and quoting James Bond villains until she is satisfied.

RJ also writes as Susan Copperfield and
Bernadette Franklin. Visit RJ and her pets
(the Management) at
thesneakykittycritic.com.

Follow RJ & her alter egos on Bookbub:
RJ Blain
Susan Copperfield
Bernadette Franklin